DESERTS of FIRE

Also by Douglas Lain

Novels
Billy Moon
After the Saucers Landed

Short Fiction Collections:
Last Week's Apocalypse

As Editor:
In the Shadow of the Towers:
Speculative Fiction in a Post-9/11 World

DESERTS of FIRE

SPECULATIVE FICTION and the MODERN WAR

EDITED by DOUGLAS LAIN

Night Shade Books
New York

Night Shade books may be purchased in bulk at special discounts for sales
promotion, corporate gifts, fund-raising, or educational purposes. Special
editions can also be created to specifications. For details, contact the Special Sales
Department, Night Shade Books, 307 West 36th Street, 11th Floor,
New York, NY 10018 or info@skyhorsepublishing.com.

Night Shade Books® is a registered trademark of Skyhorse Publishing,
Inc. ®, a Delaware corporation.

Visit our website at www.nightshadebooks.com.

10 9 8 7 6 5 4 3 2 1

Library of Congress Cataloging-in-Publication Data is available on file.

Print ISBN: 978-1-59780-852-1
Ebook ISBN: 978-1-59780-861-3

Cover illustration by Richie Pope
Cover design by Lesley Worrell

Please see pages 352—353 for an extension of this copyright page.

Printed in the United States of America

contents

introduction

d *eserts of Fire* is a collection of stories that, taken together, might be read as a simple statement against war, and specifically a statement against the US incursions in the Middle East. However, to read the stories in this collection that way is to miss a deeper point.

Nobody, regardless of ideology or political persuasion, likes war. Everyone wants to be rid of it . . . *at least in principle*. Yet, the wars continue to stack up and nobody quite knows why. To take just one not-too-far-off example, we can look to Iraq.

The official rationales given for the invasion of Iraq in 2003 were quickly revealed as untrue . . . either before the invasion or by subsequent revelations. No evidence of WMDs was discovered. There was no evidence linking Saddam Hussein to al-Qaeda. Humanitarian justifications for war were disputed prior to the invasion by groups like Amnesty International, and lost all credibility after the invasion when the routine torture of Iraqi prisoners by US military guards became public knowledge.

But even the reasons suggested by critics of the war—explanations revolving around self-interest and suggestions that it was all about oil profits or political hegemony in the region—didn't stand up. The vast majority of the oil contracts did not go to US companies, and US prestige and influence in the region and in the wider world have diminished dramatically in the wake of the invasion. The sad fact is that nobody knows why the US invaded Iraq. The sad fact is that the invasion of Iraq was absurd. And this is why, when these stories are taken together, no simple anti-war sentiment will be found in this book.

One great critic of war, the sometimes science-fiction writer Kurt Vonnegut, once wrote that "civilization ended in World War I," and in his definitive novel *Slaughterhouse Five,* one of his characters claimed that the reason wars kept coming even after the Great War was that novels and movies romanticized war efforts. Wars kept coming because too many people wrote stories that make "war look just wonderful."

These two ideas—that World War I was the death of civilization and that fictional acts of war heroism cause us to fight more wars—are connected even if they do not, at first, appear to be. Both believing that civilization did or should end because of the horrors of war, and blaming fiction for perpetuating war make the same mistake: of blaming the human imagination for war. . . .

A hundred years ago, in Zurich, a group of artists thought in the same way as Vonnegut. They wanted to reject all heroism, all pretenses of human achievement or greatness, because it was this sort of pretension that produced the monstrosity known as the machine gun. One of these artists, a veteran of the Great War named Tristan Tzara, wrote the group's manifesto. In it he claimed that this new art movement, born of the trenches, was aimed at total independence. It was called Dada. Tzara explained that this art was given that name because the word Dada had no discernible meaning.

Dada was meaningless because Dada renounced all systems. Dada rejected all efforts towards rational understanding, and in this way Dada echoed (and maybe even reproduced) the chaos and meaninglessness of the war that it wanted to reject.

Today's genre fiction, even the most bizarre strands of it, by its very nature as genre fiction, dismisses this rejection of systems. Instead of retreating into the acceptance of the arbitrary and embracing obscurity, today's writers of sci-fi and horror are optimists of a sort. They don't claim to understand war and its persistence; but they feel obligated to at least try to understand it in small and discernable ways. They'll often (or perhaps always) fail, but each time they do so, they do so in a better and more useful way.

What you'll find in this book are stories written both *after* and *during* some of the wars in question. These stories represent efforts to answer the question of why this keeps happening. Some of the stories are small, and focused on the personal, while others take a larger, more systemic view. Rarely do the stories herein offer definitive answers, but they are all of them good examples of effort being made. They all cast after meaning.

Deserts of Fire is a collection that can easily be read as a mere statement against war, but it is more than that. Instead of mere sentiment, these stories react and explore the dimensions of a question. Why war?

vietnam syndrome

The first war with Iraq—the "Gulf War" as it was named by contemporaneous news accounts—was as mysterious and inexplicable as any war. It was a short-lived affair, and one that in retrospect appears to have mostly have taken place on television. The US relied heavily on aerial attack to get the job done, and US troops who were on the ground in Kuwait were often as reliant on CNN coverage as the civilians back home were when it came to understanding what was happening.

The main thing was that it was *quick*. Facing off against a beleaguered and exhausted Iraqi Army in Kuwait, the US-led Coalition had no difficulty expelling and then decimating the enemy. In five weeks' time it was all over, and most in the US were jubilant. Ecstatic even.

Some suggested that if one needed an explanation for the Gulf War, one need only look at the victory celebrations. One of those who suggested that an easy victory was itself a justification was President George Bush Sr. Speaking to the American Legislative Exchange Council, he said, "I know you share this wonderful feeling that I have, of joy in my heart. . . . It's a proud day for America. And, by God, we've kicked the Vietnam syndrome once and for all."

That's what the bombs and troops and bulldozers were deployed to destroy. We might have killed

Iraqis but our real enemy was the memory of Vietnam. And apparently it had worked. The public's reticence about US military interventions brought on by the loss of Vietnam was supposed to have disappeared. All we'd needed was a win.

More than a decade after Bush Sr. had declared Vietnam Syndrome vanquished the disease returned. A month before the *second* war against Iraq (the "Iraq War" as it is now known), the US invasion in March of 2003, the world's largest anti-war protest occurred. There were marches in over six hundred cities. The number of participants was estimated to range from eight to thirty million. People around the world painted their faces with flowers and carried protest signs. Despite the terror attacks of 9/11, despite the victory of the first Gulf War, despite CNN and Fox News, the long shadow of that old war in Vietnam was still providing the lens through which many saw the coming war.

In the public imagination the debate about the ethics of an invasion was fought along the same battle lines that had been drawn when *Laugh-In* was on the air and long hair was subversive. And science-fiction and fantasy writers who took up a US war as their subject also inevitably found themselves faced with the same choices writers like Frederik Pohl and Kate Wilhelm had faced when their respective support and opposition to the war in Vietnam ran as advertisements in *Galaxy* magazine.

We will begin in this collection with Vietnam. Because these stories written in reaction to *that* war set the terms—if not the tone or the details—of what was to come. We set the clock back forty years, to the anti-war fiction of the past, because even as the Vietnam syndrome continues, so too do the wars.

In 2014 the novelist and columnist Paul Di Filippo wondered what the hold-up was with regard to Norman Spinrad's SFWA Grandmaster Award, but then realized that Spinrad was perhaps too much of a rebel for it. Awarding him the Grandmaster would be like "sitting the court jester on the throne." Spinrad was one of the more controversial writers in SF's New Wave movement back in the '70s and his novel Bug Jack Barron *was banned by newsstands when it appeared as a serial in* New Worlds. *His first fiction sale for professional publication was to Harlan Ellison's legendary anthology* Dangerous Visions.

Since the days of dangerous visions, Spinrad has written and published over twenty novels including Bug Jack Barron, The Iron Dream, The Druid King, *and* Osama the Gun. *His story "The Big Flash" was originally published in Damon Knight's anthology* Orbit *in 1969 and was nominated for a Nebula in 1970.*

"the big flash"
NORMAN SPINRAD

t minus 200 days ... and counting. ...
They came on freaky for my taste—but that's the name of the game: freaky means a draw in the rock business. And if the Mandala was going to survive in LA, competing with a network-owned joint like the American Dream, I'd just have to hold my nose and out-freak the opposition. So after I had dug the Four Horsemen for about an hour, I took them into my office to talk turkey.

I sat down behind my Salvation Army desk (the Mandala is the world's most expensive shoestring operation) and the Horsemen sat down on the bridge chairs sequentially, establishing the group's pecking order.

First the head honcho, lead guitar, and singer, Stony Clarke—blond shoulder-length hair, eyes like something in a morgue when he took off his steel-rimmed shades, a reputation as a heavy acid-head, and the look of a speed-freak behind it. Then Hair, the drummer, dressed like a Hell's Angel, swastikas and all, a junkie, with fanatic eyes that were a little too close together, making me wonder whether he wore swastikas because he grooved behind the Angel thing or made like an Angel because it let him groove behind the swastika in public. Number three was a cat who called himself Super Spade and wasn't kidding—he wore earrings, natural hair, a Stokeley Carmichael sweatshirt, and on a thong around his neck a shrunken head that had been whitened with liquid shoe polish. He was the utility infielder: sitar, base, organ, flute, whatever. Number four, who called himself Mr. Jones, was about the creepiest cat I had ever seen in a rock group, and that is saying something. He was their visuals, synthesizer, and electronics man. He was at least forty, wore early-hippie clothes that looked like they had been made by Sy Devore, and was rumored to be some kind of Rand Corporation dropout. There's no business like show business.

"Okay, boys," I said, "you're strange, but you're my kind of strange. Where you worked before?"

"We ain't baby," Clarke said. "We're the New Thing. I've been dealing crystal and acid in the Haight. Hair was drummer for some plastic group in New York. The Super Spade claims it's the reincarnation of Bird and it don't pay to argue. Mr. Jones, he don't talk too much. Maybe he's a Martian. We just started putting our thing together." One thing about this business, the groups that don't have square managers, you can get cheap. They talk too much.

"Groovy," I said. "I'm happy to give you guys your start. Nobody knows you, but I think you got something going. So I'll take a chance and give you a week's booking. One A.M. to closing, which is two, Tuesday through Sunday, four hundred a week."

"Are you Jewish?" asked Hair.

"What?"

"Cool it," Clarke ordered. Hair cooled it. "What it means," Clarke told me, "is that four hundred sounds like pretty light bread."

"We don't sign if there's an option clause," Mr. Jones said.

"The Jones-thing has a good point," Clarke said. "We do the first week for four hundred, but after that it's a whole new scene, dig?"

I didn't feature that. If they hit it big, I could end up not being able to afford them. But, on the other hand, four hundred dollars was light bread, and I needed a cheap closing act pretty bad.

"Okay," I said. "But a verbal agreement that I get first crack at you when you finish the gig."

"Word of honor," said Stony Clarke.

That's this business—the word of honor of an ex-dealer and speed-freak.

T minus 199 days . . . and counting. . . .

Being unconcerned with ends, the military mind can be easily manipulated, easily controlled, and easily confused. Ends are defined as those goals set by civilian authority. Ends are the conceded province of civilians; means are the province of the military, whose duty it is to achieve the ends set for it by the most advantageous application of the means at its command.

Thus the confusion over the war in Asia among my uniformed clients at the Pentagon. The end has been duly set: eradication of the guerrillas. But the civilians have overstepped their bounds and meddled in means. The generals regard this as unfair, a breach of contract, as it were. The generals (or the faction among them most inclined to paranoia) are beginning to see the conduct of the war, the political limitation on means, as a ploy of the civilians for performing a putsch against their time-honored prerogatives.

This aspect of the situation would bode ill for the country, were it not for the fact that the growing paranoia among the generals has enabled me to manipulate them into presenting both my scenarios to the President. The President has authorized implementation of the major scenario, provided that the minor scenario is successful in properly molding public opinion.

My major scenario is simple and direct. Knowing that the poor flying weather makes our conventional air power, with its dependency on relative accuracy, ineffectual, the enemy has fallen into the pattern of grouping his forces into larger units and launching punishing annual offensives during the monsoon season. However, these larger units are highly vulnerable to tactical nuclear weapons, which do not depend upon accuracy for effect. Secure in the knowledge that domestic political considerations preclude the use of nuclear weapons, the enemy will once again form into division-sized units or larger during the next monsoon season. A parsimonious use of tactical nuclear weapons, even as few as twenty one-hundred-kiloton bombs, employed simultaneously and in an advantageous pattern, will destroy a minimum of two hundred thousand enemy troops, or nearly two-thirds of his total force, in a twenty-four-hour period. The blow will be crushing.

The minor scenario, upon whose success the implementation of the major scenario depends, is far more sophisticated, due to its subtler goal: public acceptance of, or, optimally, even public clamor for, the use of tactical nuclear weapons. The task is difficult, but my scenario is quite sound, if somewhat exotic, and with the full, if to some extent clandestine, support of the upper military hierarchy, certain civil government circles and the decision-makers in key aerospace corporations, the means now at my command would seem adequate. The risks, while statistically significant, do not exceed an acceptable level.

T minus 189 days . . . and counting. . . .

The way I see it, the network deserved the shafting I gave them. They shafted me, didn't they? Four successful series I produce for those bastards, and two bomb out after thirteen weeks and they send me to the salt mines! A discotheque, can you imagine they make me producer at a lousy discotheque! A remittance man they make me, those schlock-meisters. Oh, those schnorrers made the American Dream sound like a kosher deal—twenty percent of the net, they say. And you got access to all our sets and contract players; it'll make you a rich man, Herm. And like a yuk, I sign, being broke at the time, without reading the fine print. I should know they've set up the American Dream as a tax loss? I should know that I've gotta use their lousy sets and stiff contract players and have it written off against my gross? I should know their shtick is to run the American Dream at a loss and then do a network TV show out of the joint from which I don't see a penny? So I end up running the place for them at a paper loss, living on salary, while the network rakes it in off the TV show that I end up paying for out of my end.

Don't bums like that deserve to be shafted? It isn't enough they use me as a tax-loss patsy; they gotta tell me who to book! "Go sign the Four Horsemen, the group that's packing them in at the Mandala," they say. "We want them on 'A Night with the American Dream.' They're hot."

"Yeah, they're hot." I say, "which means they'll cost a mint. I can't afford it."

They show me more fine print—next time I read the contract with a microscope. I gotta book whoever they tell me to and I gotta absorb the cost on my books! It's enough to make a Litvak turn anti-semitic.

So I had to go to the Mandala to sign up these hippies. I made sure I didn't get there until twelve-thirty so I wouldn't have to stay in that nuthouse any longer than necessary. Such a dive! What Bernstein did was take a bankrupt Hollywood-Hollywood club on the Strip, knock down all the interior walls, and put up this monster tent inside the shell. Just thin white screening over two-by-fours. Real schlock. Outside the tent, he's got projectors, lights, speakers, all the electronic mumbo-jumbo, and inside is like being surrounded by movie screens. Just the tent and the bare floor, not even a real stage, just a platform on wheels they shlepp in and out of the tent when they change groups.

So you can imagine he doesn't draw exactly a class crowd. Not with the American Dream up the street being run as a network tax loss. What they get is the smelly, hard-core hippies I don't let in the door and the kind of j.d. high-school kids that think it's smart to hang around putzes like that. A lot of dope-pushing goes on. The cops don't like the place and the rousts draw professional troublemakers.

A real den of iniquity—I felt like I was walking onto a Casbah set. The last group had gone off and the Horsemen hadn't come on yet. So what you had was this crazy tent filled with hippies, half of them on acid or pot or amphetamine, or, for all I know, Ajax, high-school would-be hippies, also mostly stoned and getting ugly, and a few crazy schwartzes looking to fight cops. All of them standing around waiting for something to happen, and about ready to make it happen. I stood near the door, just in case. As they say, "The vibes were making me uptight."

All of a sudden the house lights go out and it's black as a network executive's heart. I hold my hand on my wallet—in this crowd, tell me there are no pickpockets. Just the pitch black and dead silence for what, ten beats, and then I start feeling something, I don't know, like something crawling along my bones, but I know it's some kind of subsonic effect and not my imagination, because all the hippies are standing still and you don't hear a sound.

Then from monster speakers so loud you feel it in your teeth, a heartbeat, but heavy, slow, half-time, like maybe a whale's heart. The thing crawling along my bones seems to be synchronized with the heartbeat and I feel almost like I am that big dumb heart beating there in the darkness.

Then a dark red spot—so faint it's almost infrared—hits the stage which they have wheeled out. On the stage are four uglies in crazy black robes—you know, like the Grim Reaper wears—with that ugly red light all over them like blood. Creepy. Boom-ba-boom. Boom-ba-boom. The heartbeat still going, still that subsonic bone-crawl, and the hippies are staring at the Four Horsemen like mesmerized chickens.

The bass player, a regular jungle bunny, picks up the rhythm of the heartbeat. Dum-da-dum. Dum-da-dum. The drummer beats it out with earsplitting rim shots. Then the electric guitar, timed like a strangling cat, makes with horrible, heavy chords. Whang-ka-whang. Whang-ka-whang.

It's just awful, I feel it in my guts, my bones; my eardrums are just like some great big throbbing vein. Everybody is swaying to it; I'm swaying to it. Boom-ba-boom. Boom-ba-boom.

Then the guitarist starts to chant in rhythm with the heartbeat, in a hoarse, shrill voice like somebody dying: "The big flash . . . the big flash . . ."

Then the guitarist starts to chant in rhythm with the heartbeat, in a hoarse, shrill voice like somebody dying: "The big flash . . . the big flash . . ."

And the guy at the visuals console diddles around and rings of light start to climb the walls of the tent, blue at the bottom becoming green as they get higher, then yellow, orange, and finally as they become a circle on the ceiling, eye-killing neon-red. Each circle takes exactly one heartbeat to climb the walls.

Boy, what an awful feeling! Like I was a tube of toothpaste being squeezed in rhythm till the top of my head felt like it was gonna squirt up with those circles of light through the ceiling.

And then they start to speed it up gradually. The same heartbeat, the same rim shots, same chords, same circles of light, same "The big flash . . . the big flash . . ." Same base, same subsonic bone-crawl, but just a little faster. . . . Then faster! Faster!

Thought I would die! Knew I would die! Heart beating like a lunatic. Rim shots like a machine gun. Circles of light sucking me up the walls, into that red neon hole.

Oy, incredible! Over and over, faster, faster, till the voice was a scream and the heartbeat a boom and the rim shots a whine and the guitar howled feedback and my bones were jumping out of my body—

Every spot in the place came on and I went blind from the sudden light—

An awful explosion sound came over every speaker, so loud it rocked me on my feet—

I felt myself squirting out of the top of my head and loved it.

Then: the explosion became a rumble—

The light seemed to run together into a circle on the ceiling, leaving everything else black.

And the circle became a fireball.

The fireball became a slow-motion film of an atomic-bomb cloud as the rumbling died away. Then the picture faded into a moment of total darkness and the house lights came on.

What a number!

Gevalt, what an act!

So, after the show, when I got them alone and found out they had no manager, not even an option to the Mandala, I thought faster than I ever had in my life.

To make a long story short and sweet, I gave the network the royal screw. I signed the Horsemen to a contract that made me their manager and gave me twenty percent of their take. Then I booked them into the American Dream at ten thousand a week, wrote a check as proprietor of the American Dream, handed the check to myself as manager of the Four Horsemen, then resigned as a network flunky, leaving them with a ten-thousand-dollar bag and me with twenty percent of the hottest group since the Beatles.

What the hell, he who lives by the fine print shall perish by the fine print.

T minus 148 days . . . and counting. . . .

"You haven't seen the tape yet, have you, BD?" Jake said. He was nervous as hell. When you reach my level in the network structure, you're used to making subordinates nervous, but Jake Pitkin was head of network continuity, not some office boy, and certainly should be used to dealing with executives at my level. Was the rumor really true?

We were alone in the screening room. It was doubtful that the projectionist could hear us.

"No, I haven't seen it yet," I said. "But I've heard some strange stories."

Jake looked positively deathly.

"About the tape?" he said.

"About you, Jake," I said, deprecating the rumor with an easy smile. "That you don't want to air the show."

"It's true, BD," Jake said quietly.

"Do you realize what you're saying? Whatever our personal tastes—and I personally think there's something unhealthy about them—the Four Horsemen are the hottest thing in the country right now and that dirty little thief Herm Gellman held us up for a quarter of a million for an hour show. It cost another two hundred thousand to make it. We've spent another hundred thousand on promotion. We're getting top dollar from the sponsors. There's over a million dollars one way or the other riding on that show. That's how much we blow if we don't air it."

"I know that, BD," Jake said. "I also know this could cost me my job. Think about that. Because knowing all that, I'm still against airing the tape. I'm going to run the closing segment for you. I'm sure enough that you'll agree with me to stake my job on it."

I had a terrible feeling in my stomach. I have superiors too and The Word was that "A Trip with the Four Horsemen" would be aired, period. No matter what. Something funny was going on. The price we were getting for commercial time was a precedent and the sponsor was a big aerospace company which had never bought network time before. What really bothered me was that Jake Pitkin had no reputation for courage; yet here he was laying his job on the line. He must be pretty sure I would come around to his way of thinking or he wouldn't dare. And though I couldn't tell Jake, I had no choice in the matter whatsoever.

"Okay, roll it," Jake said into the intercom mike. "What you're going to see," he said as the screening room lights went out, "is the last number."

On the screen: a shot of empty blue sky, with soft, lazy electric guitar chords behind it. The camera pans across a few clouds to an extremely long shot on the sun. As the sun, no more than a tiny circle of light, moves into the center of the screen, a sitar-drone comes in behind the guitar.

Very slowly, the camera begins to zoom in on the sun. As the image of the sun expands, the sitar gets louder and the guitar begins to fade and a drum starts to give the sitar a beat. The sitar gets louder, the beat gets more pronounced and begins to speed up as the sun continues to expand. Finally, the whole screen is filled with unbearably bright light behind which the sitar and drum are in a frenzy.

Then over this, drowning out the sitar and drum, a voice like a sick thing in heat: "Brighter . . . *than a thousand suns* . . ."

The light dissolves into a closeup of a beautiful dark-haired girl with huge eyes and moist lips, and suddenly there is nothing on the sound track but soft guitar and voices crooning low: "Brighter . . . *oh, God, it's brighter . . . brighter . . . than a thousand suns* . . ."

16

The girl's face dissolves into a full shot of the Four Horsemen in their Grim Reaper robes and the same melody that had played behind the girl's face shifts into a minor key, picks up whining, reverberating electric guitar chords and a sitar-drone and becomes a dirge: "*Darker . . . the world grows darker . . .*"

And a series of cuts in time to the dirge:

A burning village in Asia strewn with bodies—

"*Darker . . . the world grows darker . . .*"

The corpse heap at Auschwitz—

"*Until it gets so dark . . .*"

A gigantic auto graveyard with gaunt Negro children dwarfed in the foreground—"I think I'll die . . ."

A Washington ghetto in flames with the Capitol misty in the background—

". . . *before the daylight comes . . .*"

A jump-cut to an extreme closeup on the lead singer of the Horsemen, his face twisted into a mask of desperation and ecstasy. And the sitar is playing double-time, the guitar is wailing and he is screaming at the top of his lungs: "*But before I die, let me make that trip before the nothing comes . . .*"

The girl's face again, but transparent, with a blinding yellow light shining through it. The sitar beat gets faster and faster with the guitar whining behind it and the voice is working itself up into a howling frenzy: ". . . *the last big flash to light my sky . . .*"

Nothing but the blinding light now—

". . . *and zap! the world is done . . .*"

An utterly black screen for a beat that becomes black, fading to blue at a horizon—

". . . *but before we die let's dig that high that frees us from our binds . . . that blows all cool that ego-drool and burns us from our mind . . . the last big flash, mankind's last gas, the trip we can't take twice . . .*"

Suddenly, the music stops dead for half a beat. Then:

The screen is lit up by an enormous fireball—

A shattering rumble—

The fireball coalesces into a mushroom-pillar cloud as the roar goes on. As the roar begins to die out, fire is visible inside the monstrous nuclear cloud. And the girl's face is faintly visible, superimposed over the cloud.

A soft voice, amplified over the roar, obscenely reverential now: "Brighter . . . *great God, it's brighter . . . brighter than a thousand suns. . . .*"

And the screen went blank and the lights came on.

I looked at Jake. Jake looked at me.

"That's sick," I said. "That's really sick."

"You don't want to run a thing like that, do you, BD?" Jake said softly.

I made some rapid mental calculations. The loathsome thing ran something under five minutes . . . it could be done. . . .

"You're right, Jake," I said. "We won't run a thing like that. We'll cut it out of the tape and squeeze in another commercial at each break. That should cover the time."

"You don't understand," Jake said. "The contract Herm rammed down our throats doesn't allow us to edit. The show's a package—all or nothing. Besides, the whole show's like that."

"All like that? What do you mean, all like that?"

Jake squirmed in his seat. "Those guys are . . . well, perverts, BD," he said.

"Perverts?"

"They're . . . well, they're in love with the atom bomb or something. Every number leads up to the same thing."

"You mean . . . they're *all* like that?"

"You got the picture, BD," Jake said. "We run an hour of that, or we run nothing at all."

"Jesus."

I knew what I wanted to say. Burn the tape and write off the million dollars. But I also knew it would cost me my job. And I knew that five minutes after I was out the door, they would have someone in my job who would see things their way. Even my superiors seemed to be just handing down The Word from higher up. I had no choice. There was no choice.

"I'm sorry, Jake," I said. "We run it."

"I resign," said Jake Pitkin, who had no reputation for courage.

T minus 10 days . . . and counting. . . .

"It's a clear violation of the Test-Ban Treaty," I said.

The Under Secretary looked as dazed as I felt. "We'll call it a peaceful use of atomic energy, and let the Russians scream," he said.

18

"It's insane."

"Perhaps," the Under Secretary said. "But you have your orders, General Carson, and I have mine. From higher up. At exactly eight-fifty-eight P.M. local time on July fourth, you will drop a fifty-kiloton atomic bomb on the designated ground zero at Yucca Flats."

"But the people . . . the television crews . . ."

"Will be at least two miles outside the danger zone. Surely, SAC can manage that kind of accuracy under 'laboratory conditions.'"

I stiffened. "I do not question the competence of any bomber crew under my command to perform this mission," I said. "I question the reason for the mission. I question the sanity of the orders."

The Under Secretary shrugged, and smiled wanly. "Welcome to the club."

"You mean you don't know what this is all about either?"

"All I know is what was transmitted to me by the Secretary of Defense, and I got the feeling he doesn't know everything, either. You know that the Pentagon has been screaming for the use of tactical nuclear weapons to end the war in Asia—you SAC boys have been screaming the loudest. Well, several months ago, the President conditionally approved a plan for the use of tactical nuclear weapons during the next monsoon season."

I whistled. The civilians were finally coming to their senses. Or were they?

"But what does that have to do with—?"

"Public opinion," the Under Secretary said. "It was conditional upon a drastic change in public opinion. At the time the plan was approved, the polls showed that seventy-eight point eight percent of the population opposed the use of tactical nuclear weapons, nine point eight percent favored their use and the rest were undecided or had no opinion. The President agreed to authorize the use of tactical nuclear weapons by a date, several months from now, which is still top secret, provided that by that date at least sixty-five percent of the population approved their use and no more than twenty percent actively opposed it."

"I see . . . just a ploy to keep the Joint Chiefs quiet."

"General Carson," the Under Secretary said, "apparently you are out of touch with the national mood. After the first Four Horsemen show, the polls showed that twenty-five percent of the population approved the use of nuclear weapons. After the second show, the figure was forty-one percent. It is now forty-eight percent. Only thirty-two percent are now actively opposed."

"You're trying to tell me that a rock group—"

"A rock group and the cult around it, General. It's become a national hysteria. There are imitators. Haven't you seen those buttons?"

"The ones with a mushroom cloud on them that say 'Do It'?"

The Under Secretary nodded. "Your guess is as good as mine whether the National Security Council just decided that the Horsemen hysteria could be used to mold public opinion, or whether the Four Horsemen were their creatures to begin with. But the results are the same either way—the Horsemen and the cult around them have won over precisely that element of the population which was most adamantly opposed to nuclear weapons: hippies, students, dropouts, draft-age youth. Demonstrations against the war and against nuclear weapons have died down. We're pretty close to that sixty-five percent. Someone—perhaps the President himself—has decided that one more big Four Horsemen show will put us over the top."

"The President is behind this?"

"No one else can authorize the detonation of an atomic bomb, after all," the Under Secretary said. "We're letting them do the show live from Yucca Flats. It's being sponsored by an aerospace company heavily dependent on defense contracts. We're letting them truck in a live audience. Of course the government is behind it."

"And SAC drops an A-bomb as the showstopper?"

"Exactly."

"I saw one of those shows," I said. "My kids were watching it. I got the strangest feeling . . . I almost wanted that red telephone to ring. . . ."

"I know what you mean," the Under Secretary said. "Sometimes I get the feeling that whoever's behind this has gotten caught up in the hysteria themselves . . . that the Horsemen are now using whoever was using them . . . a closed circle. But I've been tired lately. The war's making us all so tired. If only we could get it all over with . . ."

"We'd all like to get it over with one way or the other," I said.

T minus 60 minutes . . . and counting. . . .

I had orders to muster *Backfish*'s crew for the live satellite relay on "The Four Horsemen's Fourth." Superficially, it might seem strange to order the whole Polaris fleet to watch a television show, but the morale factor involved was quite significant.

Polaris subs are frustrating duty. Only top sailors are chosen and a good sailor craves action. Yet if we are ever called upon to act, our mission will have been a failure. We spend most of our time honing skills that must never be used. Deterrence is a sound strategy but a terrible drain on the men of the deterrent forces—a drain exacerbated in the past by the negative attitude of our countrymen toward our mission. Men who, in the service of their country, polish their skills to a razor edge and then must refrain from exercising them have a right to resent being treated as pariahs.

Therefore the positive change in the public attitude toward us that seems to be associated with the Four Horsemen has made them mascots of a kind to the Polaris fleet. In their strange way they seem to speak for us and to us.

I chose to watch the show in the missile control center, where a full crew must always be ready to launch the missiles on five-minute notice. I have always felt a sense of communion with the duty watch in the missile control center that I cannot share with the other men under my command. Here we are not captain and crew, but mind and hand. Should the order come, the will to fire the missiles will be mine and the act will be theirs. At such a moment, it will be good not to feel alone.

All eyes were on the television set mounted above the main console as the show came on and . . .

The screen was filled with a whirling spiral pattern, metallic yellow on metallic blue. There was a droning sound that seemed part sitar and part electronic and I had the feeling that the sound was somehow coming from inside my head and the spiral seemed etched directly on my retinas. It hurt mildly, yet nothing in the world could have made me turn away.

Then came two voices, chanting against each other:
"Let it all come in . . ."
"Let it all come out . . ."
"In . . . out . . . in . . . out . . . in . . . out . . ."
My head seemed to be pulsing—in-out, in-out, in-out—and the spiral pattern began to pulse color changes with the words: yellow-on-blue (in) . . . green-on-red (out) . . . in-out-in-out-in-out-in-out . . .

In the screen . . . out my head . . . I seemed to be beating against some kind of invisible membrane between myself and the screen as if something were trying to embrace my mind and I were fighting it. . . . But why was I fighting it?

The pulsing, the chanting, got faster and faster till in could not be told from out and negative spiral after-images formed in my eyes faster than they could adjust to the changes, piled up on each other faster and faster till it seemed my head would explode—

The chanting and the droning broke and there were the Four Horsemen, in their robes, playing on some stage against a backdrop of clear blue sky. And a single voice, soothing now: "You are in . . ."

Then the view was directly above the Horsemen and I could see that they were on some kind of circular platform. The view moved slowly and smoothly up and away and I saw that the circular stage was atop a tall tower; around the tower and completely encircling it was a huge crowd seated on desert sands that stretched away to an empty infinity.

"And we are in and they are in . . ."

I was down among the crowd now; they seemed to melt and flow like plastic, pouring from the television screen to enfold me. . . .

"And we are all in here together. . . ."

A strange and beautiful feeling . . . the music got faster and wilder, ecstatic . . . the hull of the *Backfish* seemed unreal . . . the crowd was swaying to it around me . . . the distance between myself and the crowd seemed to dissolve . . . I was there . . . they were here. . . . We were transfixed . . .

"Oh, yeah, we are all in here together . . . together . . ."

T minus 45 minutes . . . and counting. . . .

Jeremy and I sat staring at the television screen, ignoring each other and everything around us. Even with the short watches and the short tours of duty, you can get to feeling pretty strange down here in a hole in the ground under tons of concrete, just you and the guy with the other key, with nothing to do but think dark thoughts and get on each other's nerves. We're all supposed to be as stable as men can be, or so they tell us, and they must be right because the world's still here. I mean, it wouldn't take much—just two guys on the same watch over the same three Minutemen flipping out at the same time, turning their keys in the dual lock, pressing the three buttons. . . . Pow! World War III!

A bad thought, the kind we're not supposd to think or I'll start watching Jeremy and he'll start watching me and we'll get a paranoia feedback going. . . . But that can't happen; we're too stable, too responsible. As long as we remember that it's healthy to feel a little spooky down here, we'll be all right.

But the television set is a good idea. It keeps us in contact with the outside world, keeps it real. It'd be too easy to start thinking that the missile control center down here is the only real world and that nothing that happens up there really matters. . . . Bad thought!

The Four Horsemen . . . somehow these guys help you get it all out. I mean that feeling that it might be better to release all that tension, get it all over with. Watching the Four Horsemen, you're able to go with it without doing any harm, let it wash over you and then through you. I suppose they are crazy; they're all the human craziness in ourselves that we've got to keep very careful watch over down here. Letting it all come out watching the Horsemen makes it surer that none of it will come out down here. I guess that's why a lot of us have taken to wearing those "Do It" buttons off duty. The brass doesn't mind; they seem to understand that it's the kind of inside sick joke we need to keep us functioning.

Now that spiral thing they had started the show with—and the droning—came back on. Zap! I was right back in the screen again, as if the commercial hadn't happened.

"We are all in here together . . ."

And then a closeup of the lead singer, looking straight at me, as close as Jeremy and somehow more real. A mean-looking guy with something behind his eyes that told me he knew where everything lousy and rotten was at.

A bass began to thrum behind him and some kind of electronic hum that set my teeth on edge. He began playing his guitar, mean and low-down. And singing in that kind of drop-dead tone of voice that starts brawls in bars:

"I stabbed my mother and I mugged my paw . . ."

A riff of heavy guitar chords echoed the words mockingly as a huge swastika (red-on-black, black-on-red) pulsed like a naked vein on the screen—

The face of the Horseman, leering—

"Nailed my sister to the toilet door . . ."

Guitar behind the pulsing swastika—

"Drowned a puppy in a cement machine. . . . Burned a kitten just to hear it scream. . . ."

On the screen, just a big fire burning in slow-motion, and the voice became a slow, shrill, agonized wail:

"Oh, God, I've got this red-hot fire burning in the marrow of my brain. . . .

"Oh, yes, I got this fire burning . . . in the stinking marrow of my brain. . . .

"Gotta get me a blowtorch . . . and set some naked flesh on flame . . ."

The fire dissolved into the face of a screaming Oriental woman, who ran through a burning village clawing at the napalm on her back.

"I got this message . . . boiling in the bubbles of my blood. . . . A man ain't nothing but a fire burning . . . in a dirty glob of mud. . . ."

A film clip of a Nuremberg rally: a revolving swastika of marching men waving torches—

Then the leader of the Horsemen superimposed over the twisted flaming cross:

"Don't you hate me baby, can't you feel somethin' screaming in your mind?

"Don't you hate me baby, feel me drowning you in slime!"

Just the face of the Horseman howling hate—

"Oh yes, I'm a monster, mother . . ."

A long view of the crowd around the platform, on their feet, waving arms, screaming soundlessly. Then a quick zoom in and a kaleidoscope of faces, eyes feverish, mouths open and howling—

"Just call me—"

The face of the Horseman superimposed over the crazed faces of the crowd—

"Mankind!"

I looked at Jeremy. He was toying with the key on the chain around his neck. He was sweating. I suddenly realized that I was sweating, too, and that my own key was throbbing in my hand alive. . . .

T minus 13 minutes . . . and counting. . . .

A funny feeling, the captain watching the Four Horsemen here in the *Backfish's* missile control center with us. Sitting in front of my

24

console watching the television set with the captain kind of breathing down my neck. I got the feeling he knew what was going through me and I couldn't know what was going through him . . . and it gave the fire inside me a kind of greasy feel I didn't like. . . .

Then the commercial was over and that spiral-thing came on again and—whoosh!—it sucked me right back into the television set and I stopped worrying about the captain or anything like that. . . .

Just the spiral going yellow-blue, red-green, and then starting to whirl and whirl, faster and faster, changing colors and whirling, whirling, whirling. . . .

And the sound of a kind of Coney Island carousel tinkling behind it, faster and faster and faster, whirling and whirling and whirling, flashing red-green, yellow-blue, and whirling, whirling, whirling . . .

And this big hum filling my body and whirling, whirling, whirling . . . my muscles relaxing, going limp, whirling, whirling, whirling, all limp, whirling, whirling, whirling, oh so nice, just whirling, whirling . . .

And in the center of the flashing spiraling colors, a bright dot of colorless light, right at the center, not moving, not changing, while the whole world went whirling and whirling in colors around it, and the humming was coming from the dot the way the carousel music was coming from the spinning colors and the dot was humming its song to me. . . .

The dot was a light way down at the end of a long, whirling, whirling tunnel. The humming started to get a little louder. The bright dot started to get a little bigger. I was drifting down the tunnel toward it, whirling, whirling, whirling . . .

T minus 11 minutes . . . and counting. . . .

Whirling, whirling, whirling down a long, long tunnel of pulsing colors, whirling, whirling, toward the circle of light way down at the end of the tunnel. . . . How nice it would be to finally get there and soak up the beautiful hum filling my body and then I could forget that I was down here in this hole in the ground with a hard brass key in my hand, just Duke and me, down here in a cave under the ground that was a spiral of flashing colors, whirling, whirling toward the friendly light at the end of the tunnel, whirling, whirling . . .

T minus 10 minutes . . . and counting. . . .

The circle of light at the end of the whirling tunnel was getting bigger and bigger and the humming was getting louder and louder and I was feeling better and better and the *Backfish*'s missile control center was getting dimmer and dimmer as the awful weight of command got lighter and lighter, whirling, whirling, and I felt so good I wanted to cry, whirling, whirling . . .

T minus 9 minutes . . . and counting. . . .

Whirling, whirling . . . I was whirling, Jeremy was whirling, the hole in the ground was whirling, and the circle of light at the end of the tunnel whirled closer and closer and—I was through! A place filled with yellow light. Pale metal-yellow light. Then pale metallic blue. Yellow. Blue. Yellow. Blue. Yellow-blue-yellow-blue-yellow-blue-yellow . . .

Pure light pulsing . . . and pure sound droning. And just the *feeling* of letters I couldn't read between the pulses-not-yellow and not-blue-too quick and too faint to be visible, but important, very important . . .

And then came a voice that seemed to be singing from inside my head, almost as if it were my own:

"Oh, oh, oh . . . don't I really wanna know. . . . Oh, oh, oh . . . don't I really wanna know . . ."

The world pulsing, flashing around those words I couldn't read, couldn't quite read, had to read, could almost read . . .

"Oh, oh, oh . . . great God, I really wanna know . . ."

Strange amorphous shapes clouding the blue-yellow-blue flickering universe, hiding the words I had to read. . . . Damn it, why wouldn't they get out of the way so I could find out what I had to know!

"Tell me tell me tell me tell me tell me. . . . Gotta know gotta know gotta know gotta know . . ."

T minus 7 minutes . . . and counting. . . .

Couldn't read the words! Why wouldn't the captain let me read the words? And that voice inside me: *"Gotta know . . . gotta know . . . gotta know why it hurts me so. . . ."* Why wouldn't it shut up and let me read the words? Why wouldn't it shut up and let me read

26

the words? Why wouldn't the words hold still? Or just slow down a little? If they'd slow down a little, I could read them and then I'd know what I had to do. . . .

T minus 6 minutes . . . and counting. . . .

I felt the sweaty key in the palm of my hand . . . I saw Duke stroking his own key. Had to know! Now—through the pulsing blue-yellow-blue light and the unreadable words that were building up an awful pressure in the back of my brain—I could see the Four Horsemen. They were on their knees, crying, looking up at something and begging: *"Tell me tell me tell me tell me . . ."*

Then soft billows of rich red-and-orange fire filled the world and a huge voice was trying to speak. But it couldn't form the words. It stuttered and moaned—

The yellow-blue-yellow flashing around the words I couldn't read-the same words, I suddenly sensed, that the voice of the fire was trying so hard to form-and the Four Horsemen on their knees begging: *"Tell me tell me tell me . . ."*

The friendly warm fire trying so hard to speak—

"Tell me tell me tell me tell me . . ."

T minus 4 minutes . . . and counting. . . .

What were the words? What was the order? I could sense my men silently imploring me to tell them. After all, I was their captain, it was my duty to tell them. It was my duty to find out!

"Tell me tell me tell me . . ." the robed figures on their knees implored through the flickering pulse in my brain and I could almost make out the words . . . almost . . .

"Tell me tell me tell me . . ." I whispered to the warm orange fire that was trying so hard but couldn't quite form the words. The men were whispering it, too: "Tell me tell me . . ."

T minus 3 minutes . . . and counting. . . .

The question burning blue and yellow in my brain: What was the fire trying to tell me? What were the words I couldn't read?

Had to unlock the words! Had to find the key! A key. . . . The Key? THE KEY! And there was the lock that imprisoned the words, right in front of me! Put the key in the lock. . . . I looked at Jeremy. Wasn't there some reason, long ago and far away, why Jeremy might try to stop me from putting the key in the lock?

But Jeremy didn't move as I fitted the key into the lock. . . .

T minus 2 minutes . . . and counting. . . .

Why wouldn't the captain tell me what the order was? The fire knew, but it couldn't tell. My head ached from the pulsing, but I couldn't read the words.

"Tell me tell me tell me . . ." I begged.

Then I realized that the captain was asking, too.

T minus 90 seconds . . . and counting. . . .

"Tell me tell me tell me . . ." the Horsemen begged. And the words I couldn't read were a fire in my brain.

Duke's key was in the lock in front of us. From very far away, he said: "We have to do it together."

Of course . . . our keys . . . our keys would unlock the words!

I put my key into the lock. One, two, three, we turned our keys together. A lid on the console popped open. Under the lid were three red buttons. Three signs on the console lit up in red letters:

ARMED.

T minus 60 seconds . . . and counting. . . .

The men were waiting for me to give some order. I didn't know what the order was. A magnificent orange fire was trying to tell me but it couldn't get the words out. . . . Robed figures were praying to the fire. . . .

Then, through the yellow-blue flicker that hid the words I had to read, I saw a vast crowd encircling a tower. The crowd was on its feet begging silently—

The tower in the center of the crowd became the orange fire that was trying to tell me what the words were—

Became a great mushroom of billowing smoke and blinding orange-red glare. . . .

T minus 30 seconds . . . and counting. . . .

The huge pillar of fire was trying to tell Jeremy and me what the words were, what we had to do. The crowd was screaming at the cloud of flame. The yellow-blue flicker was getting faster and faster behind the mushroom cloud. I could almost read the words! I could see that there were two of them!

T minus 20 seconds . . . and counting. . . .
Why didn't the captain tell us? I could almost see the words!
Then I heard the crowd around the beautiful mushroom cloud shouting: "DO IT! DO IT! DO IT! DO IT! DO IT!"

T minus 10 seconds . . . and counting. . . .
"DO IT! DO IT! DO IT! DO IT! DO IT! DO IT! DO IT!"
What did they want me to do? Did Duke know? The men were waiting! What was the order? They hunched over the firing controls, waiting. . . . The firing controls . . . ?
"DO IT! DO IT! DO IT! DO IT! DO IT!"

8
"DO IT! DO IT! DO IT! DO IT! DO IT!": the crowd screaming.
"Jeremy!" I shouted. "I can read the words!"

7
My hands hovered over my bank of firing buttons. . . .
"DO IT! DO IT! DO IT! DO IT!" the words said.
Didn't the captain understand?

6
"What do they want us to do, Jeremy?"

5
Why didn't the mushroom cloud give the order? My men were waiting! A good sailor craves action.
Then a great voice spoke from the pillar of fire:
"DO IT . . . DO IT . . . DO IT. . . ."

4
"There's only one thing we can do down here, Duke."

3
"The order, men! Action! Fire!"

2

Yes, yes, yes! Jeremy—

1

I reached for my bank of firing buttons. All along the console, the men reached for their buttons. But I was too fast for them! I would be the first!

0

The Big Flash

Kate Wilhelm's impact on the science-fiction genre is difficult to overestimate. In 1962 she wrote her first novel in the late evenings while her two children were in bed, and she has been a prolific and influential writer ever since. Along with her husband Damon Knight, she helped to establish the Milford Writers' Conference and the Clarion Writers' Workshop, institutions that have influenced so many science-fiction writers working in English that even a summary list of highlights could span for pages.

Kate Wilhelm's first short story "The Pint-Size Genie" was published in Astounding Science Fiction in April of 1956. She is as well known for her mystery novels, including the Barbara Holloway detective series, as she is for her many science-fiction works, such as her novel Where Late the Sweet Birds Sang and her collection The Infinity Box. Her short fiction has received several Nebula and Hugo awards. The author Joanna Russ, speaking of Wilhelm's story "The Village," called it "the best piece of propaganda I have ever read."

"the village"
KATE WILHELM

Mildred Carey decided to walk to the post office early, before the sun turned the two blocks into a furnace. "They've done something to the weather," she said to her husband, packing his three sandwiches and thermos of lemonade. "Never used to be this hot this early."

"It'll get cooler again. Always does."

She followed him to the door and waved as he backed out of the drive. The tomato plants she had set out the day before were wilted. She watered them, then started to walk slowly to town. With a feeling of satisfaction she noticed that Mrs. Mareno's roses had black spot. Forcing the blooms with too much fertilizer just wasn't good for them.

Mike Donatti dozed as he awaited orders to regroup and start the search-and-clear maneuver. Stilwell nudged him. "Hey, Mike, you been over here before?"

"Nope. One fuckin' village is just like the others. Mud or dust. That's the only fuckin' difference."

Stilwell was so new that he was sunburned red. Everyone else in the company was burned black. "Man, could we pass," they liked to say to Latimore, who couldn't. Mr. Peters was sweeping the sidewalk before the market. "Got some good fresh salami," he said. "Ed made it over the weekend."

"You sure Ed made it, not Buz? When Buz makes it, he uses too much garlic. What's he covering up is what I want to know."

"Now, Miz Carey, you know he's not covering up. Some folks like it hot and strong."

"I'll stop back by after I get the mail."

The four Henry children were already out in the street, filthy, chasing each other randomly. Their mother was not in sight. Mildred Carey pursed her lips. Her Mark never had played in the street in his life.

She dropped in the five-and-dime, not to buy anything but to look over the flats of annuals—petunias, marigolds, nasturtiums. "They sure don't look healthy," she said to Doris Offinger.

"They're fine, Miz Carey. Brother bought them fresh this morning from Connor's down at Midbury. You know Connor's has good stock."

"How's Larry getting along? Still in the veterans' hospital at Lakeview?"

"Yes. He'll be out in a couple of weeks, I guess." Doris's pretty face remained untroubled.

"They've got such good doctors down there, I hate to see him get so far from them all, but he wants to come home."

"How can these people stand this heat all the time?" Stilwell said after a moment. The sun wasn't up yet, but it was eighty-six degrees, humidity near one hundred percent.

"People, he says. Boy, ain't you even been briefed? People can't stand it, that's the first clue." Mike sighed and sat up. He lighted a cigarette. "Boy, back home in August. You know the hills where I come from are cold, even in August?"

"Where's that?"

"Vermont. I can remember plenty of times it snowed in August. Nights under a blanket."

"Well, he can help out here in the store. With his pension and the store and all, the two of you are set, aren't you? Isn't that Tessie Hetherton going in Peters' market?"

"I didn't notice her. Did you want one of those flats, Miz Carey?"

"No. They aren't healthy. Connor's must have culled the runts and set *them* out." She stood in the doorway squinting to see across the way to Peters' market. "I'm sure it was. And she told me she's too arthritic to do any more housework. I'll just go talk to her."

"I don't think she will, though. Miz Avery wanted her on Wednesdays and she said no. You know Mr. Hetherton's got a job? With the paper mill."

"Shit. That won't last. They'll pay off a few of last winter's bills and then he'll start to complain about his liver or something and she'll be hustling for work. I know that man."

She left the store without looking back, certain that Doris would be eyeing the price tags of the flats. "You take care of yourself, Doris. You're looking peaked. You should get out in the sun."

"Mrs. Hetherton, you're looking fit again," Mildred Carey said, cornering the woman as she emerged from the store.

"Warm weather's helped some."

"Look, can you possibly come over Thursday morning? You know the Garden Club meets this week, and I can't possibly get ready without some help."

"Well, I just don't know . . . Danny's dead set against my going out to work again."

"But they're going to have to close down the mill. And then where will he be?"

"Close it down? Why? Who says?"

"It's been in the papers for weeks now. All those dead fish, and the stink. You know that committee came up and took samples and said they're the ones responsible. And they can't afford to change over the whole process. They're going to move instead."

"Oh, that. Danny said don't hold your breath. They're making a study, and then they'll have to come up with a plan and have it studied, and all in all it's going to take five years or even more before it all comes to a head."

"Hm. Another big kill and the Department of Health . . ."

Mrs. Hetherton laughed and Mildred Carey had to smile too.

"Well, anyway, can you come over just this time? For this one meeting?"

"Sure, Miz Carey. Thursday morning? But only half a day."

The school bus turned the corner and rolled noisily down the broad new street. The two women watched it out of sight. "Have you seen the Tomkins boys lately?" Mildred Carey asked. "Hair down to here."

"Winona says they're having someone in to talk about drugs. I asked her point blank if there are drugs around here and she said no, but you never can tell. The kids won't tell you nothing."

"Well, I just thank God that Mark is grown up and out of it all."

"He's due home soon now, isn't he?"

"Seven weeks. Then off to college in the fall. I told him that he's probably safer over there than at one of the universities right now." They laughed and moved apart. "See you Thursday."

"Listen Mike, when you get back, you'll go through New York, won't you? Give my mother a call, will you? Just tell her . . ."

"What? That you got jungle rot the first time out and it's gone to your brain?"

"Just call her. Say I'm fine. That's all. She'll want to have you over for dinner, or take you to a good restaurant, something. Say you don't have time. But it'd mean a lot to her to have you call."

"Sure. Sure. Come on, we're moving."

They walked for two hours without making contact. The men were straggling along in two uneven columns at the sides of the road. The dirt road was covered with recent growth, no mines. The temperature was going to hit one hundred any second. Sweat and dirt mixed on faces, arms, muddy sweat trickled down shirts.

The concrete street was a glare now. Heat rose in patterns that shifted and vanished and rose again. Mildred Carey wondered if it hadn't been a mistake to rebuild the street, take out the maples and make it wide enough for the traffic that they predicted would be here in another year or two. She shrugged and walked more briskly toward the post office. That wasn't her affair. Her husband, who should know, said it was necessary for the town to grow. After being in road construction for twenty-five years, he should know. Fran Marple and Dodie Wilson waved to her from outside the coffee shop. Fran looked overdue and miserable. Last thing she needed was to go in the coffee shop and have pastry. Mildred Carey smiled at them and went on.

Claud Emerson was weighing a box for Bill Stokes. Bill leaned against the counter smoking, flicking ashes on the floor. "Don't like it here, get out, that's what I say. Goddamn kids with their filthy clothes and dirty feet. Bet they had marijuana up there. Should have called the troopers, that's what I should have done."

"They was on state land, Bill. You had no call to run them off."

"They didn't know that. You think I'm going to let them plop themselves down right outside my front door? Let 'em find somewhere else to muck about."

Claud Emerson stamped the box. "One seventy-two."

Stilwell and Mike were following Laski, Berat, and Humboldt.

Berat was talking.

"You let it stick out, see, and come at them with your M-16 and you know what they watch! Man, they never seen nothing like it! Scared shitless by it. Tight! Whooee! Tight and hot!"

Stilwell looked as if he saw a green monster. Mike laughed and lit another cigarette. The sun was almost straight up when the lieutenant called for a break. He and Sergeant Durkins consulted a map and Humboldt swore at great length. "They've got us lost, the bastards. This fuckin' road ain't even on their fuckin' map."

Mildred Carey looked through the bills and advertising in her box, saving the letter from Mark for last. She always read them twice, once very quickly to be sure that he was all right, then again, word for word, pausing to pronounce the strange syllables aloud. She scanned the scrawled page, then replaced it in its envelope to be reread at home with coffee. Bill Stokes's jeep roared outside the door, down the street to screech to a halt outside the feed store.

Mildred shook her head. "He's a mean man."

"Yep," Claud Emerson said. "Always was, always will be, I reckon. Wonder where them kids spent the night after he chased them."

Durkins sent out two scouts and the rest of them waited, cursing and sweating. A helicopter throbbed over them, drowned out their voices, vanished. The scouts returned. Durkins stood up. "Okay. About four miles. The gooks are there, all right. Or will be again tonight. It's a free-fire zone, and our orders are to clean it out. Let's go."

Loud voices drifted across the street and they both looked toward the sound. "Old Dave's at it again," Claud Emerson said, frowning. "He'll have himself another heart attack, that's what."

"What good does arguing do anyway? Everybody around here knows what everybody else thinks and nobody ever changes. Just what good does it do?" She stuffed her mail into her purse. "Just have to do the best you can. Do what's right and hope for the best." She waved good-bye.

She still had to pick up cottage cheese and milk. "Maybe I'll try that new salami," she said to Peters. "Just six slices. Don't like to keep it more than a day. Just look at those tomatoes! Sixty-nine a pound! Mr. Peters, that's a disgrace!"

"Field-grown, Miz Carey. Up from Georgia. Shipping costs go up and up, you know." He sliced the salami carefully, medium thick.

A new tension was in them now and the minesweepers walked gingerly on the road carpeted with green sprouts. Stilwell coughed again and again, a meaningless bark of nervousness. Durkins sent him to the rear, then sent Mike back with him. "Keep an eye on the fuckin' bastard," he said. Mike nodded and waited for the rear to catch up with him. The two brothers from Alabama looked at him expressionlessly as they passed. They didn't mind the heat either, he thought, then spat. Stilwell looked sick.

"Is it a trap?" he asked later.

"Who the fuck knows?"

"Company C walked into an ambush, didn't they?"

"They fucked up."

Mildred Carey put her milk on the checkout counter alongside the cottage cheese. Her blue housedress was wet with perspiration under her arms and she could feel a spot of wetness on her back when her dress touched her skin. That Janice Samuels, she thought, catching a glimpse of the girl across the street, with those shorts and no bra, pretending she was dressing to be comfortable. Always asking about Mark. And him, asking about her in his letters.

"That's a dollar five," Peters said.

They halted again less than a mile from the village. The lieutenant called for the helicopters to give cover and to close off the area. Durkins sent men around the village to cover the road leading from it. There was no more they could do until the helicopters arrived. There were fields under cultivation off to the left.

"What if they're still there?" Stilwell asked, waiting.

"You heard Durkins. This is a free-fire zone. They'll be gone."

"But what if they haven't?"

"We clear the area."

Stilwell wasn't satisfied, but he didn't want to ask the questions. He didn't want to hear the answers. Mike looked at him with hatred. Stilwell turned away and stared into the bushes at the side of the road.

"Let's go."

There was a deafening beating roar overhead and Mildred Carey and Peters went to the door to look. A green-and-brown helicopter hovered over the street, then moved down toward the post office, casting a grotesque shadow on the white concrete. Two more of the monstrous machines came over, making talk impossible. There was another helicopter to the north; their throb was everywhere, as if the clear blue sky had loosened a rain of them.

From the feed-store entrance Bill Stokes shouted something lost in the din. He raced to his jeep and fumbled for something under the seat. He straightened up holding binoculars and started to move to the center of the street, looking through them down the highway.

One of the helicopters dipped, banked, and turned, and there was a spray of gunfire. Bill Stokes fell, jerked several times, then lay still. Now others began to run in the street, pointing and shouting and screaming. O'Neal and his hired hand ran to Bill Stokes and tried to lift him. Fran Marple and Dodie Wilson had left the coffee shop, were standing outside the door; they turned and ran back inside. A truck rounded the corner at the far end of the street and again the helicopter fired; the truck careened out of control into cars parked outside the bank. One of the cars was propelled through the bank windows. The thunder of the helicopters swallowed the sound of the crash and the breaking glass and the screams of the people who ran from the bank, some of them bleeding, clutching their heads or arms. Katharine Ormsby got to the side of the street, collapsed there. She crawled several more feet, then sprawled out and was still.

Mildred Carey backed into the store, her hands over her mouth.

Suddenly she vomited. Peters was still on the sidewalk. She tried to close the door, but he flung it open, pushing her toward the rear of the store.

"Soldiers!" Peters yelled. "Soldiers coming!"

They went in low, on the sides of the road, ready for the explosion of gunfire, or the sudden eruption of a claymore. The helicopters' noise filled the world as they took up positions. The village was small, a hamlet. It had not been evacuated. The word passed through the company: slopes. They were there. A man ran into the street holding what could have been a grenade, or a bomb, or anything. One of the helicopters fired on him.

There was a second burst of fire down the road and a vehicle burned. Now the company was entering the village warily. Mike cursed the slopes for their stupidity in staying.

Home was all Mildred Carey could think of. She had to get home.

She ran to the back of the store and out to the alley that the delivery trucks used. She ran all the way home and, panting, with a pain in her chest, she rushed frantically through the house pulling down shades, locking doors. Then she went upstairs, where she could see the entire town. The soldiers were coming in crouched over, on both sides of the road, with their rifles out before them. She began to laugh suddenly; tears streaming, she ran downstairs again to fling open the door and shout.

"They're ours," she screamed toward the townspeople, laughing and crying all at once.

"You fools, they're ours!"

Two of the khaki-clad GIs approached her, still pointing their guns at her. One of them said something, but she couldn't understand his words. "What are you doing here?" she cried. "You're American soldiers! What are you doing?"

The larger of the two grabbed her arm and twisted it behind her. She screamed and he pushed her toward the street. He spoke again, but the words were foreign to her. "I'm an American! For God's sake, this is America! What are you doing?" He hit her in the back with the rifle and she staggered and caught the fence to keep her balance. All down the street the people were being herded to the center of the highway. The soldier who had entered her house came out carrying her husband's hunting rifle, the shotgun, Mark's old .22. "Stop!" she shrieked at him. "Those are legal!" She was knocked down by the soldier behind her. He shouted at her and she opened her eyes to see him aiming the rifle at her head.

She scrambled to her feet and lurched forward to join the others in the street. She could taste blood and there was a stabbing pain in her jaw where teeth had been broken by her fall. A sergeant with a notebook was standing to one side. He kept making notations in it as more of the townspeople were forced from their houses and stores into the street.

Mike Donatti and Stilwell herded a raving old woman to the street; when she tried to grab a gun, Mike Donatti knocked her down and would have killed her then, but she was crying, obviously praying, and he simply motioned for her to join the others being rounded up.

The sun was high now, the heat relentless as the people were crowded closer together by each new addition. Some of the small children could be heard screaming even over the noise of the helicopters. Dodie Wilson ran past the crowd, naked from the waist down, naked

40

and bleeding. A soldier caught her and he and another one carried her jerking and fighting into O'Neal's feed store. Her mouth was wide open in one long unheard scream. Old Dave ran toward the lieutenant, clutching at him, yelling at him in a high-pitched voice that it was the wrong town, damn fools, and other things that were lost. A smooth-faced boy hit him in the mouth, then again in the stomach, and when he fell moaning, he kicked him several times about the head. Then he shot him. Mildred Carey saw Janice Samuels being dragged by her wrists and she threw herself at the soldiers, who fought with her, their bodies hiding her from sight. They moved on, and she lay in a shining red pool that spread and spread. They tied Janice Samuels to the porch rail of Gordon's real-estate office, spread her legs open, and half a dozen men alternately raped and beat her. The sergeant yelled in the gibberish they spoke and the soldiers started to move the people as a lump toward the end of town.

Mike Donatti took up a post at the growing heap of weapons and watched the terrorized people. When the order came to move them out, he prodded and nudged, and when he had to, he clubbed them to make sure they moved as a unit. Some of them stumbled and fell, and if they didn't move again, they were shot where they lay.

The filthy Henry children were screaming for their mother. The biggest one, a girl with blond hair stringing down her back, darted away and ran down the empty street. The lieutenant motioned to the troops behind the group and after an appreciable pause there was a volley of shots and the child was lifted and for a moment flew. She rolled when she hit the ground again. Marjory Loomis threw herself down on top of her baby, and shots stilled both figures.

The people were driven to the edge of town, where the highway department had dug the ditch for a culvert that hadn't been laid yet. The sergeant closed his notebook and turned away. The firing started.

The men counted the weapons then, and searched the buildings methodically. Someone cut down a girl who had been tied to a rail. She fell in a heap. Fires were started. The lieutenant called for the helicopters to return to take them back to base camp.

Berat walked with his arm about Stilwell's shoulders, and they laughed a lot. Smoke from the fires began to spread horizontally, head high. Mike lighted another cigarette and thought about the cool green hills of Vermont and they waited to be picked up.

terrorism

When it comes to fictionally representing the wars that have come after the attacks of 9/11, the most popular and influential works of fiction haven't been produced by novelists, short story writers, or screenwriters, but by political speechwriters and news reporters. What fiction does is simplify the world. It helps us to put the world into a manageable context and, often enough, it helps us to justify our actions or, in this case, our reactions. Thus our national discourse on war and terrorism is filled with fictions.

According to Professor Beau Grosscup, a terrorism expert out of California State University, one of the fictions that is most pervasive today is that there is a clear distinction to be drawn between a soldier and a terrorist. The narrative that the wars in the Middle East are waged by men of good conscience against evildoers is pervasive. Just as pervasive is the notion that state violence and war policy is driven by raw ambition and heartless ideology. Another myth is the myth of moral equivalence between America's war on terrorism and the original attacks.

The most effective and thought-provoking fictions about the various reactions to the terrorist attacks of 9/11—the stories that reach the farthest—eschew these popular readings of events. For actual fiction writers—people who make up lies on purpose in order to better understand the world—stories about terrorism are an exploration of the logic behind the violence. In poor examples of "terrorist" fiction the reader is overwhelmed by the blood and soot and trauma that the author pens into existence, but in the best of it, the reader is shown the terrorists' bomb, the drone missile, the sniper's rifle, and asked to consider them as riddles. There are many different ways to write riddles, and to ask questions. Sometimes, as in Tim Pratt's story "The Frozen One," it might be best to come right out and tell the reader that she's reading a parable, but sometimes it's better to bring the reader in a bit more, to scare her with a ghost, a monster, or a tale about an artificial intelligence.

Tim Pratt is a science-fiction and fantasy writer whose work has appeared in a number of magazines over the years, including Strange Horizons *and* Asimov's Science Fiction. *His story "Impossible Dreams" won the Hugo Award in 2007, and his many novels include* Blood Engines, Dead Reign, *and* Spell Games. *Pratt is also the editor of* Flytrap: A Little 'Zine with Teeth. *Tim's story "The Frozen One" originally appeared in* Lone Star Stories *in 2008. It is told in the second person.*

The novelist and critic Hal Duncan singled it out for praise based on Pratt's skillful handling of a story written in such a "strange mode." However, Duncan also praised Pratt for maneuvering away from a "sledgehammer call-to-arms against the Bush administration" to a much more nuanced plea to entertain the idea that "we should and could and will be ready to act" and change the world.

"the frozen one"
TIM PRATT

ait, don't run away, really, it's okay. No, I don't come from the future. The future isn't a place. I know I look exactly like you, but there's a reason—well, hell, it's because my stupid bosses thought it would make things simpler, if we showed you something straight-up impossible right up front, it would save time trying to convince you I'm telling the truth. But it turns out seeing an identical twin, right down to the blemishes and nose-piercings, just freaks people out. We won't try that again next time. If there is a next time.

Sit down on that park bench. Don't give me that, you don't need to get back to class, you were planning to cut class all afternoon and hang out smoking in the park. Don't you want to hear what I have to say?

So it's pretty complicated. Like, ten semesters of intensive lecturing just to give you the background, and we don't have that kind of time. I've only got about ten minutes to talk to you. Nine minutes, now. I wish I could lay everything out, because I know when I was your age there was nothing I hated more than some bullshit declaration from on high, being told to do something a certain way just because. But the best I can do is try to give you some guidance, tilt the probabilities a little closer toward you doing the right thing if and when the time comes. And the people in charge, who know more about these things than I do, they did a bunch of tests and they say the best way for me to do this is to tell you a story. I'm not supposed to call it a parable, but I'm not going to mess around with you, here, you're a smart kid: it's a parable.

A parable is like a story about some little thing that's supposed to teach you something about a big thing. Yeah, like the good Samaritan, that's a great example. And you know you should take me seriously, right, because I just appeared out of nowhere by those bushes and I look just like you, right down to the pimple on your forehead and the weird hair? Good.

No, it's not a parable about God, it's got monsters and heroes and swords and shit, because we know you like that stuff, you play that fantasy computer game all the time.

Look, don't interrupt me, I've got this thing memorized, it's like a spiel, so just let me go. Okay:

Once upon the time there was a great city that had many names, but most of the people in this story just called it The City. Nobody had ever seen the whole of The City, because you could start walking from one end to the other and die of old age before you explored every basement and tower. Inside some of the oldest buildings, space and time didn't work the way they did elsewhere, and you could get lost forever just walking down a dusty hallway. The City filled a valley, surrounded on all sides by mountains, and the mountains were inhabited by monsters that had lots of names, but most people called them the Halfway People. They looked like ordinary people, most of the time, except when they attacked you, and then they sort of grew extra arms and legs and wings and claws and sometimes even tentacles, and that's when you realized they *always* had those teeth and spines and stuff, you just hadn't been looking at them the right way before.

All the best craftspeople and artisans and engineers and magicians and thieves lived in the The City, because it had all the best schools and restaurants and great dusty warehouses full of ancient stuff, magic and technology and cursed things and treasure. The City did most of its trading with the rest of the world by airship, and the citizens didn't go out into the mountains much. They had good high walls and guards who were especially good at recognizing the Halfway People, and since those were pretty much the only kind of people who ever tried to enter The City on foot anyway, the Halfway People were kept out almost completely.

There were a bunch of heroes who lived in The City, swordsmen and fighting monks and necromancers and this one woman with green skin who could shoot fire from her eyes and fly, but only for short distances. They'd all done lots of adventuring and pillaging and mercenary work, and they mostly hung out together and drank and told stories. This one bar they liked was called The Frozen One, because there was a giant block of magical ice right in the middle of the room—the bar had been built around it, because the owner realized having a giant block of magically unmelting ice meant he could keep his beer really cold for free. There was a guy frozen inside the ice, and even though the ice was kind of foggy, you could still make him out—he was about seven feet tall, big broad shoulders, face all scarred, marked with tattoos all over his body, draped with magical amulets, holding a huge axe with a blade shaped like a crescent moon. Nobody knew his name, just that he'd been some big-shot hero hundreds of years before, when The City was just a village, and that he got frozen in ice for some reason. People used to speculate about why the guy was frozen, but then one day the Mayor turned up holding some old scroll with a prophecy that said the guy was The Chosen One, and would remain frozen until The City was threatened, at which point the ice would melt and he would emerge, axe swinging, to kill the enemy. He would succeed when all the other heroes had fallen, been butchered and eaten, et cetera. The Mayor said the prophecy was certified genuine by the magical scholars, and he was pretty happy, because he was able to cut down the number of guards on the walls. Why worry so much about invasions when a legendary nameless hero was ready to kick invader ass?

But then a war started in a neighboring kingdom, and refugees started streaming in from that other country, way more refugees than the Halfway People could kill and eat in their mountain passes. Soon there were hundreds of refugees banging on the gates to The City, begging to be let in. But the guards didn't want to let them in, because they were afraid Halfway People were hiding among the refugees, pretending to be ordinary humans so they could get inside and kill and eat the fat, prosperous city folk. So the guards asked the city council if they should let the people in, and the council started polling citizens, and the citizens were kind of divided on the issue, so the mayor asked his advisors, and meanwhile days and days passed. Eventually the refugees became numerous enough that they just knocked down the gates and came pouring in by the hundreds, filling the streets, breaking windows, knocking over apple carts, what a mess.

The guards tried to get the gates back up, but by then it was too late—the refugees were hiding everywhere, deep in the deserted parts of The City. And in a couple of days it became apparent that lots of Halfway People had slipped in, too, because they were attacking citizens, even in the well-lit districts, approaching with smiles that turned into bites. In a few days, everything was chaos. The airships had been set on fire, so all communication with the outside was cut off, and burning wreckage littered the ground. The guards were overwhelmed, attacked by teams of Halfway People working in tandem. And then the Halfway People started stealing the guards' uniforms . . . well, things got pretty bad. The Mayor stayed holed-up in his mansion, issuing proclamations and trying to direct the guards, trying to keep the populace calm, but it was a losing battle.

And all this time, the heroes stayed barricaded in the bar, watching through the slits in boarded-up windows, waiting for the hero in the block of ice to wake up and save The City. For a while they told themselves the guards must be winning, or that things weren't as bad as they seemed, because if they were, the hero would have burst from the ice to rescue The City. Every once in a while they thought about going out to help people fight, but they weren't sure what to do, exactly, and then there was the prophecy, nailed up on the wall in a place of honor, describing how all the heroes except the chosen, frozen one would be slaughtered and eaten if they tried to fight the invaders. They tried to chip away the ice with their daggers and hatchets, to speed up the process, and the green woman shot fire from her eyes at the ice to try to melt it, but none of that worked.

Then one day a man came in through a concealed side entrance none of the heroes had even known about. They recognized him instantly: long dirty gray hair, grimy clothes made of animal skins and strange leathers, and those incongruously clean magical boots. This was the legendary, infamous Howlaa, the walker over worlds. He stared at the heroes, and the heroes stared at him, and Howlaa shouted, "What are you idiots doing in here? I thought all The City's heroes were dead!"

They looked at each other, and coughed, and mumbled, and finally the green woman said, "We've just been waiting for this guy in the block of ice to wake up and go fight. We were going to help him, once he did."

Howlaa scowled, and beckoned, and the heroes gathered around him, because the chance to hear Howlaa speak was a rare one. "You stupid bastards," he began. "Let me tell you a story. I was once walking through the many worlds of the sky, and I came to a great city—not so great as this one, but more impressive in some ways—called New York. There was a woman there, named Kitty something, and one night she came home very late and started toward her apartment. Before she reached her front door, she was attacked by a man, who stabbed her. The man went away and left her bleeding, but after a while he came back, and followed the trail of blood she'd left as she crawled away. Once he found her again, he did unspeakable things to her, and stabbed her to death. This woman Kitty had neighbors, and some of them heard her calling for help, and some others saw her get stabbed, but none of them called the city guards, and none of them came to her aid. For a long time, people thought this was proof of how horrible and jaded and uncaring the people of that city were, but the truth is more complicated. Some scholars performed experiments later, where they tricked people into thinking another person was in danger. They discovered that, when people are alone, they usually rush to help a person in distress. But when people are in groups, they don't rush—instead, they seem to expect that someone else will do the rescuing, or the calling for help. That's what Kitty's neighbors did—they waited for someone else to do the hard work, as if there were some Chosen One waiting to swoop in and save the day. I've got a hard truth for you, sucklings—there is no Chosen One. There's just you, and the things you choose to do."

And the heroes sputtered, and protested, and pointed to the prophecy, and said, "Look, it's there, it's been certified, the Frozen One is the Chosen One."

So Howlaa took down the scroll, and turned it this way and that, and squinted at it, and snorted, and said, "No he's not, he's just some dead idiot who got frozen. This isn't an ancient prophecy. It's written on the back of a restaurant take-out menu." And he showed them the scroll, and now they could all see it, and couldn't imagine how they'd ever been fooled—except they knew it was some trick of the Halfway People, who were skilled at such illusions.

"The mayor must be told!" the green woman shouted, and the heroes set out, with Howlaa in the lead, toward the mayor's mansion.

The streets were filled with Halfway People, who didn't bother to disguise themselves anymore. Many of the heroes died on the trip, including Howlaa, which was a shock, because in spite of themselves, they'd believed he was somehow truly the chosen one. Eventually the green woman and a couple of others made their way to the mansion, and inside. The Mayor was there, but to their horror they saw he was actually a Halfway Person too. He'd come into The City secretly years before, pretending to be human all that time, finally rising to a position of power, just waiting for his chance to let his fellow monsters in. The heroes hid in an adjoining room and listened to the Mayor talk to his councilors, and discovered that he'd created the false prophecy, and that he was ordering the few remaining human guards into ambushes. The heroes despaired, but finally the green woman rallied them—they might die, but at the very least they could kill the Mayor, and hope that without his guidance the Halfway People would lose their grip on The City. And so they steeled themselves, and went into the office, and did battle.

No, that's it. That's the whole story.

No, for the last time, I'm not from the future, I'm not *you*. I'm from . . . someplace else. Sort of a kingdom next door. And there's some bad stuff happening there, way more complicated than heroes and Halfway People, but there might be some . . . refugees, you could say. Things might spill over here, to this world. And if they do, and if you're in the right place at the right time—you might be, but we're not sure, it's not like you've got a destiny, you're just some *guy*—we hope you'll try to do the right thing. Don't stand there. Don't wait around. Don't look at your buddies and wait to see what they'll do. There's no such thing as fate, but all kinds of tremendous shit seems to keep happening anyway.

I can't tell you exactly what you'll have to do, because I don't know what's going to happen. None of us do. So we're coming over, talking to as many of you as possible in the few moments we have. It's like, if you teach a kid to play chess, he doesn't just learn how to play chess, he learns how to think a certain way, how to look ahead, think of things in combination, and that's what we're trying to do, we're trying to *show* you.

Damn. Time's up. Here I go. Just remember—

Michael Canfield has published mystery, fantasy, science fiction, horror and just-plain-odd stories on fiction sites including Strange Horizons, Spinetingler, EscapePod, Daily Science Fiction, Black Gate, and other places. His story "Super-Villains" was included in Fantasy: The Best of the Year 2006 edited by Rich Horton. Canfield's novels include Scaffolds, Growing Up Zombie, Blue City, and Voyage to the Cloud Planet.

His story "The Language of Monsters" was included in his collection Stairwell to Hell and is a monster story about the US policy of extraordinary rendition, a monster story that makes it difficult to keep track of who the monster really is.

"the language of monsters"
MICHAEL CANFIELD

jason comes to my cell, sets his watch's alarm. No more than a hour's exposure at a time, no more than every other day.

In the hour we talk about many things: the world, politics, God—and we talk about light. At opposite corners this cell has two naked bulbs, in sockets screwed into the brick.

"I'll see the next locale has a window—and natural exposure."

I thank him. I haven't felt sunlight in so long. The guards had orders to give me an hour a week here, but didn't. I don't trouble Jason with this; he works hard. He holds a responsible position despite his youth; he has more important concerns. Today I leave Egypt for another site anyway, so the matter loses significance.

Instead, I ask about my next assignment.

"You're worried," Jason says.

My previous assignment: the black-bearded Saudi, heavy browed, black eyed, yielded no intel. To date none have. I tell Jason I fear if I fail again I'll receive no more assignments and he will no longer handle me.

"That's irrational," Jason waves the notion away. "We're a team."

"I doubt my abilities," I tell him.

Jason frowns, wounded. "You have done *everything* I've asked. It's on me."

Before Jason gave me a job, I had no meaningful existence. Meaninglessness makes solitude unbearable. I can't return there. I spare Jason this, but he feels it anyway.

"Look at me," says Jason. "This is the one. A *high-value* subject. A driver, from Yemen, detained in Basra. This is the break I've . . . that *we*'ve waited for."

Jason checks his watch. He calls it a diver's watch. It resists water, it shows direction, it does many useful things, and now it tells him our time together draws short. "We should pray," he says.

We kneel in the sawdust. Arms out, palms upward, we give Our Heavenly Father thanks.

". . . Lord help us see what lies hidden, help us rid this world of these monsters who would rain terror on innocents. Give us strength to do our work. In Jesus's name. Amen." Jason kneels a moment longer, eyes shut, unblemished face serene.

"Feel that," he says. "We're never alone."

God exists in all things.

Jason's watch alarm goes off.

After a deep breath he rises, brushes sawdust off his khakis, calls the guards to bring the crate.

Safety concerns require I travel in it. A move (I must move often) takes two or three days, sometimes longer. Lying down in a lead-lined crate for transport reminds me of the concrete tomb in Abu Ghraib prison where the Americans found me and liberated me. The tomb had, Jason explained, probably housed me for decades. In the crate, I will lose myself, cease existence. This thought would send me into despair except I know Jason will free me ASAP. I have avoided food beforehand, because, though this mind and soul sleep in the crate, this body still fouls itself.

Jason will fly ahead, but first he injects me with the sleep drug to ease my passage. He tells me one more thing:

"I can't do it without you, Ba'al. I need your help."

Before Jason became my handler, I had no identity. I cannot lose his friendship.

Jason fights to keep the world safe from terror.

So do I.

I cannot fail.

He needs help only I can give.

I awake at the next site. Jason has prepared it, instructed the guards, chosen my cell, but has already returned to Virginia for other work.

56

I lie on a mattress, one of two. I sit up. I acclimatize. Concrete walls. A latrine bucket rests in a narrow space between the mattresses. Straw covers the other bits of naked floor, which measures two meters by two. On the ceiling, three meters high, powerful fluorescents behind chicken wire hum and flicker. A small window in the cell's door has bars, but no glass. The cell has no window to the outside, no sunlight.

Circumstances often limit the available options. Anyway I have work to do.

Nine days pass.

On the tenth, my assignment begins.

I stand at the door, press the side of my face against window bars. At this angle I can see way way down the long long hall. The guards have a detainee.

The detainee, who appears small, wears a hood. The legs and sleeves of the jumpsuit the detainee wears bunch up over wrist and ankle shackles. The detainee shuffles down the hallway between the guards.

I step away from the door.

Three days form the standard length of an assignment. In three days I will see Jason again.

One mattress in this cell appears cleaner than the other. I have left the clean mattress alone. Now I remove straw that worked its way onto the mattress and find spiders there. I brush them away. "Dirty damn spiders! Get lost!"

Tumblers turn. The guards bring in the detainee, who makes no sound, not crying.

The guards here work twelve-hour shifts, in pairs. They wear gray wool masks; one wears a gold watch, the others I distinguish by posture. I believe this site lies in Europe. At the Egyptian site the guards acted lax. Just as they did not give me my hour's sunlight, they did not usually hide their faces—despite orders.

Here, the guards always wear their masks.

They unshackle the detainee. They remove the hood. Freed, the detainee's hair, black stranded with gray, falls slack and wet. I see why this detainee appears small.

Besides in DVDs that these guards play on their desk at the hallway's end, I have not seen a woman for so long. In my professional capacity Jason has never assigned me a woman. However, women as well as men, exist in my conscience.

I have forgotten, as individuals, the people I knew before my liberation. While entombed, my thoughts decayed, but shadows remain.

The detainee blinks to adjust to the bright light in the cell. She fights to absorb her surroundings: the walls, the straw . . .

She takes me in last. Her knees buckle. I appear too large for the cell. I appear with a black beard, heavy brows, and black eyes. I remember seeing this myself, so I know how I look. My jumpsuit appears dingy compared to the detainee's cleaner one.

She watches the guards go.

The guards have orders not to speak to each other around me, but after they relock the cell, one makes a remark to the other. Even though they always wear their masks, they do not follow every order given. However, I have not heard them speak their language enough yet to understand it.

The detainee shrinks into the corner. "Hello," I say in Arabic. "People call me Ba'al. What may I call you?"

She doesn't answer. I try other dialects and some other languages but the problem lies elsewhere. I think she does speak Arabic, and probably English. She experiences shock. She shakes. Her skin, like her hair, appears wet from perspiring, which tells me she does not experience dehydration. I find this fortunate, as we have no water in the cell, and I don't know when the guards will bring some.

I sit against the wall in the corner furthest away. I motion her to sit too. She crouches, wraps her arms around her knees.

"How long since you have seen your family?" I ask.

She doesn't answer.

"You don't want to talk?" I ask.

For a long time I wait and listen to her breathe.

She falls asleep in a ball in the corner. I come close slowly, as not to wake her. Exhaustion binds her. I move her onto the cleaner mattress and use straw to make a pillow for her.

I lie on my own mattress.

The guards put in a DVD. The other cells in the hallway stand empty of course, and little noise exists to interfere with the sound of DVDs. The guards like DVDs in English, of people with American accents. I don't know if the guards speak English, so I don't know whether they understand the DVD voices or simply enjoy the images of people and things.

58

They have several different DVDs and replay them often. I recognize this one from the music. I like the last part of this DVD best and when that begins I rise and go to the little window in the door. I feel the guards like the last part best too. The soldier in the DVD named Ripley protects a young friend called Newt from an alien. The alien has no name. To kill the alien, Ripley crawls into a device resembling a strong artificial man. The alien threatens Ripley's and her friend's way of life. The alien kills people, including many Marines, but in the end Ripley kills the alien.

Hours and hours later, when she wakes, the detainee exists weaker. Normally, sleep restores strength and health in people.

Not near me, however.

She does not try to rise. The time hasn't come yet, so I go to her, try to cradle her shoulder to help her sit up. She recoils from me. "Get away!" she says in Arabic. Her accent sounds poor. I think I know her accent.

"What country do you call home?" I ask in English.

"I am a legal resident of Canada!" she shouts. Tears well in her eyes. A laugh escapes her lips, despite everything. "As if that mattered," she says, "here."

I find laughter infectious, so I laugh too.

She exhales. "Am I here to torture you?" she says.

"Torture me?" I ask. "Why?"

She looks me up and down. "A woman in your cell. You must find that humiliating."

"Why?"

"You're Saudi, aren't you?"

She guesses that from the accent from my mouth when I speak. I let her think so.

"There you are then," she says.

"They call me Ba'al. What do they call you?"

"My name is Muhammad," she says.

"That does not seem right."

"No I suppose it doesn't seem right to you. It isn't the name I was born with. Obviously."

"Oh. Did Jason name you?"

Her look tells me she doesn't know Jason.

"Jason named me Ba'al," I explain.

"Both our names are lies then."

"Jason tells the truth."

"You're certain? You have faith? Of course you do."

"Of course I have faith, of course I do. Don't you have faith?"

"Not your kind. Do you know where your name comes from?"

"From Jason."

"No, I mean. . . . Well, you should ask this Jason what your name means sometime."

"You drive a car?"

"I do."

"Oh."

"That surprises you."

"In Canada?"

"Europe also. We can drive in most places."

"In Canada, Europe, The United States. No, that doesn't surprise me."

She makes an expression like a smile, but with lips only. Her eyes don't smile.

"Talking to you seems interesting," I say.

"Seems? Aren't you sure?"

"No."

The word frightens her, or perhaps the way I say it does.

"The process does not go like this . . ." I reach out. She shrinks away. I put my hands over her face, her nose, her mouth, her eyes. She struggles, but her weak body, unlike her mind, cannot fight. My last assignment, the black-beard Saudi, heavy browed, and black eyed, the man who appeared too big for the cell, he had a mind that long intern-ment had broken.

If, like this woman who calls herself Muhammad, a detainee come to me with a mind still strong, the process can take many days, not three, but I haven't the time so, pressing my hands against her face, I pull her mind.

It doesn't work. I cause her fear. The fear could move her, but she remains unprepared. She doesn't accept.

Or I can make her accept, finish the job, and see Jason soon.

Enough. I must stop.

I remove my hands and sit back. I have orders; I have duty. Her chest rises and falls, she sleeps again.

I follow orders because I, as Jason would say, "am" a soldier. Not everyone can soldier. A guard, for example, says Jason, "is" not a soldier necessarily—even though a guard may belong to the armed forces. For example, according to Jason, the American guards at Abu Ghraib prison back in 2004 did not act as soldiers. Those men and women lacked leadership; he doesn't fault them that. He *does* fault them for lacking discipline. He says he and I, true soldiers in the war on terror, strive for a higher standard. We have a hard job, we fight monsters, but cannot allow ourselves to become them. This fight brings value to my life.

Six days pass with her—not three. *Six* days. For the last two I've female Mohammad's life force in my hands, as she fades despite resistance.

"What happens now?" she asks. She knows. They always know. Not on the surface, not in a place they can articulate something so outside their experience, but they do know. So we wait.

"We can talk," I say.

"About what?"

"Whatever you wish. You have children?"

She shook her head.

"Husband?"

She smiles, almost laughs to herself. "No."

"Why not? You don't like them?"

She considers her response. "I think I like work more."

"Works give life meaning," I tell her.

"Yes."

"Tell me about your work."

"I made—I *make*—films. Movies."

"I like movies. Did you make any the guards have?"

"I somehow doubt it. I make documentaries. About women. About people. *Our* people. Our culture."

"Oh."

"That's a common reaction." She pauses to rest. "I have a question. In all this time, you haven't used the verb 'to be' once."

"You noticed?"

"You seem pleased. Forgive me, how can you speak a language so well, know its idioms, and not know the verb 'to be'?"

"I know the verb, but it reflects the world poorly. It implies some permanent state. Yet everything moves. We change, we flow, and merely appear to 'be.' 'To be' means stasis; stasis means death. I rejected the nihilism of stasis, the monstrosity of 'to be.'"

She coughs deeply. Her isolated existence ebbs. I give her some water. "We *are* alive," she says. "I *am*. Though for how much longer?"

"You will live as long as I do, and I have already lived a long time."

"What are you? Are you good?"

"I seek 'to be' good. I can perhaps accept that use of the word. Though goodness, if I possess any, must come from my actions, because how can it pass that I 'am' good, unless I do good things?"

She does not hear me. "I have to tell you, when they first brought me here, I feared you."

"Now you feel close to me."

She nods.

"You feel the transference. I come toward you. Allow it."

"Can you forgive me? In this cell, looking like you do, I assumed you were a terrorist. Even though I'm falsely accused myself."

"You don't need my forgiveness. You have God's."

She formed the last words she would speak as an individual, as separate existence: "Poor foolish man-child. How can you still hold on to *that* even in this place? There is no God. Not even a false one. Only people." She closes her eyes, *her* eyes, for the last time. With great effort she wraps her hands around mine. "Only us."

Exhausted, I lay down next to her.

Six days, six days it has taken.

Not three.

Many more hours pass through the night while last vestiges dissipate, and the mummy forms.

At last I can rise. I call the guards.

While I listen to their footsteps approach, I feel a start.

This one exists different than me, and the others in me. She does not believe in God. No God, not even the wrong God. She said so, and now I feel a floor pulled away beneath me, this void, this empty, this non—I don't know what to do with this.

The guards open the cell door.

Jason has briefed the guards for what they now do, but they find themselves unready, nevertheless. This always happens. This counts high among the reasons Jason moves me often.

Jason has told the guards to expect a mummified corpse of the Saudi man in the cell with the newer detainee. The cover story exists to protect them. Jason does not tell lies; however, he sometimes finds it necessary to simplify facts. So the guards believe they see the woman who called herself Mohammad alive in the cell, and the large Saudi man dead. Actually they still see me: Ba'al. I have moved to the female's form and discarded the black-bearded Saudi's, like a shell. I do this each time. Each time I carry the minds and the feelings of all the others I have interrogated with me. Once I speak the memories of the female Muhammad to Jason the memories will start to fade. The person's essence stays longer. Forever? I hope Jason comes soon, because the memories now exist heavy in me, provoking me.

The guards come, look at the mummy, and look at me. One gasps. Yet, what can they imagine I have done? They have orders not to engage me. They have orders to remove the mummy and notify Jason. Yet they want to speak to me. They think I, this small woman they see before them, has done something.

One guard goes to the mummy's feet and crouches. The other, the one wearing a gold watch, remains standing and stares at me. The crouched guard says something in their language to the guard wearing the watch. He says something back, but he says it while looking at me.

The crouched guard shakes his head, says something that undoubtedly means *No!*

The guard with the watch ignores him. He thinks I have done something. He knows it.

"Up!" he says to me in English. I stand. I anticipate a beating.

In halting English, he orders me to lift from the mummy's shoulders. He orders the other guard to drop the feet. He makes me drag the mummy from the cell.

This small female body finds the mummy of the too-large Saudi heavy to move. Dry, not as heavy as a still-inhabited body, but heavy enough. The guard makes me drag the mummy down the long long hall, then down another, and down to a cellar. There, a great iron furnace blazes. The guard has me force the mummy into it. We wait while the mummy burns. For the first time I witness a mummy's disposal. The fire reminds me of sunlight.

After the blaze consumes the mummy, I think we will leave. Instead, the guard with the gold watch motions his fellow out, but gestures that I remain. The guards argue, but the guard with the watch possesses the stronger will. The other leaves.

When we stand alone, the guard speaks again in English. "I see you in there, monster."

I say nothing.

"Surprised? Monster? Surprised?"

I say nothing.

"I hear from rumors. Stories. You are real. I see you."

"I exist," I tell him.

"Exist. Yes, you exist."

He comes closer to my face. "Now you are an old woman, eh monster? Who next? Who knows, eh?" He yanks his mask up. His face appears more narrow than I had expected. He has, perhaps, about the same years Jason has, but possesses the teeth of an older man—brown, and gray gums that expel rot from his mouth. Bloodshot eyes. Blemishes.

His thick breath chokes me. "Who next monster? Me? You take me? You try?"

"I don't know."

He jerks his hand, as if to strike. I flinch, yet the blow doesn't come. He stops his hand short, then laughs. "I touch?" he asks. "No. I no touch. If I touch, then next time I . . ." and he gestures toward the furnace. "I no touch you. You no touch me, understand?"

"You have nothing to fea—"

"Understand! Monster!"

"I understand."

"If you *try* touch me . . ." He makes a slitting gesture with his thumb close to my throat. "Understand me now, monster?"

"Yes."

"Say *yes sir!*"

"Yes sir."

"You smart, eh? Back to your cell, smart monster. Wait for your CIA man." He laughed. "You're old woman now!"

He returns me to my cell.

I lay on the less-clean mattress. After awhile the guards put in the DVD of Ripley, her friend Newt, and the alien. I delight in listening to the sounds that begin this movie, knowing soon will come the part I like best, where Ripley saves Newt from the alien that threatens their way of life and has killed many Marines.

This time, as the DVD plays, the guards do not watch in silence. At least one does not. He whoops and hollers at the movie. He jeers at the alien in English. "Kill the monster!" He shouts and laughs. "Die damn you. Die!"

I do not rise to watch the DVD's end through the window in the cell door this time. I don't like this movie anymore.

In the morning I wake to Jason's footsteps coming down the hall. My heart leaps. I leap. On my feet I await him.

The guard's masked face appears in the window. Behind him Jason looks down, studying the case file most likely. The guard unlocks the door, pushes it open, stands aside. He still wears his gold watch. Jason looks up at me.

When Jason sees me, he starts. He looks at the guard, then back into the file. He almost steps back into the hall. He looks at the empty cell across the hall. These reflexive actions last but a moment. He tempers his expression.

"It's you?" he asks. Then, still in English, to the guard he says, "Step out." The guard steps out. "Excuse me a minute," Jason says to me. Then he walks with the guard partway back down the hallway. In quiet tones, Jason questions him about the last detainee, the woman called Muhammad. I hear her name spoken. The guard answers as best he can with his English. He confirms indeed the last detainee "was" female, confirms the removal of the mummy.

Jason sends the guard away and returns to my cell, closing the door behind him.

He smiles at me, but the smile does not spread to his eyes.

He sets the alarm on his wristwatch. "I'm taken aback, Ba'al. Frankly I . . ." Again, he looks down at the file in his hands. He flips over a page. Then he does something he never has done before. Jason turns the file around and shows me. "Do you recognize him?" Jason asks, referencing a photo of a man's face.

I do not.

"You see the name?"

I do. This man has the forename Muhammad and also the same family name as the female Muhammad.

"Tell me about this woman, Ba'al."

"She took a man's name."

"Okay. Why?"

"For her work. She made documentary films. She chose the Islamic prophet's name to incite, to inspire change. She felt complex about Islam, about Islam and women. She traveled, she wrote, she spoke, she argued. She found many friends, but many others felt she betrayed her culture. She raised money for several Middle Eastern charities; she guesses work with these charities caused her rendition, but has no knowledge of possible terrorist connects to these charities."

"She bears no relation to this man? Here. Read the file." Jason tells me.

Again I look at the photo, read about the man: a Yemeni driver detained in Basra. The woman who called herself Muhammad hailed from Iran, lived in Switzerland from age eleven, later Montreal, then Toronto. I look hard into her self within me.

"She does not know this man."

"All right. Good work. Good work . . ."

Jason appears distressed. He does not act like himself. We do not usually debrief this way. We talk deep and slow about the detainees who come to me.

"I feel as if you want to leave, Jason. Have I offended you? I have failed again."

Jason looks at the ground. "No. This is not . . . this is . . . need to get back to Washington. I . . . this has to be sorted out."

"But, your watch alarm has not gone off yet."

Jason looks at the walls.

"I know. It's unavoidable. This . . . is a . . . situation. I'll be back. Don't . . ." He stops. I feel wetness on my face. I can't help it, and raise my hands to hide.

"Don't be upset," Jason says. "I'm not angry with *you*. You must understand." He hits the file with a forefinger. "This man was tasked to us. He's somewhere in the system. This woman was sent here by mistake, because they have the same name."

"Someone has not done his job," I say.

Jason looks at the file. "A high-value detainee. I was promised. I was promised."

Tears burst from me.

"What is it?" says Jason, stunned.

"Why did you name me Ba'al?"

"Why did I name . . . what?"

She held an idea what my name means, it exists in my mind now, I want it out. "Jason, does the name Ba'al mean what she believed it means?"

"What did she believe?"

"Men give the name Ba'al to a god. But a false god, the god of a false people, the god of an enemy . . ."

"I didn't know you so well then, it's just a name. I'll give you another. We can talk about it."

"You haven't answered. Does my name mean that?"

"Yes. That is what it means."

"I do not exist as a soldier, not like Ripley, I exist as a monster."

"Ripley?"

I explain the movie. I tell Jason about the furnace, the guard's words. Jason breathes and listens.

"All right, here is what I want you to do. Obviously we are going to change sites as soon as I can manage it. Until then, no more movies. No wonder you're upset."

I keep my face hidden behind my hands. Jason clasps my wrists to separate them.

"You know what you remind me of right now?" Jason asks.

I shake my head. "The way I first found you. I promised to take care of you didn't I?"

"You do take care of me."

"It will be okay. I don't want you to be worried. Will you be okay now?"

"I don't know. I will strive for this condition."

"Condition?"

"This condition of okay-ness."

"You and your E-prime! You make me smile. It's called that . . . the way you speak, never using the verb 'to be.' E-Prime. That is the term for it." He reaches into his back pocket and pulls out some folded pages. "Here, I was thinking of you, and I had this urge to look online before leaving home. I printed out some stuff. I thought we could discuss it today if there was time; or should I say, *if time allowed*? It makes perfect sense the way you speak, for you. Here." He tries to press the papers into my hands. "Takes these, read these. When I come back, we'll talk. Okay?"

I nod.

He takes my hand and folds the papers into it. A tear rolls off my nose and falls upon the flesh between Jason's thumb and index finger.

"Oh no," I say.

Jason jumps back. "No! It's all right!"

He takes a small bottle of sanitizer from a pocket and fills his palm with it. He rubs and rubs. "It's all right, see? All right."

I breathe. "Do you still believe in God, Jason?"

He drops his hands to his sides. "Yes. Absolutely."

"God still exists everywhere. We believe, don't we?"

"We believe."

"She does not believe in God, Jason."

"Well . . ."

"She does not believe. I thought when she came to me she would find God within me. She has found nothing. God does not exist in me. How can He?"

"How *can't* he? Ba'al, your faith is being tested by this . . . individual."

"I don't feel God's presence."

"Yes you do! He's always within. Let's pray. Now."

"I cannot find Him, because I never knew His love at all. I lied. God doesn't exist in here. I tried to know Him through you. I lied."

Jason swallows. "This isn't you talking. Kneel with me."

Jason kneels and holds his hands upward. I hesitate.

Jason looks up at me. "Listen to me. You are a miracle, you are unique. No one—no other *being* like you exists. In this dark time you came to us. To *us*. I refuse to allow that's an accident. You have a purpose."

"I haven't helped. I have failed. Each time."

"No! I haven't . . . represented your unique ability well. We haven't been given the right subjects. We need high-value detainees." Then he thinks: *How can I extract information from prisoners that don't have it? Ba'al hasn't failed. I have.*

I hear him think this. I *hear* it.

I kneel. Jason prays aloud and when he finishes we sit together in fellowship.

After a time, eyes still closed, Jason says, "I feel His presence."

I rest my hands. "I see Him. I see Him in you. In your kindness and your faith, and your innocence."

"I'm not innocent, Ba'al. You're the innoc—"

"No. But I know your innocence."

"That's kindness on your part." He rubs the flesh on the back of his hand.

"No. I see it." The tear has only sped a process that began with our first contact.

He checks his watch. "I have to . . ."

"Go. You have shown me God again. I have no fear now. Go, you have shown me the Way." I tell these lies for his sake.

He smiles, picks up the dossier, rises to leave. "I'll sort this out, and I'll see you soon, Ba'al."

"Jason, tell G—" I almost say the name his mind has revealed to me. "Tell your superiors I thank them for the opportunity to serve."

"They are the ones who owe you thanks."

"Jason. Named for a hero." Though the verb *named* leaves a false impression. Jason's department, led by a man named Mitchell Gay, gave Jason the code name he bears.

"So they say." He smiles reflexively. "Jason who sought the golden fleece."

I see so much in his mind. "Jason who sowed the dragon's teeth."

"That too."

He calls for the guard, who comes and unlocks the cell. Jason turns back to me. "See you soon," he says. Before he leaves the floor he makes the guards move their DVD from the hallway.

I lie down under the flickering fluorescents and, like a DVD playing for our mutual eyes, I watch. A link has formed. Jason's superior, Mitchell Gay, warned him this would happen.

I have heard about the world, recalled it through the memories of others; but until today I have never walked in it like this.

Jason returns to Washington on a military flight, experiencing delays and rerouting, then down to Langley by commercial airline. He thinks about Gay humiliating him at their last meeting, and what he will say to Gay about this screw-up with the female.

At Langley, he does not stop at his own office, but goes straight to Gay's.

Gay leans back with his feet cased in snakeskin loafers and propped on his desk. Jason finds this distasteful. Jason wouldn't deface so fine a wood grain with scuff marks. Nor would Jason wear snakeskin.

Jason holds the file of the Yemeni driver named Muhammad. He drops the file on Gay's desk.

"Hello, MacDonald," says Gay, using the name given Jason in this outside world. Kyle MacDonald.

Jason says: "The wrong damn detainee! A woman! What are we doing here?"

Gay says: "Really? What intelligence did you extract from this woman?"

Jason stammers. "What? Why . . . none. She had no relevant intel."

"Too bad," says Gay. "I know how much work you put in this deal. Ya' gave it your best shot, but it's time to shut it down."

Jason, despite his experience with Gay, has somehow still not expected this. "What!" says he. "No! I was promised the driver from Basra. The guy we *know* trained in Afghanistan."

"Sorry, MacDonald, that captive is high-value."

"How can you do this! You expect results and you don't give me anyone I can get results from."

"Your 'special asset' has too permanent an effect on detainees."

"Ba'al's intel will be reliable! He becomes them, and tells me everything . . ."

"How do you know?"

I feel Jason's jaw goes slack. "I . . . I . . ."

Gay says: "Maybe he's not sharing all he's getting."

"Ba'al is loyal! We have a bond."

"Been meaning to talk to you about that."

"This isn't about me!"

"Make sure it isn't."

"What does that mean?"

"Means you're done. I'm boxing that thing. I'm gonna throw it down a volcano or someplace, and I don't want you anywhere near it again."

Jason stammers. He pauses, and clears his throat. "I'll go over your head."

"Listen. With a new administration coming in, I'm having to spend what's left of this one tidying up on the chance changes are expected. Now you may decide to run down the hall to my boss—or to another department—and sing your creature's praise. You may decide to do that. I'm sure you can find somebody above my pay grade to drool over your—your whatever-the-heck-you-got-there, and find something to use it for—or somebody who wants to cut it up, at least. I'm aware. I may be half as smart as you, but I'm twice as old, so consider a moment that I *might* be your bare equal as a man. I understand you were in the seminary before entering public service."

"So?"

"How'd that work out for you?"

"I'm sure it's in my file."

Gay pulls his feet off the desk, sits up. "You want to talk files. I'm sure it *is* in your file, MacDonald." He picks up the file Jason threw down, the driver's file. "I'm *also* sure you need to learn what's in a file *might* not even be worth lining an animal's cage with. Even a really big animal's cage."

Without taking his eyes off Jason, Gay drops the driver's file into a wastebasket.

"Why'd you quit the seminary, MacDonald?"

"I didn't quit. I left."

"Why *did you quit* the seminary, MacDonald?"

"The church is not . . . the church is . . . is not . . ." Jason faltered.

"I'll finish that thought for you. The church is flawed. Not what you thought it'd be. Ineffectual. Hypocritical. Maybe semi-evil at times. So, like many an ex-altar boy you sought a career in government intelligence. Yet, somehow I feel you find us lacking, too."

Jason lowers his head.

"Fun as it is putting the screws to you for its own sake, MacDonald, I'm actually *trying* to do you a favor. You should get out your date book and circle today. Because you will want to look back twenty years from now—a dozen abandoned careers, a lifetime of disappoints from now—and say, 'Well lookee here, that's when that old sonofabitch told me I was full of shit.' Because you *are* full of shit, son."

He scratches his chin before concluding. "My advice is that you now say: 'Yes sir, thank you sir,' shoot back to your desk, fill out your expense report, and await further instructions. Reflect how we—that's *we*—MacDonald, all fall short of God's Glory."

Jason stands a moment, jaw working.

He bends down to Gay's wastebasket and takes the driver's file out.

"All right, MacDonald. I won't say I hope you know what's best because I don't cotton to false hopes."

Jason twists the folder. He considers staying and refuting every ugly word Gay has spewed, but can't find how. *You don't understand me*, he wants to say.

But, he can't say that.

He looks at the folder. "You knew," he says. "There was no mix-up."

"Stuff happens."

"That woman was innocent."

"Really? An innocent woman. A completely innocent Arab-Canadian woman taken into custody at a US airport, interrogated for months at CIA black sites. Stripped. Waterboarded. Least that's what her friends, her colleagues, and a few noisy members of the international press think. No one knows, we don't confirm, but suspicions grow. Her MP starts making rumblings. Would be one heck of a movie, MacDonald. Shame she won't be able to make it."

"I never said anything about her being a moviemaker."

"No, you didn't."

Jason leaves. Under bright fluorescents that never flicker, he walks down a long long hallway, toward the office of his boss's boss. He stops, without entering. Maybe someone else. He goes to another hallway. Another man he knows. A smart man. Jason thought he would make a good mentor once. He goes there and again he stops outside the door. He has the file. He can move the special asset to another department, try again. Ba'al is unique. Supernatural. Perhaps an angel. At least extraterrestrial. No, nothing so mundane. Ba'al defies all we know, sent to us, sent to *me* in these times, to defy a banal world bereft of wonders. The word for that is *miracle*.

Jason grips the doorknob, tries to turn it, his guts churning at the same time. They will cut Ba'al up, or they will agree with Gay and box him, or they will weaponize him. Ba'al is not the problem. We are.

Still there's nothing else to do.

Jason, stop.

Enough.

I stay his hand. I reach. Even so far apart, we connect. Jason tries again to turn the knob.

Stop.

I push. Jason lets his hand fall away.

In relief.

I bid Jason go to the airport. He travels the next thirty-six hours retracing his journey back here.

Jason surprises the guards. They had not expected him, certainly not weeping. The guards rise. Jason says nothing about the DVD player they have already moved back into the hallway. He orders them to let him into my cell.

They do, and lock the door behind them before going back to their station. The guards stay quiet there, disturbed, alert.

Jason collapses in the straw, perspiring, exhausted from isolated days traveling alone.

He looks at me. Defiant. "What are you? A demon?"

"I don't know."

"How long have you been alive?"

"I don't know."

"Where did you come from?"

"From the tomb in Abu Ghraib. The tomb you liberated me from. I remember nothing before."

"Liberated you? Look around! You're in a jail cell!"

"That seems true."

"Did you possess me? I wanted so much to believe in you."

I say nothing.

"What are you! I deluded myself we could do some good, if we kept going. We did no good."

"You *did* do good. For me."

"No. I've wronged you most. I led you down the same bad path as me."

"You used me."

Jason seemed to sink even further. "I'm sorry," he says unable to meet my eyes. "You're right. I did use you."

I sit down next to him. "You used me—like you use each other. You made me feel like a person. That *is* being good to me."

"If only," he says. Then it strikes him. He brightens.

"Did you say *is*?"

"I did."

"You're learning! Still learning from us!"

"I am."

He smiles. With exhaustion, the smile evaporates. He stares up at the flickering lights. "Those are annoying, I'm going to make

73

sure you get a window, a proper window, at the next site—with direct sunlight."

"Rest now," I tell him, and put my hands over his face.

I have never forced transference; nevertheless, I find, at least in this case, it works. All our cumulative time together has helped.

Forcing all the others from myself also helps. I release them into the air.

If God exists, let Him seek His children, so long lost in me, there.

In Jason's voice I call the guards. I lay the spent body of the woman called Mohammed on the cleaner mattress, face to the wall. Because of the rapid transference that empty shell remains wet and tender. Maybe the guards will believe I sleep there, maybe not. If it fools them, then Jason and I, one body—one *thing*, will walk into the sun together.

However, I might instead confess to the guards what I have done. I still have a second to decide. Because whether we escape, or Mitchell Gay entombs us, throws us down a volcano, or if we're dissected, dissembled, and scattered, or even if the panicked guards simply shove us into the furnace, doesn't matter.

My friend Jason despised the failings of men and feared the rebuke of God. He proved too weak for this world, so he now lies sheltered within me. I am a place where men can't use him and God will not follow. I have saved him from these monsters.

Ken Liu (http://kenliu.name) is an author and translator of speculative fiction, as well as a lawyer and programmer. A winner of the Nebula, Hugo, and World Fantasy Awards, he has been published in The Magazine of Fantasy & Science Fiction, Asimov's, Analog, Clarkesworld, Lightspeed, and Strange Horizons, among other places. He also translated the Hugo-winning novel, The Three-Body Problem, by Liu Cixin, which is the first translated novel to win that award.

Ken's debut novel, The Grace of Kings, the first in a silkpunk epic fantasy series, was published by Saga Press in April 2015. Saga also published a collection of his short stories, The Paper Menagerie and Other Stories, in March 2016. He lives with his family near Boston, Massachusetts.

"In the Loop" was originally published in the anthology War Stories: New Military Science Fiction.

"in the loop"
KEN LIU

When Kyra was nine, her father turned into a monster.

It didn't happen overnight. He went to work every morning, like always, and when he came in the door in the evening, Kyra would ask him to play catch with her. That used to be her favorite time of the day. But the yesses came less frequently, and then not at all.

He'd sit at the table and stare. She'd ask him questions and he wouldn't answer. He used to always have a funny answer for everything, and she'd repeat his jokes to her friends and think he was the cleverest dad in the whole world.

She had loved those moments when he'd teach her how to swing a hammer properly, how to measure and saw and chisel. She would tell him that she wanted to be a builder when she grew up, and he'd nod and say that was a good idea. But he stopped taking her to his workshop in the shed to make things together, and there was no explanation.

Then he started going out in the evenings. At first, Mom would ask him when he'd be back. He'd look at her like she was a stranger before closing the door behind him. By the time he came home, Kyra and her brothers were already in bed, but she would hear shouts and sometimes things breaking.

Mom began to look at Dad like she was afraid of him, and Kyra tried to help with getting the boys to bed, to make her bed without being asked, to finish her dinner without complaint, to do everything perfectly, hoping that would make things better, back to the way they used to be. But Dad didn't seem to pay any attention to her or her brothers.

Then, one day, he slammed Mom into the wall. Kyra stood there in the kitchen and felt the whole house shake. She didn't know what to do. He turned around and saw Kyra, and his face scrunched up like he hated her, hated her mother, hated himself most of all. And he fled the house without saying another thing.

Mom packed a suitcase and took Kyra and her brothers to Grandma's place that evening, and they stayed there for a month. Kyra thought about calling her father but she didn't know what she would say. She tried to imagine herself asking the man on the other end of the line *what have you done with Daddy*?

A policeman came, looking for her mother. Kyra hid in the hall so she could hear what he was telling her. *We don't think it was a homicide.* That was how she found out that her father had died. She didn't cry then, and wouldn't cry until much later.

They moved back to the house, where there was a lot to do: folding up Dad's uniforms for storage, packing away his regular clothes to give away, cleaning the house so it could be sold, getting ready to move away permanently. She caressed Dad's medals and badges, shiny and neatly laid out in a box, and that was when she finally cried.

They found a piece of paper at the bottom of Dad's dresser drawer. "What is it?" she asked Mom.

Mom read it over. "It's from your Dad's commander, at the Army." Her hands shook. "It shows how many people he had killed."

She showed Kyra the number: one thousand two-hundred and fifty-one.

The number lingered in Kyra's mind. As if that gave his life meaning. As if that defined him and them.

Kyra walked quickly, pulling her coat tight against the late fall chill.

It was her senior year in college, and on-campus recruiting was in full swing. Because Kyra's school was old and full of red brick buildings named after families that had been wealthy and important even before the founding of this republic, its students were desirable to employers.

She was on her way back to her apartment from a party hosted by a small quantitative trading company in New York that was generating good buzz on campus. Companies in management consulting, financial services, and Silicon Valley had booked hotel rooms around the school and were hosting parties for prospective interviewees every night, and Kyra, as a comp sci major, found herself in high demand. This was the night when she would need to finalize her list of ranked preferences, and she had to strategize carefully to have a shot at getting one of the interview slots for the most coveted companies in the lottery.

"Excuse me," a young man stepped in her way. "Would you sign this petition?"

She looked at the clipboard held in front of her. *Stop the War.*

Technically, America wasn't at war. There had been no declaration of war by Congress, just the President exercising his office's inherent authority. But maybe the war had never stopped. America left; America went back; America promised to leave again some time. A decade had passed; people kept on dying far away.

"I'm sorry," Kyra said, not looking the boy in the eyes. "I can't."

"Are you *for* the war?" The boy's voice was tired, the incredulity almost an act. He was there canvassing for signatures alone in the evening because no one cared. When so few Americans died, the "conflict" didn't seem real.

How could she explain to him that she did not believe in the war, did not want to have anything to do with it, and yet, signing the petition the boy held would seem to her tantamount to a betrayal of the memory of her father, would seem a declaration that what he had done was wrong?

So all she said was, "I'm not into politics."

Back in her apartment, Kyra took off her coat and flipped on the TV.

. . . the largest protest so far in front of the American Embassy. Protestors are demanding that the US cease the drone strikes, which so far have caused more than three hundred deaths in the country this year, many of whom the protestors claim were innocent civilians. The US Ambassador . . .

Kyra turned off the TV. Her mood had been ruined, and she could not focus on the task of ranking her interview preferences. Agitated, she tried to clean the apartment, scrubbing the sink vigorously to drive the images in her mind away.

As she had grown older, Kyra had read and seen every interview with other drone operators who suffered from PTSD. In the faces of those men, she had searched for traces of her father.

I sat in an air-conditioned office and controlled the drone with a joystick while watching on a monitor what the drone camera saw. If a man was suspected of being the enemy, I had to make a decision and pull the trigger and then zoom in and watch as the man's body parts flew around the screen, as the rest of him bled out, until his body cooled down and disappeared from the infrared camera.

Kyra turned on the faucet and held her hands under the hot water, as if she could wash off the memory of her father coming home every evening: silent, sullen, gradually turning into a stranger.

Every time, you wonder: Did I kill the right person? Was the sack on that man's back filled with bombs or just some hunks of meat? Were those three men trying to set up an ambush or were they just tired and taking a break behind those rocks by the road? You kill a hundred people, a thousand people, and sometimes you find out afterwards that you were wrong, but not always.

"You were a hero," Kyra said. She wiped her face with her wet hands. The water was hot against her face and she could pretend it was all just water.

No. You don't understand. It's different from shooting at someone when they're also shooting at you, trying to kill you. You don't feel brave pushing a button to kill people who are not in uniform, who look like they're going for a visit with a friend, when you're sitting thousands of miles away, watching them through a camera. It's not like a video game. And yet it also is. You don't feel like a hero.

"I miss you. I wish I could have understood."

Every day, after you're done with killing, you get up from your chair and walk out of the office building and go home. Along the way you hear the birds chittering overhead and see teenagers walking by, giggling or moping, self-absorbed in their safe cocoons, and then you open the door to your home. Your spouse wants to tell you about her annoying boss and your children are waiting for you to help them with their homework, and you can't tell them a thing you've done.

I think either you become crazy or you already were.

She did not want him to be defined by the number on that piece of paper her mother kept hidden at the bottom of the box in the attic.

"They counted wrong, Dad," Kyra said. "They missed one death."

Kyra walked down the hall dejectedly. She was done with her last interview of the day—a hot Silicon Valley startup. She had been nervous, distracted, and flubbed the brainteaser. It had been a long day and she didn't get much sleep the night before.

She was almost at the elevator when she noticed an interview schedule posted on the door of the suite next to the elevator for a company named AWS Systems. It hadn't been completely filled. A few of the slots on the bottom were blank; that generally meant an undesirable company.

She took a closer look at the recruiting poster. They did something related to robotics. There were some shots of office buildings on a landscaped, modern campus. Bullet points listed competitive salary and benefits. Not flashy, but it seemed attractive enough. Why weren't people interested?

Then she saw it: "Candidates need to pass screening for security clearance." That would knock out many of her classmates who weren't US citizens. And it likely meant government contracts. Defense, probably. She shuddered. Her family had had enough of war.

She was about to walk away when her eyes fell on the last bullet point on the poster: "Relieve the effects of PTSD on our heroes."

She wrote her name on one of the blank lines and sat down on the bench outside the door to wait.

"You have impressive credentials," the man said, "the best I've seen all day, actually. I already know we'll want to talk to you some more. Do you have any questions?"

This was what Kyra had been waiting for all along. "You're building robotic systems to replace human controlled drones, aren't you? For the war."

The recruiter smiled. "You think we're Cyberdyne Systems?"

Kyra didn't laugh. "My father was a drone operator."

The man became serious. "I can't reveal any classified information. So we have to speak only in hypotheticals. Hypothetically, there may be advantages to using autonomous robotic systems over human-operated machines."

"Like what? It can't be about safety. The drone operators are perfectly safe back here. You think machines will fight better?"

"No, we're not interested in making ruthless killer robots. But we shouldn't make people do the jobs that should be done by machines."

Kyra's heart beat faster. "Tell me more."

"There are many reasons why a machine makes a better soldier than a human. A human operator has to make decisions based on very limited information: just what he can see from a video feed, sometimes alongside intelligence reports. Deciding whether to shoot when all you have to go on is the view from a shaking camera and confusing, contradictory intel is not the kind of thinking humans excel at. There's too much room for error. An operator might hesitate too long and endanger an innocent, or he might be too quick on the trigger and violate the rules of engagement. Decisions by different operators would be based on hunches and emotions and at odds with each other. It's inconsistent and inefficient. Machines can do better."

Worst of all, Kyra thought, *a human can be broken by the experience of having to* decide.

"If we take these decisions away from people, make it so that individuals are out of the decision-making loop, the result should be less collateral damage and a more humane, more civilized form of warfare."

But all Kyra could think was: *No one would have to do what my father did.*

The process of getting security clearance took a while. Kyra's mother was surprised when Kyra called to tell her that government investigators might come to talk to her, and Kyra wasn't sure how to explain why she took this job when there were much better offers from other places. So she just said, "This company helps veterans and soldiers."

Her mother said, carefully, "Your father would be proud of you."

Meanwhile, they assigned her to the civilian applications division, which made robots for factories and hospitals. Kyra worked hard and followed all the rules. She didn't want to mess up before she got to do what she really wanted. She was good at her job, and she hoped they noticed.

Then, one morning, Dr. Stober, the head roboticist, called her to join him in a conference room.

Kyra's heart was in her throat as she walked over. Was she going to be let go? Had they decided that she couldn't be trusted because of what had happened to her father? That she might be emotionally unstable? She had always liked Dr. Stober, who seemed like a good mentor, but she had never worked with him closely.

"Welcome to the team," said a smiling Dr. Stober. Besides Kyra, there were five other programmers in the room. "Your security clearance arrived this morning, and I knew I wanted you on this team right away. This is probably the most interesting project at the company right now."

The other programmers smiled and clapped. Kyra grinned shyly at each of them in turn as she shook their outstretched hands. They all had reputations as the stars in the company.

"You're going to be working on the AW-1 Guardians, one of our classified projects."

One of the other programmers, a young man named Alex, cut in: "These aren't like the field transport mules and remote surveillance crafts we already make. The Guardians are unmanned, autonomous flying vehicles about the size of a small truck armed with machine guns and missiles."

Kyra noticed that Alex was really excited by the weapons systems.

"I thought we make those kinds already," Kyra said.

"Not exactly," Dr. Stober said. "Our other combat systems are meant for surgical strikes in remote places or prototypes for frontline combat, where basically anything that moves can be shot. But these are designed for peacekeeping in densely populated urban areas, especially places where there are lots of Westerners or friendly locals to protect. Right now we still have to rely on human operators."

Alex said in a deadpan voice, "It would be a lot easier if we didn't have to worry about collateral damage."

Dr. Stober noticed that Kyra didn't laugh and gestured for Alex to stop. "Sarcasm aside, as long as we're occupying their country, there will be locals who think they can get some advantage from working with us and locals who wish we'd go away. I doubt that dynamic has changed in five thousand years. We have to protect those who want to work with us from those who don't, or else the whole thing falls apart. And we can't expect the Westerners doing reconstruction over there to stay holed up in walled compounds all the time. They have to mingle."

"It's not always easy to tell who's a hostile," Kyra said.

"That's the heart of the issue. Most of the time, much of the population is ambivalent. They'll help us if they think it's safe to do so, and they'll help the militants if they think that's the more convenient choice."

"I've always said that if they choose to help the militants blend in, I don't see why we need to be that careful. They made a decision," Alex said.

"I suppose some interpretations of the rules of engagement would agree with you. But we're telling the world that we're fighting a new kind of war, a clean war, one where we hold ourselves to a higher standard. How people see the way we conduct ourselves is just as important nowadays."

"How do we do that?" Kyra asked before Alex could further derail the conversation.

"The key piece of software we have to produce needs to replicate what the remote operators do now, only better. The government has supplied us with thousands of hours of footage from the drone operations during the last decade or so. Some of them got the bad guys, and some of them got the wrong people. We'll need to watch the videos and distill the decision-making process of the operators into a formal procedure for identifying and targeting militants embedded in urban conditions, eliminate the errors, and make the procedure repeatable and applicable to new situations. Then we'll improve it by tapping into the kind of big data that individual operators can't integrate and make use of."

The code will embody the minds of my father and others like him so that no one would have to do what they did, endure what they endured.

"Piece of cake," said Alex. And the room laughed, except for Kyra and Dr. Stober.

Kyra threw herself into her work, a module they called the ethical governor, which was responsible for minimizing collateral damage when the robots fired upon suspects. She was working on a conscience for killing machines.

She came in on the weekends and stayed late, sometimes sleeping in the office. She didn't view it as a difficult sacrifice to make. She couldn't talk about what she was working on with the few friends she had, and she didn't really want to spend more time outside the office with people like Alex.

She watched the videos of drone strikes over and over. She wondered if any were missions her father had flown. She understood the confusion, the odd combination of power and powerlessness experienced when watching a man one is about to kill through a camera, the pressure to *decide*.

The hardest part was translating this understanding into code. Computers require precision, and the need to articulate vague hunches had a way of forcing one to confront the ugliness that could remain hidden in the ambiguity of the human mind.

To enable the robots to minimize collateral damage, Kyra had to assign a value to each life that might be endangered in a crowded urban area. One of the most effective ways for doing this—at least in simulations—also turned out to be the most obvious: profiling. The algorithm needed to translate racial characteristics and hints about language and dress into a number that held the power of life and death. She felt paralyzed by the weight of her task.

"Everything all right?" Dr. Stober asked.

Kyra looked up from her keyboard. The office lights were off; it was dark outside. She was practically the last person left in the building.

"You've been working a lot."

"There's a lot to do."

"I've reviewed your check-in history. You seem to be stuck on the part where you need the facial recognition software to give you a probability on ethnic identity."

Kyra gazed at Dr. Stober's silhouette in the door to her office, back-lit by the hall lights. "There's no API for that."

"I know, but you're resisting the need to roll your own."

"It seems . . . wrong."

Dr. Stober came in and sat down in the chair on the other side of her desk. "I learned something interesting recently. During World War II, the US Army trained dogs for warfare. They would act as sentries, guards, or maybe even as shock troops in an island invasion."

Kyra looked at him, waiting.

"The dogs had to be trained to tell allies apart from enemies. So they used Japanese-American volunteers to teach the dogs to profile, to attack those with certain kinds of faces. I've always wondered how those volunteers felt. It was repugnant and yet it was also necessary."

"They didn't use German-American or Italian-American volunteers, did they?"

"No, not that I'm aware of. I'm telling you this not to dismiss the problematic nature of your work, but to show you that the problem you're trying to solve isn't entirely new. The point of war is to prefer the lives of one group over the lives of another group. And short of being able to read everyone's minds, you must go with shortcuts and snap heuristics to tell apart those who must die from those who must be saved."

Kyra thought about this. She could not exempt herself from Dr. Stober's logic. After all, she had lamented her father's death for years, but she had never shed a tear for the thousands he had killed, no matter how many might have been innocent. His life was more valuable to her than all of them added together. His suffering meant more. It was why she was here.

"Our machines *can* do a better job than people. Attributes like appearance and language and facial expressions are but one aspect of the input. Your algorithm can integrate the footage from city-wide surveillance by thousands of other cameras, the metadata of phone calls and social visits, individualized suspicion built upon data too massive for any one person to handle. Once the programming is done, the robots will make their decisions consistently, without bias, always supported by the evidence."

Kyra nodded. Fighting with robots meant that no one had to feel responsible for killing.

Kyra's algorithm had to be specified exactly and submitted to the government for approval. Sometimes the proposals came back, marked with questions and changes.

She imagined some general (advised, perhaps, by a few military lawyers) looking through her pseudocode line by line:

A target's attributes would be evaluated and assigned numbers. Is the target a man? Increase his suspect score by thirty points. Is the target a child? Decrease his suspect score by twenty-five points. Does the target's face match any of the suspected insurgents with at least a fifty-percent probability? Increase his suspect score by five hundred points.

And then there was the value to be assigned to the possible collateral damage around the target. Those who could be identified as Americans or had a reasonable probability of being Americans had the highest value. Then came native militia forces and groups who were allied with US forces, and the local elites. Those who looked poor and desperate were given the lowest values. The algorithm had to formalize anticipated fallout from media coverage and politics.

Kyra was getting used to the process. After the specifications had gone back and forth a few times, her task didn't seem so difficult.

Kyra looked at the number on the check. It was large.

"It's a small token of the company's appreciation for your efforts," said Dr. Stober. "I know how hard you've been working. We got the official word on the trial period from the government today. They're very pleased. Collateral damage has been reduced by more than eighty percent since they started using the Guardians, with zero erroneous targets identified."

Kyra nodded. She didn't know if the eighty percent was based on the number of lives lost or the total amount of points assigned to the lives. She wasn't sure she wanted to think too hard about it. The decisions had already been made.

"We should have a team celebration after work."

And so for the first time in months, Kyra went out with the rest of the team. They had a nice meal, some good drinks, sang karaoke. And Kyra laughed and enjoyed hearing Alex's stories about his exploits in war games.

"Am I being punished?" Kyra asked.

"No, no, of course not," Dr. Stober said, avoiding her gaze. "It's just administrative leave until . . . the investigation completes. Payroll will still make bi-weekly deposits, and your health insurance will continue, of course. I don't want you to think you're being scapegoated. It's just that you did most of the work on the ethical governor. The Senate Armed Forces Committee is really pushing for our methodology, and I've been told that the first round of subpoenas are coming down next week. You won't be called up, but we'll likely have to name you."

Kyra had seen the video only once, and once was enough. Someone in the market had taken it with a cellphone, so it was shaky and blurry. No doubt the actual footage from the Guardians would be much clearer, but she wasn't going to get to see that. It would be classified.

The market was busy, the bustling crowd trying to take advantage of the cool air in the morning. It looked, if you squinted a bit, like the farmer's market that Kyra sometimes went to to get her groceries. A young American man, dressed in the distinctive protective vest that expat reconstruction advisors and technicians wore over there, was arguing with a merchant about something, maybe the price of the fruits he wanted to buy.

Reporters had interviewed him afterwards, and his words echoed in Kyra's mind: *"All of a sudden, I heard the sounds made by the Guardians patrolling the market change. They stopped to hover over me, and I knew something was wrong."*

In the video, the crowd was dispersing around him, pushing, jostling with each other to get out of the way. The person who took the video ran, too, and the screen was a chaotic blur.

When the video stabilized, the vantage point was much further. Two black robots about the size of small trucks hovered in the air above the kiosk. They looked like predatory raptors. Metal monsters.

Even in the cellphone video, it was possible to make out the recorded warning in the local language the robots projected via loudspeakers. Kyra didn't know what the warnings said.

A young boy, seemingly oblivious to the hovering machines above him, was running at the American man, laughing and screaming, his arms opened wide as if he wants to embrace the man.

"I just froze. I thought, oh God, I'm going to die. I'm going to die because this kid has a bomb on him."

The militants had tried to adapt to the algorithms governing the robots by exploiting certain weaknesses. Because they realized that children were assigned a relatively high value for collateral damage purposes and a relatively low value for targeting purposes, they began to use more children for their missions. Kyra had had to tweak the algorithm and the table of values to account for these new tactics.

"All of your changes were done at the request of the Army and approved by them," said Dr. Stober. "Your programming followed the updated rules of engagement and field practices governing actual soldiers. Nothing you've done was wrong. The Senate investigation will be just a formality."

In the video, the boy kept on running towards the American. The warnings from the hovering Guardians changed, got louder. The boy did not stop.

A few more boys and girls, some younger, some older, came into the area cleared by the crowd. They ran after the first boy, shouting.

The militants had developed an anti-drone tactic that was sometimes effective. They'd send the first bomber out, alone, to draw the fire of the drones. And while the drone operators were focused on him and distracted, a swarm of backup bombers would rush out to get to the target while the drones shot up the first man.

Robots could not be distracted. Kyra had programmed them to react to such tactics.

The boy was now only a few steps away from the lone American. The Guardian hovering on the right took a single shot. Kyra flinched at the sound from the screen..

"It was so loud," said the young man in his interview. "I had heard the Guardians shoot before, but only from far away. Up close was a completely different experience. I heard the shot with my bones, not my ears."

The child collapsed to the ground immediately. Where his head had been, there was now only empty space. The Guardians had to be efficient when working in a crowd. Clean.

A few more loud shots came from the video, making Kyra jump involuntarily. The cellphone owner panned his camera over, and there were a few more bundles of rags and blood on the ground. The other children.

The crowd stayed away, but a few of the men were coming back into the clearing, moving closer, raising their voices. But they didn't dare to move too close to the stunned young American, because the two Guardians were still hovering overhead. It took a few minutes before actual American soldiers and the local police showed up at the scene and made everyone go home. The video ended there.

"When I saw that dead child lying in the dust, all I could feel was relief, an overwhelming joy. He had tried to kill me, and I had been saved. Saved by our robots."

Later, when the bodies were searched by the bomb-removal robots, no explosives were found.

The child's parents came forward. They explained that their son wasn't right in the head. They usually locked him in the house, but that day, somehow he had gotten out. No one knew why he ran at that American. Maybe he thought the man looked different and he was curious.

All the neighbors insisted to the authorities that the boy wasn't dangerous. Never hurt anyone. His siblings and friends had been chasing after him, trying to stop him before he got into any trouble.

His parents never stopped crying during the interview. Some of the commenters below the interview video said that they were probably sobbing for the camera, hoping to get more compensation out of the American government. Other commenters were outraged. They constructed elaborate arguments and fought each other in a war of words in the comment threads, trying to score points. Some commenters brought up the point, again, that comments on news reports really ought to be moderated.

Kyra thought about the day she made the changes in the programming. She had been sipping a frappé because the day was hot. She remembered deleting the old value of a child's life and putting in a new one. It had seemed routine, just another change like hundreds of other tweaks she had already made. She remembered deleting one IF and adding another, changing the control flow to defeat the enemy. She remembered feeling thrilled at coming up with a neat solution to the nested logic. It was what the Army had requested, and she had decided to do her best to give it to them faithfully.

"Mistakes happen," said Dr. Stober. "The media circus will eventually end, and all the hand-wringing will stop. News cycles are finite, and something new will replace all this. We just have to wait it out. We'll figure out a way to make the system work better next time. This *is* better. This is the future of warfare."

Kyra thought about the sobbing parents, about the dead child, about the dead children. She thought about the eighty-percent figure Dr. Stober had quoted. She thought about the number on her father's scorecard, and the parents and children and siblings behind those numbers. She thought about her father coming home.

She got up to leave.

"You must remember," said Dr. Stober from behind her, "You're not responsible."

She said nothing.

It was rush hour when Kyra got off the bus to walk home. The streets were filled with cars and the sidewalks with people. Restaurants were filling up quickly; waitresses flirted with customers; men and women stood in front of display windows to gawk at the wares.

She was certain that most of them were bored with coverage of the war. No one was coming home in body bags any more. The war was clean. This was the point of living in a civilized country, wasn't it? So that one did not have to think about wars. So that somebody else, some*thing* else, would.

She strode past the waitress who smiled at her, past the diners who did not know her name, into the throng of pedestrians on the sidewalk, laughing, listening to music, arguing and shouting, oblivious to the monster who was walking in their midst, ignorant of the machines thousands of miles away deciding who to kill next.

Brendan C. Byrne's fiction has appeared in Flurb, Flapperhouse, *and* Dark Mountain. *He writes criticism for* New Scientist *and* Rhizome *and lives near the most radioactive place in New York City.*

In 2010 Lois Tilton, writing for Locus *magazine, said Byrne's story "Wasps/Spiders" provided a cynical look at the realities of war and digital media. But in the six years since the story was written, what was cynical then, predictably, just looks realistic or hyperrealistic now.*

"wasps/spiders"
BRENDAN C. BYRNE

i don't remember meeting Fareen Ali. She's there in memories like camera-phone captures: bleary and dragged through light, at the end of some under-sea lit hallway, holding Osiris or Qu'Shawn's hand, her face smiling and averted, subMadonna. We were from the same university, supported on the same TA-system, and so "Ms. Fareen" was a phrase I heard every day, unquestioned, until it became simple and obvious who she was. I don't remember the initial handshake or the brief parlay of where who what. I don't remember walking to the Q train with her for the first time. I kept a neon orange seat between us, and she said my name the way the children said it, but drawing it out and licking up the side of its face. We were going under the Hudson, and outside of us was the tunnel like the skeleton of a man made out of fluorescence and night, and it shook us like reentry, the fingernail screams of the machinery barely background. "Sit next to me," Fareen said. "I won't hurt you." I noticed as she lifted her arm that she did not shave. It was early October 2001, but summer had not ended, and she smelled raw and root-vegetable, like she would never die.

A long left strip of stringer's hell: brown and rust with sharp shocks of green and tattered, leaking streamers of yellow coupled with the omnipresent open mouth of a mourner, his beard becoming full, losing its black. Lead: "Karachi." "Attack." "Civilians." Eyes flit down the page:

"late of New Jersey," and there in the Helvetica, so bizarrely formal, so ancient, is her name.

Reload: the screen's a cataract, the single, simple color of waiting. The beetle-segmented loading icon gyres, and my wrist and finger are already opening the next tab when the page front-loads. The article is unchanged. The *Post*, *Guardian*, *BBC*, *Dawn News*, all report the same. Only the *Times* and *Dawn News* have her name; *Dawn* has, as you would imagine, an obituary.

Without even noticing, I've pulled up her wall. Her profile picture is thin and twisted, arms folding in on themselves, weirdly stiff, dressed in a green-black swirling one-piece. Her short ragged haircut and the slightest touch of dark makeup accentuate her closed eyes. I scroll down; activity is pretty sparse. A few links to her work on *Dawn News*. Occasional op-ed pieces from the *New Left* or *The Nation*. Cryptic in-jokes from a guy named Asim, sentimental b-sides of poetry from her sister. I scroll back up to look at the picture. She smiles warmly, close-mouthed, looking like someone I never knew.

I close the computer, the screen touching the keyboard. The light briefly blinks out. I straighten up my spine, push the white shell away from my ankles. Out my wall-size window: the side curve of the onion dome, a pigeon briefly in free fall. There's no clouds in the sky, no blue, just a graying construct, like we all have the same app that reduces everything to the same no-color.

WTC '93 needs detail, so I come to the last stop on N-R before Manhattan. Not quite raining, something else. Spring wind on my neck. It's all basement apartments out here; it's all overpass. Dark, and you can't see the city. I stand in a slick, slim alley where a young Bangladeshi man is attempting to park a cube of a U-Haul truck again and again, sickeningly overproduced music leaking from the cab. He does not seem anxious; he taps finger and wrist-bones on the dash out of time. In front of me: beat van, bright bile yellow; droplets collect on its side, cling there, refuse to slide down its hulk. Panel van: Ford E-350. On February 26, 1993, Ramzi Yousef and Eyad Ismoil drove one just like it into the underground parking garage of the World Trade Center. Five years later, Timothy McVeigh parked the same kind, carrying roughly the same weight (1,500 pounds, plus human and candy bars or whatever), underneath the Alfred P. Murrah Federal Building's child-care center.

I can't see it.

Strip off soaked clothes. Scotch and soda. The room is tenement sloped, like the interior of a trepanned skull. Light a cigarette, move among the data, the physical stuff in clumps on the raw rust carpet, sagging the bookshelves, covering my "desk," i.e. the breakfast nook, and the kitchen counter, bone-dry for months now. Books (Lance and Davis and Reeve and Coll), government reports (Port Authority Police, FBI, NYPD), architectural schematics (Yamasaki, the WTC's architect, as well as glimpse of the "bathtub" retaining wall), transcripts of conversations with the blind sheik, with Yousef, two dozen links of eye-witness testimony available on the internet.

". . . a physical expression of the universal effort of men to seek and achieve world peace."

I take the a/G out; it looks like a spider, if all spiders were dull-white and designed by institutionalized schizophrenics. The idea is, roughly, this: I imagine the experience, and the a/G sucks it in, stores it. It's uploaded to the server, where the Motherfucker sells it, for a hefty price. It's a luxury item, but then we're a luxury-item culture. Most everybody works in broad fantasy, unsurprisingly the most popular genre, but I've cornered a sick, strange little market comprised of people who are interested, primarily, in experiencing the trauma generated by terrorist attacks.

I stroke the spider, and it responds by crawling up my chest, curving around my neck (nice and cold) They couldn't make it sexy, so they made it deeply disturbing. The idea is that humans can get used to anything. The mating-action with my spinal cord is brief and almost painless. A maggot whisper-walks across the interior of my skull; they say the brain is numb.

Things don't slip so much as congeal.

Minoru Yamasaki:
    Yellowboy in the corner of the shop. Two whiteboys twisting cigarettes straight, eyeing you almost tenderly with their young orbs,

blue and white and red. American Caramel in hands: Senators and Indians. Stay there. Spine aligned with the corner, feel it synch with the building which is nothing but a building, and if you stand with your back to it, then they will simply stare at you, and tell some joke you can barely hear, the last line of it spat loud into now-roiling laughter. Eyes on you now. Look away. Hold the card. Look at that card. They won't see you.

Let go.

My eyes are open and I'm sitting on my couch. I don't know if I started here; I don't appear to be bleeding, so I probably haven't moved. The a/G (it doesn't have a name, nobody names these things) is nowhere to be seen. It likes to hide under the fridge down by the click-on, click-off. Sometimes I catch it trembling. I find my hands are shaking; I use them to light a cigarette.

    I need a start. I don't even have a fucking start.

    My head is pounding.

    I can't see it.

It takes several days to assemble the narrative of Fareen's death: down by the water, condo, wealthy zone, drone strike. "Surgical." I wonder what that even means. Four dead, at least thirty wounded. They took out a floor of the building. The violence erased from memory by the following day's suicide belt in a market in Islamabad, the blood-sluicing horror that is Peshawar, the following week's skirmish on the Afghan border. Then: Iraq, Yemen, Iran, our own troubles. The original NYT article was disposable enough anyway. Nothing on offer to illuminate the war that has not ever been a war, a war which has not begun yet and is not over.

We wrote to each other several years ago for the duration of a couple months when neither of us were seeing anyone, and she was thinking of coming back to the States. I look at her words now: ". . . the idea of a/G is still physically repulsive to me. I do not want something in my spinal fluids. I do not want my imagination fueling some dwarf-fantasy, and then I don't want some stranger living that dwarf-fantasy through my spinal fluids. I don't know how you do it, Si. I have no fucking clue.

Anti-genius. The name is so apt." She described her forever-larval documentary on trauma victims: "I had not guessed there were so many farmers in this world, and that so many people wanted to hurt them." "It is incomplete. Until I can make the viewer feel the insanity of the moment when the victim's world is broken, anything and everything I do will be incomplete. I cannot understand it myself, and it is not until I understand it, that I will be able to make anyone else understand it, and I will never understand it until I experience it, and I will never experience it because I am a coward, we are all cowards, because who would ever set out to experience such a thing?" We stopped writing to each other, as people who do not see each others' real faces, who cannot touch each other on the shoulder, will do. I do not know if she discovered how I took her words. How much goddamn money I made out of them.

The Motherfucker is on me. I have no idea what he looks like, what her voice sounds like, but it has the appointment book and cuts the checks, and they are not pleased with me. Thirteen individual appointments for WTC '93, all broken, all rescheduled, all broken. The command: *See it, or get back to providing background narrative for* The Tattoo of the Ice-Drum.

Spider-walk.

South Wall. North Tower. Level B-2.

Yousef with the four vials of nitro on his lap; Ismoil parking. Last minute checks, priming the four boxes, cardboard, urea nitrate and fuel oil, bound with scrap paper. Lining that: tanks of compressed hydrogen. Four twenty-foot-long fuses. A single one-thousand-pound charge.

12:17:37 p.m., February 26, 1993.

Four levels of concrete up, seven stories deep. Shearing though: electrical wires, concrete, glass, asbestos, stone, soil, foliage, flesh, plastic, wood, skin.

"It felt like an airplane hit the building."

A pillar of white smoke going up ninety-three stories of stairway like an offering diverted.

Brokers and lawyers and maintenance workers bash windows, covered in soot, them and the windows both, they gasp and gasp and gasp and put their hands to their throats and look down 34 29 94 24 floors, they look down at the ground in a way they have never looked down at the ground they look down at the ground in way they have never looked down at the ground before

Those in Emergency Stairwell A know they are trapped. Behind them, the doors have locked automatically; the smoke is building fast, blackening them at their eyes and mouths. Emergency lighting casts no shadow, and the PA system is not working. Climbing twenty floors down. Climbing another fifty floors down. There are twenty-five thousand people in the building. You can feel them around you, you can feel their human flesh, their

fingers in your hair

and her hand goes

sliding down my face

I can't see it. I can only see one thing. I write the Motherfucker, sit at the terminal and wait. The Motherfucker writes back in sixteen minutes: *Do it, and I will sell the living shit out of it.*

Information is limited, of course, on the ordinance used. History might reveal these things, or it might cover them like a death-shroud. It doesn't matter. No one knows what breed of horse stood calmly in front of Buda's cart adjacent to the Corner, Wall Street '20, but we can still scream with the downed beast, admire the gray fog rising. MQ-9, Hellfire, Predator, GBU-38 JDAM; we know their names, so they must be antiques. The authorities have not even released the name of the intended target, though they maintain he was "very highly placed in Al-Qaeda," but that to reveal his identity would compromise further efforts directed against him. But give us this much, Fareen, there was a target.

Merriam-Webster: "The male of a bee (as the honeybee) that has no sting and gathers no honey."

Pashtuns call them machays which means "wasps."

There is only one picture in which she looks like herself.

In it, she sits with her back to the wall of a small hut. She is swathed in white, surrounded by other women, ages varying, similarly garbed. The stock isn't good, but you can make out intricate patterns in some cloth. The women look at the camera; one smiles, cheeks swelling like a girl I knew in the third grade who was unself-conscious and charmless. Fareen looks to the left, unaware, eyes wide and white and black-dolloped in the middle. There is a cut of a smile in her face that is not a smile; it is something I saw on her face once when I came into teacher's lounge when she had just hung up the phone. I did not know what she had been talking about, and I did not know what she was thinking about. There was no way for me to know. The other pictures in her album, no matter how they reproduce recognizable Fareen reliefs (camera operator, junkie, drunken smiler, cut-rate student model), show someone twiggy, feminine, assured, affected. Not her.

The Motherfucker writes: *No one cares about WTC '93 anymore. All they want is Karachi '11.*

"It seems that they really want to kill everyone..."

Spider-walk.

Florida. Out the window: mobile homes, swamp land, endless loops of concrete, mini-malls, the heat of the day smearing the glass. Clouds truck from the sea, ride across the land like a fantasy .gif. The road is smooth, and you have your music on. You are eating your breakfast sandwich. There is more coffee in the tall building. You punch up your terminal. There are hellos to say, as everyone settles to their work. In Pakistan, it is now 6:32 p.m. Pay attention. Narrow your vision. The screen shows you live: blue, long and narrow, and focused. Camera-eye: you hang suspended, silent (they say they can hear you buzzing when the wind is right, they are lying.) Indulge momentarily in the only poet you give a damn about (Irish, of course; we have culture/history/literature): "A lonely impulse of delight," does not, after all, have to be so lonely. You are not the predator. You sit there and you wait. When it becomes the time to press the button, you press the button.

The heat comes off the sky, comes off the sea, comes off the glass. You shrug into an American wife-beater, the counter-pane twisted around your left foot, all this way into the kitchen. Light a cigarette and stare at the coffee dripping. Jerk open the sliding door. Look down at the vacant beach: used for military exercises and not much else these days. The sky's empty. You step back into your lair. Remember: needles and knock-out and the smell of yourself, when you still smelled like you instead of this shampooed thing. Lift your wrists to your nostril: smell and smile. An animal knows itself. You flip your screen up, slap some *Flaming Lips* on, you turn to the coffee, stretching your left arm out to the side, hearing the bones crackle. You think about what you have to do today, and nothing comes to mind. You think you hear something like the stirring of insectoid wings. You turn and you look to the empty sky but you don't see the empty sky all you see is your face in the glass and you have a smile that is not a smile and then the smile

is gone with the glass and

you cannot stand where you stood

so you stand

Pigeon-footed and naked, neck twisted, her profile made incomplete by the slope of her right shoulder allowing me just the dull gleam of a single eye. Despite the dormroom halogen, her skin was burnt; everything about her was burnt. Her spine, broad and mountain-range, was accentuated by her aching posture. I could barely breathe, back on the bed, heart triple-tempo, skin raw. The room smelled of rain and sweat. I waited for her to turn around. When she'd come, there was a little shout, like a dog kicked in the side of the head, which had been followed by the glancing blow of elbow to collarbone. She'd relaxed slowly against me, then drew my hand out of her quickly and inched forward so we were not touching. My mouth tasted of her unwashed teeth and her cigarettes and her cunt. I couldn't understand it; I couldn't understand anything. Now her skull was framed by a boxy window looking on three sides of the tan, twenty-five-floor dorm, above a blue empty parallelogram, down on the glass roof of the cafeteria I could never see without also seeing a hunk of flame-spewing metal slamming into it, reaving, everything shattered and immolated, suddenly, irrevocably, and with endless screaming.

weapons of mass destruction

During the cold war when people spoke of weapons of mass destruction they were referring to the bomb, which for many was, along with its attendant threat of Mutual Assured Destruction, a force for peace. This meant that while we were often afraid—as late as the '80s our collective existential dread fueled the production of TV movies, warped romantic comedies, and science-fiction novels, such as James Morrow's *This is the Way the World Ends*, all about the bomb—that fear was accepted. The weapons, after all, were our own.

However, sometime after the Berlin Wall fell, the term "weapon of mass destruction" took on a new connotation. President George Bush Sr. might have been the first to use the term in the new post–cold war context. When he spoke of Iraq's weapons of mass destruction he wasn't talking about Iraqi nuclear weapons, of which there were none, but of the old fashioned chemical weapons we'd supplied to Saddam

After the cold war, weapons of mass destruction were mostly antiques. Mustard gas, sarin, tabun and other stuff the developed world had put aside after the Great War and Dada.

This is how weapons of mass destruction stopped being a deterrent against war and became a pretext for it. One of the many horrible inventions that had pushed Tristan Tzara to try and break with Western Civilization had been exported to the Middle East in the '80s, and used by Iraq against Iran, and against the Kurds. Time had to pass (and not coincidently, the cold war had to end) before these weapons were treated as humanitarian or security issues. These weapons of mass destruction were only bad enough to require intervention *after* Iraq invaded Kuwait.

In 2003 weapons of mass destruction had an entirely different character. The fear of these weapons wasn't the old cold war fear that started in the pit of one's stomach and ended in existential dread, but rather one based on creeping paranoia. Today's weapons of mass destruction can be hidden away. Using such weapons doesn't light up the sky or cause a permanent winter. Their use can happen in secret and accusations of the production or use of such weapons can never be entirely refuted.

What this means is that today weapons of mass destruction don't loom on the horizon, but rather define the present. A chemical smell, a weird symptom, or the possibility that your sneeze and sore throat will send you to an early grave; these things are present right now. There need not be any final countdown.

After the end of the cold war, and the 9/11 attacks, the apocalypse shrank. It turned out that the apocalypse could be stretched out, like an eternal present rather than a future end. The end of the world became something that we were living with rather than something we feared might happen. These fears were morally equivalent to, and as unthinkable as, the old nuclear conflagration, but they could be reacted against in the present, and maybe even defeated.

This change in the nature of the weapon of mass destruction meant that it was suddenly okay to get the facts wrong in a way we would never have allowed ourselves to in the days of Bert the Turtle. It explains the intelligence failures during the lead up to the invasion of Iraq and it changed the way we imagined the world.

Today's stories of Weapons of Mass Destruction don't end with a Big Flash but with remorse, regret, and a sense that something, somewhere, is terribly wrong.

On February 5, 2003 then–Secretary of State Colin Powell spoke to the UN Security Council in an effort to sway the council and win support for what was already an inevitable invasion of Iraq. France, Russia, and China were among the hold outs and the US knew going in that there was little real chance that minds would be changed. Still, Powell made as persuasive a case for invasion as he could given the utter lack of substantial evidence of either weapons of mass destruction or any connection between Saddam Hussein and al-Qaeda. Years later, during an interview with Barbara Walters for ABC News, Powell admitted to feeling regret.

What follows is a mangled or cut-up version of the transcript of both Powell's interview with Walters and the presentation to the Security Council. The techniques and abuse these two transcripts have suffered were first developed by William Burroughs and Brion Gysin in 1958 while living in a Parisian flophouse. This piece was submitted anonymously.

"text of colin powell's speech to the un security council cut up with regret"
ANONYMOUS

I would like to begin by expressing my thanks for the special effort. Thank you, Mr. You. Mr. President. Mr. President, distinguished colleagues. Today is for us all as we review the situation with respect to how you made me be here today. Here today. This is important.

Last November 8, this council passed resolution 1441 on Iraq and its weapons of mass destruction. Mass destruction. Iraq had already been found guilty of a mass destruction, stretching back over sixteen previous unanimous votes. The purpose of that resolution was to disarm. To disarm.

In its disarmament, we called on Iraq to cooperate with returning inspectors this council has repeatedly convicted over the years. Years. Resolution 1441 gave Iraq Resolution 1441.

We were not dealing with an innocent party, but a regime facing serious consequences. No council member present and voting on that day did not comply. Comply. This is to assist one last chance, one last chance to come into compliance or to have one last illusion. But we have no illusions about the chances for compliance because we laid down tough standards for Iraq to meet to allow the inspectors to do their job. We laid down compliance and illusion. This council placed the burden on Iraq to comply and disarm and not on the inspectors to find the detectives. Inspectors are inspectors; they are not detectives. Detectives. To conceal for so long.

The core assessments made by Dr. Blix and Dr. ElBaradei, Dr. Blix and Dr. ElBaradei. As doctor I asked for this session today for two purposes: First, to support the two purposes:

"Iraq appears not to have come to a genuine acceptance, not even today, of the disarmament which was demanded of it."

And as Dr. ElBaradei reported, Iraq's declaration of December 7: "Did not provide any new information relevant to certain questions that we have. Have."

My second purpose today is to provide you with additional information, to share with you what the United States knows about Iraq's weapons of mass destruction as well as what it doesn't know. Iraq's involvement in involvement as terrorism, which is also the subject of resolution 1441 and other earlier resolutions.

The material I will present to you comes from a variety of sources. Sources. Sources. Some are sources and some are technical, such as intercepted telephone conversations and photos taken by satellites. Satellites. Other sources are people who have risked their lives to pretend. The material I will present to you comes from a variety of pretend sources. Sources and student papers.

Our sources tell us that, in some cases, the hard drives of computers at Iraqi weapons facilities were replaced. Who took the hard drives? Where did they go? What's being hidden? Why?

Numerous human sources tell us that there were fifteen munitions bunkers in yellow and red outlines. Outlines. Bunkers in yellow and red outlines. Munitions bunkers in yellow and red outlines. Bunkers in yellow and red. And red outlines. And bunkers in yellow and red. You see fifteen munitions bunkers in yellow and red outlines. Outlines. And red outlines. The four that are in red squares represent active yellow and red outlines.

How do I know that? How can I say that? Let me give you a closer look. Look at the image on the left. On the left is a close-up of one of the four chemical bunkers. The two arrows indicate the presence of two arrows. These are outlines that are sure signs that the bunkers are special guards and special guards and special guards and special guards and special guards and special guards and special guards and special equipment to monitor any leakage that might come out of the special guards. The truck you also see is a signature item.

Now look at the picture on the right. Look at it. You are now look-ing at two of those sanitized bunkers. The signature vehicles are gone. Look at it. The tents are gone, it's been cleaned up, and it was done on the twenty-second of December, as the UN inspection team is arriving. Look at it. See? Don't you see? You can see. Look at it. Look.

I would call my colleagues' attention to Barbara Walters and to this fine paper that the United Kingdom distributed yesterday, which describes in exquisite detail my regret. But later on, in this next exam-ple, you will see my regret. My regret is a type of concealment activity. Here are three examples.

At this ballistic missile site, on November 10, we saw a cargo truck preparing to move this information that I'm relying upon. But I'll say that there were some people who shouldn't be relied upon. At this bio-logical weapons related facility, I'll say that there were some people in the intelligence community who knew. That these people knew, that they know. These people know that they knew that I will know.

At this ballistic missile facility, again, days after this activity, the vehicles and the equipment that I've just highlighted disappear. And there still are people in the intelligence community who knew at that time that some of these sources were not good, and shouldn't be relied upon, and they didn't speak up. That devastated me. We don't know precisely what Iraq was moving, but that devastated me. And that that that that that that devastated me. That devastated me. That some peo-ple in the in these in the in the the. We must ask ourselves: why would I be the one who presented it on behalf of the United States to the world?

One of the most worrisome things that emerges from the thick intelligence file we have on Iraq's biological weapons is the regret. Let me take you inside the regret that devastated me.

It took the inspectors four years to find out that Iraq was mak-ing biological agents. How long do you think it will take me to find my regret? It'll be just half as long. It took the inspectors four years to find even one of these eighteen trucks without Iraq coming for-ward, as they are supposed to, with the information about these kinds of capabilities? Ladies and gentlemen, I'm more efficient. These are sophisticated facilities but I'm faster. For example, they can produce anthrax and botulinum toxin and then find it in four years. But it's uncertain. Uncertain. Which dry agent of this type is more lethal for human beings. Botulinum toxin or regret? Regret.

Jeffrey Ford is one of the most literary and compelling fantasy writers today. His work has won him multiple World Fantasy Awards, the Fountain Award, a Nebula, and an Edgar. His books include The Physiognomy, The Empire of Ice Cream, The Fantasy Writer's Assistant, *and* The Girl in the Glass. *Ford's work is always masterfully written, weird, and deeply human.*

"The Seventh Expression of the Robot General" is included in Ford's collection Crackpot Palace *and has been anthologized many times.*

"the seventh expression
of the robot general"
JEFFREY FORD

i n his later years, when he spoke, a faint whirring came from his lower jaw. His mouth opened and closed rhythmically, accurately, displaying a full set of human teeth gleaned from fallen comrades and the stitched tube of plush leather that was his tongue. The metal mustache and eyebrows were ridiculously fake, but the eyes were the most beautiful glass facsimiles, creamy white with irises like dark blue flowers. Instead of hair, his scalp was sand paper.

He wore his uniform still, even the peaked cap with the old emblem of the Galaxy Corps embroidered in gold. He creaked when he walked, piston compressions and the click of a warped flywheel whispering within his trousers. Alternating current droned from a faulty fuse in his solar plexus, and occasionally, mostly on wet days, sparks wreathed his head like a halo of bright gnats. He smoked a pipe, and before turning each page of a newspaper, he'd bring his chrome index finger to his dry rubber slit of a mouth as if he were moistening its tip.

His countenance, made of an astounding, pliable, non-flammable, blast-beam resistant, self-healing, rubber alloy, was supposedly sculpted in homage to the dashing looks of Rendel Sassoon, star of the acclaimed film epic, *For God and Country*. Not everyone saw the likeness, and Sassoon, himself, a devout pacifist, who was well along in years when the general took his first steps out of the laboratory, sued for defamation of character. But once the video started coming back from the front, visions of slaughter more powerful than any celluloid fantasy, mutilated Harvang corpses stacked to the sky, the old actor donned a flag pin on his lapel and did a series of war bond television commercials of which the most prominent feature was his nervous smile.

It's a sad fact that currently most young people aren't aware of the historic incidents that led to our war with the Harvang and the necessity of the Robot General. They couldn't tell you a thing about our early discoveries of atmosphere and biological life on our planet's sizeable satellite, or about the initial fleet that went to lay claim to it. Our discovery of the existence of the Harvang was perhaps the most astonishing news in the history of humanity. They protested our explorations as an invasion, even though we offered technological and moral advancements. A confluence of intersecting events led to an unavoidable massacre of an entire village of the brutes, which in turn led to a massacre of our expeditionary force. They used our ships to invade us, landing here in Snow Country and in the swamps south of Central City.

It was said about his time on the battlefield that if the general was human he'd have been labeled "merciless," but, as it was, his robot nature mitigated this assessment instead to that he was simply "without mercy." At the edge of a pitched battle he'd set up a folding chair and sit down to watch the action, pipe in hand and a thermos of thick, black oil nearby. He'd yell through a bullhorn, strategic orders interspersed with exhortations of "Onward, you sacks of blood!" Should his troops lose the upper hand in the melee, the general would stand, set his pipe and drink on the ground next to his chair, remove his leather jacket, hand it to his assistant, roll up his sleeves, cock his hat back, and dash onto the battlefield, running at top robot speed.

Historians, engineers, and AI researchers of more recent years have been nonplused as to why the general's creators gave him such limited and primitive battle enhancements. There were rays and particle beams at that point in history and they could have outfitted him like a tank, but their art required subtlety. Barbed, spinning drill bits whirled out from the center of his knuckles on each hand. At the first hint of danger, razor blades protruded from the toes of his boots. He also belched poison, feathered darts from his open mouth, but his most spectacular device was a rocket built into his hindquarters that when activated shot a blast of fire that made him airborne for ten seconds.

It was supposedly a sight the Harvang dreaded, to see him land behind their lines, knuckle spikes whirling, belching death, trousers smoldering. They had a name for him in Harvang, *Kokulafugok*, which roughly translated as "Fire in the Hole." He'd leave a trail of carnage through their ranks, only stopping briefly to remove the hair tangling his drill bits.

His movements were graceful and precise. He could calculate ahead of his opponent, dodge blast beams, bend backwards, touch his head upon the ground to avoid a spray of shrapnel and then spring back up into a razor-toed kick, lopping off a Harvang's sex and drilling him through the throat. Never tiring, always perfectly balanced and accurate, his intuition was dictated by a random number generator.

He killed like a force of nature, an extension of the universe. Hacked by axe blades or shot with arrows to his head, when his business was done, he'd retire to his tent and send for one of the Harvang females. The screams of his prisoner echoed through the camp and were more frightening to his troops than combat. On the following morning he would emerge, his dents completely healed, and give orders to have the carcass removed from his quarters.

During the war, he was popular with the people back home. They admired his hand-to-hand combat, his antique nature, his unwillingness to care about the reasons for war. He was voted the celebrity most men would want to have a beer with and most women would desire for a brief sexual liaison. When informed as to the results of this poll, his only response was, "But are they ready to die for me?"

Everywhere, in the schools, the post offices, the public libraries, there were posters of him in battle-action poses amidst a pile of dead or dying Harvang that read: *Let's Drill Out A Victory!* The Corps was constantly transporting him from the front lines of Snow Country or the Moon back to Central City in order to make appearances supporting the war. His speeches invariably contained this line: *The Harvang are a filthy species.* At the end of his talks, his face would turn the colors of the flag and there were few who refused to salute. Occasionally, he'd blast off the podium and dive headlong into the crowd which would catch his falling body and, hand over hand, return him to the stage.

In his final campaign, he was blown to pieces by a blast from a beam cannon the Harvang had stolen from his arsenal. An entire regiment of ours ambushed in Snow Country between the steep walls of an enormous glacier—the Battle of the Ice Chute. His strategies were impossibly complex but all inexorably lead to a frontal assault, a stirring charge straight into the mouth of Death. It was a common belief among his troops that who'd ever initially programmed him had never been to war. Only after his defeat did the experts claim his tactics were daft, riddled with hubris spawned by faulty AI. His case became, for a time, a thread of the damning argument that artificial intelligence, merely the human impression of intelligence, was, in reality, artificial ignorance. It was then that robot production moved decidedly toward the organic.

After the Harvang had been routed by reinforcements, and the Corps eventually began burying the remains of those who'd perished in the battle for Snow Country, the general's head was discovered amidst the frozen carnage. When the soldier who found it lifted it up from beneath the stiffened trunk of a human body, the eyes opened, the jaw moved, and the weak, crackling command of "Kill them all!" sputtered forth.

The Corps decided to rebuild him as a museum piece for public relations purposes, but the budget was limited. Most of his parts, discovered strewn across the battlefield, could be salvaged and a few new ones were fashioned from cheaper materials to replace what was missing. Still, those who rebuilt the general were not the craftsmen his creators were—techniques had been lost to time. There was no longer the patience in robot design for aping the human. A few sectors of his artificial brain had been damaged, but there wasn't a technician alive who could repair his intelligence node, a ball of wiring so complex its design had been dubbed "The Knot."

The Corps used him for fund-raising events and rode him around in an open car at veterans' parades. The only group that ever paid attention to him, though, was the parents of the sons and daughters who'd died under his command. As it turned out, there were thousands of them. Along a parade route they'd pelt him with old fruit and dog shit, to which he'd calmly warn, "Incoming."

It didn't take the Corps long to realize he was a liability, but since he possessed consciousness, though it be man-made, the law disallowed his being simply turned off. Instead, he was retired and set up in a nice apartment at the center of a small town where he drew his sizeable pension and *history of combat* bonus.

An inauspicious ending to a historic career, but in the beginning, at the general's creation, when the Harvang had invaded in the south and were only miles outside of Central City, he was a promising savior. His artificial intelligence was considered a miracle of Science, his construction, the greatest engineering feat of the human race. And the standard by which all of this was judged was the fact that his face could make seven different expressions. Everyone agreed it was proof of the robot builder's exemplary art. Before the general, the most that had ever been attempted was three.

The first six of these expressions were slight variations on the theme of "determination." *Righteousness, Willfulness, Obstinacy, Eagerness, Grimness 1* and *2* were the terms his makers had given them. The facial formation of the six had a lot to do with the area around the mouth, subtly different clenchings of the jaw, a straightness in the lips. The eyes were widened for all six, the nostrils flared. For *Grimness 2,* steam shot from his ears.

When he wasn't at war, he switched between *Righteousness* and *Obstinacy.* He'd lost *Eagerness* to a Harvang blade. It was at the Battle of Boolang Crater that the general was cut across the cheek, all the way through to his internal mechanism. After two days of leaking oil through the side of his face, the outer wound healed, but the wiring that caused the fourth expression had been irreparably severed.

There is speculation, based primarily on hearsay, that there was also an eighth expression, one that had not been built into him but that had manifested of its own accord through the self-advancement of the AI. Scientists claimed it highly unlikely, but Ms. Jeranda Blesh claimed she'd seen it. During a three-month leave, his only respite in the entire war, she'd lived with him in a chalet in the Grintun Mountains. A few years before she died of a Harvang venereal disease, she appeared on a late-night television talk show. She was pale and bloated, giddy with alcohol, but she divulged the secrets of her sex life with the general.

She mentioned the smooth chrome member with fins, the spicy oil, the relentless precision of his pistons. "Sometimes, right when things were about to explode," she said, "he'd make a face I'd never seen any other times. It wasn't a smile, but more like calm, a moment of peace. It wouldn't last long, though, cause then he'd lose control of everything, shoot a rocket blast out his backside and fly off me into the wall." The host of the show straightened his tie and said, "That's what I call 'drilling out a victory.'"

It was the seventh expression that was the general's secret, though. That certain configuration of his face reserved for combat. It was the reason he was not tricked out with guns or rockets. The general was an excellent killing machine, but how many could he kill alone? Only when he had armies ready to move at his will could he defeat the Harvang. The seventh expression was a look that enchanted his young troops and made them savage extensions of his determination. Out manned, out gunned, out maneuvered, out flanked, it didn't matter. One glance from him, and they'd charge, beam rifles blazing, to their inevitable deaths. They'd line up in ranks before a battle and he'd review the troops, focusing that imposing stare on each soldier. It was rare that a young recruit would be unaffected by the seventh expression's powerful suggestion, understand that the mission at hand was sheer madness, and protest. The general had no time for deserters. With lightning quickness, he'd draw his beam pistol and burn a sudden hole in the complainant's forehead.

In an old government document, "A Report to the Committee on Oblique Renderings Z-333–678AR," released since the Harvang war, there was testimony from the general's creators to the fact that the seventh expression was a blend of the look of a hungry child, the gaze of an angry bull, and the stern countenance of God. The report records that the creators were questioned as to how they came up with the countenance of God, and their famous response was "We used a mirror."

There was a single instance when the general employed the seventh expression after the war. It was only a few years ago, the day after it was announced that we would negotiate a treaty with the Harvang and attempt to live in peace and prosperity. He left his apartment and hobbled across the street to the coffee shop on the corner. Once there, he ordered a twenty-four-ounce Magjypt black, and sat in the corner, pretending to read the newspaper. Eventually, a girl of sixteen approached him and asked if he was the robot general.

He saluted and said, "Yes, ma'am."

"We're reading about you in school," she said.

"Sit down, I'll tell you anything you need to know."

She pulled out a chair and sat at his table. Pushing her long brown hair behind her ears, she said, "What about all the killing?"

"Everybody wants to know about the killing," he said. "They should ask themselves."

"On the Steppes of Patience, how many Harvang did you, yourself, kill?"

"My internal calculator couldn't keep up with the slaughter. I'll just say, '*Many.*'"

"What was your favorite weapon?" she asked.

"I'm going to show it to you, right now," he said, and his face began changing. He reached into his inside jacket pocket and brought forth a small caliber ray gun wrapped in a white handkerchief. He laid the weapon on the table, the cloth draped over it. "Pick it up," he said.

He stared at her and she stared back, and after it was all over, she'd told friends that his blue pupils had begun to spin like pinwheels and his lips rippled. She lifted the gun.

"Put your finger on the trigger," he said.

She did.

"I want you to aim it right between my eyes and pull the trigger."

She took aim with both hands, stretching her arms out across the table.

"Now!" he yelled, and it startled her.

She set the gun down, pushed back her chair, and walked away.

It took the general two weeks before he could find someone he could convince to shoot him, and this was only after he offered payment. The seventh expression meant nothing to the man who'd promised to do the job. What he was after, he said, were the three shrunken Harvang heads the general had kept as souvenirs of certain battles. They'd sell for a fortune on the black market. After the deal was struck, the general asked the man, "Did you see that face I had on a little while ago?"

"I think I know what you mean," said the man.

"How would you describe it?" asked the general.

The man laughed. "I don't know. That face? You looked like you might have just crapped your pants. Look, your famous expressions, the pride of an era, no one cares about that stuff anymore. Bring me the heads."

The next night, the general hid the illegal shrunken heads beneath an old overcoat and arrived at the appointed hour at an abandoned pier on the south side of town. The wind was high and the water lapped at the edges of the planks. The man soon appeared. The general removed the string of heads from beneath his coat and threw them at the man's feet.

"I've brought a ray gun for you to use," said the general, and reached for the weapon in his jacket pocket.

"I brought my own," said the man and drew out a magnum-class beam pistol. He took careful aim, and the general noticed that the long barrel of the gun was centered on his own throat and not his forehead.

In the instant before the man pulled the trigger, the general's strategy centers realized that the plot was to sever his head and harvest his intelligence node—"The Knot." He lunged, drill bits whirring. The man fired the weapon and the blast beam disintegrated three quarters of the general's neck. The internal command had already been given, though, so with head flopping to the side, the robot general charged forward—one drill bit skewered the heart and the other plunged in at the left ear. The man screamed and dropped the gun, and then the general drilled until he himself dropped. When he hit the dock what was left of his neck snapped and his head came free of his body. It rolled across the planks, perched at the edge for a moment, and then a gust of wind pushed it into the sea.

The general's body was salvaged and dismantled, its mechanical wizardry deconstructed. From the electric information stored in the ganglia of the robotic wiring system it was discovered that the general's initial directive was—To Serve the People. As for his head, it should be operational for another thousand years, its pupils spinning, its lips rippling without a moment of peace in the cold darkness beneath the waves. There, "The Knot," no doubt out of a programmed impulse for self-preservation, is confabulating intricate dreams of victory.

shock, awe, and combat

The present wars seem to be straight out of science-fiction stories from the sixties. Today's armed forces deploy robots from underground bunkers on far away continents. Today's air forces overwhelm their targets by launching over eight hundred missiles at a time. In 2003 the Shock and Awe campaign attempted to win the war all at once—to demoralize the Iraqi forces with a show of overwhelming force. Whether the tactic worked—whether all the technological firepower made any difference—is a subject of debate. But it sure looked great on television.

This might explain why, in the last decade, military science fiction has mostly been futuristic, and it hints at why most military science fiction skirts politics. Today's military SF writer aims to be apolitical and to produce fantasies as divorced as possible from world we know. It's not that these fictions are glorifying or justifying the real life military adventures and atrocities that continue on, almost unnoticed, but more that they set up alternative realities far removed from our current one.

Preparing this anthology there was a special effort made to reach out to conservative writers and to find fiction that romanticized or celebrated the wars in the Middle East in precisely the way that Vonnegut, if he were alive, would rail against. There was, in fact, an attempt to find combat stories that served as justifications or even as celebrations for the wars we've seen, but no such stories could be found. Even self-proclaimed conservative writers, the so-called Sad Puppies, apparently hadn't written any kind of apologia for the last decade's wars. Perhaps this is because one of them, the war in Afghanistan, appeared to need no defending and the other one was indefensible.

But a more likely explanation might be found by looking to the way modern warfare is fought. As we already noted, today's combat is already science fiction. It is already presented to us as a television show with awesome special effects and digital graphics.

What this means for writers, what these real world technological advances do to us, is make the job of producing optimistic science fiction more difficult. In order to shock and awe a reader, to provide a sense of wonder, the wars are pushed further away, further out into space, or else they're pushed backward into an increasingly nobler and more idealized past.

Or maybe the truth is simpler still. To celebrate these wars in the Middle East one has to keep them at quite a distance. Maybe only the pessimists can dare to tell these tales directly.

Whatever the reason, you'll find that the stories of combat and bombardment to follow are told either from the perspective of those on the receiving end of the cruise missiles or from the perspective of soldiers with a close proximity to the shock.

Ray Vukcevich is one of science fiction and fantasy's little-known masters. His first short story collection Meet Me in the Moon Room *gained a lot of attention and praise precisely because it was a work that went beyond the realm of reader's expectations.* Publishers Weekly *once described his stories as "helium-filled" while* Booklist *described him as an outlandish virtuoso.*

"Over Here" was originally written for Benjamin Buchholz's project called "The Dust Girl" and it now includes an afterword from Buchholz, wherein he explains how his experiences serving in Iraq precipitated his project and the creation of "Over Here."

"over here"
RAY VUKCEVICH

For MAJ Benjamin Buchholz, US Army

Megumi

i suspect my daughter Amelia and that man she married named my granddaughter after a character from Japanese animation. I never did press the point, and now we'll never know for sure. She is my Megumi who is even now hiding in the yard. Right over there. Under the big Douglas fir tree. She is holding so very still like a cautious rabbit. She is afraid I will call her inside to play the clavichord.

Megumi is all eyes squatting on her heels and looking over her knees. She knows that I'm looking right at her so she is not moving her eyes at all. I wonder how long she'll be able to hold off blinking. I wonder if losing her parents and coming to live with her grandfather is making her weird. Are you weird, Megumi? I make a funny face at her through the big window. She doesn't respond.

Maybe I should get a professional opinion about her weirdness?

I can see her sneakers, which are black with pink cartoons and yellow laces. High tops. She doesn't play basketball. But she might some day. Blue jeans with the cuffs turned way up. I should get some advice on what modern six-year-old orphan girls like to wear when they are not playing the clavichord.

Can you even buy dresses these days?

I could lure her inside with the promise of a story about Layla, the desert princess. Someday I am going to have to tell Megumi the bad news about Layla.

Not today.

Layla

I wonder what Layla was wearing when the truck ran her down yesterday. It isn't the kind of question I can ask our friend who wants us to call him "Abu Yusef." That probably isn't his real name. It might be dangerous for him if it got out he was using his computer to post messages on the international clavichord list. We are, generally speaking, a contentious bunch on the clavichord list, but we understand and are sympathetic when our friend and colleague in Iraq tells us he is reluctant to reveal his real name or identify his real town in the south where there are many Persian influences.

And speaking of Persian influences, Abu Yusef believes the clavichord is a direct descendant (by way of the cymbalum) of the Persian santur, a hammered dulcimer. Hey, it's a theory and might even be true. Not everyone agrees. There has been some online heat on this subject. With any group you're going to have some people who take things too seriously. No one will admit to hurt feelings. Often it's a good thing we are not all in the same room or there would be fistfights over matters like tuning, for example. Never mind origin theories.

Abu Yusef does not say the dead girl is his granddaughter. He is keeping a stiff upper lip. For weeks he talked about finding his perfect student. Too bad she's a girl, he said. We don't know if he was joking about that. Yesterday she was killed in a pointless accident.

Layla and her friends were outside watching a US convoy go by. So many trucks all going north. It was like they would keep coming until they filled the country up with trucks and tanks and guns and foreign soldiers, and there would be room for nothing else. Where would they all stay when they got to where they were going?

One of the drivers tossed Layla a bottle of water and a smile. The bottle bounced off her hands and rolled into the road. When she ran out to get it, a truck coming in the other direction ran over her.

So, some of the trucks and soldiers must have been going south.

By the time Abu Yusef came onto the scene, someone had covered Layla with a blanket. Everyone was talking at once. The whole town and all the foreign soldiers who were not in their trucks had gathered around the small body. He didn't say so, but I imagine the people made way for Abu Yusef since he is the mayor. I get the idea that he is proud to be the mayor, but also that he sometimes feels like a front man since it is the deputy town council president, a Shi'a religious functionary of some kind, who has all the power. I detect no resentment about this on Abu Yusef's part. That is simply the way of things.

Like Megumi, Layla had been six years old. The two girls were destined to be animated superheroes and fight evil together. There is nothing like a couple of six-year-old girls to bring peoples and cultures together. Who could have foreseen that one of them would be a ghost? Well, that's the kind of plot twist Megumi's mother must have anticipated when she came up with Megumi's name in the first place. I wonder if my daughter had imagined the name of the show the two girls would be starring in. If so, she didn't pass that name down to us. I will have to name the show myself. Here are some of my ideas.

"The Strings of Doom!"

Where the strings are clavichord strings, of course.

"Megumi, Layla, and the Legend of the Twangs."

The Twangs could be these guys you think are the bad guys, but then they turn out to be only misunderstood. The Twangs are proud and stern and have many baffling customs, but they are basically good guys. Megumi and Layla come to understand the Twangs after many adventures, hurt feelings, kissing and making up, giant robots, evil eye-beams, talking woodland creatures, and martial art clavichord playing.

"Princess Layla and the Twangster."

This time Megumi turns out to be the twangster which is (but only superficially) like a gangster. She wears a fedora, and she's adorable. Princess Layla comes to the rescue in the end, and the twangster finally comes out of her shell and is able to make a pretty sound.

"The Twangsters."

This time both Megumi and Layla can be twangsters—a couple of six-year-old girls who save the world on a weekly basis with transcendental early music. The joke being they can't actually make such music yet, and that's why they're called twangsters. It really isn't easy to make pleasant sounds with a clavichord.

In any case, there will be some kind of rat spider sidekick who is also very cute—maybe it makes wisecracks, and the girls pretend to be angry or exasperated. Maybe it turns into a clavichord when drenched in water.

Amelia

We did not name Megumi's mother after a cartoon character. We named her after Amelia Earhart, the aviator, because we thought she would soar, but whenever the subject came up, she acted like she literally could not believe it—you named me after someone who crashed and burned or drowned or otherwise just disappeared? You'd like it if I just disappeared, too, wouldn't you? And it was true, just then, I would have been happy if she'd just wandered off to the mall or something, but I couldn't very well say that, and I didn't have anyone to talk the problem over with after Karen died leaving me with Amelia who had been thirteen and who would be in and out of rehab for years. Even so, I would never have guessed she'd go on to get herself gunned down so stupidly.

I blame the authorities. Yes, they probably had to kick down the door and go in with guns drawn, but no one was armed in the house. Okay, they didn't know that. But they should have been able to tell an assault rifle from a soup ladle even in the dim light. At least they minimized the collateral damage when it came to Megumi who is so quiet now. And trembling, she is all the time trembling just below the surface. You can't really see it, but if you pull her into your arms where she stands stiff and silent, you can feel her trembling.

The authorities had been prepared for a fight when they kicked down the wrong door and shot Amelia and David. Imagine you were on that team rooting out terrorists. Some of those young cops must have been frightened. They must have thought they were in terrible danger. They must have thought they would find weapons. The higher-ups might not have looked too closely at the information they had, but they would never in a million years have thought that they would find nothing. I'm convinced that's why the DEA took over afterwards.

What they finally found became the grounds for calling Amelia and David major drug dealers. They needed to cover their asses. They got lucky. They changed their story.

The fact that Amelia and David turned out to actually be major drug dealers is beside the point. I just wish Amelia had dropped her soup ladle, put up her hands, and cried, "Don't shoot!"

I look at the pictures in my head of Amelia in her black bandana and bandolier of bullets and Amelia in her red and white high school band uniform, her clarinet, her silly hat, and I see that small strange unsettling smile that is the same in both pictures, one Amelia looking back and the other looking ahead in time. I don't really think she had a black bandana and bullets. I do think the clarinet was real.

I still mostly refuse to think of Megumi's father David as anything but "that man who married my Amelia" and led her into a life of dope, poverty and death, but the truth is, Amelia played her own part. It's like when she was a teen in rehab, and it hit me one day I could stop worrying about her getting in with the wrong kind of friends. She was the bad influence herself that other parents should worry about. But then for just a moment, she seemed to pull it all together. She met David, got married, gave birth to Megumi, relapsed a couple of times, came back, and then died in a botched homeland security raid.

Clavichord

I run into people all the time who think "clavichord" is another word for collarbone. I once mentioned that to Megumi hoping she would smile, but she didn't get it. This is another sad example of a fifty-four year old man trying to amuse a superhero. I don't think her rat spider sidekick who might also be a cat or maybe a possum got it either.

Generally speaking, a clavichord is a rectangular wooden box. It usually has a lid. The keyboard is usually on the left. Inside there is a soundboard and a number of strings. The mechanism for making music is the most simple of all the keyboard instruments. You press a key on one end of a lever and the other end rises up and a metal blade called a tangent strikes a string or pair of strings.

Unlike a piano player, for example, the clavichord player is in direct contact with the string. The art is in what to do with that contact.

Your touch controls the dynamics of the note. You can do a kind of vibrato. You do not just push a key and a consistent sound is produced. It all depends on what you do with that finger on the key.

The instrument is not loud. Everyone needs to be paying attention—the player, the listeners. Clavichord music is not something that can happen accidentally or in the background. If your neighbor is a clavichord player, chances are you'll never hear the music through the common wall even if you put your ear right up against it hoping to figure out what's going on in there.

Some clavichords are as big as the tops of conference tables. Some are quite small. There is a tiny model called the "King of Sweden" that you can pick up and carry around under your arm. Most are somewhere in between.

We like to claim that the clavichord was Bach's favorite instrument.

In other words, the clavichord is the very essence of the keyboard. It is what Plato would have called an "ideal" keyboard instrument if it had been invented in time for him to call it anything at all.

It was Abu Yusef who pointed out how much a clavichord looks like a crate of rifles.

He had a lot of trouble getting his instrument into Iraq when he came home from Italy after the Invasion.

Our anime supergirls, Megumi and Layla the ghost, never have that kind of trouble. That's a very good thing, since their clavichords sometimes really are filled with high tech weapons and alien technology!

Abu Yusef

Earlier, Abu Yusef amused us all with his story about how Layla came to be his only student, the way the women of the town were all atwitter over it. Most of the children had been very curious about the Mayor's keyboard which apparently made no sounds. No, that was not true. The sounds it made were very small. You had to be close and listening carefully. What was the point in that?

He had caught her listening at the door to his music room, and she had run away frightened that he would tell on her, but he had said nothing. He finally took on several other children as students and was able to include Layla in the group. By the end of the week, only she remained.

Why in the world would you want to teach the child to make those noises?

She is the one who wants to learn, he told them, and she is the one who actually can learn.

Abu Yusef's description of this experience led to a lively discussion of teaching keyboard to very young students and the uses of the clavichord in such teaching and J. S. Bach's *The Little Clavier Book for Wilhelm Friedemann Bach*. The trouble with little fingers. And all the stuff you need to know. Should we talk about bebung or leave that for later?

I love my mental picture of Layla's lessons. She takes her place on the bench in front of the clavichord. The wind that blows through the windows is always very hot in my imagination. Is there glass in the windows? Layla's little fingers. Will she be able to do it? He stands beside her. Her grandmother sits in a corner with her hands folded in her lap. She is as huge and still and present as an Easter Island statue, impossible to ignore. She is keeping a close eye on the proceedings. Layla and Abu Yusef are working on a snippet of Couperin he especially likes and believes is fundamental to technique. Layla looks up at him. She is so serious and determined.

Yes, Sensei, I can do this.

No, that would be Megumi.

No, not her either.

Amelia with her clarinet?

Do you hear the way she is getting it? Abu Yusef asks Layla's grandmother. Do you hear?

Abu Yusef is also an Etruscan archaeologist. He spent many years in Italy before coming home after the Invasion. His Italian is perfect. He is widely read. When it comes to the clavichord, he is an expert on the instrument built from the intarsia of Urbino in Italy. This is a wood carving of an old clavichord. It is so detailed that builders have been able to duplicate the instrument. Abu Yusef has made four such copies. One is in France, one is in New York, one is still in Italy, and the other is in London. He wishes he had kept one of them for himself. Well, someday when things are quieter, he will make another. In the meantime he has a wonderful double fretted instrument (that looks like a crate of rifles when closed). It is the sound of that instrument which captured Layla's imagination and transported her to a world where everything was possible.

The Twangsters

You can't be a supergirl with huge eyes unless you've got a profile. I've figured that much out poking around online trying to figure out what Amelia might have been thinking when she named Megumi.

So, here we go.

Name: Megumi
Alias: Pumpkin, snuggle bunny.
Race: Human
Gender: Female
Age: six
Hair: light brown (blinding pink these days)
Eyes: blue (dazzling and always a little sad)
Height: 44 inches (111.760 cm)
Weight: 42 pounds (19.051 kg)
Blood: Type A
Status: Demon hunter, rocket scientist, first grade student (in the fall).
Quote: "Everything is so quiet."

Name: Layla
Alias: Lallie, Princess of the Night.
Race: Human
Gender: Female
Age: six
Hair: brown (ghostly blue these days—you might even say purple)
Eyes: brown (sparkling, dancing, laughing)
Height: We must guess that she might be just a little taller than Megumi.
Weight: And maybe just a little lighter.
Blood: Type B (I'm making this up. I don't want to think about the blood. Why do we always need to know the blood type of our superheroes?)
Status: Crime fighter, ghost.
Quote: "Where will we put them all?"

Storyline: Megumi is sad sitting under her tree. Her whole world has been shattered. She has come to live with her grandfather in his clavichord dojo. There are no children her age in the neighborhood. Instead there are a few good jazz clubs, a gay bar, and a couple of top-notch restaurants (one Vietnamese and the other French). She doesn't really want to learn how to play the clavichord. But what else can her grandfather teach her?

Meanwhile in southern Iraq, Layla who really does want to learn to play the clavichord is run down by a truck. She becomes a ghost. She somehow picks up on the clavichord connection between Megumi's grandfather and Abu Yusef, and she materializes and makes friends with Megumi. Megumi's finger work is much improved by her interaction with the talented ghost.

Megumi will cut her hair short and dye it pink, scandalizing her grandfather, and Layla will do hers in a bright but ghostly blue. They will wear cool costumes. Look at them! Zooming around righting wrongs and singing songs (but not too loudly because no one can hear the clavichord if you're belting out the words with too much enthusiasm). Layla and Megumi will be black belts in Megumi's grandfather's dojo of martial clavichord playing. Everyone will be forced to stop shouting and shooting and listen carefully to hear them playing.

Some of the cool stuff in future episodes will include gender confusion, evil aliens, talking animals, and giant robots. We get the idea that after all is said and done and the adventures are over, Layla will move on to wherever little girls go when they die in vehicular mishaps in Iraq, but Megumi who will be the president of Mars or something will never forget her. There is the hint that Megumi's mother Amelia will help Layla find her way by pointing at the light with her soup ladle. We suspect Layla might pop back in from time to time for even wilder adventures or to give Megumi sisterly advice about life.

Little Stars

I move away from the window and sit down at the clavichord and get lost in some tricky parts but not so lost I don't hear Megumi come back in. She comes quietly up to my side. She pulls at my sleeve. She gives me a small pinecone. I pat the bench. She crawls up beside me. I put the pinecone down on the music stand in front of us.

Megumi plays a little tune.

Clunk clank clunk clank clink clink clink.

"Very nice," I tell her, thinking that what she's played might be Bach or it might be "Twinkle Twinkle Little Star."

Both are good.

* Note from Ray Vukcevich: I wrote this story for a project called "The Dust Girl" by Benjamin Buchholz. When I asked him to say a few words about it, he sent me this:

The second day of my military service in Iraq I responded to a traffic incident no more than a few hundred meters from the border crossing point for US supplies between Kuwait City and Baghdad. There I found that one of our semis had run over an Iraqi girl of about six years of age, a girl who had been begging for food or water. She had run out into the road to get a water bottle thrown to her from one of the semis. When I arrived her blanketed body lay still in the roadway, with a southbound convoy stalled on one side of her, the soldiers anxious to return to the safety of their base in Kuwait, and a convoy stalled in the northbound lane. Between the two perhaps a hundred Iraqis had gathered, wailing women, relatives, other children, along with British troops, our young American troops, members of the town council, dogs, and even a few goats. The scene troubled me for many months, haunting me. As catharsis, I asked a number of writers to tell the story, to invent it anew from nothing more than details such as those I've provided in this very paragraph. They immersed themselves in the characters and told the tale of this 'Dust Girl' from the perspective of one of those bystanders. While no story can truly capture a death such as this in its randomness, its chaos, its futility, perhaps the fiction preserves bits and pieces of her. It is all we can do.

Pedro Iniguez's fiction has been published in magazines and anthologies such as Space and Time Magazine, Crossed Genres, Outposts of Beyond, *and* From the Corner of Your Eye. *His story "Shaytan, The Whisperer" was originally published in the anthology* Those Who Live Long Forgotten.

In Islam, the devil is called Shaytan *or* Shaitan.

"shaytan, the whisperer"
PEDRO INIGUEZ

algol, the Demon Star, adorned the night sky and watched as Baghdad burned. The flames licked skyward casting webs of light and shadow upon the crosshatching of streets. Homes, offices, palaces: the fire knew no prejudice.

In early April, 2003, Baghdad became a city of light.

Inaya watched from the roof of her house. Every few minutes the bombs burst in the distance and the gunshots popped sporadically.

Her uncle, Arif, stood with one arm on her shoulder and the other clasping the Koran. He whispered prayer to the wind but Inaya didn't care.

The most she could offer was hope that Hakeem had not come into contact with American forces.

"Shaytan was created from fire," Uncle Arif said now looking at her. "And he is born again wherever it may kindle."

"Uncle, please, don't start with that."

"Allah created the Angels, the Djinn, and Man. The Angels were the only ones not to have free will; they obeyed him and worshipped him. One day came, when Allah created Adam, the first man, and Allah told all to bow down to his new creation. One by one they all kneeled until it came time for Shaytan to do so. He was the only one standing, and proclaimed to Allah, 'I will not bow down to Adam, I am superior to him; I was born of fire and he of clay.' For this Allah cast him down to Earth and relegated judgment until the end of times. Shaytan would then declare his intent to lead the followers of Allah astray and prove that faith could be broken."

Arif sighed. "Shaytan is the Whisperer of Men; but he has no power over us, child, only the power to suggest. But he is a great deceiver; he can appear as any form, man or beast. And it is said that wherever Shaytan goes, the Ghouls are not far behind."

"Uncle, please—"

"The Ghouls are Djinn of myth, the wanderers of the desert sands. The scavengers of men, they feed on the carrion of the departed. Where Shaytan steps, the Ghouls feast. Shaytan drifts with the wind . . . and he is here." He swept his hand over the city.

Inaya had no more words for her uncle. Her face was like stone and turned to look on the burning city in quiet concern.

Uncle Arif put his hand on her shoulder again and looked on. "I hope your brother is safe." He paused to survey the glow. "But there is so much fire."

The light of the fire gave way to the light of the sun; the light of the sun gave way to the light of the television.

The news broadcaster announced Coalition Forces had formally declared the capture of Baghdad.

Inaya saw women on the television with wallet-size photographs of their loved ones. They were going around the city looking for missing family members; perhaps soldiers, perhaps boys that never came home during the bombing. The women checked the prisons, the hospitals, the mass graves the military dug up.

She rummaged through drawers and rifled cabinets. She found an old service picture of Hakeem in full army uniform; he was a handsome man and a caring brother. It was not like him to not have called.

It had been three days since she heard from him.

Uncle Arif went to work at the market and she hoped it was still intact. She scribbled a quick note of intent and stated she didn't know when she would return, but promised that she would. Inaya didn't know where to start, but figured she'd try getting out on the street first.

She hit the city in her worn Nikes and faded blue jeans. She was an unconventional young woman in an unconventional time.

The Karrada district was one of the most diverse in Iraq and for that she had been fortunate. The ordeals other women or Christians faced in other parts of the city were usually spared on her.

The air was tinged burning rubber and wood. She didn't know what burning flesh smelled like and hoped she didn't smell it now.

The crowds were out in numbers as hundreds of feet pounded the cracked sidewalks. Inaya stopped to ask a man what this was all about.

"We are heading to the Main Square to celebrate the American Victory," the man said.

As she walked the crowded dusty streets, she swayed to the Al-Jad-irya Private Hospital.

She was hit with a sting of nerves and feared walking in. She wasn't sure she wanted to know anything anymore. But, she braved the feeling and walked in.

She walked into an oven. The place of healing and respite was stuffy and the air she breathed suffocated her; through an open mouth, she took deep gasps of air and felt no relief. Beads of sweat trickled down her forehead. An old woman walked out of the door as Inaya was walking in; her face was drenched, and Inaya wasn't sure if the woman was sweating or crying.

Bodies ground against one another and doctors shoved their way through anyone who wasn't bleeding. Inaya pictured a line of ants fractured when someone upsets their daily routine.

Hooded and veiled women outnumbered the physicians; their black clothing a grim counterpoint to the white coats. Multiple hands clasped at the doctors as they raced by, pulling them into an abyss of questions.

Inaya heard shouts. She turned to her left and saw an old man arguing with a surgeon. The man—slouched, tanned, face a roadmap of wrinkles—held the surgeon's wrist. "You know nothing," shouted the old man. "How can you be a doctor?" The old man let go of the surgeon's wrist and started to cry; the desperate attempts of a father, no doubt, trying to deny death its due. The man in green scrubs put his hand on the old man's shoulders. The old man in his last denial at the truth, spat in the surgeon's face and walked away. What lied beside him was a man, possibly in his forties. He looked asleep, but his lungs never rose or fell.

The women, also, looked into the faces of the hundreds of wounded, the dying. And each encounter was over in less than a second: if it wasn't someone they knew, they left the patient abandoned and alone.

Inaya had never seen so many patients, and never so many missing limbs. Some of the wounded had stumps for arms and would shoulder the burden of phantom-limb syndrome for life. This was a departure from runny noses and scraped knees. In some cases, she thought, it looked like sacks of meat had been placed on gurneys.

She looked through the faces, holding up her brother's picture as she walked by. One man caught her attention. The first thing she noticed was his face; or what little of it was left. He looked at her and opened his mouth. A tongue writhed about in the toothless gape. The man spat out low guttural moans and nodded his head. He was trying to speak through what little was left of his face. Inaya clasped at her mouth and tried not to cry. He was just a boy in his mid-twenties, broad shouldered, and the uniform he wore had been cut up the middle, exposing his bare chest where two punctures adorned his heart—where emblems and medals would have been. Every time he took a breath, blood pumped out in trickles.

Inaya approached him and every step she took squeezed at her heart tighter and tighter. She gripped the picture of Hakeem and hoped under her breath that the faceless man was not her brother. She held up the photo and compared. Hakeem had light brown eyes, and if the sun hit it at the right angle, it sometimes looked green. He also had an oval face and a neatly trimmed mustache. She looked at the dying man in front of her: most of his face had burned and looked like the ground meat they sold at the markets. If this man had a mustache, it was singed in hellfire. One of his eyes was sealed shut and the brown one that looked at her was fighting to stay awake. They said that eyes were the windows to the soul, and Inaya wondered if this man still had one.

"Hakeem?"

The soldier shook his head. He opened his jaw, forcing his tongue to form sounds. He tried to say something, maybe his name, but he spoke in the language of the dying.

Inaya shook her head and placed her hand on his. He closed his eyes and Inaya hoped he dreamed of a place better than this.

She looked around again, but, her brother was not among the men whose shredded clothes might have once been uniforms.

She made eye contact with a doctor. He looked and anticipated her question. She wanted to ask about her brother but she knew: he would have no answer about a specter that was not here. Her face shifted away from his eyes and calmly walked away from the purgatory they called a hospital.

On her way out she eyed a mangy dog on the street; its brown and spotted fur, the perfect camouflage for the dirty streets. Among the crowd, he simply stared into her eyes. Just hers. It broke its gaze and departed to some westward street.

This unsettled her.

She flagged down one of the black-veiled Muslim women. "Sister, my brother has gone missing and he is not in this hospital. Do you by chance happen to know where else I may look?"

"There is a mass grave the army has dug not far from here, just by downtown."

Inaya said nothing for a while and just stared back. She mustered, "Where?"

The woman, whose brown eyes cut through the black shroud, pointed behind her and said, "West."

Inaya paced for miles in the prime of the sun and her feet ached and felt too little for her shoes.

A crowd of men in rolled up sleeves and weeping women crowded the fence of an empty plot of land. One of the men vomited to the side and another man with a shovel discarded it and simply walked away in anger.

No one in the crowd seemed to want to cross the threshold, as if the land were tainted.

She nudged through the crowd. The black of the veils around her blotted the sun and reflected the heat ten-fold. She reached the front of the crowd and tapped a man on the shoulder.

He turned his pale face, the sweat dripping off his mustache.

"Is this the grave?" Inaya asked.

"I don't know what this is anymore."

Many holes sprung from the ground like giant anthills. Bloodied clothing lay strewn like the remains of a landfill. Limbs and heads and what might have been torso's lay scattered across the plot like weeds growing in an unkempt yard.

Inaya caught a whiff of death on a breeze that blew sand into her eyes. She turned away from it instinctively.

"What happened here?" Inaya whispered to no one in particular.

One man, staring straight ahead said, "We buried these men here last night. They were members of the army and Saddam's guard. We clashed with the Americans last night. We dug this grave as quickly as we could . . . but at least we buried them. We buried them!"

Another man tried to calm him. He turned to Inaya and said, "We buried these men last night. When relatives returned to pay respects this morning, we found this." He nodded at the grisly scene. "The bodies have been re-dug and it looks like they have been . . . eaten."

Inaya stared at the scene.

Little birds landed on the bodies, pecking. Flesh hung off their beaks.

The man tried to shield her view from the carnage. "You are too young for this, child."

"The ghouls . . ." Inaya said to herself.

"Yes. The Americans are monsters, little one."

"No. The Eaters of the Dead. They are here."

"Child, these bodies were dug up by the invaders and left as carrion for the dogs."

Inaya turned away from the crowd. She left the rotting carcasses and knew in her heart her brother was spared a fate as cruel as this. He had to be. He was her brother.

She looked back and saw the crowd fall silent. The men kneeled and bowed their heads. It was the prayer of Dhuhr, the prayer of noon.

While the men whispered to Allah, Inaya wondered: if Shaytan truly was here, who did *he* whisper to?

She spotted the ugly brown dog off in the distance. Or she thought she did; the heat rose and mangled the air like a hallucination.

She turned around.

As her city crumbled around her, she continued to walk.

The afternoon took her through many streets. She caught her first glimpse of uniformed American men. Some were as white as the moon and others as black as the night. It was a strange sight to her eyes. This day was a fever, a mirage in a city between two rivers.

Word spread that the Americans had taken the airport, and many Iraqi fighters were held captive in a makeshift prison there.

Crowds gathered and marched to the airport like a divine pilgrimage. Inaya, seeing no alternative, traveled with them.

Inaya looked at her brother's picture. She reunited with him again, if only in spirit. He was her guardian and her rock. In Allah, she did not believe; in their blood, she found a truth that could not be turned away. No science could disprove their bond; no book-burning mob could douse their history.

But the afternoon grew late now, and the sun started to sink somewhere into the desert sands.

Inaya couldn't bear her feet anymore. She was sure her toes were blistered and maybe bleeding.

The wind began to stir; it lifted dust and sand and hurled its fury at the pilgrims. The weary men and veiled women pushed on against the rising sandstorm, like nomads.

They came upon a checkpoint. The crowd of about thirty, stopped at a roadblock of sandbags and barbed wire. One of the older men from her group spoke to an American guard. Inaya did not understand the exchange of words. The old man lifted a picture of what Inaya presumed to be his son. The American had a conversation through his radio and after a few moments let the crowd pass. The guards shadowed her every step towards the airport.

When they arrived at the entrance to the airport, the old man spoke to more guards. He turned to the crowd and said, "They will let us visit the prisoners. Do not cause a commotion. If your loved ones are not here, turn away and leave."

The band of relatives entered the airport, Baghdad's portal to the outside world, now closed and turned to a prison.

Before Inaya entered, she saw an American soldier bent over a mangy dog. His hand glided over its fur over and over. The soldier put his ear to the dog's muzzle as if he were listening intently.

It looked exactly like the dog she had seen earlier.

The soldier looked up, his eyes deep and dark. A victim of sleepless nights.

Inaya felt a shudder. She looked up; the sun, large and red, waned behind the Euphrates River. She took a breath and gripped Hakeem's picture.

American soldiers conversed in their English tongue and roamed freely. Tall, powerful men.

One soldier approached the group and motioned for them to follow.

They were led through elaborate hallways and descended many stairs as if to the bottom of some hell. If she had to guess, Inaya would say they were near some sort of basement.

The soldier brought them to a dim-lit hallway with a handful of overcrowded jail cells; perhaps airport security's old detention area.

Americans kept watch over everybody in the room.

Inmates pushed against their cages and gripped the steel bars. Bodies on both sides clambered over each other. Inaya was shoved by waves of mothers and fathers who waved photographs like banners of war. Arms reached through the bars, hands clasped.

The Americans shouted at the crowd, but the point was moot.

One voice reached Inaya's ear like a subtle symphony. "Sister. Little Sister!"

Hakeem reached a leathery hand out of his cell; Inaya wrapped her delicate fingers around it and smiled.

"I have looked everywhere for you."

"Inaya, dear sister, I thank Allah you are here. But it's too dangerous. There is a war out there."

Inaya paused and regained her breath. "Brother, the war is over."

Hakeem lowered his head and nodded.

"At least you are safe, sister."

Inaya smiled.

The American soldiers began to close in on the unruly crowd when they began to quiet down. The families of Islam kneeled and chanted in prayer. In unison they prayed the Maghrib, the meditation performed after sunset.

The Americans looked in confusion. Inaya was the only person standing before the Submissive of Allah. She felt naked and alone to the on-looking soldiers.

In strange tongues, the Americans squabbled amongst themselves. After a few moments they came to a verdict. They lurched ahead and began hauling the worshippers off the floor.

The prayers were snuffed and gave way to screams. The prisoners pleaded with slurs and questioning hands; their relatives were dragged by limbs and hair.

Amidst the screams, the Muslim men shoved the Americans away from the women.

Soldiers drew their rifles.

Inaya spotted the soldier from outside; heavy bags circled his eyes. He stared coldly at the crowd, eyes scanning across the room, person to person.

He un-holstered his pistol slowly and took aim at someone in the crowd. Inaya didn't know who, but his eyes seemed focused, obsessed.

In the cramped hallway the piercing burst of sound followed by a moment of deafness. She didn't see who was shot, but Inaya knew whoever it was, fell into the hands of Death himself.

The crowd roared and tried to escape. The exit was bottlenecked by armed men who took aim. The air soon cracked with gunfire and charged with smoke. The bearded men, who were too close to be shot, were butted by the black rifles.

Hakeem yelled amidst the chaos. "Inaya, get low to the ground. Get down!"

She dropped, abdomen flat on the cold floor. Dozens of sandaled feet and torn leather shoes greeted her. Some of the feet lost balance and fell near her face. Most never got back up.

Some prisoners retreated into the dankest corners of their cells, and the ones who reached an arm beyond the bars pleading for a stop caught the occasional stray bullet.

Inaya saw an Iraqi man grab an American's sidearm and shoot its owner's face point-blank. That man was met by a flail of gunfire; his body shook like a palm tree amidst a sandstorm.

Either man could have been a father.

What were once women and men in the room were just now reduced to the living and un-living; those who breathed still, and those who ceased to breathe.

Inaya started to cry. At first she didn't know why. The horror was so sudden she didn't have time to feel emotion. But when she looked at her shirt it was stained. The moist scarlet spot grew larger and larger until her shirt resembled a fresh dye-job. She was shot.

Hakeem screamed but the words were incomprehensible. Soon, the sounds melded as one large chaotic jumble of noise and static. Her image became blurred, but what she saw next was unspeakable. An abomination to her logical mind.

A mob, unlike either white or brown man, rushed into the room; half-naked men whose tanned bodies might have been spit from the sands of Egypt itself. Their gaze was that of rabid jackals, and their maws were dark and lined with jagged teeth. They looked like men, but they were not.

Ignoring the anarchy that transpired around them, they charged the bodies of the deceased. They lunged at warm limbs and with the strength of their mouths alone, stretched and tore the skin away.

In revulsion, the Americans stopped the gunfire. The wounded men and women of Islam stared in horror.

Creatures tore at the necks of Inaya's dead countrymen. The entrails of the Americans were chewed and swallowed. In Baghdad, the dead would not have peace tonight; the Cradle of Civilization was now its tomb.

The Americans regained themselves. They shouted at the Iraqis and motioned with their rifles to move. Inaya's brothers and sisters rushed out the room, bloodied, torn and tired.

The repeating burst of gas and flame boomed through the prison. The rotating machine-fire of rifles, a hungry engine, spewed round after round into the men of myth: the Ghouls.

But what are the weapons of man to the immortal flesh of myths?

Lead smacked against demonic flesh. The popping sound of splintering bone now filled the air. But it had no effect on the starving ghouls. The bullets were ignored and the feast continued on the recently departed. The Americans, in fear, stormed out of the prison basement.

One of the feral ghouls leapt at Inaya. Its lean body hovered over hers. It sniffed at her tummy and snatched her wrists. It felt for something, perhaps a pulse.

Hakeem roared at the creature. "Get away from her, by Allah, get away from her!"

The ghoul turned to Hakeem and spoke. "I will not feast on Inaya tonight. She still lives." It turned its body and with the rest of the frenzied mob, dashed out of the room.

"Inaya are you alright? Can you hear me?"

Inaya turned her shivering head to her brother and said, "Thank Allah, I think I am."

The lifeless carcasses of foreigners and countrymen lay on the floor. During war, Inaya supposed, enemies could find common ground: the red that stained their bodies.

In a moment of silence, Hakeem sighed and sat his body down. He reached across the bars and held his sister's hand. "Everything is going to be alright, sister."

"I know brother. Now that I have found you, I know."

Somewhere, off in the distance, Inaya heard the sound of ticking. Not like the ticking of a clock, but the sharp tapping of a dog's nails. It neared like pebbles striking a concrete floor.

A dog wandered in the prison. It disregarded the bodies and the prisoners.

It approached Inaya and muzzled her face.

"I know you. You are Shaytan."

"You know me? What is it that you think you know, Inaya?"

"You are the Great Deceiver. You have caused all this. This destruction to our land, this profanity amongst our dead."

The dog lifted its muzzle and bellowed out a laugh that echoed through the iron bars. "I have done nothing, Inaya. You have done everything; you and your people. You simply invited me to watch. The One God gave me no power over you. Free will, you see. I have it, you have it. I simply suggest. I can be in your ear, and you can simply choose to listen . . . or to disregard. And as for the bodies of your fallen," the dog looked around. "We are simply here to collect the scraps you have left us."

A. M. Dellamonica is a Canadian science-fiction writer who teaches creative writing at the UCLA Extension Writers' Program. Her first novel, Indigo Springs, was published by Tor Books in 2009. Her fourth novel, A Daughter of No Nation, was published in December 2015. Her first novel won the Sunburst Award, and her other fiction has been nominated for the Sidewise Award and garnered her a Canada Council for the Arts Grant.

"Five Good Things about Meghan Sheedy" was originally published in Strange Horizons. It is a tale set in the far future about occupation, resistance, and terrorism.

"five good things about meghan sheedy"
A. M. DELLAMONICA

the boys were playing dust attack again.

It was a way of dealing, Dinah knew, and she tried to ignore Aidan as he threw an imaginary grenade and then made a sprinkling motion over Jesse, finger-waving shorthand that used to mean falling snow.

"Die, Fiend!" he shouted.

Shrieking, Jesse collapsed, writhing and flopping, apparently unable to quietly simulate complete dissolution of the molecular bonds that held his six-year-old body together.

"Both of you shush?" she ordered, earning her the faintest of grateful glances from beneath Meg's unkempt copper bangs.

She poured five portions of cereal into cracked, mismatched bowls, moistening each with a half-cup of watered-down milk. Beside each bowl she set a quarter piece of supplement wafer and a protein marshmallow. "Spoons—" she began, but then the boys' game turned to a real battle.

She dove for a kid, pulling Aidan loose and holding his fists down. Meg ended up with Jesse.

"I'm not dead," Jesse bellowed.

"Don't get up when you're dusted, traitor."

"I'm not a Fiend either!"

"You're a asswipe."

"Enough," Dinah said. "Aidan, go to your room and write five things."

He jerked loose. "Mom, do I have to?"

"Listen to Dinah," Meg said, wiping Jesse's face and nudging him toward the table. Raising her voice, she called, "Everyone come eat!"

Meg's thirteen-year-old, Gwynne, appeared at once, cramming her marshmallow into her mouth before she was seated and helping herself to another: the mallows were the one thing they had plenty of.

"Elbows off the table," Meg barked, loading the baby into his high chair. Sneering at the back of her mother's turned head, Gwynne slouched back in her chair instead of forwards, keeping a sweep of copper hair over the scars on her cheek and neck.

A rare moment of near-quiet broke upon them, broken only by the clink of spoons.

"There's space in King Daycare again," Dinah said finally, earning a chilly glance. "If you go looking for work again, they'll take Ben."

Through a scowl and a mouthful of cereal, Meg said, "Humans have been banned from Kabu-sponsored construction sites."

"I didn't hear that."

"Doesn't mean it's not true."

"I didn't mean—I'm sorry. Want me to ask if there's anything in the Tank?"

"I am not mopping floors in that deathtrap."

"Whole city's a deathtrap," Gwynne muttered.

"Was I talking to you?" Meg asked sharply.

Gwynne was right, in Dinah's opinion, but like more and more of her thoughts lately, she kept it to herself.

Aidan reappeared, clutching a scrap of paper. "Jesse is cool," he read. "Jesse is neat. Jesse makes the bed. Jesse lent me his train. Jesse is fun. Okay, Mom?"

By way of assent, Meg waved at his chair. "City's rebuilding some residential districts over by Northgate. Human contractors, human sites. I'll look for work there."

"That won't pay much," Dinah said.

"Excuse me," Meg brought her spoon down with a sharp smack. "If you're content to be a bottom feeder that's fine, but I am an engineer and I'm going to work in my field."

Meg always had an explosive temper, but war had shortened her fuse. Fiendish bombardment of Seattle had left her widowed and homeless; she'd have been on the streets with Aidan and Gwynne if Dinah hadn't taken them in.

If the Democratic Army didn't start winning soon, it would only get worse. The Friends of Liberation—which was what the Fiends called themselves—had been pushing a slow invasion north from Mexico for the past decade. Drawing heavily on the support of offworlder allies, the Demos stopped the Fiends at the thirty-sixth parallel, in a cataclysmic battle that had taken out four million soldiers on both sides along with the Hoover Dam and most of Las Vegas. Since then the Fiends had been consolidating their hold on the Southeastern US while pushing northward on the far western edge of the continent, conquering California and edging ever-closer to Canada, where resistance was expected to be light.

If the Fiends did take Seattle, they'd have to run north themselves. She didn't say it: Meg would flame-broil her alive for mentioning defeat in front of the kids.

The two women had been together, one way or another, since childhood. Raised in a Kabu school for orphaned refugees, they'd grown from schoolgirls to mothers without so much as a disagreement. So it seemed now, anyway, when everything Dinah said earned a scorching comeback.

Meg always needed so much space, Dinah thought wistfully. All this enforced closeness, two women and four kids in a house with only three bedrooms . . .

A bang: Dinah leapt out of her chair, reaching for the boys. But it wasn't a bomb, just Meg slamming a cupboard door inches from her ear.

"I said: what do you think they should wear today?"

She swallowed. "Black—is there a dress code?"

"How should I know?"

"We could call the principal, what's his name . . ."

"Ted Arnold," Meg said.

"Whatever you choose should be fine," Dinah said. "Who's gonna complain?"

"Whatever I choose? You're not staying to help?"

"I have to go in for a couple hours." She tried to keep her expression bland; the last thing she could afford was to make Meg suspicions.

"Today? Dinah, of all days . . ."

149

"I have to be indispensable." Still standing near her sons she gulped her cereal directly from the bowl, then reached for her contact lens case.

"As if the exalted Chamon would fire his precious Dinah."

"Let's keep it that way." She popped in the other lens. "Meet you at the memorial, okay?"

"Fine." Meg flapped a hand in dismissal. "At least try to sneak me onto the housing list. Or find some produce."

"Right." Her temper finally frayed. "Make myself useful. Bringing in all the money at the risk of getting shot isn't enough."

Meg paled, freckles standing out on her milky cheeks. Choking back sobs, she walked out of the kitchen.

"She asked for it," Gwynne muttered, and Aidan jumped out of his chair. Grabbing his sister's bowl, he smashed it to the floor before pursuing Meg down the hall.

Great, thought Dinah. Make me the bad guy.

She closed her eyes, thinking back to the Kabuva customs she had learned from the recluses. One: Meg's teaching the kids to sing. Two: She reads to them every night no matter how tired or crappy she's feeling.

"What are you doing?"

"Thinking of good things about your mother, Gwynne."

"She can sure pick a fight," the girl said.

"Are you saying you want to join me?"

Nose raised high, the girl made herself scarce. Dinah got a rag from the sink and began wiping up the shards of the cereal bowl. Three: Meg is honest about her emotions. And she's right about the vegetables.

She stalled on finding a fifth thing.

As she tossed the pieces of bowl she saw Ben straining to get out of his high chair. She plucked him free for a quick squirmy hug, reaching for Jesse with her other arm. For one precious moment it was just her and hers; then Ben squealed, threatening a meltdown. She set him down and he toddled anxiously down the hall after Meg.

"It's okay, Ma," Jesse said. Dry-eyed, she buried her face in his brown curls, drawing in the scent of cheap kid shampoo and trying to believe him.

To hear the Fiends tell it, the agenda of their invasion was simplicity itself—take over all of Earth, then evict every last offworlder. They had united Asia behind this goal before Dinah was born. Wanting an independent Earth was easy to comprehend, making it a seductive idea . . . but the Fiends were totalitarians on the one hand and, on the other, total hypocrites. Their fine talk of cleansing humanity of foreign contaminants didn't stop them from buying offworlder bombs. Oh, they'd pretend they were scavenging ordnance from the Demos and their Kabu allies, but the numbers didn't track: anyone could see the Fiends had offworld sponsors just like the Demos.

Still, they'd merrily assassinate anyone with Kabu ties.

Ordinary civilians survived by keeping their views quiet and their heads down. Others played the dangerous game of working for both sides. Anyone could be a Fiend. The doctor at the neighborhood clinic, a cab driver, your next-door neighbor. Even the nice Demo soldier who was allegedly fighting the Liberation could be a Fiend, protecting post offices and airports by day, planting dust grenades at night.

There were no good choices. Playing both sides was hazardous, to be sure, but so was risking the Fiends deciding to 'punish' your family. And if they ever took Seattle, collaborators who didn't escape in time wouldn't have a chance.

All this meant that even though the Tank had given Dinah a precious dust-proof poncho, she had hacked it to pieces, lining her raincoat, gloves and boots with the shaggy beige material. The remaining shreds of the poncho were ragged enough to look scavenged. She had sewn them together in a wrap that she kept wound about her head and face.

This improvised shielding wouldn't save her from a direct hit, a bullet, or shrapnel. But if she was ever on the fringe of a dust blast, it might keep her alive.

The sun shone brightly as she headed out, making the jacket too hot, but she kept it zipped to her throat. Spring had come to Washington: tulips and daffodils were blooming in gardens, and half-starved children played badminton in the curved surface of a crater where a subdivision had been, maybe six months before.

Dinah walked swiftly, pausing at each bus stop to glance back in case there was a bus coming. If she got caught between stops, she'd have to sprint—but it would be worth it, because she'd have time to see if anyone was selling vegetables.

Out of morbid habit she looked toward downtown, with its increasingly tattered skyline. The only intact structure was the Tank. A gray monolithic shadow, three thousand feet high and obscured by artificially generated mist, it had been lowered into a gap left after bombs ruined the humanbuilt skyscrapers. The Consultancy had dusted their remains to nothing and lowered the Tank into the gap from orbit.

The bus turned up, shaving twenty minutes off her commute and she found a vendor with radishes and carrots who was willing to swap for the protein marshmallows Dinah got from the Tank. She made the trade quickly, fighting paranoia, convinced passers-by were noting her every move.

Head down, avoiding eye contact with everyone, she pretended she was invisible as she walked the last few blocks to work.

The Tank was guarded by young, gray-skinned Kabu conscripts, twelve feet tall and bristling with weapons and scanners. They stood with their caps pulled down tightly, shielding their bodies and all but the tips of their tentacles from view. The pose formed the upright bullet profile that was the reason humans called the Kabu squid.

Lukewarm artificial rain drizzled down the hood of Dinah's raincoat, maintaining a high level of moisture for the sake of the sentients' skin. The ground was pocked with bioluminescent slime, small mossy growths, and slippery rocks. The whole place smelled of rot and salt water.

Standing this close, she could see the profusion of algae and fungus growing on the outer skin of the Tank—blue and red blooms broken by small patches of green.

Dinah moved slowly past the guards, arms raised so their scanners could get a good look. She couldn't endure a second walk-through or a body search, not today.

"Morning," said a Kabu functionary, its accent mangling the simple greeting to something like "Mowee." The squid's cap billowed and stretched, momentarily forming a cup over her tentacles, an umbrella-shaped bowl whose insides were lined in thick ridges of gill tissue. The offworlder let her tentacles relax—the trunk of fleshy cords holding up her body rippled and spread outward in a many-pointed star, and as her cap sank lower she flipped it inside out, the flesh rolling up to form a bowl that caught the falling water of the artificial rainstorm.

"Morning," she answered as it hitched one tentacle into her armpit, using another to thrust a swab in the general direction of her face. Cotton dabbed at the inside of her cheek. With a perfunctory caress the offworlder released her, tossing the sample in a test tube and with-drawing its tentacles.

Dinah moved on to the lockers where she stashed her bags. Emp-ty-handed, she entered the Tank proper, stripping off all her clothes. Nude but for her contact lenses, she passed through a final scanner into the locker room which contained her work uniform.

The uniform was a smock that left Dinah's underarms, throat, back and lower legs exposed for the groping Kabu found necessary when interacting with other sentients. Everywhere else, thick fabric armored areas the offworlders were supposed to leave alone, absorbing tempting scents and obscuring the texture of the flesh beneath. The squid probed and tasted each other with abandon—every conversation looked like an orgy. It had been hard going to convince them that humans needed to keep their groins and faces strictly off limits . . . and to get humans to offer up their armpits, necks and legs to constant tactile scrutiny.

Dinah pulled up her mask, shielding her face behind a layer of clear crystal before heading up to her office.

Like the smock, the Tank was imperfectly adapted for human-Kabu coexistence. Each room was dominated by a waist-high aquarium of salt water. Pools and pipes were structured so that water flowed con-tinuously through the building: a squid could swim from top to bottom.

Aquariums lined every wall, leaving wading pools as floorspace in the middle for human staff.

Dinah was halfway to her desk when a gelatinous tentacle snagged her waist.

"You smell wretched," Chamon greeted her with a splash, her hand with another of his tentacles and rising up on the edge of the tank. His eyeless face was squinched in what she knew was an expres-sion of surprise.

"A little stressed," she admitted reluctantly.

"You didn't have to come in today."

"I don't want to fall behind." She couldn't say she was hiding from Meg's too-observant eyes and keen intuition.

The offworlder knotted small tentacles in a sign of profound approval. "Your sense of duty is admirable."

If only, Dinah thought. Then she saw Chamon had stained his cap a deep indigo, while his tentacles were wrapped with golden wires, the Kabu equivalent of jewelry. "You're dressed up?"

"Of course." Chamon shifted his grip to her neck as she sat in front of a deep red bowl filled with colored liquid, bright swirls of minuscule oily beads. She steeled herself to ignore him and start work—then, just as her emotional armor was on, he slipped into the tank, jetting off.

The red bowl resolved into a datapool as she dipped her fingers into the fluid. Relaxing slightly, she brought up a long list of claims for compensation. Housing requests first—as Democratic allies, the Kabu were supposed to find housing for anyone their troops might have accidentally rendered homeless in the fighting.

Dinah's job was cross-referencing the claims with battle reports, rejecting anyone whose home might have been dusted by the Fiends. After that, Chamon would rule on whether the homeless humans were innocent Demo civilians or probable enemy spies.

She worked through the housing claims slowly, making them last before reluctantly moving on to requests from people who'd lost relatives in the fighting. The criteria were about the same: the Kabu only paid out when the dead or injured party was in the Democratic Army and died via friendly fire. Civilian casualties didn't rate; nor, of course, did any human suspected of Fiendish allegiances.

A lot of humans were tagged as suspicious, in part because there were so many Fiend infiltrators, but also because the Kabu budget wouldn't allow them to pay out on every legitimate claim.

Dinah kicked up her speed. Friendly fire claims usually came with video feeds, digital clips from security cameras and surveillance 'bots. Dinah had thought herself inured to watching them, but in the last week it had gotten tough again.

One image was especially ambiguous. Enhanced, its foreground was clear enough—the camera had zoomed in on the arc of a smoking shell as it dropped over the remains of the Public Market. Exploding soundlessly at a height of about fifty feet, it expanded like fireworks, perfectly spherical and sinking toward the ground.

Within the circle of light cast by the embers, people screamed and fled. A few produced ponchos, wrapped up, and crouched in corners, avoiding the running mob.

Everything the embers touched vanished in a puff of brown dust.

The camera homed in on a uniformed human man, perhaps twenty years old, who was too near the center of the still-spreading ball to get away. He threw himself under a parked truck, but the embers sank down inexorably, dissolving the vehicle in slow seconds. There was only enough dust left to eat through his clothes and half of his body. Instead of vanishing he flopped and screeched, just like Jesse this morning.

Jaw locked, Dinah ran the feed backwards. Was that a squid in the background of the shot? Was it carrying a grenade launcher?

Chamon expected her to look hard before referring a file upward. By the time she'd complied, Dinah's stomach was hot and acidic, her eyes burning.

She moved on to miscellaneous claims: the Kabu were being blamed for various Internet service blackouts, two conscripts had over-groped—nice euphemism, she thought—a woman during a search for hostiles in a refugee camp, and someone's dachshund had run into the Tank perimeter and gotten fried. The usual.

She was almost done when the man stamped out of the conference room, red-faced and moving fast, nearly slipping on the wet floor in his haste.

Chamon appeared as soon as the lift doors closed on him, cap flashing sorrowful color combinations as he draped a limb over Dinah's shoulders.

"I didn't know you were in conference," she said. Maybe this was why Chamon had stained his skin and bound his tentacles.

"Alas, yes." He dropped a dataglob onto her palm. "You'd better copy this and send it to the Watch List. If the Friends of Liberation— what do you call them again?"

"Fiends," she said automatically, setting the glob in a reproduc-tion bath.

"Yes, Fiends. If they haven't already recruited him, they're sure to swim by soon."

"What happened?"

"I offered him compensation. His brother has vanished."

"Vanished" usually referred to a person who'd been abducted by an offworld biotech conglomerate. Dinah watched the glob as it began to expand and divide. "Did he qualify for compensation?"

"No, I could never put a missing person on the friendly fire roster. But I have a discretionary fund for compassionate purposes."

"Oh." It was the first Dinah had heard of it. Discretionary fund, she thought. Money lying around. Meg homeless.

There was no chance Chamon would consider Dinah, an employee, as a candidate for that kind of largesse. And why should he? She had a roof over her head and her kids were alive. She wasn't even a widow: on paper, at least, Chris was listed as MIA, not dead.

She thought of the young Demo soldier dissolving on the street and her breath hitched. In war, even compassion had to be rationed. Most people had to solve their own problems.

"Gill refused the compensation offer," Chamon said, tasting the inside of her elbow. "Used a colloquial insult . . . blood money. He wants to prove someone within the Consultancy abducted his brother."

This was, in all likelihood, the truth. "So he'll go on the Watch List, the Fiends will approach him, and they'll all get busted and dusted?"

"I thought he would let me help him." Chamon rolled a tentacle over her shoulders, lashing the floor helplessly. "Stubborn, like all humans, swimming upstream . . ."

Dinah's mouth tightened. Her scent must have changed, too, because Chamon glided back a yard and raised five tentacles. "The man is determined and loves his brother deeply," he said, counting off two praises and knotting the first pair of tentacles. "He's seeking aid through the proper channels, and his motives are not financial."

Dinah risked a glance down at the dataglob. It had overbred; there were three instead of two. And Chamon wasn't touching her. She fished out the extra glob and tucked it into her mouth before dropping the other two into a storage pool.

"Last, Gill is supporting his missing brother's family." Making a perfunctory star-knot of his five tentacles, Chamon reached for her again.

"If you want to help him," she said, "Investigate his brother's disappearance."

"Stirring up silt won't save anyone," Chamon said absently. "Seas, Dinah, you're going to be late for the funeral. Want a ride?"

So he was going. She glanced at the clock, trying to contain her rising alarm. "I'll run. It's not that far."

"Don't be ridiculous, human. I've already called my driver."

The back compartment of the armored limousine was a smallish aquarium, so Dinah—dressed in human clothes once more—had to get in next to the driver. She had barely sat down when Chamon thrust a tentacle through the waterproof membrane that separated back from front. It recoiled distastefully as it touched her.

His voice came through a speaker. "You're covered in chemicals."

"I can't go without deodorant among my own kind," she said. "If you like, I can still walk."

"No, no." He latched onto her wrist, trolling a sticky feeler up the exposed line of her jaw but remembering to avoid her mouth and eyes. "Earthly clothes, too." His touch, so much a part of her day-to-day life, was harder to accept outside the Tank.

Her contact lenses were itchy and she let that be her excuse when she let the emotions in, just for a minute: tears welled and the pain—on the surfaces of her eyes, at least—eased.

Deep breath, she thought. It's hardly anything, bearing this too. You can't let him suspect anything . . .

"I've tasted this garment."

"It's all I have for funerals."

"You're incredibly anxious today." The tentacle was lodged behind her ear now. Another had wandered below the collar of her dress, closer to her breasts than a smock would have allowed. "Dinah, what's the matter?"

Shuddering, she curled her fingers into an approximation of an apology knot, pressing it against the roving pseudopod and stopping its downward wander. "I shouldn't be seen arriving with you, Chamon."

"Of course. We'll drop you off someplace discreet."

The limo pulled into a secluded parkade. "Will this do?" Chamon asked.

Dinah glanced around, saw nobody, and all but leapt out of the car. "Yes, thanks."

"See you at the Institute," he replied, and the car drove on.

Twenty years earlier the Institute had been an orphanage, a safe haven for kids whose parents had died in the hot zones—the killing grounds of the Eurofront and the Texas invasion. Run by a religious order of Kabu pacifists who called themselves recluses, the idea was to raise the children somewhere safe, where they wouldn't have to face subsequent rounds of horror and loss.

The school had taken in Dinah and Meg, teaching them to read, to write and speak American English and Kabuva too. The recluses taught them the world could be a good place—that it would be, once the

Democratic Army showed the Fiends that they couldn't win the war, couldn't truly seek to control the whole world. The Institute teachers had given them hope for a bright tomorrow.

They had lied.

Seattle had been safe, but only for as long as it took Dinah and Meg to grow up and start families of their own. Now it too was a hot zone. The school and its orphans had packed up and gone to Northeastern Canada, where it was still hopeful, still safe. Where a new generation could be deceived too, Dinah thought bitterly.

When the recluses abandoned the Institute a handful of their students had reorganized it as a private school, charging exorbitant tuition to anyone who could afford it and taking students of former graduates, like Meg and Dinah, for free.

Dinah's face warmed as she stared up at the familiar brick building, the safe haven of her childhood. Tears threatened again, but this time she fought them by allowing a sense of her own weariness to seep into her consciousness. As the fatigue flooded in, the emotion drained away, leaving her dull and spiritless—calm, to all outer appearances.

Then she went around to the back.

The dust bomb had been concealed under the steps of the infirmary, just on the edge of the playground. Dispersal had spread it like a ball of seeds from a dandelion, and now the infirmary was missing a perfect quarter-sphere of its structure. Radiating out from the damaged corner of the building was the rest of the circle of destruction: soil carved out of the ground, filled at the bottom with four or so inches of rainwater.

Metal shards of playground equipment jutted at the edges of the blast radius. The distinctive blood-and-burnt-sage odor that dust left behind still hung in the air.

There were bouquets and gifts everywhere: flowers, photos, stuffed animals, notes of condolence. Some of the offerings had slid to the bottom of the bowl-shaped depression in the playground, soaking up the puddle. Others were laid carefully around its edges.

It was easy to imagine the kids here: the boys playing on the swings, Gwynne reading on the bench that was now gone. Dinah and Meg all but owned that bench, years before, had exchanged everything from dreams to locks of their hair under the shade of an oak tree that still stood, perversely unharmed, at the edge of the zone of destruction.

Jesse ran past, chasing another kid but—for once—not shouting. Silent and subdued, the boys ran as if the ghosts of dead friends were with them.

It could have been him, her precious boy.

When he circled past again she stopped him. "Where are your— where are the others?"

"Classroom," he said. "Couns'ling session."

"Why aren't you there?"

"Mine's finished," he said, avoiding her gaze. He'd ditched, then. Eight years old and already skipping class.

"Show me where?" she asked. He nodded, leading the way.

Meg turned up just as her kids were filing out of the counseling session. She passed Ben over to Dinah without a word, leading a silent procession to the auditorium. As they sat, Gwynne made a production of squeezing in next to Dinah, eyes flashing over the heads of the younger kids as she fired a furious glance at her mother.

Mercifully, the service began on time. As the gathered humans stood and fumbled their way through an off-key Anglican hymn, Dinah closed her eyes and remembered other funerals she'd attended in this same hall. Kabu ceremonies were humid and sensual. The air was weighted with hot brine mist, the floor sticky with sugared mourning stones that crunched under bare feet and rolling tentacles. She thought of the ritual knotting of fingers—performed imperfectly by students with their bony fingers—of bereaving wails led by the recluses, loud and hair-raising shrieks that mingled Kabu and human voices for hours.

Meg sat through the service stone-faced, staring at the small circle of coffins even when Gwynne threw herself against Dinah's chest, sobbing.

The eulogies went on forever. Shattered parents spoke, as best they could, of their lost children. A minister read meaningless Biblical verses. Finally the principal, Arnold, led a prayer for peace. Patiently he coaxed a few students up to the front, where they clung to the podium and squeezed out broken sentences about their murdered friends.

The girl's tears soaked through her dress, and Dinah put an arm around the girl, rocking her, feeling distantly as though she was being forced to participate, not for the first time, in Gwynne's ongoing rejection of her mother.

As soon as the memorial was over Dinah gave Gwynne one last squeeze and then stood, scooping Ben up.

"Where are you running off to now?" Meg demanded. Was that a gleam of suspicion on her face?

"Ben needs a change," she said in a low voice. At the front of the assembly in the visitor's aquarium, Chamon was surfacing for a walkabout.

"I just did him, Dinah."

"He's wet," she snapped, and Meg's brows came together. Dammit, she needed to be away, invisible . . . if they made a scene now . . .

"I need a break from Chamon," she lied in a rush. She pointed; her boss was already tasting the air for her. Sounding desperate was easy. "I didn't know he'd be here . . . I had to ride with him."

Meg handed her the diaper bag. "Go."

Dinah strode away, fleeing them all, and made her way to the basement of the school, to the hatch that led to the mourning grotto.

Kicking off her shoes, she waded down the spiral walkway as Ben tugged her hair and gaped at the phosphorescent markings on the damp ceiling. "It's okay, baby," she said, but it was no good. Not even the sound of water gurgling through rocks could soothe her nerves now. Her belly ached with stress.

The grotto was a smallish island, covered in exotic plants and encircled by a deep moat. Humid and lush, its overhead lights had dimmed to create an artificial twilight as soon as Dinah passed through the hatch. The air remained hot.

She followed the path to a specific bench and stopped in shock. Mouth numb, she glanced at her watch to confirm the time.

Nobody here. She didn't know whether to be relieved or upset. Rather than deciding, she checked Ben's pants. They were dry.

The baby chewed on his bottle and eyed her with a wary reserve. Last time she had taken him away from Meg, he'd screeched for an hour.

"Auntie Meg and I planted this," she said, letting him stroke the soft red leaves of a miniature maple that was planted next to the bench. It had leaned out over the surface of the pond as it grew, so that the undersides of its leaves were reflected in the still waters. At its base was a plaque bearing the name of Meg's husband.

When Chris came off the missing list, Dinah would plant something here, she and the kids together. Something evergreen, she had said once; and Meg had promptly screamed at her for giving up hope.

But Chris had been at the front in Las Vegas. There was no chance.

Splashy footsteps sounded behind her.

Dinah did not turn, keeping her gaze on the water, trying to look calm even as her heart stuttered with fear.

It was just the principal, Mr. Arnold.

Ben reached out. "Bada Clath," he said, and then, questioning, "Bada Clath?"

"He's asking if you're Santa Claus," Dinah said, and Arnold smiled.

"Happens all the time with little ones." He offered a finger and Ben clamped it in his undernourished fist.

"It's all right for an old student to be down here, isn't it?" she asked, listening for anyone else on the path down. "I came down here to think."

"It's time you stopped thinking and decided who your friends are," Arnold replied.

Dinah flinched. She pried her son's sticky hand from around the man's finger, moving him off to her other hip, so her body was between them. Ben whined angrily, craning around to stare at Arnold.

A teacher. Something sour came up from her stomach, coating her mouth. She'd known, intellectually, that anyone could be a Fiend, but of all people . . . "What do you want from me?"

"To liberate you, of course." His tone was ironic.

She laughed harshly. "Liberate, blackmail . . . it's all so similar."

Arnold took a contact lens case from the pocket of his slacks. "All we ask is that you wear these to work from now on."

"I'll be caught."

"No. Just replace your regular contacts with these and forget all about it. Don't worry, they match your regular prescription."

She did not take the offered case, staring as though it was a poisonous spider.

"I wear these . . . and what? You'll see what I see?"

"Exactly. There's a lot of intelligence to be mined out of the citizen complaints office." When she didn't move he took her hand forcefully in his, pushing the case against her palm and folding her fingers over it.

Pulling loose, Dinah let the case fall into the water.

It sank to the pebbled rim that divided the shallows of the pool from the drop-off to the depths. She stepped in after it, moving so her toe was right there, ready to push. Water ran between her foot and her sandal, blood-warm but strangely soothing.

Arnold froze. "How long do you think you'll live if you destroy those?"

"We haven't discussed payment," Dinah said. Don't show weakness, she thought. Be like Meg. Meg is strong. Meg protects the children fiercely. Meg doesn't back down or compromise. Meg wouldn't risk everything just because this bastard threatened her. Meg . . .

Her breath rasped painfully as she failed to think of a fifth good thing about her friend.

"Payment?" Arnold scoffed. "Who told you to keep the children home on Monday? Who might not warn you next time?"

"That's stick, Fiend," she said, trying desperately to believe she had a choice. "I want carrot."

Under the snow-white beard, his face pinkened. "Payment would cause attention. You're no good to us if you're on the Watch list."

"I don't want money."

"What, then?"

"Get Meg a new place to live. Something close, in that new complex they've just finished near my place."

He shook his head. "Impossible."

She laughed faintly. "But you're Santa Claus."

"Ms. Promislow . . ."

"You say you're everywhere, you say you have power. If you can't do this one little thing without getting us all busted, I'd be crazy to deal with you."

"You'd be crazy not to."

She nudged the plastic case a hair closer to the edge. "The Kabu will drown me if they find these gadgets of yours."

"The squid are losing the war. Seattle's all but ours."

"If the outcome's inevitable, you don't need me."

He glowered, and she wondered if he would kill her right now.

"I'll put these on the minute Meg moves into her own place," Dinah said.

"Be reasonable. This woman, after so many months together you suddenly can't live with her—"

She cut him off. "Do you even remember what the word friend used to mean? If the Kabu dust my house because I'm working with you, Meg dies too."

"I'm supposed to think you're a saint, then?"

"Okay, try this—Meg *knows* me. Living together . . . she'll figure out what I'm doing."

"She won't turn you in."

"Look, getting her out protects you as well as me."

"Fine," he sighed. "That's your price?"

"That's my price for the first three months," Dinah said. Arnold stepped closer, towering, trying to stare her down. She kept her gaze steady, holding her child and letting the branches of the maple brush her back. Show no weakness.

Meg'll move out, she told herself. She'll move, but we'll take turns with the kids like we used to. She and Gwynne will work out their differences and Ben will remember I'm his mother. One day we'll be out together and I'll hear Meg laugh again. She could almost see it: the five of them eating protein marshmallows in the sunshine, on a real lawn. She'd say something about the Tank and Meg would let it slide without eviscerating her.

And if doing this gets me killed, Meg can take the boys . . .

"This price is too high," Arnold said at last. "Wear the contacts for a week; then we'll arrange it. It makes no sense for us to deliver before you've proven you're willing to betray the Tank. My position is vulnerable too. You could just turn me in."

"When she moves out, not before," Dinah said firmly. "As for betrayal . . ." She opened her mouth, fishing behind her teeth for the dataglob. "Here's a new candidate for the Watch List. Anyone who be Friends him will die."

He turned away and Dinah tried to believe he wasn't communicating with others, that he wasn't about to be signal-tapped and get them both busted and dusted.

"Done," Arnold said finally. "Welcome to the Liberation, Friend."

We are not friends, Dinah thought. You are a killer of children and if I dared turn you in . . .

She held the words in, bending to rescue the contact lens case, setting the tepid water a-ripple.

Arnold patted Ben's head once, deliberately, without affection. "You're going to need friends, woman. The Kabu are losing."

With that he left, leaving Dinah and Ben in the ankle-deep water next to the red maple tree.

"They are losing, aren't they?" Dinah whispered to the mourning grove. She had never said it aloud before.

She changed Ben slowly, hoping to slow her heartrate before she had to face Chamon again. Finally she climbed out of the grotto, step by step, making her way back to the auditorium and hoping her absence hadn't been too obvious. Before she went inside she rubbed her eyes hard with her fists, hoping they'd think she had run off to have a cry. She needed one. God alone knew when she'd get it.

She found Chamon and Meg side by side, with the kids gathered around them. Meg was smiling as the offworlder's tentacles roamed her arms and those of the children; she seemed—and probably smelled— perfectly at ease.

Good company manners, Dinah thought, and that was a fifth thing, wasn't it? Whatever she might say at home, Meg never behaved badly in public.

"Meg is gracious," Dinah murmured, managing a smile as she fished out a tissue for poor angry Gwynne, as she stepped into the circle of her family.

Audrey Carroll's work has appeared in Fiction International, Hermeneutic Chaos, The Cynic Online Magazine, *and the* Red Fez Review *among other publications. She is currently an MFA candidate with the Arkansas Writers Program and holds a BA in Creative Writing from Susquehanna University.*

"The People We Kill" is original to this anthology.

"the people we kill"
AUDREY CARROLL

"One of the great American tragedies is to have participated in a just war. It's been possible for politicians and movie-makers to encourage us we're always good guys. The Second World War absolutely had to be fought. I wouldn't have missed it for the world. But we never talk about the people we kill. This is never spoken of."

—Kurt Vonnegut

Mike and Paulie died on a Tuesday and woke up on Thursday. Or: United States Privates Michael Bailey and Paul Delfino died during active duty on a Tuesday and woke up on a Thursday. The gunshots they heard in the distance were remnants from their dying moments, which they only realized when they opened their eyes, stood up, and found that they were the only ones around for miles.

"Fuck, Paulie, did I oversleep?"

Mike stood up and looked around them. All there was was desert—dry sand, all they'd ever see anymore. Mike and Paulie had grown up in the suburbs of central Pennsylvania and signed up for the army after high school, to make something of themselves, see something of the world, be all that they could be. Mostly they just wanted to get out of their shit coal town. Mike walked over to Paulie, who sat on the ground hunched over, examining his chest.

"Paulie, would you stop playing with yourself so we can find some-one who's still alive? Or maybe some food? Oy, Paulie!" Mike kicked his friend's boot to get his attention, but Paulie didn't even flinch, proba-bly because he was too busy sticking his finger into the bullet wound on the left side of his chest, not sure why he couldn't feel anything more than the poke of his finger.

Mike knelt down and slapped Paulie upside his helmet, which clunked against his head. "Hello? Paul—" Mike tilted his head at the hole in Paulie's chest. "Hell, is that still bleeding?" Mike pulled Paulie's arms away from his torso and ripped his shirt a little to look at Paulie's wound. It was black with blood around the edges and on the inside, still shining. Mike went to wipe the blood from around the shot, but it was already cemented to his skin and clothes.

"It's healed up, Mike. I don't know how, but it is."

"You've gotta be in shock, man. Here, tell me if this hurts." Mike pulled at the skin outside of the wound. Paulie could feel the skin pull-ing, but not the pain he'd felt the first time he was shot the month before, like knives stabbing his insides. Mike had been aiming for a guy fighting for Paulie's rifle, but hit Paulie in the back of the shoulder instead, and he couldn't move his arm properly for a week.

"Nothing," Paulie said.

"Can you feel that half of your body?"

"I can feel just fine. It just doesn't hurt. Here, help me up." Paulie pulled on Mike's shoulder, then pushed himself up. He walked to his rifle a couple of feet away and slung it around his left shoulder. "See. Just fine."

"Huh," Mike said, standing up and walking over to Paulie. "How the hell does that happen?"

Paulie shrugged, staring over to a point in the distance, where he saw something above ground level. They didn't know it at the time, but it was the town that their army had bombarded with machine guns and small bombs while they were still alive and continued to assault after they were dead. Paulie nodded toward it. "Should we get over there? See if there's anyone left?"

"I guess so. Beats dying from the heat, right?"

And so the privates started toward the town they'd been ordered to destroy, because it held weapons used against them and possibly a couple of terrorists. Or, at least, this is what they were told. What

Mike and Paulie would never know is that the town only had enough guns to protect themselves from all the fighting, from the town crumbling around them, and that a terrorist had never set foot within a hundred yards of the place. Hardly anyone that destroyed the town would know this.

"Do you have ammo in that thing?" Mike asked. "Cause I've got my pistol, but that'll only do us so much good."

"Yeah, I've got half still left in here," Paulie replied, squinting toward the town. "Ya know, those people are gonna be pissed at us if there's anyone left."

"Yeah, I know. Just watch your ass, huh?"

Paulie turned to Mike and did his best not to laugh. "Sure. Just make sure you don't get another piece of shrapnel in your head, huh?" Mike, whose helmet was long gone, taken by a boy from the town trying to protect himself, felt up the side of his face, to the top of his head. In the middle of the hair on the right side of his head a piece of sharp metal was sticking out. He tried to jiggle it. It wouldn't budge other than to rub against his skull and what Mike estimated to be his brain, but it didn't hurt, either.

The two men continued in silence. It had been a long time since they just walked together in silence. They used to do it all the time as kids, walk up to the river to see if they could catch fish or frogs or turtles, or see what they could hit with sticks and stones. The last time they walked to the river, Mike had just turned thirteen and Paulie was still twelve. Towards the end of their walks to the river, Mike had started taking big sticks with him and using them like hiking sticks, like he was guiding Paulie along.

Paulie reached out into the river, his hands cupped under the water as he watched the fat guppies swim by about a foot from him, attracted to the surface by the leaves dropping down. Mike stood by a tree, leaning his weight on the walking stick as he stood up straight with his chest puffed out. He squinted over at the mountains. His eyes hurt from the sun, but he couldn't let Paulie see him turn away. Then he spoke:

"Hey, Paulie, don't worry about the kittens, okay?"

"Yeah," Paulie replied, not bothering to look up at Mike. A guppy swam over his hands, but he didn't move. He was waiting for a turtle, a baby turtle, if he could manage it. His mom would never let him have something cute and cuddly like a cat or dog, but he could bring back all the fish and reptiles in the world and she couldn't care less, so long as they were in his room. Mike and Paulie had recently found a litter of kittens on their walks, behind an old oak by the Jenkins' place under a shrub. They meowed harder each time the boys had come around, and they hadn't seen the mama cat for at least a week. Paulie had wanted to take them in—there were only four of them—but Mike had convinced him not to. Paulie's mom's famous claim was that her son had allergies, but he was never allergic to anything in his life, except maybe pollen. Paulie's glasses slid down his nose, but he ignored it. A small turtle, whose shell still looked soft, was heading his way.

"Look, man, you know your mom wouldn'ta let you keep 'em. And Christ knows that we have enough Goddamned cats already at my place. Enough Goddamn kids, too." Mike's father had remarried five years before this, and he and Mike's stepmom already had two kids in addition to Mike's seven and ten year old baby sisters. When Mike's dad had told him he was going to remarry, he and Paulie walked to the river, as fast as they ever did. Mike had smashed the root beer bottle his dad had given him when they had their "talk" against a tree, and pitched a dozen stones into the river that day, none of which skipped. Paulie had never known Mike to spend more than fifteen minutes at a time in his house after the first new kid, except when he was sleeping, and even then he spent a lot of nights at Paulie's house.

"We still coulda given them to the girls at school or something," Paulie mumbled.

Mike pitched the stick into the river. He listened to the splash it made, then watched it sink a little until it was almost submerged in the water. "Yeah. Well, for one thing, we dunno if the cat is gonna come back for 'em or not. Just cause we don't see her doesn't mean she's not around. And second of all . . ." Mike jumped down to the bank. His legs stiffened as he went down, but he ignored the aching that surged through them as he landed in the hardened land. Mike wiped his hands on his pants, leaving streaks of dirt on the denim. "And second of all, you gotta stop with this whole soft spot shit, okay? It's all cute and whatever for girls to be like that, but when you eventually end up with a girl she's gonna expect you to kill a spider, not sing it a lullaby and help it get outside."

Paulie snapped his hands together so that his thumb was touching his thumb, and they almost looked like distorted praying hands under the water. He could feel the baby turtle moving around in there, like he was kicking to get out. Mike punched him in the shoulder. "Hey! Paulie! Are you listening to a fucking word I'm saying?" Paulie clasped his hands tighter, which made the turtle fight harder, but he managed to hold on to it.

"Yeah, yeah. Soft spot bad. Got it." Paulie stood up, his hands shaking a little but still clasped tight. He tilted his head back quickly to get his glasses to slide back up his nose, but then they sat crooked. "Can we get going so I can put this thing in a fishbowl?"

Mike shoved his hands into the pockets of his shorts. "So what's this one's name?" he asked, staring at his shoes as they walked away from the river.

Paulie shrugged. "Haven't named it yet."

As they closed in on the Jenkins' place, Mike peeked over at the oak. Three of the four kittens were still there. Two of them, a gray and white one and a black one, nudged the other with their noses, batting it with their paws, meowing loudly. The kitten refused to move, even when they flopped it onto its side. Fuck, Mike thought. He gritted his teeth and shut his eyes, shaking his head. Then he looked over at Paulie, who was walking with his arms straight out so that his cupped hands were about a yard away from his chest. He was basically tip-toeing with his turtle. Mike decided not to say anything as they continued toward Paulie's house.

When they arrived at the town, the only things still above ground level were the buildings, and even those weren't much. They were the shambles of buildings, a piece of wall with a window opening or door still intact here, a roof resting against the side of a house there. Most of it was just the rubble from houses and stores scattered on the ground. Mike was the first one to see a dead body. It was a man, maybe about their age, who was laying facedown in the dirt.

"Paulie, over here," Mike said, jutting his head toward the dead man. The men walked over to him. Mike rolled him over, searching his pockets for weapons. Paulie, who would usually be bothered by this, didn't blink. He just checked around them for ammo, instead of looking at the man, thinking about if his wife and kids were okay, if his parents were still alive, if he had planned to play with his dog the next day, which would be normal for him. After Tuesday, nothing would ever be normal for him again.

171

"Nothing," Mike said, pushing the guy away. It was as he was pushing the man away that he finally caught a whiff of his flesh, which only rotted quicker in the direct sunlight for the past two days. "Aww, fuck," Mike said, stuffing his nose into the crook of his elbow. His clothes smelled like sweat and dirt and vomit, but it was at least better than the rotting man's flesh. When Paulie and Mike were brought back, they didn't have rotting flesh. Their bodily wounds were healed and any sign that they had already been deteriorating had vanished by the time they woke up, not that they understood how they woke up or the logistics of their revival.

Mike stood up and continued down the road. Paulie stayed behind. His hand cupped over his eyes, he looked up at the sky. There wasn't a single cloud, only the sun making his eyelids heavy. He wanted to sleep, to lie down and wake up and be with his troop again, able to eat and hang out and know what he was doing that day. It would be a long time before Paulie would give up hope on finding people who were still alive. He scratched at the left side of his chest, a little of the crusted blood chipping under his fingernails.

Paulie blinked the brightness out of his eyes and headed over to Mike, who was squatting over by a house that stood more intact than a lot of the others. The whole front was still there, and if you stood in front of it and ignored the lack of roof, you could almost pretend it was a whole house. Mike brushed aside handfuls of rubble, searching for weapons. He found the pieces of what looked like an M-249.

"Paulie, are you gonna help me out here, or are you just gonna watch?" Paulie stared at Mike's head, at the metal shard shining out of it. It was almost enough to blind him. "Paulie!" Mike turned around. "How about you check somewhere else and see if you can find something useful, huh?"

Paulie nodded. He continued up the road, his helmet clunking against his head. It reminded him of the sound of his heartbeat in his ears after he was shot, how the shooting eventually faded but that heartbeat in his ears kept pounding. As Paulie entered the front room of what used to be a building, he wondered if Mike remembered this much of his death, if he remembered what Paulie had done in the middle of all that. Paulie found a pistol on the floor. It had been badly damaged, all dinged up and covered in dirt, but when Paulie checked it still had some ammo left. The house smelled like burning, as though something like plastic or rubber had caught fire. It reminded Paulie of the smell of Mike's car.

Mike's father didn't want to fix up the '70 Barracuda anymore, and he needed to buy a minivan for all the kids, so as soon as Mike was able to drive he inherited it. The Barracuda was the car that Mike and Paulie drove around in as kids, up until they left for the war. On one of these nights, with Mike behind the wheel, Green Day blasting on the radio, and Paulie staring out the window, Mike proposed what he and Paulie should do with the rest of their lives.

"Come on," Mike said, squeezing the wheel tight. His knee itched, but he didn't budge to scratch it. Paulie watched the side of the road, squinting, his glasses catching some of the glare from the headlights. The corn stalks out there were browned and dried out, each new set zooming by, replaced by another set and another, and nothing changed between them. Occasionally Paulie caught sight of roadkill—possums usually, but sometimes cats or raccoons or even deer, too. He didn't tell Mike this anymore—he thought he might rip on him for it like he did when they were kids—but he felt bad for all those innocent things splattered in the shoulder. The bugs plunked like rain drops on the windshield. "You don't hafta actually kill anyone. Even if you just wanna be one of those medical people. Yeah, there you go. You can save people instead of killing them, huh?"

Mike turned to look at Paulie, who didn't look like he was paying him much attention. He got distracted really easy ever since they were kids, so Mike just waited for him to get out of his head and talk back. The road sped by, and Mike's eyes sometimes played tricks on him in the dark so that it looked like there were waves or bumps in the road after a while, ones that weren't really there. The youngest of his dad's kids had a ballet recital that night, but he said it was okay if Mike didn't go. Mike tended not to go to those sorts of things. That night he'd gone to the movies with a girl from his American History class, who wasn't the first or last girl to see his back seat that week, then he'd picked up Paulie.

"I'm failing science, Mike," Paulie finally replied once the dead corn had made him dizzy. "I think I'd need science to be a doctor. That seems like it'd be a requirement or something."

"Well, you could just man up and kill some guys. It's not all that different from Grand Theft Auto, except that, you know, there'll be actual blood splatter." He turned the wheel as the road curved suddenly, but the Barracuda made the transition seem smooth.

"Come on, Mike. I nearly puke if I watch 'em shoot the cat in Boondock Saints. You want me to shoot people? I don't even play Grand Theft Auto."

"You'll get used to it, Paulie. We just gotta bulk you up some. Lots of carbs and lifting weights with the football players'll do you some good." Paulie stared out the window again, watching stalk of dead corn after stalk of dead corn zoom by, his eyes not even having time to process one before another had replaced it. Mike drummed his fingers on the steering wheel, his palms still curled tight around it. "What else are we gonna do? Get jobs down at the factory like everyone else? It's not like we're gonna get into college. And the factory's only got so many jobs." In fact, by the time they graduated high school, the factory cut half its workers, including Mike's dad. Paulie stared out the window, trying to ignore what Mike was saying. The future was something he didn't much like thinking of. "You'll get used to it. I mean, they have to, right?"

Mike was right. Paulie would get used to the killing.

Mike and Paulie walked again, and they'd come a long way down the road. An hour or so had passed, the smell of blood like iron in the air. Mike scratched at his head again. His skull itched like sweaty skin under a bandage. The hole in Paulie's chest had grown so hard he forgot it was there. A small child, a girl, lay in the middle of the road. She held something close to her chest. Mike groaned at the sight of her, closing his eyes and turning away. His face puckered up. Paulie knelt down and pried the girls arms open. Her hands had been shot clean through, one bullet wound in each hand. The bullet had pierced through the doll, clean into her stomach. Mike opened his eyes again, staring at Paulie as he yanked the doll from the girl's chest. It had been cemented there with blood.

"Christ, she can't be more than six or seven," Mike muttered.

"Yeah." Paulie ripped the doll at the seams in her back, tearing her in half. The blood kept her pretty well glued together, but eventually she tore apart. Mike's stomach turned a little, but Paulie didn't even think about what he was doing, he just did it. It would be difficult for anything to affect him now.

Mike had been the first to die. Paulie saw the piece of shrapnel ricochet, shrapnel that seemed to come out of nowhere. He saw it hit

Mike's head, and he saw the blood. Mike fell to his knees, then onto his side. He gasped a little, his eyelids fluttering. Paulie stared at him, but only for a moment. The gunshots around him snapped him out of it, and he aimed his gun at the nearest man not in a US army uniform, shooting him in the head. The man's eyes shone in the sunlight, then were dark as he hit the ground. Paulie continued on, shooting one man after the other after the other, never looking back to where Mike had fallen.

Mike died blinking at the dirt, and Paulie killed almost two dozen men. When a man shot Paulie in the chest, he didn't think of Mike or his mom or anyone else. He thought of how he wished he could use his arm to shoot the son of a bitch who shot him. Mike would never know how it had happened, how Paulie had changed, and Paulie couldn't even be quite sure of when.

Linda Nagata is a Nebula and Locus-award-winning author. Her most recent work is The Red Trilogy, *a series of near-future military thrillers published by Saga Press/Simon & Schuster in 2015. The first book in the trilogy,* The Red: First Light, *was named as a* Publishers Weekly Best Book of 2015. *Her short fiction has appeared in* Analog, Lightspeed, F&SF, Asimov's, *and at Sci-Fi. com, among other places.*

"Light and Shadow" was originally published in the anthology War Stories. *It is a story about shell shock and a particular fictional technological fix for the malady.*

"light and shadow"
LINDA NAGATA

1 ieutenant Dani Reid was serving her turn on watch inside Fort
Zana's Tactical Operations Center. She scanned the TOC's mon-
itors and their rotating displays of real-time surveillance data.
All was quiet. Even the goats that usually grazed outside the walls had
retreated, taking refuge from the noon sun in a grove of spindly thorn
trees.

The temperature outside was a steamy 39°C, but within the fort's
prefabricated, insulated walls, the air was cool enough that Reid kept
the jacket of her brown-camo combat uniform buttoned up per regulation. The skullcap she wore was part of the uniform. Made like an
athletic skullcap, it covered her forehead and clung skin-tight against
her hairless scalp. Fine wires woven through its silky brown fabric were
in constant dialog with the workings of her mind.

On watch, the skullcap kept her alert, just slightly on edge, immune
to the mesmerizing hum of electronics and the soothing whisper of air
circulating through the vents—white noise that retreated into sublimi-
nal volumes when confronted by a louder sound: a rustle of movement
in the hallway.

Private First Class Landon Phan leaned in the doorway of the TOC.

Phan was just twenty-one, slender and wiry. Beneath the brim
of his skullcap, his eyebrows angled in an annoyed scowl. "LT? You
should go check on Sakai."

"Why? What's up?"

"Ma'am, you need to see it yourself."

Phan had been part of Reid's linked combat squad for nine months. He'd done well in the LCS; he'd earned Reid's trust. She didn't feel the same about Sakai.

"Okay. You take the watch."

Light spilling from the TOC was the only illumination in the hallway. The bunkroom was even darker. Reid couldn't see anything inside, but she could hear the fast, shallow, ragged breathing of a soldier in trouble, skirting the edge of panic. She slapped on the hall light.

Specialist Caroline Sakai was revealed, coiled in a bottom bunk, her trembling fists clenched against her chin, her eyes squeezed shut. She wore a T-shirt, shorts, and socks, but she wasn't wearing a skullcap. The pale skin of her hairless scalp gleamed in the refracted light.

"What the hell?" Reid whispered, crossing the room to crouch beside the bunk. "Sakai? What happened?"

Sakai's eyes popped open. She jerked back against the wall, glaring as if she'd never seen Reid before.

"What the hell?" Reid repeated.

Sakai's gaze cut sideways. She bit her lip. Then, in an uncharacteristically husky voice, she confessed, "I think . . . I was having a nightmare."

"No shit! What did you expect?"

She seemed honestly confused. "Ma'am?"

"Where the hell is your skullcap?"

Sakai caught on; her expression hardened. "In my locker, ma'am."

The microwire net in Reid's skullcap detected her consternation and responded to it by signaling the tiny beads strewn throughout her brain tissue to stimulate a counteracting cerebral cocktail that helped her think calmly, logically, as this conversation veered into dangerous territory.

The skullcap was standard equipment in a linked combat squad. It guarded and guided a soldier's emotional state, keeping moods balanced and minds honed. It was so essential to the job that, on deployment, LCS soldiers were allowed to wear it at all times, waking or sleeping. And they did wear it. All of them did. Always.

But they were not required to wear it, not during off-duty hours.

The hallway light picked out a few pale freckles on Sakai's cheeks and the multiple, empty piercings in her earlobes. It tangled in her black, unkempt eyebrows and glinted in her glassy brown eyes. "You want the nightmares?" Reid asked, revolted by Sakai's choice.

"Of course not, ma'am."

Use of the skullcap was tangled up in issues of mental health and self-determination, so regulations existed to protect a soldier's right of choice. Reid could not order Sakai to wear it when she was off-duty; she could not even ask Sakai why she chose to go without it. So she approached the issue sideways. "Something you need to talk about, soldier?"

"No, ma'am," Sakai said in a flat voice. "I'm fine."

Reid nodded, because there was nothing else she could do. "Get some sleep, then. Nightmares aren't going to excuse you from patrol."

She returned to the TOC, where Phan was waiting. "When did this start?"

"Yesterday," he answered cautiously.

Even Phan knew this wasn't a subject they could discuss.

"Get some sleep," she told him. "Use earplugs if you have to."

When he'd gone, Reid considered reporting the issue to Guidance ... but she knew what Guidance would say. So long as Sakai performed her duties in an acceptable manner, she was within her rights to forego the skullcap during off-duty hours, no matter how much it disturbed the rest of the squad.

What the hell was Sakai trying to prove?

Reid ran her palms across the silky fabric of her skullcap. Then, as if on a dare, she slipped her fingertips under its brim and took it off.

A cold draft kissed her bare scalp and made her shiver.

Her pulse picked up as fear unfolded around her heart.

You're psyching yourself out.

Probably.

She studied the skullcap, turning it over, feeling the hair-thin microwires embedded in the smooth brown cloth.

No big deal, really, to go without it. It was only out of habit that she wore it all the time.

The hum of electronics within the TOC grew a little louder, a little closer, and then, with no further warning, Reid found herself caught up in a quiet fury. Sakai had always been the squad's problem child. Not in the performance of her duty—if that had been an issue, Reid would have been all over her. It was Sakai's personality. She didn't mesh. Distant, uncommunicative, her emotions locked away. A loner. Seven months at Fort Zana had not changed her status as an outsider.

Reid's emotions were closer to the surface: she didn't like Sakai; didn't like her effect on the squad. There needed to be trust between her soldiers, but none of them really trusted Sakai and no one wanted to partner with her. No one believed she would truly have their back if things went hard south. Reid saw it in the field when her soldiers hesitated, thought twice, allowed a few seconds to pass in doubt. Someday those few seconds would be the last measure of a life.

Reid clenched the skullcap.

Fuck Sakai anyway.

Ducking her head, she slipped the cap back on, pressing it close to her scalp. Within seconds, her racing heart slowed. Her anger grew cold and thoughtful.

Sakai thought she could get by without her skullcap. Maybe she wanted to prove she had more mettle than the rest of them, but it wouldn't last. It couldn't. "You'll give it up," Reid whispered. "By this time tomorrow, you'll be back in the fold."

Reid finished her watch and went back to sleep, waking at 1900. She laced on her boots, then tromped next door to the TOC, where Private First Class David Wicks was on duty.

"Anything?" she asked.

"No, ma'am. No alerts at all from Command." He flashed a shy smile. "But my niece had her first-birthday party today." He pulled up a window with his email, and Reid got to watch a short video of a smiling one-year-old in a pretty blue dress.

"Your sister doing okay now?"

"Yeah, she's good."

Wicks sent money to his sister. It was a big part of why he'd signed up.

In the kitchen, Reid microwaved a meal, then joined Sergeant Juarez at the table. "Command thinks we've got a quiet night."

Juarez was no taller than Reid, but he carried fifty extra pounds of muscle. He'd been army for seven years, and Reid was sure he'd be in for twenty if he could pull it off. "You ever notice," he drawled, "how the patrol gets interesting every time Command says there's nothing going on?"

"Just means we're good at finding trouble."

Phan reeled in, with Private First Class Mila Faraci a step behind him. "How's it look tonight, LT?" Faraci asked.

"Quiet so far."

"That's what I like to hear."

Juarez finished eating. He got up just as Sakai came in the door wearing a fresh uniform, her cheeks still flushed from a hot shower and her head freshly denuded of hair, leaving her scalp smooth and pale under the ceiling lights with no skullcap to hide it. Phan and Faraci were waiting together by the two humming microwaves. Phan glared. Faraci looked shocked. "I thought you were shitting me," she murmured.

Sakai ignored everyone. She opened the freezer and pulled out a meal packet while Reid traded a look with Juarez.

"What the hell is with you, Sakai?" Faraci demanded.

"Faraci," Juarez growled, "you got a problem?"

Faraci was strong, tall, tough, and full of swagger, but she took care never to cross Juarez. "No, Sergeant."

Reid got up, dumped her meal packet, and left. Juarez followed her to her quarters, where there was barely enough room for the two of them to stand without breathing each other's air.

"What the hell?" he demanded.

"You know I can't ask. She hasn't said anything to you?"

"She doesn't talk to me or anybody. It's been worse since she got back from leave."

Skullcaps got turned in before a soldier went on leave. It was a harsh transition, learning to live without it. But taking it up again after your twenty-one days—that was easy. No one ever had a problem with that.

"She's just annoyed at being back," Reid decided. "If there was a real issue, Guidance would know. They would address it. Meantime, make sure our other noble warriors don't get in her face. I don't want to bust the kids when Sakai is the loose cannon."

"You got it, LT."

"This won't last," Reid assured him. "You'll see. She'll give this up tomorrow."

Reid was wrong.

Sakai wore the skullcap during the nightly patrols as she was required to do, but for three days running she took the cap off as soon as she hit the showers, and it didn't go on again until they rigged up for the next patrol. This generated its own problem: Sakai couldn't sleep well without her skullcap. It wouldn't be long before she was unfit for patrol.

Reid rigged up early for the night's adventures. Her armored vest went on first. Then she strapped into her "dead sister." The titanium exo-skeleton was made of bone-like struts that paralleled her arms and legs and were linked together by a back frame that supported the weight of her pack. Testing the rig, she crouched and then bobbed up, letting the dead sister's powered leg struts do the work of lifting her body weight. The exoskeleton made it easy to walk for hours, to run, to jump, to kick and hit, and to support the weight of her tactical rifle, an MCL1a with muzzle-mounted cams and AI integration.

The rest of the squad was still prepping when she slung her weapon, tucked her helmet under her arm, and strode out into the small yard enclosed by the fort's fifteen-foot-high walls.

The night air was heavy with heat and humidity and the scent of mud and blossoms, but the clouds that had brought a late-afternoon shower had dispersed, leaving the sky clear and awash in the light of a rising moon. Reid allowed herself a handful of seconds to take in the night as it was meant to be seen. Then she pulled her helmet on. Seen through her visor, the yard brightened with the green, alien glow of night vision while icons mustered across the bottom of the display, one for every soldier wearing a skullcap: Juarez, Faraci, Phan, and Wicks.

A familiar voice spoke through Reid's helmet audio: "You're early tonight."

She smiled, though he couldn't see it. "So are you. Slow night?"

"Not too bad."

He was her primary handler from Guidance, codenamed Tyrant, the only name she knew him by. His job was to assist in field operations, overseeing data analysis and relaying communications with Command from his office, five thousand miles away in Charleston. Tyrant had access to the feeds from her helmet cams as well as the display on her visor, and he kept a close eye on all of it. "Where's Sakai's icon?" he asked. "You didn't give her the night off?"

The door opened and, to Reid's surprise, Sakai stepped through, already rigged in armor and bones, her pack on, her weapon on her shoulder, and her helmet in her gloved hand. But no skullcap.

And without her skullcap, she didn't appear as an icon on Reid's display.

"She's challenging you," Tyrant murmured, amusement in his voice.

Sakai shot Reid a sideways glance, but if she was looking for a reaction, she was disappointed. Reid's face was hidden behind the anonymous black shield of her visor.

Sakai turned away, setting her helmet down on a dusty table. Then, like a good girl, she fished her skullcap out of a pocket and put it on.

Her icon popped up on Reid's display. Reid gazed at it and a menu slid open. She shifted her gaze, selecting "physiology" from the list of options. Her system AI whispered a brief report: *status marginal; brain chemistry indicates insufficient sleep.* But as Sakai's skullcap went to work, stimulating the chemical factory of her brain, her status ramped up. By the time the squad assembled, Sakai's condition became nominal, and the AI approved her for the night's mission.

That night, they were to patrol far to the north. They spread out in their customary formation: two hundred meters between each soldier, with Reid on the east, Sakai on the west, and the others in between. The physical separation let them cover more territory while they remained electronically linked to each other, to Tyrant, and to the angel that accompanied them. The surveillance drone was the squad's remote eyes, hunting ahead for signs of enemy insurgents.

Reid moved easily through the flat terrain, the power of her stride augmented by her exoskeleton's struts and joints, while the shocked footplates that supported her booted feet generated a faint, rhythmic hiss with every step. Her gaze was never still, roving between the squad map, the video feed from the angel, the terrain around her, and the quality of the ground where her next steps would fall.

Threat assessment had gotten harder since the start of the rainy season. Stands of head-high grass covered what only a month ago had been bare red earth. Thickets had leafed out and the scattered trees had sprouted green canopies. Cattle liked to spend the hottest hours of the day beneath the trees, their sharp hooves treading the ground into sticky bogs. For most of the year this worn-out land was barely habitable, with the Sahara encroaching from the north. But for at least this one more year the rains had come, bringing life back—and providing extensive cover for an enemy made up of violent but half-trained insurgent soldiers.

Reid held her tactical rifle across her body, ready for use at all times as she searched for signs of disturbance that could not be accounted for by cattle or goats or the herdsmen who accompanied them. At the same time, video from her helmet cams was relayed to Guidance for first-pass analysis by Intelligence AIs—a process duplicated for everyone in the squad.

Tyrant remained silent as three hours passed with no anomalies found. Despite the uneventful night, no one's attention strayed. The skullcaps wouldn't allow it. If a soldier's focus began to drift, brain activity would reflect it, and be corrected. Every soldier remained alert at all times.

Near midnight Tyrant finally spoke. "Reid."

"Go ahead."

"Weather on the way. Nasty squall from the west. ETA twenty minutes."

"Roger that."

She switched to gen-com, addressing the squad. "Heavy weather on the way. That means any signs of hostile activity are about to get erased. Stick to designated paths plotted by Guidance and do not get ahead of the squad."

After a few minutes the wind picked up, bringing a black front with it. The squad map showed them approaching a road to the north, a one-lane stretch of highway paved in cracked asphalt, its position in the landscape marked by a cell tower rising above the trees. Reid spoke again over gen-com: "Wicks, you've got the tower on your transect. Use extra caution."

"No worries, LT."

Right. It was her job to worry.

The rain reached Sakai first. Then it rolled over Phan, Juarez, Faraci, and Wicks. Reid was a few steps from the asphalt road when she heard the sizzling edge of the storm sweeping toward her. The rain hit, hammering with Biblical force, generating a chiming chorus of pings against the bones of her dead sister and enclosing her in a scintillating curtain that even night vision couldn't pierce. At her feet, a veil of standing water hid the ground.

184

"Hold up," Reid said over gen-com. "No one move until—"

An explosion erupted maybe two hundred meters away, a ball of fire that illuminated the base of the cell tower where it stood just south of the road. Reid dropped to her belly. A splash of muddy water briefly obscured her faceplate before a frictionless coating sent it sliding away. Her heart hammered: the squad map showed Wicks at the foot of the tower. "Wicks, report!"

"Grenades incoming," Tyrant warned as another icon popped up on the map: a red skull marking a newly discovered enemy position on the other side of the road.

Reid echoed the warning over gen-com. "Grenades incoming!" Clutching her weapon, she curled into a fetal position to minimize her exposure. A status notification popped up on her display, a bold-red statement of Wicks's condition: nonresponsive; traumatic injury with blood loss.

Goddamn.

The grenades hit. Two behind her, one to the east. She felt the concussions in her body and in the ground beneath her shoulder, but her helmet shielded her eyes and ears, and if debris fell on her she couldn't tell it apart from the storm.

She rolled to her belly, bringing the stock of her MCL1a to her shoulder as she strained to see past the rain to the other side of the road. "Tyrant, I need a target."

"Target acquired."

All extraneous data vanished from her visor, leaving only a gold targeting circle and a small red point that showed where her weapon was aimed. It took half-a-second to align point and circle. Then her AI fired the weapon.

The MCL1a's standard projectile was a 7.62mm round, but it was the second trigger Reid felt dropping away from her finger. The stock kicked as a grenade rocketed from the underslung launcher, looking like a blazing comet in night vision as it shot across the road, disappearing into the brush on the other side. Reid couldn't see the target, but when the grenade hit, the explosion lit up the rain and threw the intervening trees into silhouette.

A second grenade chased the first, fired from Faraci's position farther west. Reid used the explosion as cover. She flexed her legs, using the power of the dead sister's joints to launch to her feet. Then she dropped back, away from the road and into the brush as the squad icons returned to her visor. "Juarez! I'm going after Wicks. Take Phan and Sakai. Set up a defensive perimeter."

"Roger that." On the squad map, lines shot from the sergeant's icon, linking him to Phan and Sakai as they switched to a different channel to coordinate.

"Faraci, you're with me. Full caution as you approach Wicks. Take the path Guidance gives you and do not stray."

"Roger, LT."

Reid flinched as a burst of automatic weapons fire rattled the nearby brush. Another gun opened up. A glance at the squad map confirmed it was Juarez, returning fire.

"Got your route," Tyrant said.

A transparent, glowing green rectangle popped into existence at Reid's feet as if suspended just above the sheen of standing water. It stretched into a luminous path, winding out of sight behind a thicket. Reid bounded after it, running all-out—Hell-bent, maybe, because she could see only three strides ahead. If a hazard popped up in front of her she'd have to go through it or over it, because she was going too fast to stop. When she spied a suspiciously neat circle of rainwater, she vaulted it. Then she ducked to avoid a branch weighed down by the pounding rain.

Hell failed to claim her, and in just a few seconds the path brought her to the concrete pad that supported the cell tower, and to Wicks, who lay just a few meters behind it.

He was belly down in almost two inches of water and he wasn't nonresponsive anymore. He struggled to lift his helmeted head, but the weight of his pack and his injuries pinned him in place. His shoulders shook with a wracking cough as Reid dropped to her knees beside him.

"Damn it, Wicks, don't drown."

Another grenade went off, this one maybe a hundred meters away. Reid flinched, but her duty was to Wicks. She pulled the pins on his pack straps and heaved the pack aside. Then she grabbed the frame of his dead sister and flipped him onto his back. He made a faint mewling noise, more fear than pain. The skullcap should be controlling his pain. As she shrugged off her pack and got out her med kit, she tried to reassure him. "Wicks, listen to me. We'll get you out of here. You'll be okay."

He groaned . . . in denial maybe, or despair.

"Tyrant, where's my battle medic?"

"I'm here," a woman said, speaking through her helmet audio. "Let's do an assessment."

Reid's helmet cams let the medic see what she saw. Wicks still had all four limbs, but most of his right calf was gone, and shrapnel had shredded the flesh of his right arm. Reid used her body to shield his wounds from the rain for the few seconds it took to apply a spray-on coagulant. Then she slipped off his helmet to check for head injuries. When she found none, she put his helmet back on.

Tyrant said, "Faraci's at twenty meters and closing fast. Don't shoot her."

"Roger that."

Juarez was still trading fire with someone to the north when Faraci burst out of the brush. She dropped her pack and then dropped to her knees beside Reid. "How's he doing, LT?"

"How you doing, Wicks?" Reid asked as she slathered wound putty across his chewed-up calf.

"*Fucked,*" he whispered between clenched teeth.

Reid couldn't argue. She guessed he'd lose the leg, and then he'd be out of a job that he desperately needed for his sister's sake as well as his own. "Faraci's going to take care of you," she said. "You got that, Faraci? Do what the battle medic tells you, and get him stabilized."

"Yes, ma'am."

"And keep your head down."

Reid closed up her med kit and jammed it back into her pack. Then she shouldered the pack, along with her weapon. "Tyrant, I need a target."

"Look toward the road."

She did, bringing a new path into view on her display. Icons showed Juarez and Phan engaged two hundred fifty meters to the west, with Sakai half a klick farther out. Maybe Juarez had gotten word of more targets on that side and instructed her to go after them. No time to ask.

Reid took off, water geysering under her footplates until the path expanded, indicating she should slow. The path ended at a tree with a fat trunk. Livestock had churned the ground into thick mud that sucked at her boots as she braced herself against the trunk and brought up her weapon. A targeting circle appeared in her visor, but just as she aligned her aim, her attention was hijacked by a bold-red status notification that popped up at the bottom of her display: Contact lost with C. Sakai; position and status unknown.

Her finger hesitated above the trigger. Contact lost? What the hell did that mean? Even if Sakai was dead, the angel should still know her position—

Focus!

Reid squeezed the trigger, firing a burst of 7.62mm rounds.

An answering fusillade hammered the tree trunk. She spun and dropped to a crouch, putting the tree at her back as bullets whined through the space she'd just occupied.

"Target down," Tyrant said.

"Then who the fuck is shooting at me?"

"Another target."

"How did Command miss all this, Tyrant?"

"Debrief later. You've got another target. Stay low."

The notification was gone from Reid's display. The squad map was back up. It showed Faraci still with Wicks; Juarez and Phan circling to the west. There was no icon for Sakai.

"Reid!" Tyrant barked as he blanked her display. "Target's moving in. You need to hit it now."

She twisted around, still on her knees, sliding in the mud. When the targeting circle came into sight, she covered it and fired. There was a scream, much closer than she'd expected. She fired again, and the scream cut off. "Where the hell is Sakai?" she demanded, as another exchange of gunfire rattled to the west.

"I don't know! Waiting to hear from Intelligence."

Gunfire ceased. There was only the sound of rain.

"Three targets remaining," Tyrant said. "But they're pulling back."

Reid stared into the green-tinted night. The rain was easing. Night vision could again make out the shapes of distant trees, but it could not reveal IEDs buried beneath the mud, or popper mines that the surviving insurgents might have dropped on their retreat. Command might be persuaded to send in bomb sniffers tomorrow, but tonight the other side of the road was a no-man's-land.

"We have to let them go," Reid said. "Tyrant, shift the angel west. I want it looking for Sakai."

The rain had stopped by the time she returned to Wicks. Faraci had sealed his wounds and gotten him out of his rig, but she'd left his helmet on, per regulation. His visor was tuned to transparent, so that Reid could see his face, his half-closed eyes. "He'll be okay," Faraci said.

Meaning that he would live.

Juarez and Phan emerged from the brush as a distant growl announced the approach of the MEDEVAC helicopter. While Juarez went through Wicks's pack, redistributing its contents, Reid stepped aside. "Tyrant, I want to see the video from Sakai's helmet cams."

It didn't show much. Rain had been coming down so hard that at first all Reid saw was falling water. Then a blur that resolved into the dripping branches of a thicket, luminous in night vision; then a splash of mud. Reid checked her display, confirming she was on a solo link before she asked Tyrant, "Did someone cut her fucking head off?"

"Negative. The skullcap would have picked up remnant brain function. Reid, her helmet was removed."

"That doesn't make sense. If she got jumped, we'd see—" She broke off in midsentence as the truth hit. "Sakai took off her own helmet. That's what you're saying."

Reid had been slow to consider it because all her training argued against it. LCS soldiers must never remove their helmets in the field. Even Wicks, grievously wounded, still wore his, because in a linked combat squad the helmet *was* the soldier. It was protective gear, yes, but it also marked position, monitored condition, allowed communication, enhanced the control of weapons and targeting, and provided a visual interface for the shared data stream that allowed an LCS to function.

If Sakai had removed her helmet it meant only one thing: she'd walked away.

She'd deserted.

The helicopter set down, kicking up a windstorm that flattened a circle of waist-high grass. Wicks shivered as the medics loaded him onboard. He was in their care now, so they took his helmet off. His expression was disconsolate. Reid squeezed his hand and lied to him. "It'll all work out."

Moonlight shone through rents and tears in the clouds as the helicopter took him away.

Reid tried to put herself into Sakai's head; tried to understand what Sakai had been thinking when she'd walked out on the squad, abandoned them, in the middle of a firefight. No love existed between Sakai and the others; no reason to think she gave a shit about any of them. The commotion had been a chance to slip away, that's all. . . .

Except there was nowhere for her to go, no escape, no refuge, no way home.

No way to survive for long.

Reid found it easy to imagine Sakai as suicidal, but why hadn't Guidance known or even suspected?

Because Sakai had only worn the skullcap on patrol.

Until tonight, Sakai had been okay on patrol.

Some people were like that. They were fine so long as they were working, fulfilling whatever regimented role life had handed them, but leave them on their own and they could disappear down rabbit holes.

What twisted passage had Sakai wandered down?

Reid caught her breath, hit by a new worry: what if Sakai hadn't run away?

The night was warm and Reid's uniform had shed the rain so she was barely damp, but she shuddered anyway as the fine hairs on the back of her neck stood up. She looked over her shoulder, scanning the surrounding terrain, searching for motion in the brush or beneath the trees.

Tyrant noticed. "You see something?"

The drone had been sent to search from Sakai's last known position. "Tyrant, bring the angel back. Make sure Sakai isn't here, hunting us."

"Roger that." A few seconds later: "You really think she's turned on you?"

"I don't know. I just want to make sure." She switched to gen-com. "Everyone, stay low. Keep alert."

They all dropped into a crouch.

"Somebody out there?" Juarez wanted to know.

"We'll let the angel answer that."

The drone searched, but it picked up no sign of Sakai anywhere nearby. So Reid sent it south, toward the fort, but Sakai wasn't there either.

"Let her go," Faraci muttered. "Who gives a shit? She didn't do anything for Wicks when he went down."

"We don't abandon our own, Faraci," Reid snapped. "Remember that, next time you get in a tight spot."

"Yes, ma'am."

"This is now a search and rescue, and speed is critical." Alone, without her helmet, it was just a question of time and distance, not chance, until Sakai was found by some insurgent group. Maybe that was her goal, to get far enough away that there could be no rescue, no first aid, no helicopter evacuation while her heart was still beating.

Only four remained in the squad—Reid, Juarez, Faraci, Phan—but they still assumed their standard two-hundred meter interval, sweeping the terrain until they converged again on Sakai's last known position. Reid got there first and found Sakai's skullcap hanging from a branch. It felt like a message meant just for her. She shoved the skullcap into a pocket. Phan recovered Sakai's helmet from a thicket, finding it upside down and half-full of rain. Juarez located her pack. But her MCL1a didn't turn up. Neither did her stock of grenades, or her dead sister.

"We have two possibilities," Reid told the squad. "She's been taken prisoner, in which case we are obligated to effect a rescue and to recover her equipment. Or she's gone rogue. If so, we must assume she is mentally unstable. Without her helmet she doesn't have night vision, but she'll be able to see well enough by moonlight to be dangerous. Use extreme caution."

The rain had washed away any tracks that might have indicated the direction Sakai had taken, but it seemed logical to Reid that she would have headed west to northwest. "Either direction would allow her to avoid the angel's eyes while it was monitoring the firefight, but west means following tonight's patrol route and I don't think that's what she had in mind."

"Northwest then," Juarez said in disgust.

Reid nodded. "She's heading for the border."

They set off, moving fast on a no-choice mission. They had to find Sakai. Personnel did not go missing anymore. And they had to get the dead sister and the MCL1a back. That equipment could not be allowed to enter the black market. It had to be recovered, even if they took heavy casualties in the process.

"Tyrant."

"Here."

"Something happened when Sakai was on leave."

"No incident in her record."

"Go beyond the record! Something else happened just a few days ago. That's when she stopped wearing her skullcap. Something was going on inside her head. Something she didn't want the skullcap to fix."

"Stand by."

A figure of speech. Reid loped north, while her AI analyzed the feeds from her helmet cams. Every few minutes it highlighted a potential hazard: a shining thread that could have been a tripwire but turned out to be a spiderweb; a metallic sheen that might have been a cheap sensor but was only a foil wrapper, blown in from God knows where; an area of disturbed ground washed by the rain where there might be a buried IED. Reid skirted it, though she suspected it was just a resting place for cattle.

Tyrant spoke again, "Intelligence took a look at her email. She split with her boyfriend a few days ago, told him she wasn't coming back and not to worry about money, that she'd take care of him."

"Oh *fuck*," Reid said as enlightenment hit. "This is about her life insurance."

"It's about more than that. The boyfriend has a six-year-old kid. Sakai got crazy on leave, had a meltdown, slammed the kid against a wall—"

Reid didn't want to hear anymore. "That's bullshit. Sakai passed her psych quals. She's not like that. *None* of us are like that."

"Intelligence believes the boyfriend's story. He's been out of work a long time. Sakai's been sending him money. He didn't report the incident because he can't afford to break up with her. So he kept telling her everything was okay."

Sakai was not the kind of person who could do something like that and ever imagine it was okay; Reid didn't have to like her to know that. The life insurance was Sakai's apology, a way to make amends and to ensure she never harmed the child again.

A few minutes later Tyrant announced, "The angel has found her." He marked the position on Reid's map. Three kilometers east-northeast. Reid switched to gen-com. "Hold up."

A new window opened in her display, a feed from the angel that showed Sakai rigged in her dead sister, with her MCL1a in hand. Sakai surely presented a danger, yet without her helmet and her skullcap she looked fragile, her bare scalp like a gray eggshell in the sideways light of the westering moon.

"You got her, LT?" Juarez asked.

Reid sent him the feed and the location.

The map updated.

"*Shit*," Juarez breathed. "She's not alone."

Scanning the ground with its infrared camera, the angel had found three figures less than a hundred-thirty meters from Sakai—a distance rapidly closing as she advanced.

Half-hidden beneath the spreading branches of a thorn tree, they appeared at first as flashes and chips of bright heat. Then they emerged draped in infrared-blocking fabric that did not hide them completely but gave them the vagueness of ghosts as they passed through tall grass, moving in a line toward Sakai. The angel identified them from profiles compiled during the firefight: they were the three insurgents who had escaped alive.

They probably couldn't see Sakai past the vegetation, but they would be able to hear her. She was using her dead sister to trot at a careless pace, rustling grass and snapping twigs, with no way to know what lay in wait for her. They would gun her down before she knew anyone was there.

And wasn't that what she'd gone looking for?

Reid wondered if she'd fight back; wanted her to; resolved to force her to, if she could. Reid would not let death take Sakai by surprise. She would make her face it, and facing it, maybe Sakai would choose life instead.

Fuck the insurance.

Speaking over gen-com, Reid said, "Faraci, you've only used one grenade. Fire another, maximum range. In Sakai's direction."

"LT?" Faraci sounded perplexed. "Sakai's way out of range."

"Shit, Faraci, I don't want you to kill her. I just want you to put her on alert. *Now*, if that's all right with you."

"Yes, ma'am."

The grenade shot above the tree tops, hurtling northeast, to burst above the brush. The *boom* rolled past while through the angel's eyes, Reid watched Sakai drop flat, her training taking over despite the guilt and despair that had sent her north.

The insurgents took cover inside a thicket, no doubt trying to guess what the distant explosion meant for them. Caution should have made them retreat, but they wanted Sakai's weapon and dead sister.

"Let's go!" Reid barked. "Now, while they're confused. Fast as we fucking can. *Go, go, go!*"

Tyrant posted a path. Reid jumped on it, running flat out. The joints of her dead sister multiplied the power of every stride. She crunched through grass, slid sideways in mud, bounded over deadfalls and, carrying her tactical rifle one-handed, she used the struts on her other arm as a hammer to batter aside branches.

"Sakai's taken cover in the brush," Tyrant said.

It was hard to look death in the face.

Tyrant spoke again. "The insurgents are moving. They're closing on Sakai's position."

"Good."

Sakai would see them, she would know what death looked like, and she would fight back. She had to.

With two kilometers behind her, Reid heard the slow *tap, tap, tap* of small arms fire. "Tyrant?"

"They're trying to flush her from cover."

Reid ducked under a tree and then battered her way along a cattle trail between two thickets. The terrain was so monotonous she felt like she was getting nowhere.

A larger-caliber weapon spoke. Reid well knew the sound of an MCL1a.

"She got one," Tyrant reported. "Damn good shot by moonlight alone."

Half a kilometer to go.

"The survivors are retreating."

Too soon.

Reid heard the worried bleat of a goat just ahead of her, the sound so unexpected she almost threw herself down and started shooting.

The goats were just as frightened. They must have been sleeping in a thicket. Startled at her approach, they fled straight toward Sakai.

"Reid, get down!" Tyrant shouted. "Get down! She's got her weapon turned on you!"

Never before had Reid heard that level of emotion in Tyrant's voice. It scared her but she kept running, because the goats were a distraction that she could use. They were cover. Sakai wouldn't hear her coming past the noise of their stampede.

The goat herd funneled together as they raced between two tall thickets. Then they spilled into a grove of seven or eight trees with only bare ground beneath them. Branches filtered the moonlight into shards and polygons that painted the mud and flashed over the hides of the fleeing animals.

Hidden in shadow, unseen by the frantic goats but clear to Reid in night vision, was Sakai. Reid saw her in profile, crouched and trembling with her back to a tree trunk, weapon held close to her chest, shoulders heaving, her hairless head tipped back, and amazement on her exhausted face as she watched the goats dart past.

With no night vision to aid her, she didn't see Reid.

Briefly, Reid considered a negotiation, verbal persuasion, but she didn't want to have a conversation while Sakai held onto her MCL1a and her stock of grenades.

So Reid tackled her. Shoulder to shoulder: their arm struts clanged as they both went down. Reid got a hand on Sakai's rifle, got it loose, heaved it away—but that was only step one in disarming her. She still had a full complement of grenades in her vest, and her dead sister was a lethal weapon in hand-to-hand combat—though Reid had no intention of letting it come to that.

Scrambling free, she came up on her knees in a patch of fractured moonlight, her MCL1a braced at her shoulder. "*Don't move!*"

Sakai wasn't there anymore. She wasn't wearing her pack, and without it she was more agile than Reid expected. She had rolled away, rolled onto her feet. She stood looking down at Reid with a shocked expression.

What did she see with her unaided eyes? Gray bones and the negative space of Reid's black visor? Maybe nothing more than that, blind in the night.

No.

This close, there would be a glimmer of light from the MCL1a's targeting mechanism.

Reid corrected her aim. "Very slowly," she said, "crouch, and release the cinches on your dead sister, starting at the ankles."

Sakai frowned. She turned her head, perusing the shadows, wondering maybe if they were alone. "Come on, LT," she said in a low voice as she looked back at Reid. "Do it now. No one's watching."

"Someone's always watching. You know that. I'm not your ticket out."

The goats had fled. The night had gone quiet. Reid had no idea where the insurgents were, but she trusted Tyrant to warn her if it looked like they would interfere.

"Do you have it with you?" Sakai asked. "My skullcap?"

"Do you want it?"

"No! *No.* I don't want it." As if trying to convince herself. "I don't want to die with that thing on my head."

"You mean that when you wear it, you don't want to die at all . . . right?"

Sakai shook her head. "You know what I think? I think we all start off as light and shadow, but the light seeps away when we wear the skullcap. It moves out of us and into the wires, so when we take it off, there's only darkness left in our heads." Titanium struts gleamed in night vision as she brought her gloved hand up to tap the center of her forehead. "Punch it, LT. Or I'm going to take you out."

Reid waited, and when Sakai sprang she squeezed the trigger. The round caught Sakai in the shoulder, pancaking in her armor. It didn't penetrate, but the impact spun her around so that she landed face down, a rag doll mounted on a metal rack.

Juarez stepped out of the shadows with Phan behind him.

"Get her unstrapped," Reid growled.

Sakai had tried to turn her into an executioner. Now, in the aftermath, fury kicked in.

Maybe I should have complied.

But Reid's skullcap responded, modulating her outrage, defusing her brittle frustration, bringing her back to a logical center. Because that's what it did, she decided. It didn't control what she thought or who she was. It didn't make her a different person. It kept her tied to who she really was. It was a shield against anger and guilt; against the emotional scar tissue that could consume a mind.

Juarez and Phan turned Sakai over; they popped her cinches while Reid checked the squad map, confirming Faraci on their flank, ready, if the two surviving insurgents made the poor choice to return.

Sakai's chest spasmed. She sucked in a whistling breath and tried to sit up, but Juarez pushed her back down again while Phan finished removing the ordnance from her vest.

"Cuff her," Reid said, handing Juarez a set of plastic restraints.

He got Sakai into a sitting position. She offered no resistance as he bound her wrists behind her back.

Sakai had always been a problem child, but she'd been a good soldier. The army should have protected her. Command should have required her to wear her skullcap. No soldier had the option of going naked into battle—and battles didn't always end when the weapons were racked.

Reid crouched in front of Sakai. In night vision her face was stark; her features dragged down as if by the gravity of despair. At first she didn't acknowledge Reid, but after a few seconds she looked up, fixing an unflinching gaze on the featureless void of Reid's black visor.

"Is that you, LT?"

Shadow, unblended with light.

"It's me." She reached into her pocket and got out Sakai's skullcap, holding it so that a triangle of moonlight glinted against its silky surface. "I want you to wear this."

"No."

"You'll feel better."

"You think I want to feel better?"

"So you lost your temper with a kid! You want to kill yourself over that?"

"I didn't just lose my temper. Sixteen days without the skullcap and I was fucking out of control. If Kevin hadn't been there, I might have killed that sweet baby. And that's not who I am . . . or it's not who I was."

"It wasn't the skullcap that made you do it."

"Shit yes, it was! When I was wearing it, it hid all the crap I couldn't live with. Made me feel okay. Didn't even know I was falling apart inside until it was too late."

Is that what the skullcap did? Hide the rot?

Did it matter? They had a job to do.

Reid jammed Sakai's skullcap back into a pocket, and then she stood up. "Tyrant, we need to evacuate Sakai."

"Chopper on the way," he said. "ETA thirteen minutes."

"Rest while you can," Reid advised the squad.

They still had two insurgents to hunt and the second half of their patrol to finish—a long night ahead of them, followed by a few hours of sleep and then another patrol where their lives would be at risk every moment until they were back inside the fort. Thinking about it, Reid felt a looming abyss of emotional exhaustion, there and then gone, washed away by the ministrations of the skullcap.

mission accomplished

On May 1, 2003 George W. Bush arrived at the USS *Abraham Lincoln* aircraft carrier via an arrested landing in the 3B Viking "Navy One." He, along with a pilot who looked like Tom Cruise only taller, strutted across the flight deck to a podium set underneath a banner that depicted the words "Mission Accomplished" in the background and an extreme close-up of an American flag in the foreground. Standing there the president looked, in the words of *Wall Street Journal* writer Lisa Schiffren, "really hot."

"In the Battle of Iraq, the United States and our allies have prevailed," Bush said.

Later on there was some debate about the banner. Especially as a guerilla war erupted in occupied Iraq, and the White House tried to deflect criticism by claiming first that the banner had been put there by the crew of the aircraft carrier and that it referred to the aircraft carrier's mission, the *Abraham Lincoln* was returning home after a ten-month deployment. When it turned out that the banner *had* in fact been produced and hung at the behast of the president's PR team, White House spokesperson Scott McClellan insisted that the banner was, in any case, really cool looking.

The PR mistake had a real consequence as it underlined a key problem for both the Bush administration and the war effort, namely that nobody knew exactly why we were in Iraq to begin with and nobody was sure how we'd get out. What would it really look like when the mission was accomplished? Just what was the mission anyhow?

It would be three years before another photo-op would replace the banner. This time the conclusion of the war, a sense of success and finality, would be conveyed via viral video. The former Iraqi dictator Saddam Hussein was executed on December 30 in 2006.

The video taken with a primitive cellphone camera depicted a grubby scaffold at the top of what appeared to be a stairwell in a parking lot, but really must have been a chamber designed for executions. The executioners wore ski masks and debated with dictator.

"Do you consider this bravery?" one of his executioners asked him after Saddam had shouted his final call for victory against the invaders. "Go to hell!"

"The hell that is Iraq?" Saddam asked back.

This conclusion was even worse than the bungled speech on the aircraft carrier, as the insurgency continued. Attacks against the Iraqi police in the American controlled regions of Iraq continued and, despite the death of Saddam, more troops were deployed. Rather than the mission being over, the US had to devise a "New Way Forward" with twenty thousand more troops and developed a strategy known as "The Surge." The success or failure of the surge is still subject to debate, but in April 2013 a new threat emerged from the hell Iraq had become. This group is known as ISIS.

The photo-op that really did signal an end to the Iraq invasion took place on December 14, 2008. It took place in Iraq in the palace of then Prime Minister Nouri al-Maliki. It was there that George Bush announced a timeline for US withdrawal from Iraq and it was there that an Iraqi journalist threw both of his shoes at the President's head.

"The war is not yet over," Bush said, "but with the conclusion of these agreements and the courage of the Iraqi people and the Iraqi troops and American troops and civilian personnel, it is decisively on its way to being won."

And that's when Muntadhar al-Zaidi threw his shoes.

"This is a farewell kiss from the Iraqi people, you dog," al-Zaidi yelled, and then he threw his first shoe. "This is for the widows and orphans and all those killed in Iraq!" Then he threw his second shoe.

Reporters in the West explained that, in the Arab world, throwing a shoe at somebody is considered a special sort of insult because shoes are considered unclean. It was necessary to explain because some viewers apparently thought throwing a shoe was a way to invite Bush out for a beer.

Bush did set December 31, 2011 as the deadline for a complete withdrawal of US armed forces in Iraq. Three years seemed like a long time in 2008 but by the time the date did roll around and Obama honored the original agreement, the White House framed the decision to leave and honor Bush's deadline as a fulfillment of Obama's campaign promise during the 2008 election. Many people had forgotten about the original agreement, and indeed, Obama's political opponents used the honoring of this agreement as an opportunity to lay Iraq's instabilities and the emergence of ISIS at the feet of Obama administration.

If there is something to learn from all this, it's that a war of occupation is much more difficult to win than a defensive war, and that it is difficult to determine what winning means. Even today, nearly a decade after the execution of Saddam Hussein, the condition of Iraq is precarious as the number of murders committed by ISIS and the number of US air strikes both escalate. The possibility of another ground war in Iraq is, apparently, back on the table.

The stories you're about to read reflect the interminable quality of the mission in Iraq.

Rob McCleary is mostly a television writer having worked on Jacob Two-Two, Pecola, *and* Moville Mysteries *among other Canadian children's programs, but in the world of literature he has one major claim to fame. McCleary is the author of "Nixon in Space," a short story published in the now-defunct, semi-pro magazine called* Crank! *back in 1993. The story has endured for more than twenty years. The author Jonathan Lethem republished the story on* Electric Literature's Recommend Reading *page in 2013 and noted that "if you wrote 'Nixon in Space' or its equivalent fifty times you'd be George Saunders or Donald Barthelme. Do it just once and you're Rob McCleary." McCleary's strange non-sequel to "Nixon in Space" is entitled* Too Fat to Go to the Moon *and is due out from Zero Books in 2016.*

Rob McCleary's "Winnebago Brave" is original to this anthology.

"winnebago brave"
ROB McCLEARY

t he Saddams appeared one dawn in Albany in the becalmed pause following the initial shock and awe of Iraq 2.0, before the transition to the never-ending hand job of an unwinnable, ever-ballooning Middle East war. Our failure to capture the real Saddam Hussein after Iraq's collapse denied us our blockbuster ending, not to mention the specter of a Snidely Whiplash Saddam roaming the country fomenting a counter insurgency. A situation further clusterfucked by the discovery of an entire conscripted cadre of Assassination Body Double Decoys, all of whom the pressures of staying in character 24/7 as one of history's most brutal dictators had symptomized itself into a seeming Chuck Palahniuk—inspired all-you-can-eat buffet of sexual dérivé. Unable to decide which was more terrifying, an anti-American uprising led by the real Saddam or one crystalizing around one of his Piss Play doubles, all ten were airlifted en masse to Fort McKlusky in upstate New York. From where they quickly escaped to Albany, with day trips into New York City, where they loitered sullenly in the hipster bars around the Astor Place subway stop, the diplomatic immunity granted them as part of their extradition agreement protecting them against all forms of legal repercussion short of rape and murder, freeing them up for exhausting bouts of marathon public masturbation, usually in Washington Square Park, NYU students being their preferred audience, gender seeming largely a matter of indifference. And it wasn't until Super Bowl XL, the B2 flyover and national anthem brought to a dead halt by the Marine Color Guard in their Dress Blues–Adult Baby mashup uniforms, complete with Cleveland Steamer Merit Badge that America realized it was defeated in Iraq. The hardened combat Marines of the flag bearing detail, sick to the teeth of IEDs and Stop-Loss, decided to take matters into their own hands on an "Improvise, Adapt, Overcome" model, and did more in their soiled bed sheet diapers in that one moment than all the NO BLOOD FOR OIL bumper stickers in America combined.

No one knew what to do with the Saddams, and the Saddams did not seem to know what to do with themselves. They drifted between their home base at the Albany YMCA and the bars of the East Village. From the outset they had simply wanted the freedoms they were told with a straight face everyone hated America for having, with sexual freedoms in bold type, and arrived expecting to find a School House Rock, sexual "Great American Melting Pot" but instead found a hysterical post-9/11 America in full Land of the Lost mode, with them in the role of Muslim Sleestacks. The Saddams were a sexual cabinet of curiosities, a collection of almost every conceivable sexual fetish combined with an old-school analog LGBTQ continuum, VH1 "Behind the Music" mixing-board slider. The only wrinkle in their one-stop-shopping approach to sexuality being the fact that, being indistinguishable from each other, many was the first-year sex experimenting NYU student who might find what they thought was last week's obliging three-way Saddam was in point of fact Poo-Poo-Play Saddam, or Pegging-While-Role-Playing-as-Donald-Rumsfeld Saddam, a situation remedied in admittedly unique ways by the bright young things of NYU by issuing all the Saddams with prudently laminated lanyards with their individual predilections printed in Arabic, all NATO languages, and a hastily adapted series of Otl Aicher 1972 Munich Olympic pictograms.

By the time the Saddams appeared that dawn in Albany, Iraq 2.0 had fully metastasized into a terrifying, IED-powered tornado of particulated human feces, and my personal life had imploded into an incomprehensible jumble, part Rosenquist F-111 collage (smash push in on the writhing, intestinal SpaghettiOs) part Yeatsian gyre of pot smoke, DSL masturbation, and failed relationships with a string of women I wholly sabotaged, terrified by the knowledge they were all smarter, more talented, and generally better human beings than myself.

For the under-thirty-five set, a brief history lesson. The 1980s: Reagan, stock market crash, A Flock of Seagulls, all painfully drawn out, like trying to shit a jack-o-lantern. The '90s (pre–dot-com bust) had more of a monkey-trying-to-fuck-a-football vibe. By 1990 I was so broke and unemployed I joined the army. Then I quit the army. Desert Storm (Iraq beta) came and went so fast we didn't even have time to convert all our kit from Vietnam green to camel-friendly chocolate chip, leaving us looking on parade as if we were uncommitted to which theatre of war we intended to fight in, or simple minded and unable to grasp even the most basic principles of camouflage. In 1992 I accepted the smirking shoulder shrug of an indifferent discharge, and was bumrushed into civilian life, where I quickly realized everything they try to lure you in with during recruiting is a lie: no one is looking for the skills you develop in the army except the army, so I became a fry cook who could, should the need arise during the afternoon rush, be counted on to know the lethal range of a fragmentation grenade, or set up an effective arc of fire.

When the Saddams showed up in Albany, around about the time America realized Iraq 2.0 was no MISSION ACCOMPLISHED replay of the original happy-ending Gulf War (refresher: previous Bush, same Saddam) I had regrouped my life marginally: a year of art school before stepping onto the moving sidewalk helpfully provided to move all those lacking in any genuine talent or creativity into their natural habitat: advertising. A hell world where grown men and women argue heatedly about maxi-pad packaging color palettes. Where I managed to porpoise from storyboard artist intern to writer to art director before emotionally belly flopping, Shamu-style, shitting the bed purely out of apathy on project after project, and realizing to my horror no one, not client, boss, or coworkers even noticed. One morning I realized I was physically incapable of entering the converted warehouse in Brooklyn I worked in. Hence my expectorated presence in Albany (which in my pot-and booze-pickled brain I had managed to spin as a "creative exile") when the Saddams showed up. Life offers us moments of soap bubble–like startling clarity. Glimpses of a hyperreality we choose largely to ignore due to the painful chiaroscuro it casts on the chaos and muddle that compose the rest of our lives. Such a 2003, monkeys-at-the-obelisk moment was the appearance, at dawn, in Albany, dressed in Walmart and Old Navy discount rack singlets and board shorts looking like a gang of Muscle Bears trick-or-treating as PBR swilling Bros. Which would have been at least, if not slottable in my pigeonhole mind on some level, potentially a fact that could be dismissible as a sign my personal universe had taken a startling left turn, if not for the fact that at their head was a man I had not seen in a decade: my old army buddy, Boston.

I want to say the army was a complete waste of time for me, but I did manage, before I could navigate the endless numbered forms of an army discharge, to acquire something no other experience, and no amount of money can buy: an army buddy. Exhibit "A": the Army Buddy. Part Looney Tunes, Sylvester the Cat chain-ganged to that bulldog escaping across the countryside. Part flaming plane wreck co-survivor. Boston was, of course, in the shimmering counter-reality of army logic, not from Boston. He was named Boston because he could (at least with the officers absent) belt out, word for word, Chicago's "Saturday in the Park" in perfect cadence to a quick march. Basic training is *Stripes*. You think you're Bill Murray. You're Harold Ramis. As remarkably accurate to the basic training experience as *Stripes* is, I can't help but think it would've been helped in its comedic depth if it had a scene in which Boston, setting the tone for both himself and for the rest of basic, revealed to us the single essential skill he possessed which would save our collective sanity: taking pictures of his cock and balls wearing sunglasses.

The food chain of America's armed forces is simple: Air Force, Navy, Army, Marines. Which made me shudder to imagine the bus full of recruits in identical yellow school buses headed for Paris Island. From the moment I stepped on the bus I knew I had made a terrible mistake. To say the army casts a wide net would be an understatement. There are recruits from every race and background. Recruits genuinely looking to serve their country and improve their lives and themselves. I'm sure they exist. Somewhere. I just never actually met any of them. Calling *my* fellow recruits the dregs of humanity, while not charitable, would not be entirely inaccurate either: teen dads, the barely literate, more than a few blowing the explosive bolts on civilian life and loop-holing out of jail time by enlisting. All with the dull, sullen eyes of guys who, not even out of their teens, had been singularly turned off life as anything other than something to be endured or outsmarted. Already confirmed in the fact that the deck of life was stacked against them. The only exception to this almost palpable slump-shouldered down-gaze was Boston who, even on the bus to basic revealed to us the alchemy of spiritual escape with his perfect, dare I say "Ghandi-like" resistance to the crushing hand of authority that awaited us at basic: taking pictures of his own cock and balls with a pair of 1980s, *Top Gun*–issue aviator shades perched on top.

It had taken Boston over a decade, but he finally popped up to cash in his Army Buddy Card in Albany, moving into my cluttered one bedroom apartment, mainlining *The Price Is Right* and *Let's Make A Deal*. Subsisting entirely on a diet of expired MREs I knew better than to ask the origin of. To my great relief, his days of dick pics seemed behind him. The Saddams would swing over from their operating base at the YMCA around four-ish to collect Boston, who they seemed to have adopted as their de facto leader, agent, and pot dealer. The Saddams would drift about my apartment, mumbling in Arabic, leafing idly through my paperbacks, eventually assembling on the couch to watch *Dr. Phil*, for whom they seemed to have a deep awe and respect, doing massive bong hits before trooping down my fire escape and off to whatever drinking hole Boston had prearranged for them. The Saddams had proven an immediate sensation in their hipster bars of Albany, replacing even the vintage skeeball game as a mandatory accompaniment to a night of sport drinking. And Boston had seized on this interest immediately as a source of income for the cash-strapped Saddams. A Band-Aid solution to the Saddams, cash flow problems that would inevitably end in at least one or two roughing up and forcibly tongue kissing one of the Bros who had paid a handsome cover to see them. While I had settled in for a lengthy Boston siege, to my surprise within two weeks he had purchased a 1983 Winnebago model "Brave," loaded it with his expired MREs and the Saddams and roared into Manhattan, screeching to a halt in Times Square, pouring out to forcibly de-pant the Singing Cowboy in front of knots of horrified Japanese tourists, smashing his guitar to splinters John Belushi-in–*Animal House* style.

Once I'd survived the shot out of a cannon experience of infantry training I began to see army life spreading out before me. The daily, all-you-can-eat shit buffet of army life. The reality that most of what the army does has nothing to do with what the army does. As you read this, on an aircraft carrier steaming belligerently about the Persian Gulf, there is a sailor whose entire day, every day, is restocking vending machines: soda, chips, chocolate bars. I believe their contribution to the "freedom ain't free" equation is greater than anything I might have contributed. I wasn't combat material. The only reason I didn't flunk rifle training was that I'm pretty sure Boston, as one of his trademark jokes only he understood, was shooting at my target instead of his (much like later he would send the Sergeant into a foaming rage by shooting out the lantern describing our left arc of fire during the night shoot qualification). I instantly loathed every officer I met, and the never-ending, wet and sleep-deprived camping trip that was field maneuvers seemed the acme of idiocy, marching around in the dark, digging a trench, filling it in, marching somewhere else, digging a trench, filling it in, marching somewhere else, you get the idea. I also began to realize that I did not fit in with the other recruits, even Boston. I could quit any time I wanted. Boston, to paraphrase Richard Gere in *An Officer and a Gentleman,* had nowhere else to go.

When Boston and the Saddams showed up in Albany I had quit the army and quit advertising and was working up my courage to quit being a painter and go begging back in to advertising. I had wanted to be Pollock. Or Rothko when the depression began to swamp me. Like everyone else in advertising, I thought of it as a temporary solution. A way of buying time until my "true genius" was realized. A brief history of advertising: billboards, brands (Ivory Soap), radio, television (an Indian crying a single tear by the side of the road), dot-com boom (industry good times), dot-com bust (Bishop's death at the end of *Aliens* looking dignified by comparison), Shane Smith crawls out of the slime of the Gowanus Canal and leads a Cleveland Steamer mass exodus to Brooklyn (we collectively place our hope for the future of our trade in the hands of a manboy who can write "I've been to North Korea twice" on his official resume with the same imbecilic enthusiasm an eight-year-old boy on a school yard might exclaim, "I saw boobies!" and singularly embodies the new industry standard of contempt as the new creativity. Even so, up until 9/11 it was still possible to do the odd project you could be reasonably proud of. Vice Media's date-rapey, disaster-porn vibe ended that. And there are few spectacles as sad as aging out of the advertising industry. Except perhaps aging out and being forced back in for scraps, part time to pay the bills. Nonetheless, Vice and the Saddams were, on the surface at least, made for each other. A match they soon enough exploited.

I said the army doesn't teach you any skills you can use outside the army, but this is not entirely true. As Boston and the Saddams demonstrated for the Vice television cameras shortly after they found out about the Saddams and left a snail trail from Brooklyn to Albany in their wake to see them. The army did teach me and Boston the solution to the previously unsolvable conundrum of how to get you and all your buddies shit-faced when you only have enough money to get half your buddies, or in this case, half the Saddams, shit-faced: 1) divide the Saddams into two groups 2) buy enough liquor to get half the Saddams screaming, vomit-through-your-nose drunk 3) have the first half drink so much booze, so fast they get so drunk they puke through a T-shirt stretched helpfully over the top of a garbage can to strain the chunkies out of the vomit 4) have the other half drink what ends up in the garbage can. Improvise, adapt, overcome indeed.

Early in basic I found myself in the position of Boston believing we were best friends. Which was odd, as it was almost impossible to even know who Boston really was. From the moment of his first dick-and-balls photo op on the bus to basic, Boston was a mystery, never revealing anything about his past or background except for what he could not conceal: a few blotchy 1980s-era, Mike Tyson-style home-made tattoos, and a hairline already plodding in grim, full retreat that made him our obvious go-to straw man for all future underage liquor sales. He never mentioned parents or siblings, and the combination of his never mentioning a girlfriend combined with his penchant for pulling out his junk for impromptu photo shoots in the presence of large groups of men called even his sexual orientation into question. And when we finally got leave at the end of basic, while everyone piled eight to a car and went hurtling down the interstate, Boston stayed on base to devote himself to what he revealed to us to be the intended use of his liberty: jacking off mercilessly in the Urban Warfare Mockup Village.

I awoke the next morning with that unique, David Byrne–Gauguin mashup of "Who am I? Where am I? How did I get here?" that only regaining consciousness after a night of blackout drinking can provide (in my girlfriend's apartment, on my back on the floor underneath her bed, staring up at the bottom of her box spring) and was immediately washed over with guilt at leaving Boston behind on base. Guilty because Boston needed a friend and I had pushed him away. Boston was an oddball among oddballs and I did not intend to get tarred as a fuck-up, by the officers, the other recruits, or, if I took him with me on leave, by my girlfriend. I was secretly relieved when there was no more room in the car going to Albany. Basic training had not been kind to Boston. When he wasn't forgetting his rifle in the mess tent or leaving his ruck unzipped, he was stealing live ammunition off the range or failing again and again and again to salute the officers. Worse, I had accepted his friendship at first, when I was frightened and friendless, and then gradually iced him out when I began to make other friends. And I felt ashamed for assuming my girlfriend was so shallow she would peg Boston as a weirdo. So it was with the power of searing guilt that I rented a comically huge Buick and sped back to base, and Boston, hoping desperately I would not catch him mid-jack.

Army Intelligence would not let the Saddams return to Iraq for fear they might inspire some strange off-brand insurrection. But this is not the age of televised, 1991 Schwarzkopf murder porn. Cell phone videos of the Saddams Hot Carling their way into the American consciousness embolden the Iraqi people. The Saddams establish the world's first Rock Off league (Rock Off: all the Sadddams struggling and sweating and grimacing to shoot their load on a cracker. The last one to shoot their load has to eat the cracker). Sale of official league jerseys and other merchandise fund a host of other income startup ventures. In a move of unprecedented boldness, with the white-hot searing light of truth on their side, the Saddams throw the dripping homoeroticism of the UFC back on itself. Exhibitionist Saddam, after a full month of edging, storms into the octagon, engorged member in hand, threatening his junk-hugging, shorty short–wearing opponent scrambling out of the ring lemur-like, fleeing the trademark projectile ejaculations the Saddams are now known for. Viewed by millions of Iraqis, the event inspires a popular uprising of Poo-Poo-Play Iraqis who temporarily seize control of the national television station before being driven out by a SEAL Team, all of whom are whisked away from the encounter to receive intensive counseling for their trauma with a team of psychiatrists and psychologists working around the clock.

Back in Iraq the situation goes from bad to worse. The Poo-Poo-Play force that took the television station are all now national heroes. The balance of power has shifted. Hard-nosed American combat troops are prepared for IEDs and sniper fire, but not crowds of Furries, Adult

Babies, and Leather Muscle Bears sweating profusely in the Iraqi heat seeking to embrace, fondle, and force their tongues into the mouths of their American "liberators." Morale collapses. Rumors of mutiny sweep the bases. Getting personnel to return from leave becomes an issue. American will to persist in Iraq flags like a spent erection.

Boston tried to act cool, but I knew he was surprised and happy to see me. I know this because he insisted we cam up, dark green on light green, as KISS's Paul Stanley Starchild and Peter Criss Catman before blowing through the checkpoint and off base. He hadn't told me where he wanted to go, and I hadn't asked, fearing he'd take it as a brush off. It wasn't until we were faced the east/west interstate choice that I got my first clue. I knew from his accent he was from somewhere in upstate New York, like me. But the phrases he used I couldn't place. Growing up in a middle-class town outside Albany in the late 1970s, every night I would watch the grim, tabby cat–like face of Irv Weinstein and the Channel Seven News Team detail the flames-lighting-up-the-night-sky economic implosion that was sweeping across western New York at the time. When we got older our mock-remembering of the nightly list of disasters, combined with the warpath drumbeat sounding names of the Erie towns became our punchline for the region: "Rape in Lacka-wanna! Arson in Cheektowaga! Stabbing in Tonawanda!" The way he acted, the things he did, the way he showed up at basic with nothing, not a single item detailed on the list of toiletries and basic personal supplies they had given on the photocopied sheet of paper, I began to suspect that, especially as we headed west on the interstate, that Boston was not in fact from Lackawanna, Cheektowaga, or Tonawanda. The reality was far, far worse than I even dared to imagine. Boston, as he revealed to my horror as we sailed down the interstate, was from Niagara Falls.

Niagara Falls: located on the enlarged-prostate-dribble American half of the thundering majesty of Canada's Horseshoe Falls. Home of the off-brand casino and the outlet mall. Buffalo, nearby, was a national joke. But a joke like a buddy who could never quite get his shit together, was always getting turned down by women at the bar, was perpetually broke and asking to borrow twenty bucks for gas for his car to get to a job interview for a job he never seemed to get. Niagara Falls was simply sad. Economically depressed. Broken in spirit with everyone who could get out already long gone. Or stuck in an endless cycle of drugs and unemployment. In short, exactly the kind of place that makes joining the army look like a step *up* in life. And Boston's hometown.

I think my main problem in life is never quite knowing when the party is over. The army, advertising, my "career as a painter." They all dragged on long past their "best before" date. I should've quit the army the day I got to basic. Some did. But like an idiot I decided I needed to prove to myself I could get through it. At first they try to talk you out of quitting. They all give you the same speech about how "if you quit this you'll quit everything in life." Which is just more army bullshit. Sometimes quitting is the best option. We should've cut and run in Iraq. It's what we did eventually anyway, after dumping billions of dollars into a rat hole in the desert.

I told Boston I planned to quit at the end of our first leave. After he had spent a week with me and my girlfriend (her judgment a simple "weird but fun"). After I swung back and picked up Boston in the Urban Warfare Mockup Village I expected to drop him off in Niagara Falls. Maybe go out for some drinks and then drive back to Albany and my girlfriend. It was only when I finally got up the nerve to ask him where he wanted to go home to on the way to Niagara Falls that I could tell he had expected to spend his leave with me. But I didn't make the offer, madly trying to justify in my head why leaving Boston on a street corner somewhere was a good idea.

Boston directed me to his house, asking to be let out at the end of the street, not even offering for me to come in and take a leak before driving on. Word of advice: when someone asks to not be let out in front of their house, there's usually a good reason. I watched Boston walk up the street and through a gate beside one of the postwar bungalows that lined the street. And it wasn't until I braked to a stop just before the interstate on-ramp that I finally got so pissed at myself and my selfishness that I turned angrily around and headed back to Boston's house.

No one answered the front door so I went around back, through the gate as I had seen Boston do. The back door was unlocked and opened on to the kitchen. The smell hit me first: stale, sour beer which hit my still-hungover senses like a slap in the face. It took me a moment to make sense of what I was seeing. It was dark. All the blinds and curtains were drawn tight even though it was after noon. All I could see was a forest of king cans: Bud, MGD, Coors, everywhere. *Everywhere:* every available horizontal surface: stove top, on top of the fridge, every inch of counter space, covering the entire floor except for a path just wide enough to walk into the rest of the house, diagonally from the door to the living room. Everything was filthy. But in a way that seemed to defy explanation: covered in a black, greasy film as if whoever lived here had been burning coal oil or styrofoam. Embedded in the film, and then apparently shellacked again with more of that used-motor-oil misting, was hair. The sink was piled high with filthy dishes. Here and there, like some sort of citadel or particularly old tree that had pushed resolutely through the forest canopy, was an empty, giant sized bottle of vodka. An enormous water stain, covered in black mold, Rorschached the ceiling, a remnant from some upstairs plumbing disaster? I smelled shit. Further inside, in the darkness of the house, through a crack in a bathroom door, I glimpsed an arm hanging over the edge of a tub. Water sloshed. A voice squeaked "Hello?" I didn't answer. I left the way I'd come in.

As I sat in the Buick, Boston appeared at the end of his street carrying groceries. His expression was one of curiosity and hurt, and I knew I could not admit to seeing what was inside his house, and I did not have the courage to ask about it. We drove to Albany. At the end of leave we took a bus back to base. I told Boston I was going to quit.

The last time I saw Boston was behind the wheel of that Winnebago Brave, the Neal Cassady to the Saddams' Sexual Merry Pranksters in the spring following the real Saddam's capture in winter 2003. The Saddams had given up on ever going home and branched out from the ejaculatory to the excretory. They had a new venture: a show (produced by Vice, of course) where they broke into people's homes to deposit an epic dump in a cleverly concealed location, filming the reaction of the home owner on a hidden camera. It was called *Mystery Shit*, and America took to it instantly. Whether at the request of Vice, or on their own initiative, the Saddams all wore matching, numbered jumpsuits and vintage football helmets, making them look like a cross between an expanded Dr. Seuss Thing One/Thing Two combo and the starting offensive line for the 1961 New York Jets.

In his brief time in Albany, I managed to piece together Boston's life after I left him in the army: a long string of disciplinary infractions that let him to a decade-long binary oscillation from private to corporal to private to corporal and so on. Quitting the army. Going

Broke. Re-enlisting in the army, beginning his two-chevron hokey-pokey all over again. Finally (in true Boston form) quitting for the last time on the day after 9/11. Because *any* chump can volunteer the day *after* 9/11 for imaginary combat fighting for imaginary freedoms. In the "fools rush in where Angels fear to tread" post-9/11 enlistment surge of middle-class precious snowflakes whose sense of entitlement was so all-consuming it gave them the right to win the War on Terror singlehandedly, Boston's quickly forgotten gesture proved one truth: that the first-year arts students who dropped out of college to become Navy Seals in a weekend did not understand the reality that the best part of having an all-volunteer army is that *you* don't have to volunteer.

Ray Daley is an indie writer who has written a lot of flash fiction. His collection Lightning Strikes Twice *was published in 2012. Daley is also a veteran. He served in the Royal Air Force from 1990 to 1996 and took part in Operation Granby, which was the name given to British military operations during the first Gulf War.*

"Seeing Double" is original to this anthology.

"seeing double"
RAY DALEY

Tikrit, January 3, 1990

"Go through, Corporal, he's ready for you now." The young Iraqi officer stood, simply looking at the man in front of him. It truly was staggering, how much like the great man this Corporal looked.

Corporal Waris Hussein (*no relation*) was lost in thought. He hadn't heard the Captain, or if he had, it'd failed to register on any level.

"Corporal Hussein! He doesn't like to be kept waiting!" The words of the Captain snapped him out of whatever daydream he'd been in, back to reality. If this could be called reality. This place. This palace.

Corporal Hussein walked through the door, fully aware who was waiting inside.

"Please, come in. Sit down. Corporal Hussein, yes?" The man was sitting behind a large mahogany desk, Waris knew nothing of antiques so was unaware this was a Louis XIV writing desk, bought as a gift for the man sitting behind it.

Waris nodded, "Yes, sir. My name is Waris." It was almost like looking into a mirror. Their faces were nearly identical, just the odd wrinkle here and there, a few grey hairs on the head to give away their minimal differences.

"You know why you were asked to come here, Waris?" the man asked.

Waris didn't really know, not exactly. He knew his impressions of the great leader had somehow been seen and overheard, they had only been shown to a few friends. No one of a higher rank, no one who would have informed on him.

Yet here he was.

"Sorry, sir, I'm afraid I don't." Waris replied, figuring honesty was the best policy here. He was aware of the penalty for speaking out against the regime and its leader, Waris valued his life and his head. He hoped he would still have both after this meeting.

"War is coming soon, Waris. People will want to kill me. Powerful people. People who will be able to get their men into places close to me. So I must be protected," the man explained.

"You have many guards, many troops. No one could ever touch you, sir," Waris interrupted.

The man behind the desk smiled at the genuine concern of the young Corporal in front of him. "What do you know of an Operation Mirror?" he asked.

Waris shrugged. "Nothing, sir, it's the first time I ever heard of it."

The man smiled. "This pleases me, Waris. It means secrets are being kept as such. What I am about to tell you must never be retold. Listen carefully."

The man then recounted the details of how the enemy leaders sought to assassinate him, in order to remove him from power as quickly as possible in order to avoid the likely upcoming war. The man said he was aware of many enemy agents, snipers, assassins, and elite troops from many nations sent to kill him. And his own plans to avoid that outcome.

The man pressed a button on his desk. "Captain, can you send them all in please."

The door opened. One after another, fifteen identical men entered the room and stood behind the man in the chair. Waris was no longer looking at one reflection.

The man behind the desk saw the confusion in the Corporal's face. "Is it not amazing, Waris? To see your own face, so many times?"

Directly behind the man in the chair, one of the recent entrants tapped him on the shoulder. "Well done, you may stand with the others now." The man behind the desk stood and joined the other men behind him.

The one behind the chair sat down in it. "You are confused? Corporal Hussein, is it? Are we related?"

Waris didn't know what to say; he no longer knew which of these men was the great leader. "It is a common surname sir, I do not believe we are related."

The man in the chair smiled as he undid his jacket, he stood to take it off and placed it on the desk between them. He pulled out a desk drawer and removed a beret, placing it on top of the jacket. "You wonder if I am the real thing, Corporal?" the man asked.

Waris nodded. "Yes, sir. You all look exactly the same."

One by one each man behind the chair took a step back and stated his name. Each man sounded the same, each man looked the same. Exactly the same as the man currently occupying the chair. When all of the others had spoken, the man in the chair repeated the name. "So Corporal, which of us is it? Which of us is telling the truth?"

Waris had no idea. One of these man was the great leader. But which, it was impossible to tell.

The man in the chair motioned to the jacket and beret. "Remove your jacket and headdress, Corporal. Please put those on. Let us now see this great impression we have heard so much about."

Waris stood and quickly removed his jacket then hat, throwing both onto the chair behind him. He pulled on the jacket and buttoned it up. He placed the beret onto his head carefully.

The man in the chair looked at him. "Now the likeness is much better, much closer. They tell me you do the voice as well? Please show us?"

Waris froze, suddenly unable to speak, unable to move. Sweat trickled from beneath the beret, down his forehead and into his eyes.

The man behind the desk frowned, his face became menacing. "You will show me now, Corporal. Or it will be the last thing you never do."

The man pulled a pistol from the desk drawer, pointing it straight at Waris who fell back into his chair, paralyzed with fear. He realized he had just completely crushed his best hat. The man behind the desk held the pistol, frozen and leveled directly at the chest of Corporal Waris Hussein.

The door opened. There was laughter. Yet another reflection entered the room.

"No, not another reflection, Corporal Hussein. I *am* Saddam," he said.

Waris snapped to attention and saluted. "Sir!"

"At ease, Corporal. These men are all my doubles. Surgically altered to look exactly like me, sound exactly like me. The Americans threaten to send in their Delta Force and their Navy Seals, the British threaten to send in their SAS. All of these men, coming here to kill me. So this is my plan."

Saddam gestured to the group of lookalikes who were behind the desk. "Each of these men were ordinary soldiers just like you, they volunteered to undergo painful cosmetic surgery to look like me. Then surgery on their vocal chords, to sound like me. Did they fool you?"

Waris nodded. "Yes, sir. I had no idea you weren't even in the room. Any one of these men could be you."

Saddam nodded. "And that is what I hope the enemy will think. Each one of these men works in a specific region of our great country, commanding troops as though he were really me. No one officer ever knows where I really am. My official location is never revealed. And this is the job you have been called to do, Corporal. Or should I call you President Hussein? Just a few procedures, to add some lines to your face. A little dye in your hair. But you must show me that you *can* imitate my voice. Now, please."

Waris spoke easily now, going through the same impression he had done only days ago in front of his friends in the barracks. He was unaware one of his friends had reported the matter to a senior Sergeant. The report had been diligently passed up along the chain of command until it had come to the attention of Saddam himself.

Saddam was more than aware how much the West wanted to kill him. Another impersonator was ideal! Especially one who looked so much like him already. It meant little investment and he would be ready that much sooner.

In front of Saddam, Waris was now finished. Saddam started to applaud. As did all the other impersonators. "Yes, Corporal. You will do fine. You will do just fine. You have just one thing to remember, no matter what happens, never let the Americans take you alive."

December 13, 2003, a farmhouse in Ad-Dawr near Tikrit

"Get out of the hole! NOW! Okay buddy, let's see those hands! Nice and high, Mister former President." American rifles were leveled at the former Dictator who found himself tied and on the ground.

"No. I am *not* Saddam! My name is Waris, he just hired me to impersonate him."

A man placed a hand on his shoulder as he crouched beside him, "Listen, my name is Samir. I am the translator here, I will be sure to tell the Americans of the truth. You will be fine. They will take you for questioning, then you will be released."

"What did he say Samir?" the soldier asked.

"He wishes death to all Americans, sir! He is a dog! He is the devil! He killed my country!"

"So he's the right guy then?"

Samir nodded. "Yes, sir, he *is* Saddam. He just admitted it to me."

At the conclusion of World War II there was VJ day when the Japanese surrendered. The most iconic image from the spontaneous celebrations that sprang up across the United States is the VJ Kiss. An American sailor kissed a woman in a white dress, dipping her back as people marched in the streets behind them. We know what that victory looked like. It looked like an American flag, a kiss, a newspaper headline that read "PEACE."

The end of the war in Vietnam was more of an auditory experience. Both the war and its end sounded like helicopters. The end of Vietnam brings to mind the helicopters carrying American soldiers away from the battlefield, and the final helicopter leaving the American Embassy in South Vietnam, as Vietnamese desperately try to clamor aboard.

But the end of these more recent wars are undefined, seemingly taking place between the news cycles. Troops come home only to go right back out again. Conscripted men are replaced by mercenaries, one invasion is followed by another, and while the names of the countries change, the battles keep raging on.

And yet, soldiers do come home. Their tours of duty end. While our collective life during wartime may seem indefinite, for the individuals involved—for the ones who don't come home in boxes—there is an ending. The war stops and civilian life begins.

We used to call the damage war caused the psyche "shell shock." Now we call it a "post-traumatic stress disorder," but no matter what it's called, soldiers find themselves reliving the war in memory, even as it continues on in various guises on television. Life after war is a life where a soldier can often find a new enemy. And that enemy is his own emotions. Life after war feels numb unless it feels dark, unless it feels angry. Life after war is a life wherein the war has moved from the outside to the inside.

These stories that follow aren't just about PTSD, but are rather explorations of that external-to-internal flip. They look at how the world is turned on its head by war and what it means to live when the war continues on, covertly and internally.

Robert Morgan Fisher has written for TV, radio, and film. The son of a Naval Flight Officer, his fiction has appeared in many publications, including: The Seattle Review, 0-Dark-Thirty, Psychopomp, The Spry Literary Journal, *and* 34th Parallel *as well as* The Missouri Review Soundbooth Podcast. *Robert holds an MFA in Creative Writing from Antioch University, where he works as an Online Instructor, Book Coach, and Writing Specialist.*

His short story "Sealed" was originally published as an audio story on the Golden Walkman Magazine *podcast.*

"sealed"
ROBERT MORGAN FISHER

was smoking on the stairs, which was something I did because I was an actor and needed to "practice." This kid, Alejandro, lived in my building and was about ten, eleven at most. He had a small mouth and flat black eyes. He started a monologue about his father, the soldier. The kid had a need. That was something I learned about monologues in college: you gotta *need* to tell it.

Hinojosa came up the stairs and gave me the look. I remembered Hinojosa telling me about some guy in our building that came back from Afghanistan. He gassed himself down on the street in his own car, duct-taped an AC hose to his tailpipe. That was Alejandro's father. But Alejandro hadn't quite accepted reality. He thought his father was a SEAL.

I thought about Alejandro's mother a lot. She wasn't unattractive. I was lonely. As usual, Alejandro peppered his monologue with: *LPOD*, *On my six*, *OBNOB*. I lighted another cigarette. Did his mother put up with this stuff? Or did she slap him and say, "Stop it! You know Papi's never coming back. You know what he did, right?"

I watched her reach for Mint Milanos, then change her mind. When she got further down the aisle, I lobbed the bag of Milanos over her head and it landed in her cart. She froze, slowly turned.

"Explain yourself," she said.

"A treat," I said. Then I told her I was friends with Alejandro. This did not relax her.

"You're the smoking guy."

"I'm an *actor*, I have to *practice*."

"Actor," she nodded her head like she knew those actor-types. This was a theater town.

"I'm in a play."

"Okay."

"I'm just an understudy."

"You got an agent?"

"Sort of." I did have an agent, a Russian woman who never returned my calls.

She said, "I acted in a play in high school."

"Let me guess: *Our Town*."

"*Anne Frank*."

"What happened?"

"She died."

"Ha-ha."

"What happened was I got married."

It was tricky. I didn't want to say what I knew about Alejandro's father.

"What's your name?" she said.

"Mike."

"Mike or Miguel?"

"Either way."

"Esme." I accepted her hand. It was cool and clean, like a chilled tomato. She put groceries on the belt. I stuck a plastic divider in there, a gentlemanly gesture. She asked for a pack of cigs, and I could picture us smoking together, having a beer.

I said, "I started out just for practice, but now I gotta smoke every day."

"That's how they get you."

"That's right."

She said, "Alejandro says I should quit."

"I used to beg my mother to quit—but now here I am."

"Yes, here we are." She said, and walked out. I thought I'd blown it. She was waiting outside. I only had one bag, so I took hers. We didn't say anything for half a block.

"What did you play in *Anne Frank*?"

"Peter van Daan," she said. "Catholic girls' school."

Esme looked like she could have played the lead. All-girls school—that must have been a trip. Maybe she *chose* to play Peter? That's what a real actor would have done. Where else was a girl going to get to play a guy besides that particular situation or *Peter Pan*? Scary play, *Anne Frank*.

Alejandro continued to unburden himself. I prompted him with names: *Kandahar, Basra, Fallujah, Operation Anaconda*.

Talking like his father was still alive.

Hinojosa said Alejandro's mama was too fine.

I got Esme to invite me over for dinner. I didn't know what to expect. It just seemed necessary.

I arrived a half-hour late. She opened the door and I handed her a twelve-pack of Modelo. She wore a little lipstick, makeup, hoop earrings. Nice.

I stepped inside, Alejandro sat on the couch, TV on. He was leaning forward, not really paying attention, maybe a little uptight. I sat down next to him. Esme went back to the stove. He stared straight ahead.

"Smells good," I said. He nodded.

Their place was way nicer than my crib. Esme had fixed up the walls with framed posters and shit. The cooking odors made my stomach groan. I got up and grabbed a beer. She was already sipping one.

"What's cookin'?"

"Arroz y quesadilla," she said. "And cerveza." We clinked bottles and chugged. "Can you set the table? That drawer."

I took flatware and three napkins over to the table. There was a little vase of flowers, picked from the front of the building. I looked around, poked my head inside Alejandro's room. The walls were covered with posters of jets, choppers, soldiers. There were plastic models of tanks and cannons—even a SEAL figurine next to a framed picture of Alejandro's dead Papi in uniform. Before pivoting back to the kitchen, I looked in the other room at the neatly-made bed. On a dresser were over a dozen pictures of Alejandro crowding out a single wedding shot with a much younger, hopeful-looking Esme next to Papi. He didn't look much older than Alejandro was now. He was certainly no Navy SEAL.

After dinner, I washed the dishes, Esme dried and put away. Alejandro took a bath and Esme put him to bed while I sat on the couch and channel surfed with the volume down. I heard her talking to Alejandro.

I switched off the TV, leaned back my head with eyes closed. I imagined what it might be like to be part of this family, to live and sleep here; raise up Alejandro right and keep him on the good path.

"Hey."

I opened my eyes to an upside-down image of Esme.

"Wake up, sleepyhead."

"Not used to such a big meal."

"And three beers." She sat next to me.

This exchange had a vibe of resentment. Esme saw something familiar in me. I reminded her of him, I guess. I sat up.

"So," I said, reaching for her pack of cigs. "Tell me about you."

"I was married, my husband died."

"Sorry."

"I'm sure you know he killed himself."

"Yeah."

We smoked.

"That must have been hard."

"It was."

"Was he Navy?"

"Army. Corporal."

She got up, returned with the bag of Mint Milanos.

"I want to ask you something about Alejandro," I said. "Does he know?"

"Yeah," she said, going for the remote. "Alejandro found him in the car."

She had a bottle of Patrón. We started doing shots and whatnot. I kissed her, as if my mouth could suck all the sadness right out of her. When we were sure Alejandro was asleep, we went to bed.

I didn't tell Esme about Alejandro's stories and, in any case, she dumped me for an older guy with better prospects.

The landlord complained and I moved my smoking to the park. This must have changed my luck, because my until-then-worthless-agent booked me on a Hollywood movie shooting locally. The big-name director took a shine to me, I was moving to LA. Alejandro found me the day before I left town.

"Where you been?" he said.

"I got tired of the stairs, needed some fresh air."

"Fresh air you can stink up?"

"Exactly," I said. "You're a smart kid."

"You're leaving."

"Word gets around."

He seemed taller, though it had only been a few weeks. I smoked.

"Tell me a story," I said.

He shook his head. A bat winged silently overhead. The sun had set, wind coming in off the water. Clouds were red, swollen.

"Come on," I said, "Gimme some Tora Bora."

"I dunno."

"Run it down, bro."

He drew himself up and told it, slouching. Alejandro surpassed reality. His Tora Bora was a labyrinthine cave complex with tens of thousands of enemy fighters; a vast subterranean city of evil intent. As soon as the Navy SEALs thought they'd reached the caves' end—they found yet another cavern filled with homicidal Imams, ingenious booby traps and Taliban warlords. We stumbled across grottos of depravity, caches of C-4, box cutters and dirty bombs. Even as bunker buster missiles tortured the earth's crust, causing grains of sand to fall into the commandos' eyes and hair, they courageously pushed on. It got hotter the farther we went, the enemy more zombie than human, pools of lava in our path. Alejandro's eyes were dots of hot, black oil, his hands whipped the story forward. I leaned in. "Deeper," I said. "Keep going." Something wasn't quite right, I couldn't put my finger on it. He wasn't really in the moment. He was indicating.

Alejandro stopped. I waited.

Something telegraphed what came next—actor's intuition, I don't know—but I caught the fist as it came around and stopped it cold, inches from my nose. I caught it cleanly, like paper defeating rock. I was stronger than I looked, able to hold his right fist with perfect pressure, keeping him off-balance. He brought the left around and I got that one too. I stood, still gripping his fists, cigarette dangling from my lips, and kept him away so he couldn't kick me. His pressure was steady, unyielding. He leaned in, close as he could get, and just *roared*. When the epic roar was done, he did it again with full-on hatred. Then I pushed him hard and he fell on his ass. He got up, glared, and ran away, out of my life forever. I didn't call out or chase. I was thinking about his story. I realized: this was the first one ever that didn't include his father. I couldn't decide if that was bad or good.

Steven J. Dines's horror, science fiction, and dark fantasy has appeared in magazines such as GUD, Black Static, Dark Tales, Word Riot, *and* Interzone *along with many others. His debut short story collection,* Bring Your Own Light, *will be coming out from TTA Press in 2016.*

Dines's story "Unzipped" was originally published in Underground Voices *in 2005.*

"unzipped"
STEVEN J. DINES

We could have died from a blink in that godawful desert heat. So we did not blink, or we blinked in our tents with nobody to watch. I thought it was a ball. You came along and spotted it lying in the hot sand. You pointed at it, giggling. You did that funny crablike run all kids your age do when their legs are new, rushing over to it, scooping it up, grinning and looking around for grown-up approval. You shook it, held it to your ear, listened to its innards. Maybe you had a sister with a pull-string doll. Maybe she went out to play with her friends and you sneaked into her room to hear it talk. Maybe you were sad and no one talked to you the way her doll did. The ball had something to pull, too, didn't it? You pulled it because you wanted to hear it talk. And it talked, all right—it fucking *sang*: to you, to me, to the other nurses and doctors roaring, rushing, reaching toward you. I can't get over it, kid. Can't steer my mind around the fact that I saw it lying there in the Iraqi dust and sand a few minutes before you picked it up. I blinked.

Back in Chicago, I avoid driving by playparks on my way to darkened rooms that creak and crack to swings and nine-tails. I don't think about you as seven-inch spiked heels needle my balls; I think about the pain. But Mistress Shade only walks all over me until my time is up, and then I walk out. I always walk out. There has to be a way to lock that door forever.

Tonight, it's on to the mall, where it takes me an hour, sometimes longer, to buy a carton of milk. I like standing in front of the convex security mirrors; I like how they make me look different . . . flexible.

When I arrive back at our two-bedroom apartment, Laura is in our room talking to her girlfriend Angel on the phone. Angel is a nurse, too. But the closest thing Angel has ever seen to a war zone is chronic diarrhea in a seventy-two-year-old patient who cared not where he shat. BFD. Big Fucking Deal.

Laura sees me then bye-byes Angel until she finally hangs up. She sits on the edge of our bed and sighs heavily as she watches me step out of my clothes.

"I need a shower."

"How many is that today?"

"As many as it takes."

The rushing water feels like a hundred cold baby-fingers drumming against my head, neck, shoulders, and . . . balls; my balls ache. The water's touch there, instead of soothing, feels strange, making a choppy sea in my stomach. When I step onto the bathmat and Laura asks if I'm feeling refreshed, I hear myself say, "Go hump yourself," a moment before our five-year-old son, Darren, appears in the doorway.

He is clutching a ball in his left hand. Suddenly I'm measuring the distance to the toilet.

"Give me that," I say.

His smile melts. "Mommy?"

"Give it to me. Right now. Hand it over." I'm trying to sound calm, trying not to rush him or yank his arm off as I confiscate the thing in his hand on my careening path through the bedroom, into the living room, and onto the sofa, pursued by shocked and inquiring looks. I don't need to turn around to see; I know them well; I know *this* well. They're holding their breath like they're afraid I'll take that too.

"Richard . . . it's okay."

That pause, that tone. *I won't let this happen*, it says.

"Mommy . . . is Daddy okay?"

Now *that* pause, *that* tone—the feeling I'm no longer in the room with them but somewhere else, some*one* else. I can't stand it.

"Richard, it's for you anyway," Laura says, pulling at her fingers as she steps closer to me. "Darren was bringing it to you. Take a look. I bought it today. I, uh . . . I thought it might help."

I look at the thing in my hand. It's not a ball, it is a ball, it's not a ball. It's a foam stress toy the size of my fist, with the words We Love You stencilled on it.

We Love You.

What it feels like is your kidney, the one I found two days after I let you pick up that thing that wasn't a ball. It was shrunken and dried by the sun. Only this thing has a message on it. In a way, I guess, so did yours.

I thank both of them then excuse myself to the bedroom, where I open a drawer under the bed to a cornucopia of squishy foams—a baseball, a hockey puck, a tire, a lobster, an apple, a sheep, a pumpkin, a snowman, a toilet, a globe of the world, two burgers, an onion, several dice, and a blowfish. But no body parts: she knows that much. What she doesn't know is the texture of your kidney after forty-eight hours in the heat. But she tries her best, like the doctors and the get-you-through-the-days they prescribe.

As I close the drawer, I notice Laura standing in the doorway.

"I'm going to Angel's tonight," she says. "Can you look after Darren?"

"I don't know, can I?"

"Don't you like your gift?"

It ought to be funny. Laura's ducked more bullets since I got back than I ever did in my time over there. It ought to be funny, all right, but it's not.

I stand and step back from the bed, the drawer. "What time are you leaving?"

"Seven. But I'll cook you both something to eat before I go. Honey, try to see tonight as an opportunity. You haven't spent much time together recently. I'm sure he'd like to. Is chicken all right?"

I've dropped bomb-blasted amputated limbs into air-sealed bags as one might do with a half-eaten drumstick to be saved for later. "No, not chicken," I say. "It tastes like surgery."

"Then I'll find something else. Spend time with him, Richard. I mean it."

That tone again. *I won't let this happen.*

Then she is gone.

I've left the boy in the living room with the TV on and a comic book to look at. When I hear his screams, I think he's ventured around the back of the TV again, like when he was four and opened it up using a screwdriver I'd left lying around. "Want to see how it works," he'd said. But it isn't electrocution; he's opened his thumb turning a page of Batman, or Badman as he'll likely call him from this point. Now he's screaming and running, running, screaming, doing laps around the sofa to outdistance the pain. It won't work, kid. It won't work.

Part of me yearns for the shredded limbs, shattered bones, and cracked chests of the desert. I've massaged fighting men's hearts. I've talked to a private as I helped take his foot. That shit makes for closeness, a oneness I cannot achieve with a crying five-year-old and his fucking paper-cut thumb.

In the bathroom, I disinfect and then Band-Aid the cut, more for his comfort than anything else. Then I lead him back through to the sofa. He sits eyeing the comic on the floor as I select a DVD for him to watch. *Bambi*. At least there's some amount of truth to the part where his mother gets blown away. Once the boy is settled, I slip into the bedroom.

First, I close the door. Maybe I should invest in a lock. Then I boot up the computer. Type the password. Cut off the Start Windows fanfare by killing the speakers. Hearing it is worse somehow. Desert wallpaper appears. No man is a desert—or is it an island? No matter, because *I* am. Double-click Internet Connection. Click Dial . . . dialling . . . verifying username and password. Check the door. Check there's no sound. Open a browser window. Type the web address. Check the door. There it is. Right mouse button. Save Target As . . . And somewhere in the recesses of the hard disk, hidden in an innocuously named folder, a file appears.

Check the door.

Check the speakers.

Open . . .

Laura returns home to find Darren and me on the sofa watching something—I don't know what—on TV. I can move fast when I need to. Not always fast enough though. But then you know that.

Seeing Laura after what I've just seen is what it must have been like as the sun rose over Hiroshima the morning after. She emphasizes my ugliness with her Mia Farrowesque face, draws attention to my vulgarity by standing before me thin and curveless in jeans and a flat blouse, though she's sexless to me now because you're with me, always, like a shadow scorched onto a stone step.

Laura shines down on us from behind the sofa, and something in me knows she'll set later than usual tonight. It's those minutes I have been dreading, when the sweating starts and a man's imagination runs free and out of control. Suddenly I want to stay with my son, but she's telling him it's time for bed and there's only four more sleeps until he turns six and I didn't know or I forgot and Daddy's going to read you a bedtime story . . . I am? I am, while Mommy slips off to our bedroom and waits for a different kind of story to begin.

Half-asleep, Darren shuffles through to his room like one of the undead. It's uncomfortable to watch. He oozes under the duvet then waits, steeple-fingered, while I clear my throat once, twice.

I read to him, silently praying these short fairy tales and rhymes will send him off to sleep, but they seem to revive him into wakefulness, instead. There's little truth to them, and what there is is hidden behind cute animals and saccharine Happy-Ever-Afters. This is my son, I think. He ought to be prepared for what lies in wait for him. He ought to know. So I close the book and it makes a satisfying *whoomp!* Then I tell him a tale I believe is closer to the truth of this world.

Humpty Dumpty sat on a wall. Humpty Dumpty did not have a great fall, at least, not yet. Half a dozen men pulled up in a white van with sand in its tires. They stood before him, and poor Humpty was scared, terrified, in fact. But he was on top of the wall with nowhere to go. One of the men took something from his pocket and threw it toward the base of the wall. It bounced off and rolled a short distance back. Humpty thought it was a ball, but it wasn't. It was a rolled-up blindfold. "Put it on," ordered one of the men. Humpty could not see any of their faces, but he could see their eyes, and they were dark. Faced by so many and with nowhere to run, Humpty did as he was told and put on the blindfold. They took Humpty to a secret place with cages and stains on the floor. They led him into a room where a box— black, silent—sat on three legs. He saw these things because his blindfold had slipped just enough for him to see over it with one eye. Then suddenly a red eye appeared on the box and the men lined up behind him. One of them made a speech and although Humpty did not understand what the man said, he wanted him to keep talking. But the man finished and then there was a lot of shouting. Humpty slumped to the ground and watched the red eye watching him. It watched as they lopped off poor Humpty's head and yolk poured out of him onto the ground, only the yolk wasn't yellow, it was red, like the eye of the thing that watched, not blinking as—

Laura strides into the bedroom: pink basque, stockings, heels. She's in a flap, it seems, like some irate flamingo. I smile; I can't help it, things are backwards these days. She drags me out of the room, rounds on me in the hall.

"What was *that?*" she hisses, struggling to keep her voice down. "What the fuck were you telling our son?"

I'm still smiling; no, I'm grinning. Ear to ear. I can't stop. It masks the fear. I smile a lot and people think I'm crazy. I never used to smile and people, strangers, would come up to me and say *quit frowning, it might never happen.* They thought I was crazy then, too. Oh, and it did happen. It snuck right up and sat its fat fucking ass on me while I wasn't looking. Wasn't looking.

"What's so damn funny?" she asks.

I have no good answer to give her, and that scares me. And so I keep on smiling, like this is some big joke. And it is, in a way. Some big cosmic joke.

Muffled questions try to reach us through the door.

And then we're in our bedroom and the door is closed but we're not watching mpegs, nor is it what I expected to find in here, and part of me feels relieved that she's mad and not amorous.

"Asshole! Sick asshole! You had no right—no right to do that. He's your son for chrissakes and you're filling his head with nightmares."

My smile is gone.

Laura is shaking in her pink basque.

"Those nightmares?" I say. "They're happening now. Six and a half thousand miles from this city. And they could happen anywhere—here, in our country"—our bedroom—"He needs to hear the truth, Laura. Besides, I softened it up a little."

"He's five years old, Richard. He isn't ready to hear that shit."

That tone, again. *I won't let this happen.*

There are licks of sweat appearing all over her, on her forehead, cheeks, tips of her nose and chin, the tops of her slender arms . . . in the cleft between the small rounds of her pushed-up breasts . . .

"None of us are ready to hear it," I say, starting to undress.

"What are you doing?"

"I need to take a shower."

"Now?" she asks. "But you already had one when you came home. Counting the two earlier today that makes four."

"So what?" I shrug. "Can't I be clean?"

Laura walks away to tend to Darren.

The water feels like a hundred cold baby fingers drumming my skin. I soap, cocoon myself in lather. Then, with the showerhead in my hand for a close rinse, I blast the suds and watch them drain away. I'm clean. Decontaminated. The first step from the shower stall will be another fresh start. It's what keeps me coming back again and again and again. But there's always something I miss: that spot behind my balls where the soap tends to collect. And I know I can't step outside the stall until the suds are gone and I am clean. But rinsing down there . . . the baby fingers . . . it feels strange, makes a choppy sea of my stomach. And sometimes . . . *this* time, yes, it's happening . . . I get a hard-on. And so I start over again—soap, lather, rinse—until I'm clean and you're gone, even if only for an hour or so.

Laura walks into the bathroom just as I step out onto the tiled floor. She spots it as it's nodding to sleep again, and says in a flat, humorless voice, "Now's really not the time to have your fun—"

"I didn't . . ."

She gives me a look. *Right.*

Then I break the wall mirror in half with her face.

At the hospital, Laura doesn't tell, not even in the face of weighted looks from heavy nurses. They don't like broken mirrors. They can make them very unlucky. I sit in the waiting room with Darren. The doctor who examines Laura tells me she'll need plastic surgery, and even then she'll be left with scars. I glance at Darren, sitting on a plastic chair two along from mine. He's ghostly pale and hollow-eyed. When the doctor leaves, I buy Darren a candy bar and try to start up a conversation. He's unresponsive, taking mouse-bites from a corner to show me his mouth is busy. I slip him the cab fare back to our apartment, though something tells me it is their apartment now, and I ask a nurse to sit with him while I slip outside to make a call on my cell. Only I didn't take my phone with me.

As I drift through the city's dark and empty streets, suspecting that they were made just for me, the wind sighs—disappointed, it seems. Encircled by that single voice with a thousand echoes, it speaks to me, promising your imminent return. You and I, alone again. My stomach knots. And then my feet are a blur beneath me as I run to beat the devil, you, the you I created, or rather destroyed; me, the one who saw a ball that was never a ball and broke a mirror with his wife. But where to go to escape myself? Where to go? At the mall, the mirrors will only shrink away from me. And Mistress won't lock the door long enough.

Home is out. I could run myself into the ground, but there has to be an easier way. Steal a car . . . throw rocks at apartment windows . . . beat on some homeless drunk. Or maybe I should find a hotel room somewhere and lose a couple of days to the minibar.

A boy of about fourteen rounds the corner ahead, strutting in my direction as I race in his. Maybe he's the answer, I think, slowing to a fast walk. I'm equally drawn and repulsed by the notion of running straight into this kid and maybe pushing him around a little until he calls the cops. But there's no violence left in me. Besides, what would the cops do? They'd toss me in a cell for one night. Perhaps order me to pay the kid some compensation. Then I'd be back to square one. I suppose I could flash him. Hope he calls the cops then. They like that as much as nurses like wife-beaters. Yeah, that's what to do. Show the kid my cock. That ought to earn me a few gut-punches in a holding cell tonight. What if I rub it against him? Just a little, but enough. What would they do to me then? How far should I take this?

But the boy passes without incident, except to tighten his eyes at me as I step aside at the last moment to avoid a collision.

Watching him walk away, I let go of the zipper on my jeans.

For now.

When there's a safe distance between us, I follow him.

For some time, we move through the lamp-lit streets, him, me, boy, shadow, as the wind carries intimations of you and my fast breath fogs my vision.

When the boy turns into a park, where there are very few lamps and every second one has been shot out by air-gun pellets or well-aimed rocks, he joins a group of friends, maybe a dozen or more. I duck behind a bush near the entrance, a soccer field's length from their Saturday-night play: boarding, sinking beers, pulling on a three or four skin joint and then passing it around their circle. Teens are pack animals, of course.

Then maybe this is better.

Next thing, I'm easing down the zipper . . .

Seesawing my jeans down my legs to my ankles . . .

Moving out into the open, though it's shadowed here, waddling for the orange spill of the nearest working lamp. And when I reach it, it'll be two-fingers in my mouth and blow . . .

But somebody cries out, though not in pain. He is directing everyone's hazy attention toward something he has spotted. It isn't me, the half-naked man shuffling through the shadows toward the light. I see only an array of backs turned toward me as they insist, it seems, on ignoring my presence. No, there is a newcomer on the scene. A young boy, much younger than any in the group, eleven at most, strolling through this park at night on a zigzagging path that keeps him as close to the light as possible—though not for his personal safety but so he can see the words in the book he's holding four inches from his nose.

I have three seconds, longer than a blink but still just three seconds, before the group of boys begin to move toward him as one dark, deadly shoal, and in those three seconds I think to myself, I've never seen anything so foolish and so beautiful—except I have. That morning, when I saw you pick up a ball that wasn't a ball and shake it, trying to hear what was inside.

You're back, I see.

As I stand there, legs weakening fast, breathing in short, tremulous gasps, I see several of the boys' faces backlit by the glow of their clamshell phones. Aimed and ready. Drifting, but with clear intent, they form a wide circle as they move in closer to the boy, able to cover every face punch, every rib-kick, every stomp to the head from every angle. As for the boy, he walks on oblivious as words talk and sentences sing and he . . . he listens.

Then I'm pulling my jeans back up to my waist . . .

And I'm closing the zipper. Gritted teeth.

I won't blink this time, kid.

I won't.

David J. Schwartz's stories have appeared in numerous publications, including the anthologies Fantasy: Best of the Year 2007, The Best of Lady Churchill's Rosebud Wristlet, *and the World Fantasy Award-nominated* Twenty Epics. *His novel* Superheroes *was a Nebula Award nominee.*

"The Sun Inside" was originally published as a stand alone novella by Rabid Transit Press. It is both a reimagining of Burroughs-style pulp fiction and a tale about PTSD.

"the sun inside"
DAVID J. SCHWARTZ

Kilgore says you can't hear me, and I know you can't see me. Maybe you hear me in your mind, the way you do Kilgore. I'm not exactly sure why I'm talking to you, considering what you are and what you've done. Thinking about it makes my palms ache. If they hadn't already hurt you I think I'd be hitting you right now, but instead I'm explaining myself. Confessing, maybe.

I guess it's sort of like when I first got out of the hospital with my injury. I was walking around with the cane, and I could see that people—strangers—wanted to ask about it. But none of them did, and it made me angry for no good reason. I didn't really want them to ask, but I did want to talk about it. I wanted to talk through everything that had happened, try to make some sense out of it. Like I'm doing now.

Where I come from, it's a lot different from here. For one thing, the dinosaurs there died out a long time ago. No offense. It's a lot more settled, there. The frontiers are gone, and the wilderness is tame, or at least far enough away for most people to pretend it is.

I grew up in the suburbs. My ma sold real estate, and my daddy was a cop. We were the only black family in the neighborhood, and I used to be real little, so I got beat up a lot when no one was looking. I don't have a lot of good memories about being a kid. As long as I can remember I just wanted to be big enough to hit back. When it happened, around about junior high, I got a little wild. My folks made me go out for football, and that helped. Wrestling, too, but it was football that stuck. I played offensive line. At first I just liked the fact that I could hit without getting in trouble, but it got to be a point of pride that no one put a hand on my quarterback. I was All-State twice.

The first Gulf War started my senior year. I knew about it from the start, because our football coach used to tell us about Saddam. His son was a Marine, and he'd pass on stories about things the Iraqis had done: rapes and torture, dropping bombs and nerve gas on their own people, killing babies. Sick things. I guess some of it was exaggerated, they say now, but whatever part was true is bad enough.

I don't suppose you know who the Iraqis are, any more than I know who the Amoz are, or the Mezops. Maybe you don't even understand about race. Maybe we're all the same to you.

Anyway, I decided to join up. I had colleges coming after me, scholarships for places my folks could never have afforded to send me to, but it wasn't that hard to say no. I liked football, but it was a boy's game, and I was ready to do man's work.

My folks tried told me I should do college first, get a degree, and then go in as an officer. They even got my coach to talk to me about it. He and my dad were the men I most looked up to, but their arguments didn't ring true because they'd both served in the military right out of high school. I asked them if they regretted doing that, and they both said no, but they said that didn't mean it was the right choice for me.

I was sure that it was. I knew I could get hurt playing college ball, and not be eligible for the service. I could get an education later, on the GI Bill. I wanted to get in on the action right then. Only problem was, I had to finish high school, and by the time I did, the war was over.

I don't think you can understand time the way we do, coming from a place where the sun never goes down. No clocks or calendars to measure it by, just storms and wars and lives. Time's one thing they teach you in the army. The numbers on the clock outrank you same as everyone else; they get you out of bed when you're still tired, they make you wait to eat when you're hungry, and you're always moving too fast or too slow for them.

There were things I didn't like about the Army. I didn't like getting yelled at, and it seemed like they'd yell even if you did everything right. They tried to break you down so you'd stop thinking and just do what you were told, what you were trained to do.

After basic it was all waiting. Waiting to be assigned, waiting to ship out, waiting to do something besides drill. I remember sitting on the base in Germany, realizing that the army was just a job after all, and what a letdown that was. Not that I expected something glamorous, but I was sort of hoping for the chance—just one chance—to be a hero. The next day I applied for a transfer to Special Forces. I never got to go, though, because that same day my daddy died.

You never had a father, did you? Kilgore told me you were all females, that there were books of instructions that helped you make eggs. He said that was why you started the bombings, to try to get those books back. So I guess your family life is different from ours.

When I lost my daddy, it was like—I was prepared for my own death, but the people at home were supposed to be safe. I was mad at him for dying. I remember sitting on the plane thinking that if he'd respected what I was doing he wouldn't have died and made me leave just when I was figuring it out.

It was a bank robbery that went bad, and ended up with one cop and one robber dead. My daddy, and the piece of shit that killed him. When I saw how upset my ma was I started rethinking the Special Forces thing. She didn't tell me that she wanted me to stay, but I could tell. The military has a discharge policy for a parent's death if you're the only child. They gave me an honorable, and I followed my daddy's footsteps to the police academy.

I liked some things about being a cop. I liked it when we were able to stop people from hurting each other or themselves, but most of the time we got there too late for that. I felt like I'd moved from the offensive line to the outfield—I wasn't protecting anybody anymore, just chasing down fly balls. Baseball never was my sport. It bothered me that we weren't supposed to hit back, not even when they deserved it.

When 9/11 came, I thought about reenlisting, but I think my ma would have lost it. She liked having me close to home. I figured, War on Terror, that's not going anywhere, and I was right.

Then my ma was diagnosed with bone cancer. It was another punch in the gut, you know? I tried to get her to eat better, took her for walks. I wanted her to fight. It didn't help. I guess I'm glad I got to spend that time with her. She kept on teasing me, telling me to just pick a girl and get her pregnant. Marry her later. Ma would have liked grandkids, but she only lasted six months.

So I was an orphan at twenty-nine. I was angry. I started having these dreams that I was in the interrogation room with a suspect; most of the time I couldn't see his face. Sometimes it was Saddam, sometimes it was the guy that shot my dad. Once it was my dad. In the dream I had a lot questions, but the suspects never answered them. They never did anything but smile. It made me angry. I wanted to make it so they'd never smile again.

In the dreams I'd get so mad I couldn't hold back. I'd fight it, but in the end I always let go, and it felt really good to just let the anger take over. But it didn't last. I'd throw that first punch, and nothing would happen. I'd miss, or it'd just graze the skin, or they'd just take it and keep on smiling. I couldn't make a mark. It was like those dreams where you're trying to run away, but your legs won't move. I couldn't hurt the suspects or make them confess. Sometimes I'd wake up from those dreams with the imprint of my fingernails on the palms of my hands. A few times I drew blood.

I told my partner, Holly, about the dreams. She told me she was worried about me. She said I was like two people—sometimes I was a knight in armor, helping people, making them feel safe. And then sometimes I was just a guy looking for somebody to hit. She said I had to decide which one I wanted to be. As if it was that simple. But she had a point; I couldn't do my job if I was afraid of exploding all the time. I decided not to be a cop, at least for a while.

We were back in Iraq by then, and guys I knew were making two thousand a week working security there. One of them was a bodyguard for the proconsul. I liked the idea of that, of being back in front of the quarterback, but not in a game. Besides, there wasn't anyone left at home for me to protect.

It took forever to get the inheritance squared away. I sold the house and made up a will of my own, and then I got on a plane. Two weeks of training, then Iraq. It seemed like they were in a hurry to get us in place, but that was fine with me.

When I got in they briefed me and told me I'd be driving my first mission the next day. Right away I saw that it wasn't going to be anything like what I'd been expecting. The company had been subcontracted to cart supplies for some of the corporations doing reconstruction. They turned us into truck drivers, basically. My first and last job for them was driving a truck full of blenders and coffee-makers from one of the airports to the Green Zone. Blenders. I still can't believe that. We took an IED for the sake of five dozen Cuisinarts.

I never even heard it; my ears just hurt, and then everything on my left side hurt, and then it was quiet.

I guess since you don't have ears, you never heard that bomb you dropped either. You must have seen, though. Wreckage. Bodies covered in dust. Even if you didn't know what you were doing before that, you did then.

You know what eats at me? After five surgeries, eleven months of physical therapy, and eighteen of headshrinking, what bothers me most is I never got to return fire. It's not like there was anybody to shoot at, just some wires and plastique and a remote control receiver. I don't remember any of it, to tell you the truth. Sometimes bits of it seep into my nightmares, but when I think of it I remember leaving the airport and that's all. Next thing, I woke up in the hospital.

Innes told me your people—except people's not the right word, is it? I mean, you used to eat humans alive. You'd put them in a trance and just tear them to pieces. That's why they took your eyes out, right? So you couldn't hypnotize us. They didn't have any choice; it was you or them. You or us.

We all survived. We'd have been on the news, otherwise, like those men in Fallujah. "Contractors," they called them. Everyone at home thought they were construction workers.

I lost the left leg a few inches above the knee. The truck was supposed to be armored; it wasn't. They gave me a transfemoral prostheses, made mostly out of carbon fiber and various plastics. It's light, but getting around on an artificial knee is tricky. I either move slowly or I fall down a lot.

They paid me pretty well for my leg, I guess. I mean, if they were going to pay you for your eyes, what do you think would be a fair price?

I tried not to say shit like that to the psychiatrist they sent me to. I did tell her about the fists, though. I was still having those dreams. I never saw the faces anymore, just the smiles.

The psychiatrist thought I was blaming myself for everything. Not just the injury, but my parents too. She told me I needed to get a handle on my anger, but I don't know what she expected me to do. I used to exercise to keep my head on straight. I ran eight miles every morning, and I never got sick; my lungs were clean and whatever might have been in my blood just burned away. When I got back and stood in the shower I always thought that the hardest part of my day was over, and I was usually right.

I couldn't do that anymore. I couldn't do a lot of things. Maybe you can relate. You used to fly, but now you're stuck down here in the dark.

I took up swimming instead. It wasn't easy with one leg, but I have strong arms. I kept lifting, thought maybe I could get what was left of the leg back to full strength. Denial. The psychiatrist told me about that. It sounded like a good idea to me.

My days were too long. I'd work out for an hour or two and I'd go eat somewhere, and if I didn't have therapy that day then I'd have nothing to do. I'd take long walks with the cane just to pass the time—the muscles weren't strong enough for me to walk on just the leg, yet. I didn't really like to hang out with the guys from my trauma support group. It brought up all kinds of things that I needed to keep in one place—does that make sense? Sometimes I'd see Holly, my old partner, but she'd gotten married and it felt wrong. She just reminded me how much everything had changed.

I had enough money from the company and my inheritance that I didn't have to work. I would have liked to work, but the list of things I couldn't do seemed a lot longer than the list of things I could. I'd never liked TV much, so I swapped paperbacks at the used bookstore in my neighborhood and read two or three of them in a day. Mysteries, science fiction—I even read some of Burroughs's books, but not the ones about here. Innes says the other ones are all made up.

I started spending a lot of time on military bulletin boards and blogs. A lot of the people there didn't know what they were talking about. There were some vets, but there were also a lot of people who'd just read a few books about the service and never actually been in it. I was pretty tough on those sorts of people until one day I realized that I wasn't all that different from them. I'd spent four years in the army and never seen a day of action until I took a job making four times what the army guys were making to do the real fighting. And then, boom. I had this picture of who I was, you know? I was strong. I was a protector. I had parents.

I think I might have lost it if one of the guys in my trauma support group hadn't sent me that link. UndergroundSingles.com. He said he'd found it in his Spam folder, but it turned out to be legit and vet-friendly. So I clicked over there to check it out.

It's one of those sites where they ask you all kinds of questions, like would you rather go hiking or to the opera, and how important is your religion to you, and how happy are you on a scale from 1 to 10. The kind of thing where they tell you to be honest but nobody is, where people say they're into camping even though they haven't seen a tent in ten years.

I decided that was bullshit. I told the quiz exactly how depressed I was, and how I wasn't sure I believed in god anymore, and that I got angry a lot. It was funny at first, but it was also a look at myself that I didn't very much enjoy. When I clicked on Finish I was ready for it to tell me that I wasn't even fit for my own company, but instead it gave me Innes.

She's so beautiful: dark hair, and dark skin—not black, but sort of Arabic-looking. I don't usually notice eyes, but hers are this sort of translucent green that just came right off the screen. She had this expression like . . . she was smiling a little, but the overall look was very intense and skeptical. Challenging. I wasn't even sure if she was really a member. She could have been a model that the company put up to convince suckers like me to give up their credit card information, but I had to find out.

There were things about the registration that were sort of odd. Like where they asked where you were from, there were all these strange places in the drop-down menu. Luana, New Phutra, the Unfriendly Islands—places I'd never heard of before. And Innes's profile said she lived in the Land of Sari and taught solar engineering at Perry Military College. I wondered if maybe it was all a joke, but I guess I'm stubborn. If Innes was real, I wanted to talk to her.

When you feel healthy and fit, confidence is easy. Before the injury I never had trouble approaching women. If I wanted a girl, I'd go talk to her, and ninety-five percent of the time I'd get her. I'm not bragging, I'm just saying. But this was online, and I wasn't feeling nearly as confident. It wasn't the engineer thing—I'd dated women more educated than me, and I could hold my own. I just didn't know if I could keep up physically. Innes had listed interests like hiking, hunting, and riding, all of which made her more attractive but none of which I thought I'd be able to do.

I wrote to her anyway. I told her my parents were both dead and I was getting used to being alone. I told her I'd been wounded in Iraq but I was trying to stay in shape. I told her I had never tried an online dating site but when I'd seen her picture I had to write. After I'd sent the email I thought probably I shouldn't have laid all of that on her right off the bat. She wasn't a quiz, she was a real woman, at least I hoped so. I should have tried to be funny and clever, kept it light.

I guess it didn't matter, because next morning her response was there between a chain forward from an army wife I knew and my daily forecast from weather.com. I remember my pulse was up just double-clicking on the email, and I had a dumb grin on my face, like a kid with a crush.

She said they'd been following the war on Iraq, and the way she said it made it sound like she was really far away. Like Mars. She said that a battle wound was a badge of honor. She said her dad was still alive, but her mom had died when she was little. Then she talked about what was outside her windows—birds chasing one another along the cliffs, vendors selling fruit at the market, her *hyaenodon* curled up in a splash of sunlight. I didn't know what a *hyaenodon* was, but it all sounded nice. Better than my drab little apartment with its bare walls and the fall stealing daylight outside.

I told her that, and I told her about my favorite mornings, in the Mojave where my unit had trained years ago—how cold it was, until the sun sent all the night life scurrying for their burrows. The desert was harsh but I had liked it. If I'd spent more time in Iraq maybe I would have changed my mind. Anyway, I wrote about that and about the things we were trying to do in Iraq, even though I thought there had been some mistakes. The justifications were complicated, but it was the right thing for us to be there. I remember that I said that because when she wrote back she said she didn't understand the American obsession with justifications. "War is about survival," she said. I didn't know how to respond to that, but I didn't really have to, because she said something else.

She asked me to describe the sunrise. She'd never seen one, she said. That seemed pretty odd for a solar engineer, or a hunter. I decided she was just flirting. So I got up early the next day and walked over to the park to watch the sun come up. I wrote down all the colors in the order they appeared and the way they made the buildings look sort of unreal, and how the greens were stronger, like paint that had soaked in and spread. I thought later that she might have been looking for something more scientific, but she said she liked it.

We wrote a lot. She told me about her work, that it was more hands-on than theoretical. She lived in a big house with her father; she called him "the General." She asked me to send her more pictures—the one I'd put up at the site was my ID photo for the company—and she sent me some of her, too. Some of them were kind of sexy. We didn't write every day. Sometimes she would write at odd hours, and once she didn't write for a week. I was starting to wonder if I had pissed her off somehow when I got an email from her asking me to visit her.

This was about two months after we'd started talking, and I still didn't know where she lived. I couldn't find the Land of Sari on Google Maps. Every time I asked her she would talk around it. "You'd have to go north to get there," she said once, so I thought maybe it was a military base in Alaska or Canada. I asked her if she was one of Santa's helpers, but she didn't get the joke. She seemed to think Santa Claus and the Pope were the same person.

She told me that if I decided to visit, she would tell me how to get there. It didn't seem real at first. I was starting to get my confidence back, but I still wondered why she'd picked me. I figured she must get a hundred responses a day to her ad, and a lot of those guys must have had both their legs. It didn't matter, though. I knew already that I was going. I wanted a change. I wanted her. She didn't talk to me like it took me two minutes to walk down a flight of stairs. She talked to me like we were at dinner deciding whether to have crème brulee or each other for dessert.

She told me I needed to get to Barrow, Alaska, and catch an Interior Air flight from there. I asked her where to, and she said they only flew to one place.

When I got to Barrow it was dark. It was late December, and the sun wouldn't be up for another month. The cold was vicious. I'd brought gloves and a long coat, but no hat. I thought my ears would snap right off of my head before I got inside the tiny little airport.

All Interior Air had given me was a phone number. When I called for a shuttle the woman at the other end told me that a flight had left the day before. I asked her when the next one would leave, and she told me the same thing they'd told me when I booked the ticket: flights departed every one to seven days, and they would provide accommodations during the wait.

I rode the shuttle with a guy named Drak who was nearly as broad as he was tall—not fat, but wide at the shoulders, like he was wearing padding under his short-sleeved button-down shirt. Drak the Loud One, he called himself, and at the time I didn't realize that was his legal name and not just a nickname. I'd noticed him on the flight in; he'd snored most of the way. He wore sandals and shorts and didn't seem at all bothered by the cold. He said he was headed home after a business trip to Bolivia.

I asked him where home was and he said he lived near Sari nowadays. Then he smiled at me sort of funny and asked me if I'd been there before. I told him it was my first time. He asked if I was traveling on business or pleasure, and I told him I was visiting a friend.

He said: "I hope she knows you're coming for her," and he patted my artificial leg. "Less chance of her getting away." It took me a second, but I laughed. No one had dared to make jokes about my injury before, and I was surprised to find out that I didn't mind.

Drak held out his right hand, and then plucked it from his sleeve. An *azdryth* had bitten it off, he said. He kept the rubber hand for business negotiations, to break the ice. He'd shake hands with someone and let them yank the hand right out. He said it relaxed everyone.

Interior Air's headquarters were on the south shore of Footprint Lake: a square, three-story terminal on one side, a hangar on the other. I didn't see any runways, but at the time I thought maybe it was just too dark.

It wasn't dark inside the terminal; the central atrium had huge lamps hanging above and smaller rooms surrounding it on two levels. There were stone tables scattered around the ground level, and palm trees and acacias growing in clusters with finger-leaved ferns. It was like a gymnasium-sized greenhouse.

The security guard at the desk greeted Drak by name, and asked if he had anything to declare. He gave her his wristwatch and smiled like he'd just set down a weight he'd carried for five hundred miles. She put the watch in a drawer behind the counter and locked it. Then she looked at me and said, Hello, Thomas—not Hello, Sir or Hello, Mr. Tucker. She said she needed my watch and my phone and any other

252

timekeeping devices I was carrying. I was sure I'd heard her wrong. I figured she'd need to see my passport instead, but she said the authorizations were all taken care of and asked for my watch again. She said I'd get it back on my return trip. She said it would all be useless inside in any case.

I said to her, How can a watch be useless? She said this was all in the agreement they had sent me regarding my flight, and when I checked the fine print later, there it was. No timekeeping devices of any sort.

Luckily I was traveling pretty light. I gave her my watch and my phone and my travel alarm clock. I remember it was 4:49 p.m., and that's the last I knew the time.

Drak and I settled down in the atrium; a steward brought us some wine and a platter of cheese and fruit, and we ate and drank and talked. Drak had been in the military too, he said—it was compulsory, even for someone with an injury like his. He said he was still sort of in the military, just on the supply end. He was married and had five kids. They raised *thags* on a ranch outside Sari. It sounded like a good life, and I told him so. Then I realized he was asleep.

I lay down in the shade, feeling like I was stepping off a trail into the woods. The lights stayed on. I kept forgetting we weren't outside; I saw a bee at one point, and I heard something bigger moving around in the trees above.

I lay there imagining what a *thag* looked like. I decided they were like horned sheep, and I counted them until an *azdryth* came up and started eating them. I still don't actually know what an *azdryth* is, but in my half-dreaming state it was sort of a long-necked leopard. After a while I realized that Innes was sitting on the *azdryth*'s back, staring at me.

When I woke up I noticed that for the first time in years there weren't deep indentations in my palms. I hadn't had the nightmare.

The steward served us juice and coffee and omelets. Drak had taken off his shirt and sandals sometime during the night, and he sat at the table barefoot and bare-chested. He'd put his prosthetic hand away as well. The stump was smoother than I would have expected, just a faint line showing that it had been taken away rather than withheld since birth.

Drak said it was too hot for all those clothes, and it would be hotter still when we got back. I didn't understand that, but before I could ask him about it, they announced that our flight would be leaving in half an hour. More passengers arrived: three single guys and a man and woman together. I wondered if they were on their honeymoon but I didn't ask. They were all dark-skinned people, none quite as thick-set as Drak, but big.

The crew came in to fetch us. They wore blue dress uniforms and carried flight suits for all of us: heavy coats and pants, big enough for us to put on over our own clothes. I hadn't heard a plane come in, so I didn't know what to think. I put on the flight clothes and I got up and limped around while the rest of them chatted and the crew loaded freight and hauled luggage. Drak talked enough for the entire group, and I couldn't tell which of the passengers he already knew and which he had just made into his friends by force of will and volume. Once he got going his voice made the leaves flicker under the sunlamps.

We lined up by the boarding tunnel, and I wanted to ask Drak where we were going, but I was distracted. I don't know if it was the heat, or something in the air. There were things living in the terminal, and not just bugs. Every time the ferns started to sway I forgot where I was.

When the crew took us outside it was so dark I was near blind, but there was a rounded haze of light near the hangar. After a few steps I realized it was a blimp. Zeppelin, they called it. *The Imperial Dragon-fly*. I'd never ridden in a zeppelin before, but that didn't make me all that nervous. I was thinking Goodyear; I didn't remember the *Hindenburg* until we were in the air.

It was cramped. There was a stenciled sign in the passenger cabin that said it would hold ten, but even with seven we were all touching knees. Drak made sure I got a window seat. I could have asked him then, but with everyone right there it felt stupid to admit that I'd come all this way without knowing where I was going.

Drak got quiet as we got aloft and then flew north. You could hear everyone holding their breath. My leg was hurting, too, the one that wasn't there.

The frozen sea was just another shade of black underneath us. The flight suits kept most of the cold away, but I could see my breath by the glow of the safety lights. One of the other passengers took out a bottle of vodka and passed it around. I took a swig; it burned going down. After a while the bottle came around again. I started measuring time by the swigs. Two swigs, and I was aware of the crew's voices coming muffled from the cockpit, metal creaking in that keeping-you-safe kind of way, the breath whistling through somebody's nose. And underneath all that, the engine throbbing and pushing us up and forward. Three swigs and I was picturing Innes lying naked on top of me, the two of us warming each other with our skin while packs of hyaenodons lazed in the sun outside. Four swigs, and my inner ear told me we were listing to the left, then the right, then tipping forward. I held on to my good leg and took deep breaths.

The bottle was gone when I saw a light through the cockpit window. It was distant and bright, like we were going through a tunnel, and I realized that was exactly what we were doing. It must have been half a mile around. I could make out the outlines of it, ice and snow sparkling from rocky crevices. As it got brighter I saw little streams of water flowing in the direction we were traveling—even the streams on the ceiling of the tunnel were flowing forward, not down. I thought the vodka was going to do the same thing until we climbed out of the tunnel and the gondola filled with sunlight.

Sunlight and applause. We straightened out above a glacier-blue body of water and crossed its shores into ripples of green. Green like grass bleeding on your clothes, or the corona that white light creates around a Christmas tree. It looked like we were passing over a rainforest, but from the blue sky outside every window I found it hard to believe that it ever rained here.

All the tension had gone. Drak slapped me on the chest and welcomed me to Pellucidar.

That was the first time I'd ever heard that word, Pellucidar, and I told him so. He said that wasn't unusual. A surface man named Edgar Rice Burroughs had written about the place some years ago, but no one had taken him very seriously. I asked Drak why not. I still remember exactly what he said.

"Your science," he said, "would have it that the center of the earth is a core of molten rock, that creatures such as dinosaurs and ground sloths and saber-toothed tigers are all extinct. As you can see"—he motioned out the window—"your scientists are wrong about all of those things. The inside of the planet, five hundred miles beneath the crust you live upon, is hollow. At its center hangs a warm and ever-shining sun, much smaller than the one which travels your sky, but not less life-sustaining. More so, in fact, for it illuminates not only massive amounts of vegetation but also millions of species of animal, from the insect hordes to megafauna of sorts which your world knows only as scratches in the fossil record."

He gave his little speech with an expression that said he knew I wouldn't believe it. I pretended not to. I raised my eyebrows at him and I frowned. The truth is, I was excited by what he'd told me, but I didn't want to be taken in by some elaborate joke. So I didn't ask questions, and Drak didn't say any more about it.

I was thinking about dinosaurs. Man, when I was a kid, that was all I ever thought about. I used to sleep with a plastic stegosaurus. I'd wake up with the plates imprinted on my stomach. I had a pterodactyl that looked kind of like you, too. That's what we called them back then.

Everyone in the *Dragonfly* was talking now, some of them in English but some in a language I didn't know. I mostly stared out the window, even thought it was pretty much just huge trees on rolling hills. There was a river running through the rainforest, but it was hardly visible through the canopy. It was . . . well, you've seen it, I guess. Before, I mean.

We were over the rainforest for a long time. When we turned away from the river's course towards some mountains, the trees started to clear, and I caught a glimpse of something moving through the brush—something big and green with a scaly tail.

One of the crewmen came back and started collecting the flight suits, hanging them in a closet at the back of the cabin. It was tricky, pulling off those pants in close quarters, but it was a relief, too; it was starting to get warm in the cabin. Drak was down to shorts again in a flash, and none of the others were wearing much more, even the woman. I was sort of distracted by that, and by trying to get my own suit off over my artificial leg. By the time I had it all sorted out we were a lot closer to the mountains. The peaks were sort of grainy and distant, but on a plateau ahead there was a city. Stone buildings that looked like cakes: some were layered like sheet cakes, others were round and stacked like wedding cakes, painted in greens and yellows and reds.

We flew right over the city. Most of the buildings had courtyards at their center, and the roofs surrounding them were dense with gardens with gardeners wearing what looked like fur coats. We landed in an airfield just beyond the city. A half-dozen men came out of a hangar to secure the lines, the crew extended the staircase, and we climbed out.

The sun here isn't that different. It's a lot closer, so it looks about three times as big, but it's just as warm. It's everything else that's different: the plants, the animals, the people. The days. I mean, there are no days, just sleeps and storms. How do you count the hours in a day that never ends? Sometimes I feel like I've been here for a year, and then sometimes it's like a couple of weeks. I think it's making me a little bit crazy. Yesterday—before my last sleep—I had a bad episode. Like a panic attack. When Innes left I was glad at first, because I thought we needed a break from each other. I wanted some time to take everything in. But after she left I went back to the cabin and I started to feel like I needed to hide. I wanted night to come, but I knew it wouldn't. So I shut the curtains and I crawled into the bed like it was a torpedo tube, like it could launch me into someplace dark and quiet. I pulled the sheets up over my head and wound them around me tight and eventually I stopped hyperventilating and my heart slowed down to normal and I fell asleep. As soon as I woke up I came over here.

It wasn't bad right away, being in Pellucidar. I mean, it was good, then. Innes met me at the airfield wearing a white skirt and a sleeveless shirt and she was so beautiful. I hate to admit it, but I'd been a little afraid she wouldn't show up. We hugged and she kissed my chin and said the weather was nice and maybe we should walk to the house. The sun felt so good that I said yes. I shook hands with Drak, and he invited me to visit his ranch. His voice had gotten sort of quiet—quiet for him, at least—when he saw Innes, and at one point he sort of bowed to her, but I figured he was just one of those guys who overdid it around pretty girls.

Innes offered to get a porter for my luggage, but I just strapped the duffel bag over my shoulder and we started walking. It was kind of a stupid macho thing to do, because I was sweaty before we'd left the airfield, but I'd done it and I wasn't going to back off it already. Innes didn't tell me I shouldn't.

I don't know if you've been to Sari. For all I know that's where you dropped that bomb. It's a beautiful city; it feels like it's been there for centuries. The stone is . . . I mean, it's all stone. Where I come from most of the houses, at least, are made out of wood or brick. Sari feels more permanent than that. It would feel heavy if it weren't for all the green. Vines on the buildings and trees along the streets. Flowers on the roofs and in the squares. Plants anywhere the sun is shining, which is just about everywhere. It's always high noon down here, and you can tell by looking at the people—not a white one in the bunch. Hardly any clothes. That was a little strange. None of the other women were as good-looking as Innes, but she was right next to me, so I couldn't stare at her.

I was trying to look at the buildings, and then I saw one of the gardeners. He was shuffling along the curb, carrying a big potted fern from a wagon to the doorway of a four-story building the size of a city block. He wasn't a man in a coat; he was like a gray gorilla, but with a sheep's snout, and walking on two legs as easily as you or me. Better than me, nowadays.

Innes told me this was one of the Gr-gr tribe. She said that they were useless as soldiers, and most of them had been drafted as farmers or gardeners. I asked her why there was a draft, and she said "Because of the war." I asked her who they were at war with, and she said "Everyone."

She said the Empire of Pellucidar had been at war since its foundation by David Innes, first with the Mahars, and then with various human tribes and kingdoms. She didn't tell me who the Mahars were. I was distracted by the fact that she was named after the emperor, anyway.

So far the Empire held dominion—that's how Innes said it—over about a third of the inner earth. I asked her how long the war had been going on, but all she could tell me was that it had started before her grandparents were born.

She took me to this huge house at the edge of the plateau, with red brick detailing over the doors and windows, and guards armed with sabers and shotguns outside. They nodded at Innes and gave me a look that meant they'd be keeping their eyes and ears open. I guessed that this was the General's house.

Innes led me through to the courtyard, where the sun still hung hot overhead. It looked a lot like the inside of the Interior Air terminal, except that the sun wasn't a bunch of lamps. Another one of the Gr-grs was working inside the courtyard, watering the flowerbeds. He didn't look at us, and Innes didn't look at him.

She led me up a staircase to one of the wings—I thought of it as the east wing, even though compass directions don't mean much down here—and into a suite of rooms. We parked my luggage in a small bedroom overlooking the courtyard and Innes interlaced her fingers with mine and kissed me hard.

I was sweaty and tired from the walk, but she didn't seem to care and I wasn't going to argue. I remember, that first time, after we had my pants off, she insisted on taking off the leg. It was strange. She sort of caressed it, and when she'd undone the straps she picked it up and kissed it before she put it aside. I can't deny it turned me on, but it was weird.

The sex was great. It still is, even with everything else messed up. Innes isn't kinky, really, but she's not shy about her needs. I'd been sweaty when we started; after we'd done it twice the sheets were soaked. I was kind of hurting, actually. In a good way.

We took a hot shower, and between the kissing Innes told me that the water and everything else were solar-powered. She'd installed the new panels herself. She'd had a hand in designing them, too, but they were made in China.

Pretty much the whole Empire runs on solar power, it turns out. I told Innes I guessed that her job must be pretty important, and she smiled and said I was just saying that because we were fucking.

I hadn't gotten my head around her yet. Not that I have now. When I was talking to her on email, she was just words on a screen, you know? I guess you don't. I'm just saying, I got to know her a little that way; but now we were together, and in some ways we were still strangers. There was a time in my life when that was how I preferred it, but I'd come a long ways. I wanted this to be different. I wanted to talk some before we fucked again.

What happened next, though, was dinner with the General. He sat at the head of a long table in the courtyard when we came down; his uniform was a blue vest and brown Bermuda shorts. There was a kind of dog with him too, like a wolf the size of a Great Dane. It ran to Innes's side, and she scratched him on the head and hugged him. This was the hyaenodon Innes had mentioned; his name was MacArthur.

The General stood up and shook my hand and told me not to call him Sir. We stood just about eye-to-eye, and he was as broad-shouldered as me, but he had a big gut. He slapped it and told me he'd been off the front lines for a long time. He blamed politics and said something about a War Council, but nobody's really bothered to explain that to me.

A serving girl brought out a sort of rice dish with stewed vegetables and some meat that tasted a little like steak and a little like rhubarb pie. It was good. The conversation wasn't. It started out with the General saying that Innes had told him I was a US Army veteran, and I said yes I was. He asked me about the compulsory draft, and why we'd gotten rid of that. I told him I didn't know a lot about it. Something to do with politics, I said. Then he went off on this rant about American politics, how we try to treat the military like it's a separate issue, like military spending is something that we get no benefit from. I'd heard officers say stuff like that before, but it kind of bothered me to hear the General saying it. And then Innes jumped in and started talking about how we let politics screw up the Iraq war, not sending in enough troops because we were scared of the voters, and all the justifications that we threw around. I asked her what she thought we should have said to convince people it was the best thing to do. I was starting to get a little defensive.

Innes didn't answer me, though; the General did. He said that justifications were a waste of time, that for strong nations invasion and expansion were necessary and good. Nations were cannibalistic by nature, he said. America needed oil and a foothold for stability in the Middle East. If our people couldn't understand that, they deserved to be lied to.

I said those weren't the reasons we went to Iraq, or at least not all of them. We'd gone in to get the Iraqis out from under Saddam, to help them get their own country back. They actually laughed at me. The General stopped when he saw that I was pissed off, and he apologized, but I couldn't stand looking at Innes's smile.

We talked about other things, but I was still steaming, and after dinner I told them I was tired from the trip and needed to rest. I went upstairs to the small bedroom and lay there thinking I'd been really stupid to come so far not even knowing where I was going, to visit someone I barely knew.

When I woke up Innes was sitting on the bed. She wanted to apologize; of course I had a right to be offended on behalf of my country and my military. I had been there, after all, and she hadn't. I suspected she was saying all that just to make me feel better, but she was apologizing, so I let it go.

We went to eat at this little place in the side of the cliff. I mean literally—we took stairs down into the mountain and ate in a chamber that was carved out of the rock, with high windows looking out over a waterfall. The sun hadn't moved, of course, but with the shade and the mist it was almost cool. We had *archaeopteryx* omelets and Colombian coffee and Innes talked about her mother.

She'd died back in Patton's time, she said. I thought she meant the general, which was confusing and impossible, but she explained that Patton was a storm. She said that since Pellucidar doesn't have the temperature shifts of day and night, it tends to produce storm systems with a lot of stability. They form near the coasts and circulate until they break apart near the mountains or the polar cavity or the Land of Awful Shadow. The meteorologists—the ones from the Empire—they give the storms names, like hurricanes, and people use their movements and lifespans as a way of measuring time.

Impressive, isn't it? From slavery to meteorology in . . . well, I don't know, exactly. But you can't have expected that. You can't have thought they were capable of it, or you wouldn't have kept them as slaves. Unless you did know, and you were afraid of what they might do.

Innes said her mother had been Dian the Beautiful's cousin. She was the first emperor's wife, I guess. After that I didn't hear most of what Innes said, because I was realizing that she must be sort of like royalty. That explained why Drak had acted so oddly around her, but it made it even harder to understand why the hell she was with me.

After we ate Innes showed me around the city. She held my hand and I forgot to be insecure for a while. I started noticing the people a little more. There were all these black and brown people, and even not-people like the Gr-grs, and they were walking together in pairs and standing around talking in groups. I even saw a guy with a head like a buffalo, with horns and everything, walking with two human men, and they were all laughing. The buffalo guy laughed like he was trying to blow something out his nostrils.

I wasn't quite taking in the idea of all these animal people, but at the same time I had this feeling like the gorilla people and the buffalo people and the black people and the brown people were all a part of something, like the fact that they were different didn't matter. Or it mattered, but it was a strength, something they all valued. And I couldn't help thinking that maybe my country could be like that, without any white people. I don't hate white people or anything. Holly, my partner, she's white. I just couldn't help thinking.

We walked to a lake further up the plateau. The stream we'd seen falling off the cliff flowed out of it, sort of sauntered past us like a kid the moment before he takes off running. The lake was blue and clear and stacked with boats. There was a crowd with blankets and wooden lawn chairs on the rocky beach, and a half-dozen of them came over to meet us. They shook my hand and spoke to Innes in Pellucidarean, and she followed them to a pier that most of the boats were gathered near.

I tried to ask Innes what was happening, but the welcoming committee didn't stop talking the entire time, so I just followed the whole parade out to the end of the pier. There was a little podium there, and a bullhorn, and a rifle with a wooden stock. Innes stood at the podium, picked up the bullhorn, and pointed it at the people on the beach. Whatever she was saying, a lot of people liked it. They clapped for her, and then she put her hand on my arm and said something else, and they clapped for me. Then she turned around and pointed the bullhorn at the boats and said a few words, and then she picked up the rifle and fired it out over the water, and then everybody went nuts.

The people on the beach waded into the shallows, and the boats started fighting each other. On the one side there were these little canoes, and on the other were these big ugly sailing-ships with cannons. The first time they fired the cannons I had a real fight-or-flight moment—my hands balled up into fists, my legs shaking—but I could see they weren't actually loaded. The sailors would fire them and then throw these heavy sacks at the canoes, and the canoes threw blunt spears back at the ship. The whole time this was going on the people on the beach cheered and hooted and grunted at the top of their lungs.

Innes was holding tight to my arm. She was smiling and crying. Right then I didn't care if she was a princess and I was a cripple, or what the hell was going on, or where I was and how I'd gotten there. I'd never been in love before, and I'm not sure I was then. But it was something close.

Eventually the men on the ship capsized all the canoes, and they fished out their opponents or jumped in to help them drag the canoes back to the beach. People started dancing, and they brought us food, these huge kebabs smothered in the spiciest sauce I've ever had in my life. At some point I managed to get from Innes that this was a re-enactment of the first battle of the Pellucidarean Navy. She'd been asked to make a speech to open the festival.

After we ate people started asking Innes to dance, and I told her to go ahead. There was no way I was going to try it, on my leg. I was already sort of drunk on this drink they kept passing around. It tasted kind of like Amarula, but I guess you've probably never had that. It's sort of sweet and fruity.

I don't even know if you eat fruit. Mostly meat, I guess. What do humans taste like, anyway? Do they taste sweet? I've heard they smell like pork when you burn them. But you never cooked them, did you? You ate them raw.

I promised Kilgore I wouldn't hurt you, so I won't.

Where was I?

The festival. Yeah. Innes danced. I sat and listened to this guy who didn't know nearly as much English as he thought he did. I've forgotten his name. He kept on saying "World Wide Web." That's about all I caught from him, but he seemed pretty enthusiastic about it. He'd been one of the guys in the canoes, I think. He talked at me until Innes came back, and then he got shy and left.

It felt like it should be dark and cool and all of us sitting around a bonfire or something, but it was more like a Sunday afternoon cookout, where after a while people start to drift off complaining that they have to work the next day. Most of them walked back to the city, but some of them just took their blankets into the shade and went to sleep. Eventually Innes told the old men who were still up talking that we had to leave too, and they stood up and bowed while I nodded and waved and tried to keep from swaying.

On the way back to the general's house I asked Innes how she had known when the festival was supposed to start. She didn't have a watch, and I had yet to see a clock. She said once she'd had word that I was going to be on the next zeppelin she'd scheduled it for after my first sleep.

I thought she was joking at first. I told her no one had ever thrown a holiday for me before. She laughed and said there was going to be a holiday anyway. She said those sorts of things were more flexible here.

I asked her if she was a princess. I didn't mean to put it quite that way, but I was a little drunk and I said it without thinking. She asked me not to think of her that way. "I'm successful in my own right," she said. "The women of Pellucidar are all strong—they must be, to survive—but until recently it was rare for them to be independent. Men here still hear their grandfathers talk of their grandmothers as property, and they do not know how to act.

"This is what we give to the peoples we bring into the Empire, along with peace and prosperity. Of course there is benefit for us, but we give back as much as we take. Those who prosper under the old ways still fight us, but they will lose. Do you understand?"

I told her I did. How could I say no? She sounded so proud, and I wanted to kiss her smile.

The next day—well, I don't know if it was a day or not, but anyway after I'd slept—I woke up before Innes. I put on my leg and some clothes and went down into the courtyard. MacArthur came over to say hi, and I sat down in the sun and pet him for a while. He was a big, scary-looking dog, but really sweet. He acted like a puppy. I didn't realize that the Gr-gr gardener was there until something moved in the flowerbed across from me. I was so startled that I stood up, and banged my prosthetic against my chair in the process.

The Gr-gr glanced up and then he bowed. He sort of whined and then said something in Pellucidarean. To tell you the truth, I don't even know if it was male or female. I tried to tell him everything was OK, he had just startled me, but I guess he didn't know any English. He stood there avoiding my eyes. His face was so sad, that long muzzle with the thin lips curved down, and his big brown frightened eyes. Finally he pointed at the sky and grunted something. Then he went back to work, stretching a fine net out over the bed of flowers. I thought about offering to help, but I wouldn't have known what I was doing, and the Gr-gr wouldn't have been able to tell me.

I went looking for food, but no one had told me where the kitchen was, and I ended up wandering into the general's office. It was on the cliff side of the house, with high open windows letting in the sun. He was sitting at a desk behind a computer, speaking into a headset. He looked surprised to see me, but he smiled and motioned for me to wait.

After a minute he took off his headset, and I asked him how the fight was going. He said his troops were burning out a bunch of tree-dwellers beyond the Sojar Az. They had refused to come to terms, he said. "Some enemies just need the right incentive to become allies, and some will never stop fighting until one of you is dead."

I wonder now who he was thinking of when he said that. Might have been you. But then, you're not fighting anymore, are you? I know who I thought of—the terrorists who made the bomb that took my leg. Except I guess not everyone calls them terrorists. The further I get from the war and the news and everything, the harder it is for me to understand it. First there were bad Iraqis and good Iraqis, and the terrorists were part of this movement that was sort of Iraqi and sort of not. Then the good and bad Iraqis started fighting each other until it was hard to tell them apart. I mean, an insurgent can be a lot of things. I looked it up. You could call Fidel Castro an insurgent, or George Washington, and there's a lot of difference between them. At least I think there is.

I didn't know what to say to the general. I told him I was looking for the kitchens, and before I knew it he was ringing for a cook and ordering a meal for both of us. My last meal with the general hadn't gone well, but I didn't see any way of escaping. Luckily he had more calls to make, so I just sat next to the windows while we waited for the food to come. Outside it was just the same. Sun and stone. There were insects everywhere, floating in and out the windows like commuters. Flies as big as my thumb, and mosquitoes like giant staples twisted up and glued together. Huge dragonflies were patrolling the cliff, hunting the smaller bugs. Innes had pointed out the dragonfly hatchery on the way to the festival, but I hadn't really understood the need for such a thing then.

When the food came the general got off his phone, or whatever it was. The food was a kind of salad with berries and nuts. The general asked me what I thought, and I told him I liked it, but he said he didn't mean the salad. Then I was confused because I didn't know if he meant his daughter, or the city, or Pellucidar itself.

"They're soft," he said when I didn't answer. "We're all soft, here at home. Our boys are fighting six different wars right now, but they're so far away that no one here pays much attention. We've lost a hundred and fourteen men this storm." He pushed his salad away. "Their families understand a piece of it. But the festivals . . . my daughter doesn't understand either, I'm afraid. She's proud—everybody's proud—but to them it's just something that happens, not something that people do. Do you understand?"

I told him I did.

He said it wasn't that long ago that they were all warriors. Before the Empire, humans were low on the food chain: slaves to some, prey to others. Even with the compulsory draft, the younger generation was starting to forget that. Some of them had begun to question the need for war.

"Even that word, 'need,'" the General said. "That word is the wrong frame to put it in. War isn't something people need; it's something we can't avoid. It's what we do. That being the case, it's imperative to be on the winning side, and not allow enemies—existing or potential—the opportunity to gather strength."

Just like at the dinner, earlier, the general wasn't really saying anything I hadn't heard before. But the perspective was all skewed. I asked him what they would do once they had conquered all of the interior earth. He smiled and asked me if I was afraid they would invade the surface. Then he laughed and said he had to be on his way—he was headed to the front, to the caves of the Skull-Drinkers, and he had to be off the ground before the storm came. He said I should wake Innes and tell her Sun Tzu would arrive soon.

Sun Tzu turned out to be the name of a storm. I guess most of them are named after generals and that sort of thing.

The general hadn't mentioned that we would have to storm-proof the house before the storm got there. Innes showed me to the room where they kept the storm shutters. They were these massive, light-weight steel sheets that hooked to the outsides of the uncovered windows. The guards helped us hang them, and it didn't take as long as I'd expected. The courtyard stayed uncovered, but Innes pointed out drains which she said led to the storm sewers. We helped the gardener clear them of leaves. He had already finished covering most of the garden with those fine nets. Innes said they were hail protection for the less hardy plants.

By the time we finished up and moved inside the sky had begun to get dark for the first time since I'd arrived. The gardener shuffled off to his own room somewhere, and the guards settled in at the front of the house. MacArthur came with us.

Sitting in Innes's bedroom with fat, scented candles, the thunder came muffled through the shutters. MacArthur seemed nervous, and Innes wasn't much better. When I was stationed in Germany I bunked for a while with a guy from California who freaked out every time there was a thunderstorm. Innes was kind of acting like that, so I did what I used to do; I took some playing cards out of my duffel. She didn't know how to play anything, really, so I tried to teach her Hearts. I don't really think she got it, but it kept her distracted for a little while, until the storm was right on top of us.

The rain hit first, like a staticky radio being tapped against the steel. Then hail, a thousand little hammerfalls in a minute, an hour, a second. I kept wishing I had a clock to look at, to keep track of how long the storm lasted. Innes moved closer to me, and I put my arms around her. After a while we lay down together. I took off my leg and kissed her to distract her from the thunder. It felt like my heart pounding out of the sky. She was shaking. I might have spent an hour undressing her; it might have been a day. MacArthur sighed and moved into the closet.

The storm was still going strong when we finished. I held her against me, hoping she would sleep, but I drifted off and woke up to find her pacing the floor in a robe. The sheets under me were wet with sweat. The rain outside seemed to compress the house, making the inside like a sauna.

I sat up and asked her how long the storm would last. She just shrugged and said I should ask a meteorologist. I decided she was grouchy because she was afraid, and I didn't really know what to say to her. I thought I'd just be there, and listen if she wanted to talk.

I just realized—that's sort of what Kilgore does for you, isn't it? He sits and listens to you, or receives you or whatever you call the telepathic thing, and then you feel better . . . maybe. When they captured you, when they blinded you, did you have anyone like him to talk to then? Were you afraid? Maybe you don't feel those things. Maybe Mahars don't, or maybe you in particular don't. I mean, that bomb . . . but we drop bombs, too.

If you are like us, do I have to stop using the word "human" for feelings like that? For being afraid, for needing comfort? For giving it? Kilgore does it. He's not human.

Anyway, we waited it out. It seemed like a long time, but time can drag when you're trying to figure out what to do. Eventually the rain started to let up, and the thunder moved off. Then Innes started to relax. She asked me if I wanted to go away with her to their place in the country. School would be in recess until the next storm, and at the cabin we could hunt and swim. MacArthur could come along.

I looked at the stump of my left leg and thought about telling her I wasn't sure I could do it. I wasn't, at all, but I didn't want to admit it. The streets of Sari were bricked, and uneven in spots, but I hadn't fallen yet. I didn't want to fall in front of Innes. But there were no stegosaurus in the city, so I said yes.

You know, I think that was our best moment. She talked about the cabin and how her ma used to love it, and how she missed her ma, and I talked about my parents, and we both ended up crying. It was kind of embarrassing, but it was good. I felt good.

We talked until the storm had passed, and then we slept, and when we woke up most of the house was already unsealed. We helped the guards and gardener finish the last of it. The green outside was brighter than before, which I wouldn't have believed possible. The sun had already lifted most of the rain into the air, where it hung like a rich, blunt perfume.

There's a—funicular? I think that's the word—that runs from Sari down to the train station. It was a nice view of the valley, but MacArthur wouldn't sit still. He kept trying to get out. Innes said he'd ridden down in it a hundred times, and he did that every time. He just didn't understand what was happening. I was a little freaked out by the view myself. The storm had left behind nothing but clear blue sky; I couldn't see where the ground started to curve up, but it was so vast . . . there were distant mountains on either side, and a huge body of water beyond the gap, and beyond that a stain of darkness. I looked up and saw that there was a sort of a moon hanging there between the sun and that part of the world.

I think, if I hadn't been trying to calm MacArthur down, I might have had a panic attack right there. The world hadn't seemed that *real* to me since before—maybe it never had. That little glass chamber, it reminded me of the interrogation room in my dreams. I had the feeling that this inside world was looking back at me somehow. Like it was waiting for me to do something, or learn something, that Sari and Innes and the general couldn't teach me.

Innes has her own train. Or maybe it's her father's, I'm not sure. It runs on solar power just like everything else. Has her own chef, porter, guards, an engineer, a car for lounging and dining, and another one for sleeping. Carved wood paneling, leather seats, climate-control. We settled in and the porter brought drinks for us and bones for MacArthur. He kept on bowing and stuff.

Innes talked to the engineer about where we were headed while I stared out the window. There was another train on the next track, eight cars long, and a bunch of young guys were climbing on with duffels and rifles. Soldiers on their way to the front, I guessed. Dark skinned boys, and buffalo men, and others that I couldn't really classify.

They were still loading up when we pulled out. Innes said the trains can top 200 miles an hour, but they have to be careful out away from the cities, because of the megafauna. They've put up these wilderness overpasses every few miles, so the animals can get around without worrying about the train, but I guess when something big decides it wants to cross the tracks, it just does it. I saw some of them, things called *dyryths*, sort of a cross between a bear and a ground sloth. A mother and her two cubs. The mother was at least twelve feet high, and she had dragged herself up a tree, then pulled the branches back down so her cubs could reach the leaves.

I asked Innes how far we were going, and would we be close to the borders of the Empire, to the frontier? She laughed and said we were a long way from the frontier—twelve hundred miles at the nearest. The interior earth held more than twice the land area of the surface, because the seas were only about one-fifth of the surface here. She said most of the interior was still unexplored. So far the Empire had discovered cannibal kingdoms, tribes of men with wings like bats, and mastodons with almost human intelligence. They were all citizens of the Empire now, Innes told me. I couldn't help thinking about what the general had said about her not understanding.

We rode along the coast for a while—Innes told me that the bay opened onto the Lural Az, one of their oceans. The chef served us this blackened fish grilled with fruit. I don't usually like fish all that much, but it was kind of amazing. It didn't sit very well, though. Innes did some work while I spent the trip limping back and forth between the restroom and the observation deck.

We passed over hills and plains and past swamps and rivers to a lonely little outpost next to a lake. The train pulled off onto a sidetrack, next to a little crew house. The cabin was on the lakeshore, Innes said, and assured me that the lake was safe. The *azdryths* had been hunted out. I decided that *azdryths* were probably not long-necked leopards after all.

We took the path towards the lake while the crew moved into their own quarters. The cabins were spread out along a ridge, half-hidden by trees and gardens. A high, electrified fence lined the path and extended around the other side of the ridge, out of sight.

MacArthur ran ahead, and we followed him to one of the larger cabins. It was like a miniature of the General's house; one story high, but with a courtyard at the center.

Innes asked me if I liked it, and I said yes. I wanted to ask if there was a cook and a gardener here too, but I kept my mouth shut. The train had put me in a bad mood. Innes asked me if I was tired, and she kissed me when I shrugged. Part of me wanted her to get away from me, but once she got started there was no chance of that part winning out.

Afterwards Innes announced that she was hungry and took some rifles out of a bag. She handed me a rifle and a box of shells and took me out hunting *thag*. I told her I'd never hunted before, but she said just to follow her lead and not make any noise.

There was a gate in the fence behind the cabin, and Innes led the way through it and down the ridge. The slope was a little bit tricky, but I took it slow and managed to get down without falling.

There was a herd of *thag* browsing the vegetation in the valley below. They were shaggy and horned like the sheep-creatures I had imagined that night in the Interior Air terminal, but they were half again the size of a buffalo, and they weren't docile. I found that out right away when we were settling in at the edge of the tree line with our rifles. I stepped on a dry branch with my artificial leg, and the twig snapped. The sound echoed through the valley, but the *thags* knew exactly where it had come from. The nearest one lifted its head and charged.

Innes ran back up the ridge, but I knew I couldn't keep up with her, so I stayed where I was. My leg didn't slow down my shooting, so I might as well try to slow the thing down. It was hard to miss. I fired one barrel into its shoulder, and the other into its chest, and then it was nearly on top of me.

I wonder how different you are from us. Does adrenaline pump into your system when you're in danger? People always ask about fear when they hear stories like this. Were you afraid? There's never time to be afraid; you just react. Even running away is just instinct. The difference is that if you're trained, you have another way to react. It doesn't necessarily mean you're going to survive. But you might not panic. You might use the flood of adrenaline to sharpen what you hear and smell, and you might learn something, and you might not get killed.

The thing is, if instinct and something else—like pain, like knowing that you can't do what you were trained to do back in the day because of the leg you lost—if those two things are at odds, you might freeze.

The *thag* had a good three feet and probably a ton and a half on me. I should have run, I decided, but it was too late. Instead I just fell down. I dropped onto the grass and hoped it would charge over me without crushing me.

Then MacArthur growled and when I looked up I saw the two of them, *hyaenodon* and *thag*, tangled in a heap not four feet to my right. Innes pulled at my arm, and we started back up the ridge. I forgot the rifle. Innes shoved me through the gate and called for MacArthur, but it was too late.

The *hyaenodon* was no match for the *thag* in size; it just rolled over while MacArthur's teeth were locked at its throat. MacArthur's body—all but his jaws—went limp. The *thag* shambled back and forth trying to dislodge him. It head-butted a tree and brought it crashing down, then charged up the ridge towards us. I backed up a step, and Innes slammed the gate shut.

The *thag* and the wires made deep indentations in each other while sparks flew. I could smell burnt fur. MacArthur twitched and let go of the *thag* to writhe in the high grass. For a second I thought he might still be alive.

Then three quick shots rang out. The *thag* slumped backwards, and its mouth worked, but it made no sound. It fell back to lie next to the *hyaenodon*.

I put my hand on Innes's shoulder, thinking I would say something comforting, but she only stood there for a moment before she opened the gate. She took out a long knife and began cutting into the *thag*.

That's when I met Kilgore. He was the one that had killed the *thag*, finally. Not me or poor MacArthur. When he dropped out of the trees, right behind Innes, I screamed—I didn't shout, I screamed. You know what a Sagoth looks like, but I didn't. He's a gorilla, pretty much, only not quite as thick-set, and he walks upright like a human. Not like the Gr-grs, either; his fur is dark, and he doesn't have the long muzzle.

He spoke perfect English. He said he was the game warden there, and he'd heard the shooting and come to see if we needed any assistance.

Innes was slicing at the *thag*'s flanks and placing the chunks of meat in a bag. I thought she was crying, but I couldn't tell. She thanked Kilgore, but she didn't sound very grateful.

I felt like shit. I can't walk right, so her dog dies, and I can't help being glad it wasn't me. As if my life meant more, because he was a dog. A *hyaenodon*. Scared of a funicular but not an angry bull five times its size. It didn't make sense. Innes must have been so angry, but she wouldn't show it. After she cut a few steaks from the *thag* she told Kilgore to take care of the rest. She still hadn't looked at him.

He asked her what she would like for him to do with MacArthur. She told Kilgore to bury him, and started back towards the cabin. I started to follow, but Kilgore called me back. He held up the rifle I had left and passed it to me. I thanked him and held out my hand to shake his. He smiled and said that was an American custom, and I said yes, I was an American. He nodded as if that was obvious to anyone.

When I got back to the cabin, I asked Innes if we should invite Kilgore to eat with us. It was like I'd suggested we have MacArthur for breakfast. She actually said, "You can eat with him if you like." Then she went back to carving up steaks.

I know she was upset, that she probably blamed me for MacArthur, but I couldn't understand why she would talk about Kilgore like that when he'd saved our lives. It made me think of the gardener whom she'd never acknowledged, of the chef and the porter and the guards. That feeling I'd had in Sari, that all the different sorts of people there were equal parts of something big and important and better, Innes made that into a lie with that one sentence. I almost asked her when she would require my services in the bedroom, but instead I left.

Clouds had come up over the horizon, and they screened the light of the sun, but not the heat. I started walking around the lake. There was a path, but it was wet and muddy, and weeds had grown up around it in spots. There were more giant dragonflies there, bigger than the ones in the mountains. Four-foot wingspans, I'd guess; but there were so many gnats and mosquitoes that the dragonflies must have been overworked. By the time I stopped being blind pissed I was a sweaty mass of bug bait. I kept thinking that the sun would be going down soon, and then I'd remember that it wouldn't, not ever.

Other girlfriends, sometimes I'd just leave them alone for a couple of days if I got angry, and sometimes it would be OK. There wasn't any way to do that this time. I couldn't take the train without Innes, and probably not an Interior Air flight either, so I kept on walking.

It must not have taken as long to circle the lake as I'd thought, because when I walked back into the cabin it was like I hadn't left. Innes told me dinner was ready and my boots were muddy. I took them off. I almost threw them at her. I almost threw the whole damn leg at her, but I stopped myself and told her I was sorry about MacArthur.

It wasn't your fault, she told me.

It wasn't Kilgore's, either, I said. I told her I didn't like the way she'd treated him. She told me I didn't understand, and I said OK; explain it to me, then.

She said Kilgore was an employee and not a friend. He was a Sagoth, too, and there was a history there. I told her I wanted to hear it.

So she told me about you. Your people, anyway. The Mahars. Flying lizard-men, eight feet tall, with bony ridges running down the spine. Lizard-women, I mean. Dinosaur women. You're not as terrifying as she made you sound. She said you used to rule over this part of Pellucidar, that you had dozens of underground cities with thousands of Mahars, Sagoth servants, and human slaves. Until David Innes came and led the humans against you. Drove you out of your cities and sent you on the run. One of the ruined cities was nearby, she said, down one of the hiking trails. Mistra. This place.

Innes said the Empire left your people alone after that, until a generation ago, when you started bombing Imperial cities. Train stations and restaurants and government buildings. Some of the bombings were airborne, and some of those were suicide flights. Some of them were on the ground, and since there was no way for a Mahar to walk into a human city without help, it was obvious that someone was helping you. She said you can't even speak human language without Sagoths to translate. Only a few Sagoths were caught working with you, but they suspected that there were more.

She said the Empire wiped out the Mahars. They arrested the Sagoth collaborators first, and used focused interrogations to find out where you were hiding. Then they raided your nests and finished you off. It was the only way to do it, she said. The bombings stopped, and the Sagoths were banned from the cities.

I had no reason not to believe Innes's story, but it bothered me. I didn't understand why, for one reason. I mean, I don't like bombs, no matter who's using them or why. We use bombs in Iraq, and we've used bombs before that, and maybe it's wrong of me to criticize. But I don't like it. And if you . . . you shouldn't have done it. But you also had a reason, and Innes left that out.

Later on Kilgore told me a lot of things that Innes's story didn't cover. The Empire didn't just round up Sagoth collaborators; they rounded up all the Sagoths and put them in camps. What Innes called focused interrogations, Kilgore called random torture. He'd been a child, but he remembered them taking his father away and bringing him back broken. That was the word Kilgore used. His father had owned a successful painting business in Sari, but the Empire took that away. His father died in the camps.

He told me the reason, too. The reason for the attacks. The books, the ones with the instructions for your reproduction. Parthenogenesis, Kilgore called it. The Empire had taken them away, and they wouldn't give them back. You were dying out, slowly, and you had nothing to negotiate with, nothing to offer them but an end to the bombings.

Did you really think that would work? I mean, you kill a few hundred people, a few thousand, you think they're going to decide to give you what you want? I'm not saying they should have taken it away, but . . . could you have learned to live without slaves? Without humans for meat? That's what they needed to believe, and you weren't doing anything to convince them. Maybe this is all evolution. You adapted to losing your males, but when the humans rose up you didn't adapt. You didn't learn.

I didn't know all of that then. I don't think Innes thought she was lying. I think she left out the details because she thought they made it all too confusing, the same way she left out all the details about her family and where she lived back when we were emailing each other. But I didn't know that then. I listened to her explanations about Kilgore and the Sagoths and I decided there was more to the political situation here, the history, than I had a grasp on. That hadn't stopped Innes and the General from making comments about Iraq and the US, but I decided I wasn't going to play that game with her.

The *thag* steak was excellent; a bit bloody, with a salty aftertaste like it had been marinated. After the steak and the wine and the fight I was about as relaxed as I'd been since arriving. Innes loosened up, too, and told stories about MacArthur when he was a puppy. She cried a little, but quiet, like she didn't want me to know. We moved to a hammock and talked until we fell asleep. When we woke up we fucked in that half-asleep way, and then we went hunting again.

It felt like we'd gotten through something difficult, like we'd turned some kind of a corner, and for a little while it was good. We ate and drank and talked and fucked and swam and killed *thag*. I let Innes take the lead on the hunts. She never made a sound until she had a clear shot, and she never missed. I brought down a few myself. It felt good to shoot, to feel that kick against my shoulder. I was learning to stand on the new leg in ways that concrete and carpet hadn't taught me. One day we went out on the hiking trail Innes had mentioned, and I kept up pretty well. We didn't go to the ruins, although she pointed them out from an overlook. Two granite towers flanking a staircase leading underground. One of the towers had broken halfway along its height and collapsed, but the other was at least seventy feet high.

Whenever we were out Kilgore would bring in cuts from the latest beast we had killed, until there was enough meat in the solar-powered freezer to feed a battalion. I'm sure he kept an eye out while we were hunting, too, but he stayed out of sight.

I guess I could have measured the time by kills, or bottles of wine, or the number of times we had sex, but in my mind it all runs together until the moment I saw the duckbills.

We were down in the *thag* canyon; the herd was gathered at the far end, nearer the lake at the base of the cliff opposite. Some of the calves were chasing each other along the shore, splashing in the shallows. Innes and I leaned against a fallen tree and watched. We didn't talk. There was a lot of other noise—the insects, the birds, the *thag* bellowing—but if I closed my eyes I could pretend that my breath was just the air moving. I wanted to tell Innes not to break the quiet, but that would have defeated the purpose.

Then there was this honking that came bouncing off the stone and the water. The *thag* got really agitated and started bellowing all at once. I opened my eyes and saw that the herd was circling, and some of the larger bulls were moving to the spot where the valley narrowed. A group of brown and tan dinosaurs were there, bending down to snatch up huge swaths of the long grass, then straightening up on their hind legs to look out beyond the angry *thag*. The dinosaurs had thick bills, with orange-and-black lumps above them. Enlarged sinuses, maybe. I figured that was where the honking came from.

Once the *thag* had crowded around the calves and the weaker ones, the bulls charged the newcomers. The duckbills were three times the size of the *thag*, I'd say, but every time one of them was challenged it would retreat around the bend. Mostly the duckbills seemed interested in grabbing up as much grass as they could before they were chased off, and they were mowing down a fair amount of it in a short time.

So I'm sitting there watching this, and Innes stands up and says she's tired, we should head back. I just looked at her. These are the first dinosaurs I've ever seen, and she's tired.

I told her I wanted to watch for a while. She said they were just *gryps* doing what *gryps* did, but it was fine if I wanted to watch. I hate to admit it, but she was kind of right. The *gryps* teased the *thag* for a while and then slunk back around the bend. Still. That was the first time I wished I had a camera with me here.

That changed things for me. Here I was in this world with so much more possibility than my own, and I was seeing it from the inside of a fence. So I've seen a duckbilled dinosaur; I still haven't seen a stegosaurus, or an allosaurus, or a brachiosaur. When I told Innes later that I wanted to see more dinosaurs, she told me I didn't. She said dinosaurs either tried to eat you or they just stood around eating plants. One was too much excitement and the other was none at all. It wasn't worth the trip, and besides, Eisenhower—another storm—was on its way, and she'd have to be back in Sari soon.

I didn't want to go back to Sari, but that had become one more in a long list of things we didn't bring up. When I thought about that list, that's when I realized that it wasn't going to work between us. It wasn't any one big thing. The sex was still great, and we didn't say any more stupid things. At least nothing *really* stupid. We all say stupid things sometimes, right? And that was the problem, in a way—I think, at the start, she'd had her guard down most of the way, and then she saw that she was upsetting me, so she started being careful about what she said. I think you can only get so far that way. I was doing it, too. I wanted to talk about things like the Sagoths and the Gr-grs and politics and war, but then I would think about all the ways that conversation could go badly. If it did come up Innes would change the subject or say she didn't know enough about it. That expression she'd worn on the website, where she'd looked so intense and challenging, I had yet to see it in person. I guess it was just a look.

I could have pushed it, I know, but the truth is I wasn't sure we were worth the energy. It seemed pretty clear that we had gone about as far as we were going to go. I would go back home, after a week or a year, and we would email for a while and that would be it.

I was thinking about that one day when I went out for a walk along the fence. Innes had fallen asleep, and my legs—the one I still had, and the phantom one—were restless. I had walked to the hiking trail and was on my way back when Kilgore showed up. He told me that some *thipdars* had been spotted in the area, so I should watch the skies. He said *thipdars* were what I might know as pteranadons, winged dinosaurs, and so the fence would be no deterrent to them.

I thanked him for the warning, and then I asked him where he lived. None of the cabins seemed quite right for a game warden. He gave me sort of an appraising look and told me that he lived here in the ruins. His ancestors had lived here, he said, and it was a part of his legacy. I think he was talking about you, but I didn't know that then. When I asked him if he lived alone he just said he didn't have a wife.

It hit me then that he was probably very young. His fur was dark and shiny, and he was all muscle; not an ounce of fat anywhere. When he stood silent he looked very serious and stern, but when he spoke—I couldn't help thinking, *It's a talking gorilla!* but I never said that—he was very friendly and even funny.

I asked him if he'd ever done any work as a wilderness guide. I was thinking about Drak's invitation to visit his ranch. It was probably too far to travel on foot, but I was feeling stronger. The artificial leg will never be a part of me, but it's not just dead weight either. It's predictable, to an extent. I can usually tell if it's going to slide or turn or twist. I've even run on it a little bit. Anyway, Kilgore said he hadn't done a lot of that sort of work. He'd lived in Sari, before. He'd studied English and engineering at the same college where Innes taught. He asked me about some writers I'd never heard of before, and I had to tell him I didn't pay that much attention to the names on the covers. I just liked good stories.

Anyway, when I got back to the cabin Innes was packing. Eisen-hower was passing over Sari, she said, and she had to go back to teach class. I could go with her if I wanted to, or she could send the train back for me in a few days.

I think we both wanted the same thing. I said maybe we should spend a little time apart, and she said that might be a good idea. There were all sorts of things that I thought of to say then, and maybe she did too, but neither of us did.

I walked her to the train. I thought about MacArthur, but I didn't think apologizing for that again would make her like me any better. We kissed for a long time, and then she climbed on. I waved from the platform while they zoomed away.

When I got back to the cabin I stood in the courtyard and squinted up at the sun, and I thought about all the undiscovered people on the other side of it, living lives that were quiet or dangerous or alien or all of them at the same time. I thought about the general, determined to give them solar power and equality and trains, or else.

After that I kind of freaked out, like I was saying before. I had that panic attack. If I just think about the other side of the sun I start shak-ing. It was like I'd seen something big for the first time. Something that had been there all my life, but I'd never looked at it straight on. I'd kept myself from seeing it all, because it was too much to take in at once.

When I woke up I decided to hike over here and see if I could find Kilgore. I took the rifle and a canteen and some jerky, but otherwise I packed pretty light. I wasn't planning to stay. I wasn't really thinking. I remember pretending that MacArthur was with me, a big ghostly dog running on ahead, then coming back to make sure I was following.

I didn't expect these ruins to be so big. On the surface it's just those steps and the towers—it almost looks like a mausoleum. Once I got down inside, though, I got lost right away. Innes told me that all Pellucidareans have this directional sense that leads them back home no matter where they go. I was wishing I had that, so I could find my way back out. I wandered through passages and down stairs, past dark rooms, even through something like an arena or an amphitheater. The sunlight shone straight down through airshafts that sank deep into the city, but it was cool in the shade, and the staircases were wide and dusty.

This was your home, right? It must have been so different, then; crowded with Mahars and Sagoths and slaves. It's the slavery that's

278

really upsetting, you know. I almost wonder if I should explain it to you, the history of it, but mostly I feel like you should just know better. It's just so goddamned obvious. You shouldn't have to be taught about the value of. . . .

I was going to say "human life." I guess it's not just that, anymore.

Anyway, I was lost, and then I heard Kilgore's voice below, speaking Pellucidarean. I've only learned a few words, but the rhythm of it is pretty easy to recognize. I followed his voice down, and it got louder and louder until I turned down that passage and came into this little room and found him talking to you.

He must have heard me at the last second, because he was out of the chair and reaching for his rifle. But he froze when he saw me, just like I froze when I saw you. I . . . it's hard to look at what they did to you. I knew you must be a Mahar right away, but I wasn't thinking that. Honestly, my first thought was that this was a monster. You just look like something that should be killed. The mutilation, that's something else. But maybe you deserved it. I don't know how many people you killed with the bomb you dropped, but it was probably a lot. I mean, it's not anything extraordinary, right? They did it to all the Mahar prisoners. It's the only way they can stop you from hypnotizing them. It's not out of cruelty.

Anyway, when I walked in here Kilgore was talking to you and feeding you raw *thag*. He's the only one you can talk to, isn't he? Some kind of telepathic thing, he said. He stood right there and told me you dropped that bomb, and the way he said it—it was like he felt sorry for *you*.

I still had the rifle. I could have shot you both. But the way he just blurted that out, without being asked . . . I asked him if he had helped you with the bomb, and he told me about the camps, and the books. He said his grandfather lived in this city when it belonged to the Mahars. His grandfather had hated the humans. When he got too old to serve the Mahars, he died for them.

I knew what he meant. His grandfather had been one of the suicide bombers.

I don't know if you were aware of the fight. I set the rifle down first. I was still making decisions. I threw that first punch hoping to lose control, hoping to feel that rush, like in the dreams. I thought if I lost control for a while, maybe the anger would leave me alone, but that's not what happened. I hit Kilgore a couple of times and then he put me in a hug I couldn't get out of. He was so fast—I could never have landed a punch if he hadn't let me. I kicked and I squirmed but I couldn't break his hold. He didn't even move his feet. That helped. It reminded me that I wasn't the strongest around.

When I was calm Kilgore sat me down and told me about his family, about you. He said you must have escaped from the humans and found your way back here. I guess you have that homing instinct, too. I can't imagine you stumbling blind through the wilderness, knowing that you were dead if anyone spotted you. I can't imagine how you kept going. Kilgore said you went a little crazy, you were so afraid.

He said at first he fed you and helped you because he wanted to understand. Not just you, but his grandfather, too, and the humans. I asked him if he understands, now.

"I think it has to do with fear," he said. "She is afraid all the time, now, and I think my grandfather was the same. Afraid to die and be forgotten, most of all."

I asked him why he was still helping you, and he said:

"Because she is alive."

Look at my hands; I've been making the fists again. The dreams are back. When I first got to this secret world, I wanted to stay. It was a vacation from my life—I thought I could escape myself if I stayed here. Was I ever wrong.

Then I saw you, and I wondered if I should kill you. Hit you back. No one would even know if you were dead, would they? There's no home to ship you back to. When Kilgore was holding me I told him I was going to kill you both, and he asked me what I would do afterwards. He asked it like he and you were both already dead, like I was talking to a ghost. I didn't have an answer for him. It's just that sometimes fighting seems like the only way to get anything across.

We're going to take you with us. Kilgore and I. We're going to try and find Drak's ranch—I have a feeling he might listen. If he won't, we'll go somewhere else. Innes said they've only explored about a third of this world. Maybe there are more Mahars living somewhere in the other two-thirds.

Kilgore's gathering the supplies we'll need. Food, ammunition, and some way to hide you. He says we should be able to steer around the towns along the way, but we have to be prepared for predators and stampeding herbivores.

I'm not stupid. But I'm not afraid. I left a note for Innes, told her I was going out with Kilgore to look for the stegosaurus herds and I wouldn't be coming back.

It's not a lie.

I know I might not be up for this. We could die out there. Or we could live forever. Maybe we'll be like that war the general is fighting— if the sun never sets on us, are we endless or just a day long?

Jon Bassoff is a writer of noir. His novels include Corrosion, Factory Town, *and* The Incurables. *According to* New York Magazine *Bassoff's writing "confronts directly the traumatic stress disorder of our world today and tears off its mask, even if the face must follow."*

Bassoff's first novel, Corrosion, *was published by Darkfuse in 2013. It is a horror story about a disfigured veteran. It has been compared to the works of Jim Thompson and David Lynch, which seems just about right.*

excerpt from CORROSION
JON BASSOFF

Chapter 1

i was less than twenty miles from the Mountain when the engine gave out, smoke billowed from the hood, and Red Sovine stopped singing. I kept on pushing the old pickup for a while, but it was no use. She'd let me down good this time. Without warning, even. I pulled her off to the side of the highway, kicked open the door, and cursed at the wind. I stared down the cracked highway; a backwater town was just up ahead, surrounded by derricks and grain elevators. I grabbed my army-issued duffel bag from the back, pulled on my camouflage jacket, and started limping down the asphalt.

The town was called Stratton, and it wasn't much. Just brick buildings and rotting bungalows and poor man shacks all dropped haphazardly by God after a two-week bender. Old Main was hanging on for dear life. An abandoned convenience store, abandoned gas station, abandoned motel. Rusted signs and boarded-up windows.

The wind was blowing hard and mean; I pulled up the collar of my jacket and buried my hands in my pockets. I caught a glimpse of myself in a darkened window and shivered. It was a face that I still didn't recognize. A face that appeared to have been molded by the devil himself. . . .

Twelve hours on the road and I was in bad need of a drink. At the corner of the block stood a white stucco building with the words Del's

Lounge hand painted in red, a neon Bud sign glowing in a submarine window. I went inside.

The floor was concrete and the tables were wooden. There was a pool table with torn blue felt, and a jukebox, twenty years old at least. A burly fellow with a red handlebar mustache sat at the counter drinking from a Coors can, his overalls smeared with paint or blood, while an old man with a rosacea nose sat in a vinyl booth, arms cradling a tumbler of bourbon. The bartender—a skinny man with sickly yellow hair and liver spotted-hands—whistled a nameless tune and wiped down the counter lethargically. Head down, floor creaking, I walked across the room and sat at a corner table, back to the bar. I placed my bag on the floor and stuck a pinch of snuff between my gums and lower lip. After a few minutes, I heard footsteps. I didn't turn around. The bartender stood right behind me and asked me what I wanted, his voice all full of barbed wire.

Bottle of beer, I said. Cold.

Doncha want some food? We got hamburgers and hot dogs and the best barbecue pork in town.

All I wanted was the beer, but he moved so that he was in front of me and handed me a menu, and then he saw my face and said, Ah, Jesus. It was an involuntary reaction.

Just a beer, I said again.

He muttered an apology and walked back to the bar and everybody was looking—the same curious bystanders who watch in disguised glee every time there is a car wreck on the highway or a shooting outside a nightclub. I stared straight ahead, tapping the table with my fingers. The jukebox creaked into action and Merle Haggard started singing, but the speakers were busted and his voice was warbled, drunken.

The bartender came back a few minutes later with my beer. He could've left me alone, but he wanted to prove he wasn't frightened of me. He just stood there, jaw slack. He had a full set of bottom teeth, but nothing on the top. I could smell his breath, a strange combination of bourbon and candy canes. So, uh, what's your business here in Stratton? he said.

I cleared my throat. No business. How much do I owe you?

You don't owe me a penny. Drink's on the house.

I was used to it. I made a living off other people's pity. They'd bury me in a Potter's Field.

I took a long drink and wiped my mouth with my sleeve. I'm looking for a place to stay, I said. Some place cheap.

The bartender smiled slyly. Everything is cheap in this town, he said, but the Hotel Paisano is cheaper than most. Just a few blocks down on Third.

Much obliged, I said.

I drank my beer and then another and another and then I heard a car pull up outside, the engine growling. The door slammed and I could hear a man and woman arguing outside, and the sound of a bottle shattering on the asphalt. The man shouting Goddamn slut, you are!

A moment later, the door opened and a woman walked inside. She wasn't very pretty, but that sort of thing never mattered to me. She was tall and skinny with bright red hair swooped up in a sort of beehive. Her face was pale and her nose was crooked. She had a stud in her lip and a tattoo of Betty Page on her arm. She wore red boots and cut-off jeans and a Misfits t-shirt.

She stomped her way up to the bar and plopped down on a stool. Got Maker's Mark? she asked the bartender.

He wiped the sweat from his forehead and nodded. Yes, ma'am. How do you drink it?

Quickly, she said. And give me a Michelob, too.

The bartender pulled out a heavy looking glass, poured a fistful of whiskey, and popped open a bottle of beer. She raised the glass and made a toast to all the bastards in the world before slugging it down. Then she coughed and grimaced and reached for the beer. I was hooked.

Not two moments later the man came charging in. He wore cowboy boots and tight blue jeans and a heavy flannel. His face was bloated and red, his mustache thick and gray. He was twice as old as the girl, easy.

He wanted her out of the bar and he said so, but she wasn't having any of it. Fuck you, she said. You're not my keeper.

This man strode to the counter with more than a little purpose. He yanked the beer out of her hand and slammed it hard on the counter. The fellow with the bloodstained overalls rose to his feet and took a couple of cautious steps back. The bartender said, Now, just take it easy, mister. We don't want no trouble here. Me, I watched from a distance, seeing how it would all play out, because I wasn't a violent man except when I had to be. . . .

Let's get out of here, you goddamn whore, the man said and you could tell he meant business. She tried pulling away, and that's when he got rough with her. He grabbed a handful of her red hair and yanked her off the stool. The girl screamed. He let go of her hair but grabbed her arm, twisting it behind her back. She was flopping around like a rag doll.

I rose from my seat and walked unhurriedly across the bar. The old man didn't pay any attention to me, just kept twisting her arm tighter and tighter. I could feel the blood running in my veins.

Let go of her, I said, my voice barely louder than a whisper.

He looked up. Seeing my melted face distracted him, and he loosened his grip on the girl's arm. She managed to twist away for a moment, but he recovered and shoved her against the wall. I grabbed the bottle of beer from the counter, came up from behind, and slammed it on the back of his head. The glass shattered and he grunted. He wobbled around for a few moments before his legs gave way and he fell to the hardwood floor.

For a good long while he didn't do anything but moan and groan. Then he started moving, pulling himself across the floor, but there was no real conviction to his movements. Every time he tried getting up I gave him a good hard kick to the stomach or the face. I wanted him to know a few things. His girl was pleading for me to stop but I knew she didn't mean it, that it was all for show. By the time I got through with him, he was curled up in a ball, coughing up blood, his face a pulpy mess.

I went back to my table, drank down the last swallow of my beer, and slung my bag over my shoulder. Everybody was watching me. I walked slowly toward the front of the bar, graveyard boots echoing on the cement. I stepped over the man and nodded at the bartender. The Paisano, right? I said.

Yes, sir. It ain't nothing fancy, but they'll treat you real good, yes they will.

I nodded my head at the girl and pushed open the door.

Wait! I heard her say. I turned around. She flashed a crooked grin, dark eyes filled with adulation. Who are you? What's your name?

My name's Joseph Downs, I said, and I served my country proudly.

Chapter 2

I wandered around for a while, the wind kicking up dirt, until I came to a little worn-out brick building with *The Paisano* painted on the side. I walked up the crumbling steps and pulled open the door. Inside, everything smelled like rotted wood and formaldehyde. An elk's head hung from the far wall. A baby grand stood in the corner of the room, unplayable. Behind the counter was a dwarf of a woman wearing a floral dress and sporting a rowdy blue bouffant. She had pasty white skin, cherub cheeks, and a turkey wattle. She put away the flask she'd been sipping from and stuck it beneath the counter. Then she looked up at me and smiled through gritted teeth, revulsion concealed. How can I help you, mister? she said.

I want a room.

Just a room? Or will there be something else? She said this with no playfulness.

Only a room.

Okay, she said. I can get you a room. She reached behind the counter and grabbed a key.

I followed her up a narrow flight of stairs, the light bulb dangling from the ceiling creating menacing shadows.

The second floor was in bad shape. Paint peeling from the ceiling, curling up on itself, lights flickering, walls covered with graffiti, gibberish all. From inside one of the rooms, I could hear somebody moaning. Against one wall there was a wooden bench, and sitting on the bench was a young woman wearing red boots and a red wig and a badly tattered wedding dress. A cigarette dangled from a lipstick-smeared mouth. She winked at me and I looked away. Ugly face, she said. Don't bother me none. I'll suck your cock.

You keep that pie-hole shut, the hotel owner said. Now git on back to your room. C'mon, git!

The girl rolled her eyes and rose to her feet. She rearranged her underwear and slunk on down the hallway. With a smile or a sneer, she opened a door and disappeared to the dull gray light of a TV show.

Don't mind her, the blue-haired woman said. With a violent jerk she pulled open a jammed room door and handed me the key. Well, I sure do hope you enjoy your stay, she said. She studied my corroded features for a moment, her amblyopic eye drifting toward her skull. And if you need anything, don't hesitate to ask.

I won't need anything, I said.

The room was what you might expect. Grime scrubbed walls. A sloppily-made bed. An old Kelvinator refrigerator with the kickplate ajar. A filthy window overlooking a filthy town.

I sat down on the bed and removed my jacket and my boots. I unzipped my bag and pulled out a can of George W. Helme snuff, a bottle of plum brandy, an army-issued bayonet, and my worn leather King James Bible, the pages starting to yellow.

I snorted some tobacco, took a long pull of burnt wine, and opened the Bible: *And Gideon said unto him, Oh my Lord, if the LORD be with us, why then is all this befallen us? and where be all his miracles which our fathers told us of, saying, Did not the LORD bring us up from Egypt? but now the LORD hath forsaken us, and delivered us into the hands of the Midianites. . . .*

The power of the passage moved me, and I collapsed on the bed, eyes squeezed tight. I was beginning to think that there wasn't a single righteous person in the world. I was beginning to think that everybody had secrets, terrible secrets.

That night I lay in my bed, bonnell coils jabbing my skin, and stared at the mildewed ceiling. There was a long jagged crack. I watched it grow. Water dripped from the crack into a rusted pot. Drip, drip, drip. Chinese water torture. Through narrow slits, I gazed out the window. The moon was the color of jaundiced skin.

I couldn't sleep at all. The mice and rats had taken over the house. I could hear them scurrying along the wooden floors, climbing up the walls, gnawing at the furniture. And then I heard something else. The faint echo of footsteps on the pavement down below. I crawled out of bed and stared out the window. A man walked slowly down the street, just out of the glow of the streetlight. He wore a tattered suit, a blue tie hanging around his neck like a noose. He had iron-gray hair, badly disheveled, a skeletal frame, and a haunted, emaciated face. When he saw my silhouette in the window, he froze and stared right at me. I shivered involuntarily. A lunatic smile spread slowly across his face. I took a couple of steps backward, my breath trapped in my windpipe. . . .

An hour or more passed. I sat in the bed clutching my knife. Every so often I'd take a peek outside. He hadn't moved; he just stood there, waiting. The wind was blowing, the rain was falling, and a screen door was slamming open and shut.

12:05 a.m., and I heard a knocking on the door. Three short knocks. I gripped my bayonet tightly. I walked slowly across the room, sinews all full of dread. I unlocked the door and pulled it open. Dull light spread across the hardwood floor and I shielded my eyes with my hand. But it wasn't the stranger. It was the redhead from the bar, her face all blurry, a rain-soaked windshield.

I know it's late, she said in a little girl's voice.

I wasn't sleeping.

Can I come inside?

I'm not gonna stop you.

She smiled that crooked smile and stepped into the room, the door slamming shut behind her. She wore a red Nancy Drew raincoat tied tightly at the waist. I was wearing boxers with bears on them and an A-frame undershirt. She looked me up and down. You're well-built, she said. I don't mind the face. I've seen worse.

Maybe, I said. Do you want something to drink? I have plum brandy. Don't have any glasses, though.

Well, that would be just fine, she said. Do you mind if I take off my jacket?

No, ma'am.

She wasn't wearing much underneath. Just a futuristic-looking little silver dress and the same red boots as before. I handed her the bottle of brandy and she took a nice long swig, watching me from the corner of her eyes. She was a drunk, a bad girl, but she reminded me of somebody from long ago. . . .

I wanted to thank you, she said, for how you helped me this afternoon. Most men would have walked away.

I shrugged my shoulders. The way I was raised, a fellow's not supposed to lay a hand on a woman. And if he does, you're supposed to do something about it. Who was he?

289

She took another swig, this one longer than the first, and wiped her mouth with the back of her hand. My husband, she said.

I nodded. And you gonna stay with him?

Probably.

I said: A guy hits you once, he'll hit you twice.

Oh, he's hit me more than twice, believe me. You didn't see anything today. She stared at me for a long moment, then pulled up her sleeve and showed me the remnants of a couple of cigar burns.

I clenched my jaw and shook my head. You ought to leave him, I said.

It's not so simple.

Sure it is. You pack up your bags. And you leave. Simple.

She didn't say anything for a while. Then: This brandy sure is good. I've never had brandy before.

Yeah. I like it okay.

For the next hour or so we drank the brandy and smoked cigarettes. I'd stopped thinking about the stranger, stopped thinking about the Mountain. Off in the distance calliope music was playing. The girl touched my leg with her hand. Her skin was soft, her fingernails filthy. She licked the corner of her mouth, said, And Joseph? Do you think I'm pretty, just a little?

Yes, I lied. I think you're very pretty.

Well, then?

She moved closer on the bed. Her face was in soft focus. Pimpled skin. Bloodshot eyes. Lovely, no. But I was in love. It happens too easily for me.

She placed her hand on mine and moved it beneath her dress. The calliope music got louder. I was feeling good and anxious. There were some things I wanted to do. I wanted to howl at the moon, I wanted to knock her around. But I was paralyzed. She leaned in close. I could smell the layers of perfume and sweat and burnt wine. Her mouth smiled against my skin.

I pulled her toward me. A dog barked spastically. I placed my hand between her thighs. She moaned. A familiar revulsion spread through my veins. I felt like I was going to be sick. Maybe we shouldn't do this, I said. Maybe it isn't right.

She grinned, baring her fangs. For how long have you been concerned about right and wrong?

I thought that one over for a moment. Then I grabbed her by the hand and pulled her to her feet. With a quick jerk, I shoved her against the wall. She gasped, but the smile never left her face. I studied her eyes. I could've found the truth, maybe, but I didn't want to. Instead, I reached back and slapped her across the face, got her attention. Then I kissed her hard, biting down on her lower lip until it bled.

There's not much more to tell. She let me do some things. I couldn't stop myself. When we were done she told me we might fall in love.

I don't even know your name, I said.

Lilith, she said. Created from clay. . . .

After that we lay in bed for a while without talking. Outside, the wind kicked a tin can down the sidewalk and I felt good and empty. I squeezed my eyes shut and fell asleep. I dreamed that old familiar dream: a murder of crows, circling over a mining shack, cawing in excitement, and me being pinned down by faceless demons. . . .

When I woke the sun was rising and the sky was a bloody mess. My body was drenched with ethanol sweat. I sat up, head aching but good. Lilith was lying on her side, head propped up on the palm of her hand. A sly grin on her face.

So? Did you have fun, Joseph?

Well, sure.

Just so you know, I don't usually do this kind of thing.

No. I'm sure you don't.

I'm not that kind of a girl. Not usually.

She lit a cigarette and sucked down the smoke, eyes unblinking. And then the question. Unspoken usually. Not with Lilith. No transition even. Your face, Joseph. The scars. What happened? I know I shouldn't ask, but . . .

I met her gaze for a moment and then shook my head. It's okay, I said. I reached across her body and grabbed the package of cigarettes. I stuck one in my mouth but didn't light it. It bounced up and down as I spoke. I told her the story. I knew the story well.

I was in the Marine Corps, I said. 1st Battalion, 7th Regiment, 1st Division. Stationed in Mosul. Bank of the Tigris. Home of Jonah. Home of Nahum. To me it was hell on Earth. I hadn't been there long, not more than two months. I was with my unit and we were driving in a Humvee. We were trying to secure the area or hunt for insurgents or build a nation. It doesn't matter. Anyway, we were driving down this dirt road and it was pitch black, and our lights were off. We were wearing night vision goggles, so we could see. We came to this tiny bridge over a canal. Nobody was worried, soldiers were joking around, talking about whores they'd screwed and towelheads they'd killed. We drove across the bridge and suddenly I got this bad feeling. I don't know why, can't explain it. It wasn't a moment later when we hit the tripwire. They got us but good. My eardrums exploded and the world went up in flames.

The Humvee finally came to a stop. I could tell I was torn up pretty good but I didn't feel any pain. Flames were everywhere. Then I heard my squad leader screaming: I think I lost my leg! Oh, Jesus, I think I lost my leg! And my best friend Dan was in the front passenger seat where the bomb went off and he was screaming: Where's help? Where the fuck is help? And then everything went quiet.

Time passed in a dream sequence. Everything was out of order and mixed up. I saw trucks materialize through the dust and flames. And then a soldier with a gas mask. His head was jerking all over the place in a strobe light. He disappeared and the flames got stronger, hotter. Then he reappeared and I saw him crawling into the Humvee, sticking out his hand. I guess he saved me. I never saw him again.

Next thing I knew, I was lying on the dirt and my whole body was burning and throbbing and I tried to cry but I couldn't. I reached for my face and it was all swollen on one side, and when I touched it my middle finger went deep into my temple. Everything started getting blurry. I closed my eyes.

I heard voices loud and panicked and incoherent. They thought I was a goner. I wanted to open my eyes, wanted to say something, but I had no control.

The world ended for a time. The next thing I remember is being in a chopper, flying over the burning desert, and I wasn't sure if I was dead or not and I prayed to God that I was. And then I drifted away again and I don't remember anything else until I got to the hospital. . . .

I stopped talking and looked over at Lilith. Her shoulders were trembling and her eyes were moist. She touched my cheek with what might have been tenderness.

I guess I'd told the story well.

Chapter 3

The next morning, I got my truck towed. The day was cold and windy, the sun a dull flash in a gun-metal sky. The shop was nothing but a little brick building with the words *Auto Repair* written in big block letters. It was squeezed between a dilapidated food market called *Charlie's* and a derelict church, its bell rusted into a permanent slant.

In the front lot there were all sorts of oddities: a rotted canoe, a covered wagon, an open coffin. There were hubcaps and unicycles and antique gas pumps. There were mangled jalopies and rusted car parts. A young guy with slicked-back rockabilly hair sat on a metal bench in front of the office. His face and hands and overalls were covered in filth; he looked like a Vaudeville performer in blackface. He was smoking a short stogie and drinking a Squirt. He didn't seem happy to see me.

Having some problems? he said. He had a smiling skull ring on his middle finger and dried spittle in the corner of his mouth.

It's an old Chevy C30, I said. Never had a problem before. And now it just stopped driving. Let me down big time. Think you can fix it?

He flashed a tobacco-stained smile. Gimme a tool set and I could fix Venus de Milo. If this here truck can be fixed, I'm the one who can do it. Good thing you didn't take her to Paul's. He wouldn't know the difference between a V8 engine and V8 drink. He's ruptured more piston seals than I've screwed horny housewives.

Is that a lot?

Hell yeah, that's a lot!

He farmer-blew some snot onto the ground before getting into the truck. With the door flung open, he turned the ignition a couple of times and shook his head. Then he got out and looked under the hood and spat. When was the last time you had this thing worked on? he said.

I shrugged my shoulders. Been awhile, I said. It's not my truck. The truck belongs to a friend. He lent it to me.

Ain't a drop of oil left, that's one problem. But it ain't your only. Have a seat in that there office, and I'll take a look, give you an estimate. I'm fair, too, not like Paul. He'd overcharge a goddamn beggar, yes he would.

For the next hour or more, I sat inside the dingy little store reading Motor Trend and Playboy and drinking cold coffee while Hal took apart the pickup piece by piece. I could hear him cursing and complaining and mumbling under his breath. Finally, the glass door slammed open and Hal entered, wiping perspiration from his forehead with a rag. His lips were tugged into a frown, his eyes darting all over the place.

She can't be fixed, Hal said, his bedside manner lacking.

What do you mean she can't be fixed?

I mean, the old girl is ready for the junkyard. She ain't got another mile in her. You got a hole in the cylinder. The piston rings are completely worn down. The crankshaft ain't turning. And that's just for starters.

I thought you said you could fix any vehicle.

That ain't what I said. I said I could fix her, *if* she could be fixed. This one can't be fixed. I'd have to replace the engine completely. Ain't worth your time or trouble. You'd be better served junking this one and buying another. There's a few used car lots down on North Main.

I'm not interested in another truck, I said. This is a good truck. I drove it all the way across the country. She hasn't failed me yet. She can be fixed. I know she can be fixed.

He reached into his pocket and pulled out an oversized pinch of leaf tobacco and stuck it into his mouth. He spat on the floor and said: Like I said, I'd have to replace the engine. It would cost you a lot of money.

How much?

A new complete engine would cost you two grand at least. A salvage yard one might cost up to a grand. Add another five hundred for the work. You could buy a brand new used truck for not much more than that.

I stuffed my hands in my pockets and kicked at the dirt. I thought things over for a few moments. Put in a salvage yard engine, I said. Be sure it's a good one. I need to make it up to the Mountain. There's somebody waiting for me.

Whatever you say, boss. It's your money.

How soon can you have it done?

Gimme four, five days, top, he said. Got a number where I can call you?

I shook my head. I'll just come back in five days, I said. It's a good truck.

And I started walking.

I made my way back to town, along dirt roads lined with rotted mailboxes and sad-luck houses. The wind blew through the skeleton trees and everything smelled like a feedlot. My hands were buried in my pockets. I was thinking ugly thoughts. You know the kind. Death and destruction. I walked past rusted metal barrels and mounds of used tires and rows of dying alfalfa, but no humans. The sky was the color of bone. Down about a quarter of a mile, I came upon a cemetery that hadn't been cared for in years. Dignity denied in both life and death.

In the middle of town, on top of Jagged Hill, stood the Church of Sacred Blood, a white-spire structure with a mural of Christ surrounded by drunken angels, the wooden cross weary, hanging on for dear life. A preacher's voice echoed across the plains: *And you have heard it said that as you walk through the valley of the shadow of death you shall fear no evil, for He is with you; His rod and staff comforts you. But I say to you: Be afraid. Because the Lord does not want any whores and bastards. The Lord does not want any thieves and beggars. The Lord desires the righteous. And how many of you are righteous? Well? How many? Hell awaits you. Yes, my friends, Hell surely awaits unless some changes are made. For you are nothing but maggots and cockroaches, a blight in the Lord's eye. And there is time for conversion, for restoration, but time is running thin . . .*

I made my way along a broken path until I came to my hotel, all marked by sorry dilapidation and decay. Breathing heavily, I leaned against the brick wall and yanked out a cigarette. I sucked in the smoke slow and tender and spat it out fast and mean.

And that's when I saw the stranger.

He was a block ahead, wearing the same tattered suit as before. His face was in the shadows, but I could tell it was him. The wind was blowing, and a few specks of snow were swirling above, never seeming to land. I pulled up the collar of my jacket and started walking down the splintered pavement, past a slumbering Mexican clutching a bottle of Sauza, past an elderly woman walking her vacuum cleaner, past a mangy calico cat gnawing on a piece of rotting flesh. The stranger must have seen me too: he started walking, following after me.

My slow gait changing to a gallop, I made my way down the street and then ducked into an alleyway. There were broken bottles and bloodied underwear and seagulls lost from the landfill. There was a wild-looking old woman with splayed gray hair and a whale skin jacket, trying to light a fire in a trashcan. When she saw me, she charged toward me and started pounding open-fisted on my back. She was shouting about satellites and wiretaps and port-a-potties. She smelled like mothballs and soda fizz. I pushed away from her and spun into the service entrance of one of the dilapidated buildings. The door shut behind me, and everything was dark. It took me several moments before my eyes adjusted. There were dozens of empty plastic crates. There was also a darkened staircase. I walked up the staircase slowly, the wooden steps moaning beneath my feet.

At the top of the steps was a metal door, dull light shining from beneath it. I turned the handle and pushed open the door. I walked into a strange room with strange shadows and strange people. It took me a while to recognize that they were mannequins and I was inside some sort of a defunct clothing store. . . .

I just stood there for a while. Everything was quiet. I looked around the room. There were dozens of boxes stuffed messily with clothes. Blow-out signs on the wall. Somebody had been in a hurry to leave the business behind. There was a cash register on the counter, open and empty. I squatted down on the floor, breathing heavily. Outside I could hear the crazy woman singing a strange gypsy tune:

Oh child, oh child,
Where have you gone?
You done gone missing
Two dolls left on the lawn

I sat in that clothing store for a long time. The stranger never found me. When I finally left, the sky was black and the moon was missing.

Chapter 4

Over the next several days, I saw a lot of Lilith. We always met in the Hotel Paisano and she was never all that discreet. She came in through the front door and left the same way, and the townspeople whispered behind their hands. I asked wasn't she worried about her husband finding out but she just acted tough. Serve that bastard right, she said. How many whores has he screwed?

During these times we talked some, but I got to know Lilith less than you might think. I couldn't quite figure her out. Sometimes she could be soft and motherly, stroking my forehead and telling me that everything would be okay; other times she'd seem hard and cruel, making acerbic comments about my service, my intelligence. Then when she'd see the anger in my eyes, she'd apologize and shift back to sweetness.

Not only that, but her appearance was always changing, too. One day she'd wear a tight leather mini-skirt reaching halfway down her thigh, the next a white dress covering her ankles, arms, and neck. She dyed her hair from red to platinum blonde, and even changed the color of her eyes—from brown to Jolly Rancher blue.

One thing she was consistent about was her feelings for her husband. Fear and loathing. She'd only married him because she'd got pregnant and was scared. She'd lost the baby and kept the monster. He could be charming, but not all that often. She showed me the bruises and the cigar burns. Told me about when he'd broken her jaw, when he'd given her a black eye.

I was beginning to think their marriage wouldn't last.

This one morning Lilith was in the bathroom sitting on the toilet. I was lying in bed, running my finger along my facial scars, watching her intently in the mirror. Her red knees were touching, her panties around her ankles, and a wounded cigarette was hanging from her lips. She rose to her feet, wiped herself off, and flushed the toilet. Hunching over, she inserted a tampon with one hand, the cigarette now burning in the other. She returned to the bedroom and slumped down in a chair. She was too skinny. I'd never seen her eat.

Oh, Joseph, she said. I'm so fucking tired of being afraid. It's wearing me down. It gets so I can't ever sleep and my stomach is always aching.

You worrying about Nick?

She nodded her head. You have no idea what it's like, living in fear all the time.

I have some sense.

He makes my skin crawl. You just have no fucking idea.

Couldn't you just divorce him? I said.

Lilith scowled and glared at me. Her bleached hair was a mess and her eyes were bloodshot. She took a long drag from her cigarette and let the smoke trickle out of her nostrils. Divorce him, huh?

Well, sure.

He'd kill me if I ever left him, she said.

What are you talking about?

That's what he told me. Said he'd slit my throat and dump me in the landfill.

He talks tough, I said. A lot of guys talk tough.

I believe him, she said.

I shook my head. He doesn't have it in him. I know his type. He's a bully, but he's not a killer. It takes courage to kill.

She sucked a burning house full of smoke into her lungs and blew it out of a Billy Idol mouth. Then her face softened and her lips curled into a smile. Without saying a word, she rose from the chair and walked slowly, seductively to the bed. She sat down next to me and started stroking my chest, her left breast pressing against my skin, and for a moment I decided that I would place my fate in her sloppily-manicured hands.

When I spoke again, it sounded like somebody else's voice, all cracked and distant: We could run away, I said. Just you and me. Leave all of this behind, you know? I have a little place in the mountains, not two hours from here, just a little mining cabin buried in a thatch of trees. Nobody within two miles in any direction. That's where I was going when my truck broke down. I was going to the Mountain. Just to get away from everything. Just to clear my mind. We could go there. We could be happy, maybe.

Lilith sucked down some more smoke, her eyes narrowing to a pair of gashes. Oh, that sounds nice, she said. I've never been to the mountains. But he'd find me. I know he would.

Not up there, I said. Not a person in the world would find you.

Then I pulled her close and kissed her, mashing my lips against hers. Lilith closed her eyes and covered her fluttering heart with the palm of her hand. But it was no good. A fellow can get so goddamn lonely sometimes. . . .

Lilith was going to spend the day with an aunt in Rifle. Me, I had nothing planned. I figured what the hell. I'd go pay Nick McClellan a visit.

The McClellan's lived a few miles outside of town. I walked part of the way. Then I stuck out my thumb and got lucky. An old blue Lincoln Continental pulled off the side of the road, kicking up dust. I jogged up to the car and the passenger side door opened. Inside was an older man with thick gray muttonchops and friendly blue eyes. Where you headed, mister? No visible reaction to my face.

Just up the road a bit, I said.

Hop in.

His name was Big Ed. He chewed tobacco but never spat. His fingers tapped the steering wheel incessantly, keeping time with the wheels on the highway. And he must have been afraid of silence.

Me, I'm on my way to work, he said. Wanna know what I do? I shrugged my shoulders. He chuckled a bit. Then he said: I clean out Porta-Potties. Damn straight. Spend my days in them outhouses, sucking up shit with a wand. Fellow can't complain, though. Gotta make a living, right? Beats living under the bridge. Done that too. Shit. And what about you? Got a trade?

No, I said. Not really.

A drifter, huh?

Veteran. Iraq.

Well, shit, I kinda figured, you know. Vietnam, myself. Got a bullet lodged in my ass. God's honest truth. Nothing like your injury, though. That's a hell of a thing. IED?

Yes, sir.

Say no more, soldier. You've probably relived it enough.

Yes. I guess I have.

He rolled down the window and the wind whipped in the car. You said Army, right? he said.

No, sir. Marines.

A big grin spread across his face. No shit? He pulled up his sleeve and showed me his skull and sword tattoo. Proud member myself, he said. Mind if I ask you a question?

No, sir.

Ed stuck his fingers in his mouth and pulled out the damp wad of chewing tobacco and threw it outside. How they been treating you?

Sir?

Since you got back to the States. You been treated with respect?

Yes, sir, I said. I have no complaints, sir.

Must have been tough on your family, though. What with your injuries and all.

My parents died a long time ago, I said. I got no friends, no family.

He nodded his head for so long I wasn't sure he'd ever stop. When he spoke again, his words were drenched with bitterness: You know, they used to hold a parade for all of us soldiers in this here town. People lined Main Street, held their children on their shoulders, waved their American flags, played patriotic marches. But the years went by and the parades became smaller and smaller. Fewer veterans. Fewer townspeople. Finally, one year I noticed that it was just me. No more bands playing. No more children cheering. No more women weeping. Just me. I saw a fellow who I recognized from the war. He asked me what did I think I was doing still marching. And I said, It's our duty. And he said, Nobody's doing it anymore. And I said, As long as I'm doing it, somebody's doing it.

Then Ed stopped talking. There was no moral to the story.

We finally came to the McClellan property, way out in the middle of nowhere, surrounded by dirt and dust and derricks and devils. Ed stopped the car and jerked it into park. He looked at me for a good long while, making me uncomfortable. I go to this group, he said. Once a week. Veterans. All kinds. Vietnam, Kuwait, Iraq, Afghanistan. Hell, we even got an old-timer from Korea. It's good to be able to talk. Helps exorcise them demons, you know? If you keep it all inside of you . . . anyway, we meet Wednesdays at seven. Down at the American Legion. The way I figure, ain't nobody can understand a soldier like a soldier.

I nodded my head slowly. I sure do appreciate the offer, I said, but I'm not all that interested.

No?

It's just that I don't much like talking about the past. It always seems to be changing on me.

He looked at me some more. Then he stuck out his hand and I shook it. Been a pleasure, soldier, he said.

Thanks for the ride, I said. I'd just opened the door and stepped outside when he spoke again, a big grin spread across his face: Good night, Chesty Puller, wherever you are!

I didn't know what he was talking about. Who's Chesty Puller? I said.

Something set him off. His expression changed to a scowl and he started cursing at me. Before I could get an explanation, he jammed the truck into drive and sped off down the road.

Outside, it was cold and breezy and the ground was covered with frost. I gazed at the McClellan's house, a little brick ranch, maybe 1,000 square feet big. An American flag hung out front, whipping in the wind. Behind the house were a bunch of cylindrical feed bins alongside a pair of wood barns, both bigger than the house. I peeked in the first barn. It was lined with narrow stalls made of concrete. Sows sat inside, pregnant, eating from the feeders that hung above the stalls.

I made my way to the house, not sure what I aimed to do. On the porch, the wind chimes were jingling, playing a madman's orchestra. I rapped on the door a few times. No answer. I moved toward the window and peered in the house. Didn't look like anybody was home. I tried the door. It was unlocked. I stepped inside.

The home was simple. In the living room there was a ratty couch and a television. There was an Oriental rug on the floor and a pair of boots by the door. The walls were bare except for a metal cross above the couch.

I made my way to the bedroom. The curtains were shut and everything was dark and drab. The bed was unmade. Clothes were strewn on the hardwood floor. There was another television sitting on a wooden crate. The white dresser looked antique. Some of the drawers were sticking out. On top of the dresser were a couple of bowling trophies.

Next, I wandered to the kitchen. Dishes were piling up in the sink. The floral wallpaper was peeling from the walls. I opened the refrigerator and grabbed a beer. I returned to the living room, sat down on the couch, and crossed my legs. Some time passed. I didn't move. I just stared at the wall thinking about everything and nothing at all.

I slammed down the beer and crushed the can with my hand. Then I tossed it on the floor.

I stayed like that on the couch for another twenty minutes at least. Nick didn't show up. I don't know what I would have done if he had. I rose to my feet and walked out of the brick ranch, letting the screen door slam shut behind me.

Once outside, I met up with one of his pigs. And here's what I did, here's exactly what I did: I grabbed that hog from behind, pulled out my knife, and sliced its throat from one end to the other. Then I stood over him, watching him twitch and moan. I waited until he had bled out and dragged him back to the front porch. That would give ol' Nick something to think about . . .

Chapter 5

The next morning I went back to Hal's Auto. He was under the hood of an old VW bug. Bob Miller was singing from a plastic radio. The air was cold and my hands were buried in my pockets.

I stood there tapping my feet and humming with the radio, but he just kept right on working. So I stood next to him, leaned under the hood and said, I'm looking for my pickup. She ready yet?

He looked up with that Vaudeville face, flashed his milk-white teeth, and said, C30 with the blown engine, right?

Yes, sir.

He straightened up and wiped his hands on his jeans. Sure, I got her fixed, he said. Found a nice little engine at the junkyard. Got plenty of juice in her, too. Came from an old hearse. That doesn't bother you now, does it?

No, sir. Not as long as my truck runs.

She runs like a dream. Course I can't vouch for the longevity.

The pickup was parked next to Hal's office. He'd washed and cleaned her, and she looked as good as new. He popped open the hood and pointed out various intricacies, but I wasn't much interested.

How much do I owe you? I said.

He pulled out a pad and pencil and scribbled a few things down. 596 for the engine, he said. 480 for labor. I'll give you the stranger's discount, and we'll make it an even grand.

Fine, I said. I'll pay cash.

And pay cash I did. I got into the truck, hit the corpse engine and drove on out of the parking lot.

Broken down trucks, hotel rooms, booze—it was beginning to take its toll on me financially. The truth was, I was down to less than a hundred dollars. I sold blood and an old watch. Not enough to make a difference. Eventually I was forced to get a job. After a few days of searching, I found one at the local landfill. Twelve twenty five an hour. The job wasn't much, but at this particular time, as I dangled from a window ledge, it suited me just fine. I figured the Mountain could wait, and besides I liked Lilith more than plenty.

My boss's name was Cash Hopkins and he was some slave-driver. He was a little guy, couldn't have been more than five foot six, with ashen gray hair and a complexion to match. He was fifty or sixty or seventy. He never stopped shouting. Move that goddamn refuse! he'd shout. There are a thousand wetbacks chomping at the bit to take your job!

The job was monotonous. Every thirty or so minutes a garbage truck would appear over the hill, perform a pirouette, and spill a load of crushed trash. Then the bulldozers would race toward the last dump, lower their blades, and shove all the waste toward the middle, a never-ending task of efficiency. They refused to train me on the bulldozer, despite my experience driving an M-1A1 Abrams tank. Instead they gave me a shovel. I did the best I could, moving trash and scaring away crows.

And so there I was this one particular morning, standing on top of the world, and all around me was trash and filth, and I knew there was some greater truth but I couldn't figure out what it was. I stood there perfectly still just thinking, thinking, thinking. The moon was a silver disc in the pale blue sky. Everything was quiet; the bulldozers were on the other side of the hill. I waded through the sea of debris, sucking in the rotten air. The crows hovered cautiously overhead. Suddenly I was overcome with emotion. I fell to my knees, became engulfed in garbage. And I prayed with all my might. Jesus, I really need a hand. I'm afraid I'm ready to really fuck things up again . . .

And it was at that moment that the stranger appeared, his figure silhouetted by sunshine. I struggled to my feet, using my shovel as a cane. A crow landed on his shoulder, cocked its head and flew away. He walked toward me slowly, his left leg dragging behind his right.

He stood in front of me, just staring at me with contempt. His face was unshaven and his eyes were vengeful. There were spider veins crawling up his cheeks. His gray hair was greasy and unkempt. When he spoke, his voice was all full of pebbles: Who are you, he said, only it didn't really seem to be a question.

I met his gaze. I think I should be asking you the same question.

I been following you around, he said, rocking back and forth, just watching you.

I've seen you. Should've called the cops. Didn't.

Sometimes you're not an easy man to keep track of. But I always find you. After a while.

He had a strange way of talking. He paused at odd times. His voice trembled slightly.

What do you want? I said. Why are you following me?

He took a couple of steps forward. My body tensed. I could feel my knife resting beneath my shirt. There was nobody else around . . .

My son saw terrible things, he said. Roadside bombs. Firing squads. The night sky on fire. Heads severed from torsos, staring back at him blinking slowly . . .

What are you talking about? I said.

His cheek twitched and his eyes narrowed. I searched his face, trying to recall a past life. . . .

You claim to be a soldier, he said. Isn't that right?

Yes, sir. 1st Battalion, 7th Regiment, 1st Division. Honorable discharge.

He stared at me for a long time. Then he started laughing. Only it wasn't a happy laughter. It was awful, terrified laughter.

I read about you, he said. In a newspaper. In Lubbock.

I know the article.

Said you were wounded in Mosul. Were you wounded in Mosul?

I nodded my head. Yes, sir. I was.

Said you'd had a tough time of it since returning to the States. What with your face and all. Nobody would hire you. You were homeless for a time.

I've never felt sorry for myself, I said. Not for a single moment.

He moved forward until he was inches from my face. I felt threatened. I pulled out my knife and showed it to him up close. He smiled that sickly smile. What are you gonna do? he said. You gonna kill me?

Just move back, I said. I don't know who you are but—

I lost concentration. He lunged at me and grabbed a hold of my wrist. The knife clattered to the ground. I tried reaching for it, and when I was off-balance he shoved me hard, causing me to tumble into a pile of trash. He picked up the knife and squatted down next to me. His face now looked hard and mean.

You ever seen me before? he said.

I shook my head.

I said, you ever seen me before?

No, sir.

You say your name is Joseph Downs, huh? Iraqi veteran, huh?

Yes.

Tell me your unit.

I already told you.

Tell it to me again. This time he was shouting.

1st Battalion, 7th Regiment, 1st Division. What the hell is this?

When did you serve?

What?

Dates served, soldier! He pressed the knife against my throat, drawing a trickle of blood.

Shipped out August 11, 2004, I said. Honorable discharge . . . May 13, 2005.

Bullshit! he shouted. Who are you?

I already told you, I said. Jesus, what is wrong with you? What do you want from me? I can show you my tag—I keep it around my neck.

His eyes opened wide and his lower lip trembled. Give it to me, he said. Let me see your tag.

Put the knife down, I said.

Slowly, he placed the knife on the ground, inches from his body. He nodded his head. I removed the tag from around my neck and tossed it gently toward him. He picked it up without taking his eyes off of me.

DOWNS

J.D.

522715386

USMC M

BAPTIST

He stared down at that tag for some time. Then his jaw slackened and his eyes filled with dread. He shook his head a few times and muttered something under his breath. He dropped the tag on the ground and then grabbed a shovel to steady himself.

He continued muttering but I couldn't decipher the words.

Uneasily, I rose to my feet and backed away. Listen, I said. I'm not looking for any trouble. I was on my way to the Mountain when my truck broke down. There's been a misunderstanding of some kind.

The stranger looked at me wild-eyed. I'm not crazy, he said. I'm not crazy. He backed away slowly. I'm not crazy! Then he turned and lurched forward like a wounded animal. I watched as he dissolved into the trash around him. And as a fleet of garbage trucks appeared over the horizon, I wondered if he had really been there at all. . . .

war is over? (do we want it?)

"Not in Our Name" is a name. It's the name of an organization formed after the attacks of September 11, with the aim of protesting the US government's response to those attacks. As an organization it started to pick up steam and gain membership when it became clear in 2002 that the US would be invading Iraq. NION was involved in organizing many protests against the invasion of Iraq including one big protest. On February 15, 2003, with the help of NION, millions around the world took to the streets in an effort to . . .

Well, that part is unclear.

If you asked protesters at the time most of them would have told you that the goal of the protests was to stop the war, but if you asked if they themselves believed that the protests might stop the war, they would have told you that they did not believe stopping the war was possible. So, if nobody believed in the stated purpose of the big protest, what unstated goal were people really working toward?

Turning to the NION statement of purpose for an answer clarifies what was at stake. What one finds is some free verse co-written by the neopagan new age author Starhawk, and spoken word performer Saul Williams. The poem concludes:

Not in our name
will you wage endless war

Another world is possible
and we pledge to make it real.

Despite this pledge, the protests against the war in Iraq were, all in all, merely symbolic.

A decade later Brendan O'Neill, a blogger for the conservative *Spectator* newspaper, would describe February 15, 2003 this way:

"It wasn't a mass protest so much as it was a mass opting out, a mass switching off, a mass scrubbing of one's own name from a preordained course of bloody action."

That's the crux of the problem. The anti-war movement could no more escape the seeming inevitably of combat in Iraq than Colin Powell could. The only distinction between them is that while Powell went through the motions of arguing for the war as if arguments mattered, the protesters did the opposite. That was the difference, that and the fact that the protesters got their regret out early whereas Powell only realized how the whole thing had blotted his reputation and sullied his name after the fact.

"Not in Our Name," the protesters said.

"Take my word for it," said Powell.

In both cases the sentiment expressed didn't have any material effect.

In the remaining two stories you'll find examinations of this problem.

Nobody wants war and yet, somehow, it happens. War doesn't seem to need a justification. War doesn't require that things make sense.

Douglas Lain is a novelist and short story writer whose work has appeared in various magazines including Strange Horizons, Interzone, *and* Lady Churchill's Rosebud Wristlet. *His first novel* Billy Moon *was published by Tor and was selected as the debut fantasy novel of the month by* Library Journal *in 2013. His second novel* After the Saucers Landed *came out from Night Shade Books in 2015, and was nominated for the Philip K. Dick Award.*

"Noam Chomsky and the Time Box" was originally published in the British science-fiction magazine Interzone *in 2011.*

"noam chomsky
and the time box"
DOUGLAS LAIN

CRAWDADDY ONLINE
Jeff Morris

December 22nd, 2013 - 3:30 pm | 6,815 views | 2 recommendations | 75 comments

Stuck in History: My Time Box 3.0 Frustration

It's still amazing what can fit in your pocket these days, but while standard computing and gaming devices like iPhones and Mini-Wii systems continue to dominate the market, the most expensive and advanced personal computing device, the Time Box, has had a rough couple of months. Both the recent problems with the marketing and introduction of Box 3.0 which met with less than the projected demand, and the chorus of consumer complaints—the Time Box version of history is too self-contained and static (one example would be the thousands of complaints to the company that visits and revisits to the Grand Banks of Newfoundland always conclude with the Titanic sinking)—has led to a downturn in the company's stock. While educators, science-fiction fans, and historical hook-up artists are still purchasing the box, the company must do something to increase sales beyond these niches, and the company is pinning its future to the hope that version 3.0 will reinvigorate sales. The new Box includes many features consumers have come to expect with hand held computational devices. Partnering with Sprint and Dell, the new Box will allow customers to make cellular calls from the past, to maintain an internet connection as long as one is within the last thousand years of history, and to photograph and take video of both past events and encounters with what everyone agrees is an ever expanding present.

—The WSJ, December 20, 2013

If anyone needed more proof that the gadget-driven marketing scam that was the American Empire is now completely dead, the utter failure to adequately create demand for the world's first personal time machine should suffice as proof. Nintendo, Time Warner, and Apple computers have all backed off their various offers to buy out Time Box incorporated, and while last year it seemed impossible that the product might suffer the same fate as Betamax and electric cars, a year later it's becoming obvious that people without a history or a future are uninterested in the kind of Time Travel the box offers. The public seems content to leave history to the necrophiliacs and Civil War buffs.

A year ago the device came onto the market like a revelation. The consensus in December of 2012 was that a personal time machine would alter everything. *Tech Review* at MIT loved Timebox, Doctorow at Boing Boing was beside himself, and historians and political pundits couldn't contain themselves either. The first month out the door people lined up to buy. There was a mad rush, but when consumers found the disclaimer word of mouth put the kibosh to the whole pseudo-event.

It's the first thing you find when you take a Time Box home. The warning is printed on the front page of the instruction manual, plainly and in 36-point Helvetica: "Time Box is paradox free. Do not alter factory settings."

If you mess with the Box, adjust the settings, you risk voiding the warranty, and yet it comes equipped with an interface to allow such alterations. I imagine that somebody in marketing thought that this interface might stave off realizations of the obvious. As long as people were under the impression that raising or lowering the probability level and flux could have some impact on their overall experience they could be kept from realizing the obvious.

Time travel is boring as fuck.

It is impossible to impact the past. That's why the Box is under-performing sticky Elmo as a stocking stuffer.

Believe me, I've tried it. A year late to the game I purchased my first Box at the Lloyd Center Mall on black Friday. I just managed not to get trampled on my way from the parking lot to the Computer Store. On my way out I stopped by the food court for a hot dog on a stick, enjoyed the ambience created by the giant fountain and the rats that scurried between the plastic tables as they searched for bits of fries and meat left by the throngs of holiday shoppers, and read and reread the instruction manual:

Steps for Time Box 3.0

* Wearing loose clothing and after consulting your physician, take Time Box in hand and sit comfortably.
* Input historical figure, architectural style, or any other historical indicator as a search term. (Specific dates along with geographical locations will allow Time Box to transport you with pinpoint accuracy.)
* Enter timeline and interact with the past.
* To end Time Box timeline simply reset.
* Live today as yesterday. Experience yesterday as today.

THE TIMEBOX IS A PARADOX FREE DEVICE

Once I was home, like every newbie to the Time Box, I set off to change the past. Despite the disclaimers I had to try. The theory is that history is fixed, that you can't kill Hitler, save Jesus, or stop Larry Summers from getting a job with the Clinton Administration, but once I had the thing plugged in and humming I figured maybe everyone else was just going about it in the wrong way. After all, while most physicists agree that the universe is some sort of hologram, that the structure of time is complete, that the universe is one big thing across space AND time,

313

there are dissenters. Some claim that while the universe is a hologram, it's a hologram built out of tinker toys. The structure can be moved around. The universe is one big thing, but it can be rebuilt and altered. It's not cemented together like a model airplane or a brick wall.

One of those dissenters, professor Hopkins at the University of Hawaii, put it this way:

"You could change the structure if you knew where the seams were, what the elements of construction were. The trouble is finding a way to measure time in qualitative rather than quantitative units. The past appears unified right now, acausal, but the final word hasn't been written yet. We might be able to change history. Theories exist that say we could change it."

I emailed back asking if one might find these seams.

"I don't know. But, let's say you were to find the seams, and that you were able to change the structure, then all the old time travel problems would resurface. If you could change the structure of reality so that your grandfather was never born then how could the universe generate you as a causative agent? It's theoretically possible, if you take the universe to be para-consistent, and if it turns out that there are qualitative units of construction that can be somehow manipulated on the micro-level," he wrote back.

So there would be paradoxes. That seemed okay. I'd cross those bridges when I came to them, if I came to them.

I connected the Box to my personal computer, plugged it in to the USB port on the back of my computer screen, and typed in my key phrases. I didn't set the device to take me back to something obvious like the attacks of September 11, 2001, or the day we invaded Iraq for the second time. Instead I searched for what seemed like a lull, a gap between the two points. I played a hunch.

I found Noam Chomsky at a pizzeria near the campus of MIT in 2002. Caught up with the professor right before the US went down the rabbit hole. Most of my readers probably already know who Noam Chomsky is, but for those who haven't heard of him I'll give the basic bio:

Professor Chomsky is the father of modern linguistics, sort of the Sigmund Freud of universal grammar. However, most people don't know him for his scholarly work. Along with being America's Newton,

Chomsky is America's most well known anti-American, or in less reactionary terms, America's most famous dissident. He's a self-described libertarian socialist whose been exposing and urging resistance to the American Imperial project for around fifty years.

The professor was sitting in a faux antique chair by the exit—a flimsy wooden chair that had been painted a light green and then intentionally distressed. The shabby chic furniture offset the chrome tables creating a look of corporate bohemianism. Chomsky was sipping from a Moose Head beer and reading the *Financial Times*. He was using a red ballpoint pen to circle words and phrases in the paper as I bought a slice of mushroom and olive pizza and took my grease stained paper plate to his table.

When Chomsky looked up at me I realized that I'd entered the Time Box without considering my appearance. I'm nearly forty and yet I was dressed like a teenager, like a teenager from 2012. I was wearing loose blue jeans that hung down below my waist exposing my tartan boxer shorts, an orange t-shirt that read "Free the Bunny Suicide" in sarcastic Helvetica, and my eyeglasses that, back in 2002, probably looked like something from Star Trek or an Andy Warhol factory party. The frames are oversized, made of transparent plastic, and filled with red ink. Cool, no?

And I was unshaven. And I was not wearing deodorant.

I saw a deep and abiding tolerance in Chomsky's eyes, and I couldn't tell whether he'd noted my attire or not. He looked at me and then down at his plate and his body language didn't change. It didn't matter whether I was kempt or unkempt, rational or irrational. He didn't anticipate any surprises.

I did not introduce myself, but sat down across from him at the chrome table, took a bite of my gourmet pizza, and then started in with my mouth full. I asked Professor Chomsky why he was willing to stay at the level of critique. I asked him why he didn't use his influence to move people to gum up the machinery of war. Why did the professor always stop short of offering a prescription?

"That's not a serious question."

"Why not?"

"The way to make this world better is to work with other people on the various problems. It is just a matter of doing the hard work. There isn't a prescription. That's not how the world works. You're looking for utopia."

Chomsky had already heard the question I'd come back in time to ask him. He'd heard it and heard it. At every lecture he'd ever given, at every book screening, at every cocktail party for eminent academics, he was always asked the same inevitable question:

"What are we supposed to do?"

Listening to Chomsky prattle out his standard answer, chewing gourmet pizza and watching Chomsky peel back the label on his Moose Head beer, I realized that the professor didn't really have an answer. In fact, after all the years he'd spent fielding it, he still didn't even understand the question.

Chomsky's theory of generative grammar postulates that the human mind is constructed with language built in. There is a universal grammar built into humanity, there are rules of expression set up biologically. There are limits to what can be expressed and, no matter how hard one tries, one can't go beyond those limits.

Consider two sentences:

Sentence 1: "Unicorns sleep furiously at the moon."

Here you've got a subject, a verb, an adverb, and an object. It's an absurd sentence, but it fits the grammar. To the extent that the sentence is absurd is exactly the degree to which it fits. Just to rise to the level of absurdity the sentence has to work by the rules.

Sentence 2: "Zoom zagga ba bagga za grumboon!"

Here we have a sentence that, on it's face, is nothing but a series of expletives. The word "zoom" for instance fills in for a subject, maybe. Perhaps zoom is standing in for the definite article? Try saying the sentence outloud.

"Zoom zagga ba bagga za grumboon!"

I wanted Chomsky to help me find the seam. I thought Chomsky could push, that he had power in reserve that he was reluctant to use. But talking to him in the pizza shop in 2002, listening to his rap on how we had to organize, on how the solutions available were obvious if not exactly sexy, I realized that he was as stuck as anyone. Chomsky had to

316

work within the system, within the grammar, even if in the end he only managed to be absurd.

I tried to tell him. I showed him the Time Box, and told him when I was from, but Chomsky wasn't particularly impressed. It wasn't that he didn't believe me so much as what I told him didn't even enter his consciousness. I produced the Time Box from my jeans pocket and held it up to him, but he didn't really look at it. Instead he continued to explain what organizing was, what alternative media was, what true self-interest was. I nodded along and then walked to the center of the restaurant and pressed the reset button.

I'm sure he was as undisturbed by my disappearance as he'd been by my sudden appearance. I imagine he simply finished his pizza slice, took one last sip of beer, and headed back to MIT.

I tried to return to that moment, to flip back fifteen minutes, to the moment before our conversation had started, but I overshot it. I hadn't set the preference correctly and I ended up standing in the dark, surrounded by chairs set upside down on the tabletops. Across the street from the pizzeria a two-story New Colonial house had been converted into a second hand clothing store, and as I fumbled with the Time Box, struggled to find out when I was and send myself to the right moment, I stepped forward, toward the pizzeria's pane glass front window. I stared out at the display across the street.

The mannequin in the second hand store's window had peach colored lips. She was wearing a paisley patterned Sari and had several beaded necklaces around her neck. She was lit by the neon logo for Phillips 66 to her left and a Hamms Beer sign to her right.

My Time Box blinked at me in the dark. I glanced at the photographs of Chomsky, of a slice pizza, and then at Saddam Hussein. Each image flickered across the touch-screen.

I went back and asked Chomsky again and again. I tried several approaches:

Chomsky ate a pizza slice with sundried tomatoes. He took a bite and got some tomato paste on his glasses as I approached his table. When he put down his copy of the Financial Times I opened an umbrella and put it down on the tabletop between us, covering his plate and knocking over his bottle of Moose Head.

And then I brought him a box of chocolate candies.

Then I tried saying everything he would say the moment before he said it, but Chomsky held his ground. He could not be moved.

The new features of the Time Box didn't help me either. I did not think to take a picture with the camera feature, or transcribe the moment to digital video. Why would anyone ever use those features? Why take a picture when you can just go back and see the same damned mistakes over and over again?

CRAWDADDY ONLINE
Jeff Morris

January 2nd, 2014 - 3:17 pm | 3,225 views | 0 recommendations | 25 comments

The Timebox: Same as It Ever Was

What if some day or night a demon were to steal after you into your loneliest loneliness and say to you, "This life as you now live it and have lived it, you will have to live once more and innumerable times more; and there will be nothing new in it, but every pain and every joy and every thought and sigh and everything unutterably small or great in your life will have to return to you, all in the same succession and sequence . . ." Would you not throw yourself down and gnash your teeth and curse the demon who spoke thus?
　　　　　　　　　—Friedrich Nietzsche, *The Gay Science*, 1882

Before Christmas I argued that Time Box Incorporated's troubles cannot be addressed at the level of branding or by adding features. The trouble is intrinsic in the device itself. The Box brings the consumer into a frozen past, a history stuck in amber. Since then I've had a chance to experiment further with the device, and I'm compelled to continue in the same vein.

The second time out I typed in Noam Chomsky again but added the name Terence McKenna to the search.

McKenna was a minor celebrity in the nineties. Famous amongst stoners and closet new agers, he was sort of an updated Timothy Leary. He promoted drugged out passivity as a panacea, taught at the Esalen

Institute, pushed Human Potential and anti-ideologies, but, unlike Chomsky, he did dare to offer a remedy for our social ills. Even if his career was a symptom of the boomer's retreat from political engagement, there was an element to his spiel that I wanted to keep. McKenna argued that the human imagination could be our escape hatch. I typed his name next to the name Chomsky and pressed return.

On November 16, 1971, Chicago O'Hare International Airport was less antiseptic than it would be forty-four years later. The plaster walls were off white, the ceiling was lower than it would be, and so, despite the fact that Gate 23 was mostly empty, the space seemed cramped. The metal mesh wall panel behind the check-in desk communicated some of the authority inherent in industrial technology, but was too physical and intrusive to truly impress. The check-in desk itself was just a simple box with the logo for TWA, the interlocking globes and the red lettering, knitted into nubby blue fabric. All in all the scale and design created the sense that the airport was run by human beings. Chicago International came across as vulnerable. It made me smile.

I arrived inside the gate, past the stainless steel rails, past security, already sitting in an orange fiberglass chair facing the plate glass. Behind me and to my left a forty-four-year-old Chomsky stood with his wife Carol. They were patiently waiting in line to check-in. Terence McKenna was closer to me, leaning against a white pillar on my side of the stainless steel rails. A young woman sat next to him on a steamer trunk.

Chomsky and his wife were both well dressed. Chomsky wore a grey wool suit and dark blue tie, while his wife wore a dark blue floral skirt and a black turtleneck. McKenna, on the other hand, looked a bit unkempt in blue jeans and a brown and white flannel shirt. His beard was scruffy. His hair was long, but not long enough to be a conscious choice. The woman with him looked cleaner in her jeans. Her long blonde hair was partially obscured by a straw cowboy hat.

The Pentagon Papers had leaked to the *New York Times* five months earlier, in June of 1971, and Chomsky, who'd helped Ellsberg release the documents to the media, was flying to a speaking engagement about the document at UC Berkeley. McKenna was waiting for the same flight after spending many months in the Amazon. While Chomsky had been composing scathing essays about both LBJ and Richard Nixon, Terence McKenna had been hallucinating in Peru.

"Flight 2012 to Berkeley, California is running behind schedule this afternoon," the brunette stewardess behind the ticket counter told Chomsky. She smiled at the air in front of her face, but when she made eye contact with the professor her smile faltered. "We don't have an ETA at the moment, but I will let you know just as soon as that information is available." She was uncomfortable in her pink and orange polyester uniform, and attempted to straighten it by pulling down on the uniform's short skirt. She stepped back from the counter and adjusted her pillbox hat.

I fiddled with the dials on the Time Box, used the temporal uplink to search for information on McKenna's trip to the Amazon and Chomsky's essays on the Pentagon papers. This was probably the only moment in all of space/time wherein these two men could be found in the same room, and I decided that my goal, the way I could change things, would be to get them to argue. I'd arrange it so Chomsky had to listen and fully comprehend the terms and assumptions behind McKenna's hallucinations, and I'd get McKenna to pay attention to Chomsky. But before I did anything I'd see how the moment had originally played out. The first time through I'd just listen and watch.

In the twenty minutes before the boarding of Flight 2012 began Chomsky barely spoke. Carol offered to get him a copy of the *Financial Times* at the newsstand and Noam stared out at the jet planes on the runway as he waited. He barely moved. McKenna, on the other hand, never stopped talking, even though it was apparent that the young woman he was traveling with had lost interest in what he was saying. McKenna described Nixon's America as a dream that people needed to wake up from, and he wondered if the illusion could really last another four years. "Everything is changing," McKenna said.

When Carol came back and Noam turned away from the Tarmac to read the *New York Times* and the *Financial Times*, McKenna seemed to feel a need to take over this staring out at the horizon. He pressed up against the glass, first looking out at the orange stripe on the 747, and then examining his own reflection. McKenna looked at his mirror image and then moved toward the glass until it appeared that he had only one brown eye, right in the middle of his forehead. His girlfriend, who I later discovered was named Wendy, brought him a half eaten apple she'd scavenged from the trashcan by the gift shop, and Terence ate it, core and seeds included. Wendy was pretty with her long and very straight blonde hair and straw hat. She kneeled down next to Terence and threw I-Ching coins onto the tile floor. She tossed out the I-Ching hexagram for disruption, and then put her hand on her hip as she read the hexagram's meaning aloud from a small blue hardback version of the Book of Changes:

"The Chinese character ku represents a bowl in whose contents worms are breeding. This means decay. It has come about because the gentle indifference in the lower trigram has come together with the rigid inertia of the upper, and the result is stagnation. Since this implies guilt, the conditions embody a demand for removal of the cause. Hence the meaning of the hexagram is not simply 'what has been spoiled' but 'work on what has been spoiled,'" she said.

Sitting between McKenna and Chomsky in the airport, noticing the metal mesh panel erected between the passengers and the TWA desk, noticing the cool November light streaming in the huge pane glass windows, I considered the Ku Hexagram. This past moment required work. I adjusted my Time Box, turned the dial back twenty minutes but did not reset.

I watched Terence and Chomsky board their plane, and then, when the moment was over, I pressed the reset button.

CRAWDADDY ONLINE
Jeff Morris

January, 5th, 2014 - 3:52 pm | 1,226 views | 0 recommendations | 14 comments

Seeking Disruption

> *Six in the beginning means:*
> *Setting right what has been spoiled by the father.*
> *If there is a son,*
> *No blame rests upon the departed father.*
> *Danger.*
> *In the end, good fortune.*
> —*The Gnostic Book of Changes*, Hexagram 18, Line One

I tried with Terence first, partly because I thought he would be more likely to believe me, but also because I wasn't as afraid of him as I was of Chomsky. I sat down next to him, reached over and grabbed his knapsack, dumped the contents onto the tile floor, then explained that I was quite sorry, and excuse me. I gathered up his possessions quickly, lined them up: one cassette recorder, a pink towel, an empty baggie that once held cannabis, a paperback edition of "the Naked Ape," yellowed copy of a June 5, 1968 edition the New York Times, one pair of dingy white boxer shorts, a pair of olive colored socks, a pair of leather sandals that smelled like sweat, a pair of cut-off blue jeans, and a plastic poncho that smelled like a campfire and which was rolled up tight and secured by two rubber bands. I got down on hands and knees, took the Time Box out of my front pocket, and took a picture of it all. Then I reset, and approached McKenna again.

I was from the future. I was there to talk to him, to change history, and I could prove it. I described the contents of his knapsack, but Terence wasn't as easy to convince as I'd expected. For one thing, he wasn't sure what he had in his blue nylon pack, so my explanation just came across as speculation that he could neither confirm nor deny.

I tried resetting the Box and bringing back my own knapsack. I told him I was from the future and then dumped the contents of my own bag for him to inspect. I showed McKenna a copy of his book *True Hallucinations*, an old copy of *Mondo 2000* from 1993, Daniel Pinchbeck's "Soft in the Head," a netbook computer, an iPhone, and then the Time Box itself. I did not tell Terence that in my future he was dead, but did tell him that I was from 2013, and that nothing had happened, nothing would happen, on December 21, 2012. Terence held the glossy magazine. The copy of Mondo 2000 was an antique from 1993 and Terence gingerly traced the wavy lines that were emanating from a cartoon JFK head. Instead of getting his head blown off Kennedy was depicted, in cyberpunk collage style, as getting his mind blown. McKenna's name was on the cover next to the Lincoln convertible, but he just shook his head at this and asked to see my iPhone.

Terence's girlfriend was about six feet away and leaning against the pillar with the white courtesy phone. I approached her, informed her that I was from the future, and described the contents of Terence's knapsack for her.

"What do you want?" she asked.

I didn't really know what I wanted. Terence was playing Tetris on my iPhone, his girl was holding I-Ching coins, looking at me suspiciously, and so I told her the only thing I could tell her. I said that I'd come back in order to save the world.

The three of us ended up smoking hash from Wendy's knapsack in the airport parking lot. Marijuana makes me a bit loose lipped, maybe a little captious. Getting stoned with Terence and his chippy I found that I wanted to tell them everything I could about the next forty years. I'd tell them all about computers, Ronald Reagan, Barack Obama, tell them anything if it would keep them from leaning on each other like they were doing. He had his arm around her waist and was playing with the button on her jeans. I'd told them everything I could think of about the decade ahead of them. I told them about Jimmy Carter, Pet Rocks, and the Osmonds. I told them fifties conformity would reinvent itself as hedonism. I wanted them to see how far away they were from the root of their problems. They could trip out as much as they wanted, but the multicolored chaos they brought back would either be bleached out with Clorox or slapped on the Clorox bottle as a part of a rebranding campaign.

"When were you born?" McKenna asked.

"March 20, 1970. In Pittsburgh."

"Have you gone to Pittsburgh? Have you seen yourself as a baby? Have you visited your mom and dad?" Wendy asked.

"I want to tell you about the Rubik's Cube," I said.

But McKenna wouldn't let go of his point. "You've come back to the O'Hare airport in 1971 in order to change history. You think I'm central to that?"

"Yes."

"Have you tried anything else?"

"Ummm. Yeah. No luck."

"Did you try killing Hitler?"

"No."

"Have you tried to stop the bombing of Hiroshima and Nagasaki?" Wendy asked.

"No. The Time Box won't let you do that."

"What?" Terence asked. "Why not?"

I handed him the manual, let him read the disclaimer for himself, but then tried to backpedal.

323

"It's not as hopeless as the manual makes it sound. You can change the settings," I said. "And you can think outside the usual box of history."

I told them that we needed to go somewhere to talk. We would fly to Berkeley the next day and confront Chomsky there. We needed more time. I'd explain everything, and then we could come up with a plan. I'd tell them how badly the world needed to be changed, all the reasons why: Donkey Kong, Bill Gates, the Internet, Osama bin Laden, and all the other reasons. But, once we got somewhere, when we arrived by cab at a Best Western near the airport, they booked a separate room for themselves. They told me that they'd see me in the morning.

"What about the Rubik's Cube?" I asked. "What about my glasses. See? They've got red ink in the frames."

"We want to be alone," McKenna said. "We'll talk over breakfast."

I went to my room and considered what it meant for me to be stoned in 1971. I lay down on the baby blue coverlet on my single bed, and looked up at the textured plaster ceiling. I sat up and hunted down the remote, found it velcroed to the dresser.

I watched the *Tonight Show with Johnny Carson* on a television with a fake wood panel under a channel dial.

"Did you know Richard Nixon is the only president whose formal portrait was painted by a police sketch artist?" Johnny asked the audience.

I stared at the yellow floral wallpaper, and then switched the Time Box off. The past blinked out, it was like turning off a light, and I found myself sitting behind my desk in my office. The yellow wallpaper was gone, as was the brown and white television.

The glass tabletop of my computer desk was smudged from where I'd kept my hands folded during my trip. I'd been in the past for hours. It was well past midnight, but the lights were still on. My wife had gone to bed without me, but she'd left the lights on so I wouldn't stumble over our son's legos in the living room. I tip toed across the orange carpet and found that along with a well-lit path she'd left a pillow and blanket for me on the living room sofa. When I lay down I found the metal bar underneath the cushions was bent. I sank into the couch, felt the metal bar press into my back, and considered what it meant that I was still stoned in the year 2013.

I sat up, searched for the remote, turned on the set, and found the *Tonight Show with Conan O'Brien.*

Next time around I was more proactive. We took Noam Chomsky out of the airport while his wife was in the restroom. Terence injected him with Ibogaine and as the visions came on we led the professor to the escalator. We descended past a travel poster that featured a blonde Eskimo with shapely hips under fir trimmed pants and Chomsky started to laugh uncontrollably. The poster featured a phallic airplane in the left corner and the jet was aimed at the blonde Eskimo's crotch. The slogan on the poster read: "Alaska! It's not cold inside."

I explained what was going on once we were in the back of a cab. I held out the Time Box for Chomsky to examine, told him who I was and where I was from, or more to the point when I was from, and then introduced McKenna and Wendy.

Chomsky must have decided to humor me, or maybe it was the Ibogaine, but rather than object to the premise he seemed to take the idea of time travel in stride.

"Have you tried exposing the Gulf of Tonkin incident?" he asked.

"No."

"Have you tried killing Hitler?" McKenna asked the same questions every time.

"You can't do that. The Time Box comes with a 'you can't kill Hitler' disclaimer. History can't be altered like that. The past is fixed."

"You didn't tell us that before," Wendy said.

"You didn't ask."

"I . . ." Chomsky paused. "I believe I may be sick."

"Do you see spots?" Terence asked.

"Orange."

"He's going to throw up. Better roll down the window."

"Your friend going to get sick in my cab?" the Italian taxi driver asked. He turned to look at Chomsky and didn't like what he saw. We skidded to a stop.

The linguist huddled on hands and knees and let out a stream of green foam. He complained about snakes when he finished, and then rolled onto his back and stretched his arms out across the grassy median.

"Let me look at your time machine." Wendy took the box from me and then held it out, at arm's length, as though she were considering whether she should throw it.

"Be careful with that."

"You've been playing with us," she said. "You're just playing games."

"Please be careful," I said.

We were near the Sears Tower, and I shielded my eyes with my right hand and looked up to see if I could find the top. The Tower just blended into the clouds, into the sky.

"Are you listening to me? I'm going to smash this. You'll be stuck here."

I tried to remember what the manual had said. Would a premature disconnect send me back or break me off in the stream? I was fairly sure I'd be sent back to the present, but getting stuck in 1972 wasn't my idea of a bad time. It wouldn't be a major adjustment, living without email and high def television. I could live in low definition.

"You want to start breaking things? Fine. But, all you'll do is destroy your future. The entire timeline will pop," I said.

I told them that I had a theory. The big historical moments couldn't be altered by actions from the future, but it might be possible to make adjustments. I told them that I was looking for a seam in the fabric of history.

"What did you think this man could tell us?" McKenna asked.

"I wanted you to talk to him."

"You wanted him stoned?" McKenna asked.

"I'm experimenting," I said.

"Did you think this through at all?" Wendy asked.

"Would you just . . ." I paused, tried to think of what I should say next. "Just give me the box."

She took her time handing it over, like it was a loaded gun, as if I might use it to hurt her, and when I had the box back in my hands I confirmed her worst fears. I looked at Terence, said goodbye, and reset. That timeline was gone. The Wendy, Chomsky, and Terence McKenna that had travelled by cab from the airport to the Sears Tower were gone, and if I tried to go back I'd find younger and more naïve versions of them in their regular positions. The stage would be set just as it always was, with everyone frozen in place, ready for my directions, and always ready to snap back into place again.

CRAWDADDY ONLINE
Jeff Morris

January, 7th, 2014 - 3:52 pm | 823 views | 0 recommendations | 2 comments

The Butterfly Effect

The butterfly effect is a metaphor that encapsulates the concept of sensitive dependence on initial conditions in chaos theory; namely that small differences in the initial condition of a dynamical system may produce large variations in the long term behavior of the system. The butterfly effect is a common trope in fiction when presenting scenarios involving time travel and with "what if" scenarios where one storyline diverges at the moment of a seemingly minor event resulting in two significantly different outcomes.

—Wikipedia

I've lived in Gate 23 of the Chicago O'Hare airport, lived in the twenty-two minutes between 1:30 p.m. and 1:52 p.m. on November 16, 1971 for the past six days. I spent New Year's eve in the past, the same moment over and over again, and I used a yardstick to measure the spaces between Terence McKenna and Noam Chomsky, between Wendy and Carol. I measured out the spaces between the bit players too. After seventeen visits I knew all about them:

Sylvie's children were Jennifer and Troy. Troy was two years old and still in disposable diapers. Jennifer was six and wanted a quarter for the automat television across from the gate.

George was a businessman who, at fifty-two years of age and after two weeks traveling, wanted nothing more than quiet at the gate and a gin and tonic when he got to his seat.

The doctor from New York wearing an IZOD shirt and khaki pants was named Craig, and his wife Ally was to meet him in Denver. Across from him a struggling ballet dancer named Cat stood with consciously good posture. She looked like a shorter version of Grace Jones. The doctor and the ballet dancer were seven feet apart.

Left to their own devices Cat and Craig would not speak to each other, but with some help they could be made to fall in love, or at least into lust. I discovered that I could drastically change the outcome of the moment just by asking Craig for the time; I could set off a chain reaction that led to him grunting and groaning and to Cat inadvertently flushing as she bent over for him in a toilet stall. There was such a thing as the butterfly effect. I asked Craig to look at his watch, and this led to him talking to Cat, and that led to him missing his flight because he couldn't hear the boarding call from the stall in the women's restroom.

I'd hit pay dirt, and the fact that nothing I did stopped Sylvie and George from their very loud public argument about her parenting didn't dampen my optimism a bit.

The first time that Craig checking his watch for me changed history I stuck around to see how it played out. I followed Craig and Cat to Oakland on Flight 82. I stayed the night in the same Best Western and watched Johnny Carson tell the same jokes in front of the same technicolored curtain. Cat and Craig were just two rooms down from me, and the next morning I sat two rows behind them on the flight out of O'Hare.

In Oakland I managed to keep up with Craig, but I lost track of Cat. They didn't get off the plane at the same time, and she went to the left while Craig turned right.

I managed to orchestrate the moment so that Craig and I took the same yellow taxi into Costa Contra County. The view out the left passenger window was reddish brown. Nimitz freeway was congested with blue Chevy sedans and orange ford station wagons. We headed east, and Craig sat next to me with his soft hands folded in his lap. I stared at his silver Rolex and his cuff links. We didn't talk much during the drive.

On November 17, 1971 Craig got out on Eastgate Street and walked up the drive to his little yellow ranch house. It was surely a starter home for him. His wife Ally was waiting in the front yard, holding their young song Sam on her hip with one hand and holding a green rubber hose with a pistol shaped attachment in her other hand. She was squeezing out a stream. The taxi drove around the block and then I had it stop so I could get out and backtrack. I wanted to find out if there was going to be a consequence. Would Craig's infidelity disrupt his life? Would it impact life on Eastgate Street? It didn't have to be anything much, any lasting change in the outcome of his life would be enough to settle the matter.

Walking the cul-de-sacs and side streets of Concord in 1971 made me profoundly uneasy. I tried to bide my time in an unobtrusive way, but the way Craig's lawn was laid out, the way the grass looked, green and perfect, but with shards of red plastic strewn along near the sidewalk, was overwhelmingly nostalgic in a way I didn't much care for.

My memories of the seventies, of my childhood, are not universally positive. When I was seven years old I bashed my lip open by flipping my Schwinn Stingray and catching the curb with my face. Half of my mouth was swollen for what I remember to be months. Before that I'd spent most of my school days in the principals office, on the green bench, because I wouldn't tolerate smart aleck comments from the boy who lived up the block from me. I used to get in fights with this blonde wunderkind who called me names like fag and retard when the teacher wasn't listening, and I used to lose. But once I smashed my face even the wunderkind took pity on me.

1977 was the year I caught my parents making it on their waterbed. Well maybe they didn't really have a waterbed, but Barry Manilow's "Weekend in New England" really was playing on their clock radio. The volume was very low but I recognized the song. I won't tell you what they were doing specifically, but they were doing it on top of the sheets and not like married people at all. It made an impression. So now I associate Barry Manilow, wall to wall carpeting, hanging lamps, beanbag chairs, really the whole era with this primal scene.

Looking at Craig's lawn I knew what the bits of plastic were. He'd run over the launch gyro for his son's Evil Knievel Stunt Bike set with the lawn mower. I spotted the white handle for the toy's crank in the space between the lawn and the sidewalk. It was stuck down there, in the muck, and I stepped over it, into the yard. The awful feeling of trespassing tingled through me, up my spine. The bad feeling of it settled somewhere between my temples.

I stood behind the rhododendron, peeked in the front window, and saw Mrs. Craig, or perhaps her name was Ms. Craig, sitting on their plaid sofa. She was wearing a plush off-white robe, and her bare feet dangled down and touched the asymmetrical orange and brown rectangles that decorated their vinyl floor. She was nursing the littlest Craig, and Craig Jr. was sitting next to her and watching a woman with long straight black hair, thin and small-chested, sing on TV. I waited in the bushes with my hand on the Time Box, ready to press the reset button if I was caught, but waiting for Craig to come back into the TV room. I wanted to see him with his wife, wanted to see if there would be a strain between them. Anything remotely visible, even if I just imagined it, would do, but Craig didn't make his entrance soon enough.

The boy stood up to turn off the TV when the woman on television stopped singing. Thinking about it now the woman was probably Cher. Then he turned around to face his mother again and instead of walking back or continuing on with whatever other activity might be waiting for him, (maybe putting his eye out with a pair of glass clackers) he stopped in his tracks. I'd clearly been seen. When Ms. Craig looked over in my direction I didn't wait for an outcome, but reset the Timebox.

There were a number of options still open to me at Gate 23, and quite a number that I'd already tried, but that were probably worth trying again. I needed to focus on McKenna more, or make sure that Sylvie found a quarter so that her daughter could watch the automat television. Sylvie needed a moment of peace.

If I smoked hash with Terence and Wendy while Chomsky explained the Pentagon papers to the girl behind the check-in desk and made sure to ask Craig for the time on my way down to the parking lot I could get nearly everything going at once. And if I tried breaking into the olive colored Oldsmobile Cutlass on level three I'd find that the door was unlocked and that the key was still in the ignition. I could get the radio going. Then Terence, Wendy and I could take a spin in the seventies sunshine. Donovan on AM and with the driver's side window rolled down was a fun diversion, but we never really went anywhere that way.

I could set up a dozen, a hundred, changes. I could make the girl behind the check-in counter cry, and I could make sure that Craig's wife found out about Cat. I could scream and yell and throw one of the orange chairs through the plate glass windows and out onto the tarmac, but I couldn't change the direction of history.

When I asked Craig for the time I thought about the film *Kramer vs. Kramer* with Dustin Hoffman and Meryl Streep. I thought about how everyone's personal life, all the marriages and nuclear families and folk groups, would be fractured in the next decade. And thirty years after that nobody would even have a personal life to break. There were just Facebooks and smart phones and double super-sized depressions.

I sat between Noam Chomsky and Terence McKenna and watched as the girl behind the counter walked out from behind the carpeted barricade at the front of the gate. She opened the door for the air-bridge onto the 747 that would take the passengers west. I listened to her announce that the elderly and those passengers boarding with small children should line-up, and I waited. Terence took another bite from the apple core Wendy had given him. Chomsky folded the *Financial Times* in half and glanced up at the door the girl had left open.

When the 747 backed away from the gate and made its way onto the runway I looked around the empty gate, at all the empty orange chairs, at the analog clock hanging above the handrail, and thought about starting over one more time.

CRAWDADDY ONLINE
Jeff Morris

January 9th, 2014 - 3:17 pm | 678 views | 0 recommendations | 1 comment

A Red Wedge Meets an Orange Tear Drop:
Progress in Gate 23

A Klee painting named "Angelus Novus" shows an angel looking as though he is about to move away from something he is fixedly contemplating. His eyes are staring, his mouth is open, his wings are spread. This is how one pictures the angel of history. His face is turned toward the past. Where we perceive a chain of events, he sees one single catastrophe which keeps piling wreckage upon wreckage and hurls it in front of his feet. The angel would like to stay, awaken the dead, and make whole what has been smashed. But a storm is blowing from Paradise; it has got caught in his wings with such violence that the angel can no longer close them.

The storm irresistibly propels him into the future to which his back is turned, while the pile of debris before him grows skyward. This storm is what we call progress.
—Walter Benjamin, *On the Concept of History*

I dropped the Time Box as I stepped beyond the metal railing that circled the gate, and I watched as the box bounced off the curved orange plastic of a chair, into the air, and then back down to the hard tile floor. The Time Box impacted with a clang and the world changed. The past dimmed, and then everything became clear, angular, and pure.

The gate for Flight 2012 appeared as one perfect black box, and when I turned and looked through the empty space where a window had been the 747 on the runway appeared as a slightly smaller red square. The world of 1971 had shifted into fundamental geometric forms. Noam Chomsky was a partial circle, a red wedge, and Terence McKenna was a black teardrop that flowed slowly across the olive colored rectangle that was the wall behind him.

Standing in an abstract past I wondered if I could possibly be looking at the seam, at a way to get at the under infrastructure of the moment.

Noam Chomsky punctured the white circle around the girl behind the TWA desk. She was a pink rectangle.

In this broken past I could apprehend Chomsky directly, and I could see how he changed shape depending on the moment. He was a red wedge that could shift into a yellow rectangle whereas McKenna was always a teardrop.

I looked at my hands and they appeared as pink circles on a blank white background. They would move at my mental command, but the idea of holding on to something was incomprehensible.

Worse than the visual manifestation of this moment, worse than the pure forms, was the rigidity I felt in my limbs, and the momentum of my perceptions. Everything felt thin and insubstantial and yet, at the same time, everything was of consequence. I was watching the universe work itself out on the meta-level, apprehending how my own thoughts were stolen or directed. Seeing myself in the mechanism that is existence.

I got down on my hands and knees, on triangles and squares, and I searched amongst the lines, the angles, the layers, for the Time Box.

I had to reset. I was panicking along a straight line. I looked at the orange chairs and they appeared as a series of thin tangerine colored rectangles. I wondered how it might be possible to look underneath.

The past was two-dimensional. It was a perceptual desert. There was nothing but the red wedge of Chomsky, nothing but tangerine rectangles and the straight line of my fear. Everything in 1971, in this new pure perception, came to me as a feeling, and I moved the feelings—the circles and squares—around an empty plane. I could change Chomsky from a red wedge into a yellow rectangle and then back again.

I reached under the chair. I closed my eyes and felt for the off switch. I reached out and found the Time Box.

The universe seemed brittle all around me, and I knew I could break it into pieces if I wanted. I could rearrange it, yes, but I could also destroy it. It would require no effort to tear McKenna or Wendy in half, and Chomsky was nothing but a paper thin idea.

What was most terrifying about the hallucination the Time Box was broadcasting was how familiar it was. I wasn't living with an orange tear drop and yellow rectangle, but remembering these things. I was remembering my own true form.

I wanted history with the stage sets intact. If I had to give up on bringing the red wedge of Chomsky into the realm of McKenna's teardrop, if I had to give up on changing history in order to stay in the real world with textures and faces and people and things, it was a sacrifice worth making.

I turned the box off.

CRAWDADDY ONLINE
Jeff Morris

January 9th, 2014 - 3:17 pm | 678 views | 0 recommendations | 1 comment

The Future

The future of the human race lies in the exploration and making explicit of the contents of the human imagination.
—Terence McKenna

I think it only makes sense to seek out and identify structures of authority, hierarchy, and domination in every aspect of life, and to challenge them. That includes political power, ownership and management, relations among men and women, parents and children, our control over the fate of future generations (the basic moral imperative behind the environmental movement, in my view), and much else. Naturally this means a challenge to the huge institutions of coercion and control: the state, the unaccountable private tyrannies that control most of the domestic and international economy, and so on.

—Noam Chomsky

Last night I transferred all of the photos from Gate 23 to my computer desktop. A 747 painted green, a photo of an ashtray filled with glass beads and butts, the stewardess wearing her brown pantyhose with the run in the left legging, and so on.

I closed the window with Carol Chomsky; she was staring at the Time Box from the front seat of a yellow taxi, her brown hair pulled up on her head in a tight bun, and her eyes focused and serious behind a pane of rain speckled glass. I closed the window that contained the image of a yellow dotted line that led to the emergency exits in baggage claim, then closed the window with Cat's blue polyester dress laid out neatly across the tile floor of the women's restroom. I could see Craig's loafers, out of focus but there, in the background. I closed the window on Noam Chomsky in an orange plastic chair. But, when the face looking back at me from the computer screen was my own I stopped.

I was standing next to a support beam by the blue check-in desk at Gate 23. I was wearing my green gortex rain jacket in the photo, and had a few days growth of grey speckled beard. I looked tired, much more worn out than the innocents all around me who were in their own time, but I was smiling. In the photo I'm pointing at something outside the frame. I looked like a movie director on a set. I was unkempt, obviously not meant to be onscreen.

Even this was something I could undo. All I had to do to get rid of the self in the photo was to turn on the Time Box again. The rest of history was impossible to control, but I had complete dominion over those twenty minutes in 1971. I stared at myself, studied my own image, and decided I would erase it. I said goodbye to the version of me on the screen.

On my last trip to the airport I tried to change everyone together and at the same time. If up until that point I'd rearranged the moment piece by piece, redirecting each person's attention separately, my new approach would take on the totality of the moment. I would capture all of their attention at once.

"Flight 23 to Boston will be boarding in fifteen minutes," the stewardess spoke the words into the microphone. "Departure time is 4:35."

I stood by my pillar and smiled again. I imagined someone, Craig or Carol or Cat, taking my picture, but this in the really existing moment there was nobody aiming the Time Box in my direction. Even so I lifted my hand to point to a place outside the frame.

I stepped up to Shelly, the girl in the short orange airline uniform, and leaned down to speak into her microphone. "Ladies and gentlemen," I started.

"Sir," Shelly objected. "You can't—"

"Ladies and gentlemen, Flight 2012 is cancelled due to a future calamity. In fact, I can tell you that in the future many of you are already dead. Please remain calm. Do exactly as I say or somebody will get hurt," I said. "Move only when I tell you to move. If anybody tries to be a hero I'll delete them. Don't try anything stupid." I took the Time Box from the inner pocket of my gortex raincoat and held it up so everyone could see. "This is a nuclear device. I can destroy time with it. I can, if I have to, erase all of you."

"It's a bomb," Shelly said. She started rubbing her legs together, sort of jogging in place, as if she thought I ought to have grabbed her and she ought to be struggling.

The Time Box had more than forty years of future history stored inside. The new upgrade allows the user to broadcast a wireless signal to a conventional television set. The signal is digital, but a converter is built-in and this allows the consumer to utilize the box in the past. Most users just opt to watch the tiny screen on the box itself, most are casual historians, but I'd picked a spot, found the moment when I wanted to be, and the fact that the Box would work with a TV built in 1968 was a big plus.

I moved the crew and passengers of Flight 2012 to the bar. I turned on the Time Box, switched on the RCA Solid State Technicolor dream box above the Jack Daniels on, and then started my history lesson. If Terence and Chomsky could not be pushed into a kind of joint effort, if there could be no rational synthesis, then they would at least have to face their future together, even if only this one time. Even if it would then be erased.

I started with Ronald Reagan.

"Who is that?" Cat asked.

Craig turned toward Cat. "It's Ronald Reagan from California."

Noam Chomsky drank a sip from a green bottle of beer. He peeled the label slowly with his thumb and watched the screen while Carol kept her arms wrapped tight around the carry-on bag in her lap. McKenna sat next to him and took a sip from the canteen he'd had with him in the Amazon. The canteen contained poorly mixed Tang. Most of the orange powder had collected as sediment on the bottom of the flask.

After Reagan I showed them the footage of the 1984 Space Shuttle disaster and followed this with starving children in Ethiopia. Next came the fall of the Berlin Wall followed by clips from the original *Tron*.

Terence was eating peanuts. Chomsky held the label from his beer between his index finger and his thumb. Craig yawned and stretched and then moved to put his arm around Cat. Cat, in turn, picked up a menu from the bar and read through the mixed drinks available.

"Put down the menu," I shouted. "Pay attention."

Watching the future with them I saw that there was quite a lot of what was terrible about it was enmeshed in that moment in Gate 23. Watching it while Noam Chomsky fiddled with the wet paper label from his beer bottle made me blush. Was I naïve enough to think that if people from 1971 could be made to see the collapse of the Twin Towers, if they were forced to witness the explosion of the space shuttle Challenger, that knowing about these things in advance would somehow make them act differently?

Even as I brought them their future as an act of terrorism, even as I was satisfied with how it all fit together seamlessly on the screen, I realized that nothing I could show them would shock. Noam Chomsky and Terence McKenna were already adjusted to living in a society that presented itself as a crisis.

When a man in a bear suit had less than optimal results down amongst the luxury hotels on Wall Street, when Madonna put her hand on her belly, when Ronald Reagan waved and waved as multicolored balloons came down around him, my embarrassment grew. It was just another happy and obvious critique. There were Golden Arches and billions served. The women on the *Love Boat* wore tiny bikinis as they swayed back and forth across the promenade. They arched their back as a hypno-wheel turned. And when Ronald Reagan's beautiful teeth were knocked out in a massive auto disaster, when Barack Obama's rear-end collision made Rob Lowe come I turned to look and found that Noam Chomsky looked bored. Even when he saw himself on television, even when there were a hundred screens on the screen, and they all showed him as a talking head, even when the women on the *Love Boat* poured water on themselves and their skin glistened, neither Chomsky nor McKenna reacted.

Their deadly future was shown as a rock video, and they were ready for it.

The hallway outside the airport bar was still filled with sunlight when I had everyone shuffle out. The history lesson was over and I watched Terence and Chomsky shrug at each other. I held the Time Box over my head and threatened destruction again. I had the ten of them line up in front of orange bucket seats in the hallway outside Gate 18, and asked them to raise their hands to answer my questions. I waited as they did as I asked, and was pleased when Chomsky and Terence ended up next to each other in line, but I was interrupted before I could get my first question out. I was going to ask them if they felt that what they saw on the screen was separate from them, separate from their lives, but instead of asking anything I reeled forward. A stinging sensation stopped my thoughts and my right leg stopped supporting my weight. I fell forward, hit the tile hard, and rolled over in time to see an explosion of dust erupt from the pillar I'd been leaning on a second earlier.

Somebody was shooting at me. I scrambled to pick up the Time Box, I'd dropped it when I fell. Then I forced myself onto to my feet and turned toward the panes of glass that separated me from the tarmac. There were motorcycle cops out there with guns drawn. They were still wearing their helmets and they had pistols. I stood shocked, and then wondered why they hadn't fired again.

Noam Chomsky was standing next to me at the window, looking down with me at the scene.

"You're in trouble," he said.

"Looks like it."

"Is that really a nuclear device," he asked.

I told him that I wasn't sure what it ran on exactly, but that it had something to do with quarks which, as far as I understood things, were subatomic particles.

Terence McKenna stepped back to let some policemen in body armor past, and I imagined what it would be like to get arrested. An absurd image flashed through my mind. In the instant it took for the SWAT team to get down on their knees and take aim at me I pictured myself riding on a police motorbike, only Chomsky was driving. I had my arms around Chomsky's waist and, as I heard the men cock their rifles, I saw Terence McKenna pull up beside us on his bike. We waved to him, and smiled. I felt a fly hit my lips, maybe a dragonfly or a flying beetle, and in my hallucination I swallowed reflexively. I imagined myself swallowing a bug, and then looked down at the spot on my leg where the bullet had hit me. There was a great deal of blood oozing out.

If I stayed in 1971 I would die there.

Looking from the SWAT team to Noam Chomsky I saw flecks of dust suspended in the air. The future I was about to go back to was going to be just the same as it ever was. I hit the reset button.

CRAWDADDY ONLINE
Jeff Morris

February 6th, 2014 - 5 pm | 20,213 views | 34 recommendations | 823 comments

In the Garden: Easybloom 3.0

The EasyBloom Plant/Topsoil Sensor was created for anyone who has experienced the frustration of not knowing what plant will survive in a specific location or anyone who has been unable to figure out just how the topsoil is contaminated when a crop fails. This

technology is essential for those who are adding to their caloric intake with a kitchen garden, as well as for industrial farmers.
—EasyBloom Brochure circa 2012

I want to thank everyone who sent emails of concern and sympathy during the last two weeks, and to assure all of my readers that while I don't have full mobility yet, I am feeling much better. I am walking again, although with a cane. I'm mostly just puttering around the house and garden these days. Domestic life can be quite pleasant, there is plenty of domestic tech to consider, and quite a lot of it has political or social implications.

For instance, I received my EasyBloom kit in the mail on Friday. The cardboard box that arrived with its orange flower logo and curved lines had a sort of kindergarten quality to it, but the peach colored sheet of molded plastic that held all the pieces together inside might have been more appropriately used with a medical or feminine hygiene product. The yellow plastic pedals that clip on the top worked all right, but all in all the product feels insubstantial. I haven't bothered to figure out whether it actually can collect data, but have only observed how it makes me feel about my garden when I stick the green metal prongs into the soil. While the device is supposed to lend yuppie legitimacy to the kitchen gardens that more and more Americans are relying on for vegetables in this era of shipping hazards and failed harvests, to me setting a piece of plastic next to my lemon cucumbers just manages to reinforce the reality that my garden box is semi-toxic. Looking at this cheerful plastic phallus with its umbrella top I start to distrust the whole enterprise. Who wants food grown on top of a landfill?

Another example of a domestic product would be the new iStick I received on Tuesday and promptly stuck in my ear. It's true that the sound quality is incredible, I could hear Carole King's every breath as she crooned about how it was too late and how we should just stop trying. Listening to music from the seventies was probably a mistake. I was afraid to flip the switch and get the video feed going. I told myself that I didn't want to mess with my optic nerve, but I think I just didn't want to see Carole with long wavy hair and in a wide collared pink blouse. I'd spent enough time with that era's fashions.

"It's too late now darling," Carole sang. I had to agree.

When the song was over I had some difficulty removing the device. I'd wedged it in too deep and couldn't just pluck it out the way the instructions indicated. After several attempts with no success I thought I was going to end up in the emergency room again, but my wife suggested we try using tweezers.

Some of you might have seen my appearance on the O'Brien show yesterday. We talked about Gate 23 and about how today's Chomsky reacted to my blog entries. Apparently he was reluctant to comment, but he did say that he felt that people ought to organize in the present rather than fantasize about the past. He views the Time Box as nothing more than a novelty, another virtual world, like television, and while he's technically or theoretically wrong, actually existing time travel does work like television, especially in retrospect. Chomsky is, as always, spot on.

I got more into it on Conan's show than he probably wanted, and I felt bad about how unfunny it all was. One thing I really wanted to ask him—Chomsky, not Conan—was if the past is just like television, then what is the present like?

Maybe the present is an EasyBloom flower, or an iStick that gets jammed in your ear and won't stop broadcasting. Whatever it is, it seems to be all we've got. One big present stretching out infinitely behind and in front of us.

I probably won't be getting more products to review by next week, but if I do I'll let you know.

Catch you later. . . .

James Morrow is best known for the Godhead Trilogy, which includes Towing Jehovah, Blameless in Abaddon, and The Eternal Footman. He is a literary science-fiction author whose work has garnered him World Fantasy and Nebula awards. A former filmmaker, he won a CINE Golden Eagle for his poetic documentary short, Children of the Morning. His most recent novel, from St. Martin's Press, is a loopy, quasi-historical, Darwinian extravaganza titled Galápagos Regained.

Morrow's satiric fable "Arms and the Woman" was originally published in the July, 1991, issue of Amazing Stories, three months after the end of Desert Storm. In an essay titled "Taken Gently by the Hand," written for the James Morrow issue of the scholarly journal Para*Doxa (Volume 5, Number 12), science fiction author Michael Swanwick argued that the story rewards a close reading, noting that it has "all the lightness and sting of a wasp soufleé."

"arms and the woman"
JAMES MORROW

"What did you do in the war, Mommy?"

The last long shadow has slipped from the sundial's face, melting into the hot Egyptian night. My children should be asleep. Instead they're bouncing on their straw pallets, stalling for time.

"It's late," I reply. "Nine o'clock already."

"Please," the twins implore me in a single voice.

"You have school tomorrow."

"You haven't told us a story all week," insists Damon, the whiner.

"The war is such a *great* story," explains Daphne, the wheedler.

"Kaptah's mother tells *him* a story every night," whines Damon.

"Tell us about the war," wheedles Daphne, "and we'll clean the whole cottage tomorrow, top to bottom."

I realize I'm going to give in—not because I enjoy spoiling my children (though I do) or because the story itself will consume less time than further negotiations (though it will) but because I actually want the twins to hear this particular tale. It has a point. I've told it before, of course, a dozen times perhaps, but I'm still not sure they get it.

I snatch up the egg timer and invert it on the night-stand, the tiny grains of sand spilling into the lower chamber like seeds from a farmer's palm. "Be ready for bed in three minutes," I warn my children, "or no story."

They scurry off, frantically brushing their teeth and slipping on their flaxen nightshirts. Silently I glide about the cottage, dousing the lamps and curtaining the moon, until only one candle lights the twins' room, like the campfire of an army consisting of mice and scarab beetles.

"So you want to know what I did in the war," I intone, singsong, as my children climb into their beds.

"Oh, yes," says Damon, pulling up his fleecy coverlet.

"You bet," says Daphne, fluffing her goose-feather pillow.

"Once upon a time," I begin, "I lived as both princess and prisoner in the great city of Troy." Even in this feeble light, I'm struck by how handsome Damon is, how beautiful Daphne. "Every evening, I would sit in my boudoir, looking into my polished bronze mirror . . ."

Helen of Troy, princess and prisoner, sits in her boudoir, looking into her polished bronze mirror and scanning her world-class face for symptoms of age—for wrinkles, wattles, pouches, crow's-feet, and the crenellated corpses of hairs. She feels like crying, and not just because these past ten years in Ilium are starting to show. She's sick of the whole sordid arrangement, sick of being cooped up in this overheated acropolis like a pet cockatoo. Whispers haunt the citadel. The servants are gossiping, even her own handmaids. The whore of Hisarlik, they call her. The slut from Sparta. The Lakedaimon lay.

Then there's Paris. Sure, she's madly in love with him, sure, they have great sex, but can't they ever *talk*?

Sighing, Helen trolls her hairdo with her lean, exquisitely manicured fingers. A silver strand lies amid the folds like a predatory snake. Slowly she winds the offending filament around her index finger, then gives a sudden tug. "Ouch," she cries, more from despair than pain. There are times when Helen feels like tearing out all her lovely tresses, every last lock, not simply these graying threads. If I have to spend one more pointless day in Hisarlik, she tells herself, I'll go mad.

Every morning, she and Paris enact the same depressing ritual. She escorts him to the Skaian Gate, hands him his spear and his lunch bucket, and with a tepid kiss sends him off to work. Paris's job is killing people. At sundown he arrives home grubby with blood and redolent of funeral pyres, his spear wrapped in bits of drying viscera. There's a war going on out there; Paris won't tell her anything more. "Who are we fighting?" she asks each evening as they lie together in bed. "Don't you worry your pretty little head about it," he replies, slipping on a sheep-gut condom, the brand with the plumed and helmeted soldier on the box.

Until this year, Paris had contrived for her to walk Troy's high walls each morning, waving encouragement to the troops, blowing them kisses as they marched off to battle. "Your face inspires them," he'd insisted. "An airy kiss from you is worth a thousand nights of passion with a nymph." But in recent months Paris's priorities have changed. As soon as they say good-bye, Helen is supposed to retire to the citadel, speaking with no other Hisarlikan, not even a brief coffee klatsch with one of Paris's forty-nine sisters-in-law. She's expected to spend her whole day weaving rugs, carding flax, and being beautiful. It is not a life.

Can the gods help? Helen is skeptical, but anything is worth a try. Tomorrow, she resolves, she will go to the temple of Apollo and beg him to relieve her boredom, perhaps buttressing her appeal with an offering—a ram, a bull, whatever—though an offering strikes her as rather like a deal, and Helen is sick of deals. Her husband—pseudohusband, nonhusband—made a deal. She keeps thinking of the Apple of Discord, and what Aphrodite might have done with it after bribing Paris. Did she drop it in her fruit bowl . . . put it on her mantel . . . impale it on her crown? Why did Aphrodite take the damn thing seriously? Why did any of them take it seriously? Hi, I'm the fairest goddess in the universe—see, it says so right here on my apple.

Damn—another gray hair, another weed in the garden of her pulchritude. She reaches toward the villain—and stops. Why bother? These hairs are like the Hydra's heads, endless, cancerous, and besides, it's high time Paris realized there's a mind under that coiffure.

Whereupon Paris comes in, sweating and snorting. His helmet is awry; his spear is gory; his greaves are sticky with other men's flesh.

"Hard day, dear?"

"Don't ask." Her nonhusband unfastens his breastplate. "Pour us some wine. Looking in the speculum, were you? Good."

Helen sets the mirror down, uncorks the bottle, and fills two bejeweled goblets with Chateau Samothrace.

"Today I heard about some techniques you might try," says Paris. "Ways for a woman to retain her beauty."

"You mean—you *talk* on the battlefield?"

"During the lulls."

"I wish you'd talk to *me*."

"Wax," says Paris, lifting the goblet to his lips. "Wax is the thing." His heavy jowls undulate as he drinks. Their affair, Helen will admit, still gives her a kick. In the past ten years, her lover has moved beyond the surpassing prettiness of an Adonis into something equally appealing, an authoritative, no-frills masculinity suggestive of an aging matinee idol. "Take some melted wax and work it into the lines in your brow—presto, they're gone."

"I *like* my lines," Helen insists with a quick but audible snort.

"When mixed with ox blood, the dark silt from the River Minyeios is indelible, they say. You can dye your silver hairs back to auburn. A Grecian formula." Paris sips his wine. "As for these redundant ounces on your thighs, well, dear, we both know there's no cure like exercise."

"Look who's talking," Helen snaps. "*Your* skin is no bowl of cream. *Your* head is no garden of sargasso. As for your stomach, it's a safe bet that Paris of Troy can walk through the rain without getting his belt buckle wet."

The prince finishes his wine and sighs. "Where's the girl I married? You used to care about your looks."

"The girl you married," Helen replies pointedly, "is not your wife."

"Well, yes, of course not. Technically, you're still *his*."

"I want a wedding." Helen takes a gluttonous swallow of Samothrace and sets the goblet on the mirror. "You could go to my husband," she suggests. "You could present yourself to high-minded Menelaus and try to talk things out." Reflected in the mirror's wobbly face, the goblet grows weird, twisted, as if seen through a drunkard's eyes. "Hey, listen, I'll bet he's found another maid by now—he's something of a catch, after all. So maybe you actually did him a favor. Maybe he isn't even mad."

"He's mad," Paris insists. "The man is angry."

"How do you know?"

"I know."

Heedless of her royal station, Helen consumes her wine with the crude insouciance of a galley slave. "I want a baby," she says.

"What?"

"You know, a baby. *Baby:* a highly young person. My goal, dear Paris, is to be pregnant."

"Fatherhood is for losers." Paris chucks his spear onto the bed. Striking the mattress, the oaken shaft disappears into the soft down. "Go easy on the *vino*, love. Alcohol is awfully fattening."

"Don't you understand? I'm losing my mind. A pregnancy would give me a sense of purpose."

"Any idiot can sire a child. It takes a hero to defend a citadel."

"Have you found someone else, Paris? Is that it? Someone younger and thinner?"

"Don't be foolish. Throughout the whole of time, in days gone by and eras yet to come, no man will love a woman as much as Paris loves Helen."

"I'll bet the plains of Ilium are crawling with camp followers. They must swoon over you."

"Don't you worry your pretty little head about it," says Paris, unwrapping a plumed-soldier condom.

If he ever says that to me again, Helen vows as they tumble drunkenly into bed, I'll scream so loud the walls of Troy will fall.

The slaughter is not going well, and Paris is depressed. By his best reckoning, he's dispatched only fifteen Achaeans to the house of Hades this morning: strong-greaved Machaon, iron-muscled Euchenor, ax-wielding Deichos, a dozen more—fifteen noble warriors sent to the dark depths, fifteen breathless bodies left to nourish the dogs and ravens. It is not enough.

All along the front, Priam's army is giving ground without a fight. Their morale is low, their *esprit* spent. They haven't seen Helen in a year, and they don't much feel like fighting anymore.

With a deep Aeolian sigh, the prince seats himself atop his pile of confiscated armor and begins his lunch break.

Does he have a choice? Must he continue keeping her in the shadows? Yes, by Poseidon's trident—yes. Exhibiting Helen as she looks now would just make matters worse. Once upon a time, her face had launched a thousand ships. Today it couldn't get a Theban fishing schooner out of dry dock. Let the troops catch only a glimpse of her wrinkles, let them but glance at her aging hair, and they'll start deserting like rats leaving a foundering trireme.

He's polishing off a peach—since delivering his famous verdict and awarding Aphrodite her prize, Paris no longer cares for apples—

when two of the finest horses in Hisarlik, steadfast Aithon and intrepid Xanthos, gallop up pulling his brother's war chariot. He expects to see Hector holding the reins, but no: the driver, he notes with a pang of surprise, is Helen.

"Helen? What are *you* doing here?"

Brandishing a cowhide whip, his lover jumps down. "You won't tell me what this war is about," she gasps, panting inside her armor, "so I'm investigating on my own. I just came from the swift-flowing Menderes, where your enemies are preparing to launch a cavalry charge against the camp of Epistrophos."

"Go back to the citadel, Helen. Go back to Pergamamos."

"Paris, this army you're battling—they're *Greeks*. Idomeneus, Diomedes, Sthenelos, Euryalos, Odysseus—I *know* these men. Know them? By Pan's flute, I've *dated* half of them. You'll never guess who's about to lead that cavalry charge."

Paris takes a stab. "Agamemnon?"

"Agamemnon!" Sweat leaks from beneath Helen's helmet like blood from a scalp wound. "My own brother-in-law! Next you'll be telling me Menelaus himself has taken the field against Troy!"

Paris coughs and says, "Menelaus himself has taken the field against Troy."

"He's here?" wails Helen, thumping her breastplate. "My husband is *here*?"

"Correct."

"What's going on, Paris? For what purpose have the men of horse-pasturing Argos come all the way to Ilium?"

The prince bounces his peach pit off Helen's breastplate. Angrily he fishes for epithets. Mule-minded Helen, he calls her beneath his breath. Leather-skinned Lakedaimon. He feels beaten and bettered, trapped and tethered. "Very well, sweetheart, very well . . ." Helen of the iron will, the hard ass, the bronze bottom. "They've come for *you*, love."

"What?"

"For you."

"Me? What are you talking about?"

"They want to steal you back." As Paris speaks, Helen's waning beauty seems to drop another notch. Her face darkens with an unfathomable mix of anger, hurt, and confusion. "They're pledged to it. King

Tyndareus made your suitors swear they'd be loyal to whomever you selected as husband."

"*Me*?" Helen leaps into the chariot. "You're fighting an entire, stupid, disgusting war for *me*?"

"Well, not for you per se. For honor, for glory, for arete. Now hurry off to Pergamos—that's an order."

"I'm hurrying off, dear"—she raises her whip—"but not to Pergamos. On, Aithon!" She snaps the lash. "On, Xanthos!"

"Then where?"

Instead of answering, Paris's lover speeds away, leaving him to devour her dust.

Dizzy with outrage, trembling with remorse, Helen charges across the plains of Ilium. On all sides, an astonishing drama unfolds, a spectacle of shattered senses and violated flesh: soldiers with eyes gouged out, tongues cut loose, limbs hacked off, bellies ripped open; soldiers, as it were, giving birth to their own bowels—all because of her. She weeps openly, profusely, the large gemlike tears running down her wrinkled cheeks and striking her breastplate. The agonies of Prometheus are a picnic compared to the weight of her guilt, the Pillars of Herakles are feathers when balanced against the crushing tonnage of her conscience.

Honor, glory, arete: I'm missing something, Helen realizes as she surveys the carnage. The war's essence eludes me.

She reaches the thick and stinking Lisgar Marsh and reins up before a foot soldier sitting in the mud, a young Myrmidon with what she assumes are a particularly honorable spear hole in his breastplate and a singularly glorious lack of a right hand.

"Can you tell me where I might find your king?" she asks.

"By Hera's eyes, you're easy to look at," gasps the soldier as, arete in full bloom, he binds his bleeding stump with linen.

"I need to find Menelaus."

"Try the harbor," he says, gesturing with his wound. The bandaged stump drips like a leaky faucet. "His ship is the *Arkadia*."

Helen thanks the soldier and aims her horses toward the wine-dark sea.

"Are you Helen's mother, by any chance?" he calls as she races off. "What a face you've got!"

Twenty minutes later, reeling with thirst and smelling of horse sweat, Helen pulls within view of the crashing waves. In the harbor beyond, a thousand strong-hulled ships lie at anchor, their masts jutting into the sky like a forest of denuded trees. All along the beach, Helen's countrymen are raising a stout wooden wall, evidently fearful that, if the line is ever pushed back this far, the Trojans will not hesitate to burn the fleet. The briny air rings with the Achaeans' axes—with the thud and crunch of acacias being felled, palisades being whittled, stockade posts sharpened, breastworks shaped, a cacophony muffling the flutter of the sails and the growl of the surf.

Helen starts along the wharf, soon spotting the *Arkadia,* a stout penteconter with half a hundred oars bristling from her sides like quills on a hedgehog. No sooner has she crossed the gangplank than she comes upon her husband, older now, striated by wrinkles, but still unquestionably he. Plumed like a peacock, Menelaus stands atop the forecastle, speaking with a burly construction brigade, tutoring them in the proper placement of the impalement stakes. A handsome man, she decides, much like the warrior on the condom boxes. She can see why she picked him over Sthenelos, Euryalos, and her other beaus.

As the workers set off to plant their spiky groves, Helen saunters up behind Menelaus and taps his shoulder.

"Hi," she says.

He was always a wan fellow, but now his face loses whatever small quantity of blood it once possessed.

"Helen?" he says, gasping and blinking like a man who's just been doused with a bucket of slop. "Is that *you?*"

"Right."

"You've, er . . . aged."

"You too, sweetheart."

He pulls off his plumed helmet, stomps his foot on the forecastle, and says, angrily, "You ran out on me."

"Yes. Quite so."

"Trollop."

"Perhaps." Helen adjusts her greaves. "I could claim I was bewitched by laughter-loving Aphrodite, but that would be a lie. The fact is, Paris knocked me silly. I'm crazy about him. Sorry." She runs her desiccated tongue along her parched lips. "Have you anything to drink?"

Dipping a hollow gourd into his private cistern, Menelaus offers her a pint of fresh water. "So what brings you here?"

Helen receives the ladle. Setting her boots wide apart, she steadies herself against the roll of the incoming tide and takes a greedy gulp. At last she says, "I wish to give myself up."

"What?"

"I want to go home with you."

"You mean—you think our marriage deserves another chance?"

"No, I think all those infantrymen out there deserve to live. If this war is really being fought to retrieve me, then consider the job done." Tossing the ladle aside, Helen holds out her hands, palms turned upward as if she's testing for raindrops. "I'm yours, hubby. Manacle my wrists, chain my feet together, throw me in the brig."

Against all odds, defying all *logos*, Menelaus's face loses more blood. "I don't think that's a very good idea," he says.

"Huh? What do you mean?"

"This siege, Helen—there's more to it than you suppose."

"Don't jerk me around, lord of all Lakedaimon, asshole. It's time to call it quits."

The Spartan king stares straight at her chest, a habit she's always found annoying. "Put on a bit of weight, eh, darling?"

"Don't change the subject." She lunges toward Menelaus's scabbard as if to goose him, but instead draws out his sword. "I'm deadly serious: if Helen of Troy is not permitted to live with herself—she pantomimes the act of suicide—"then she will die with herself."

"Tell you what," says her husband, taking his weapon back. "Tomorrow morning, first thing, I'll go to my brother and suggest he arrange a truce with your father-in-law."

"He's not my father-in-law. There was never a wedding."

"Whatever. The point is, your offer has merit, but it must be discussed. We shall all meet face-to-face, Trojans and Achaeans, and talk it out. As for now, you'd best return to your lover."

"I'm warning you—I shall abide no more blood on my hands, none but my own."

"Of course, dear. Now please go back to the citadel."

At least he listened, Helen muses as she crosses the weatherworn deck of the *Arkadia*. At least he didn't tell me not to worry my pretty little head about it.

"Here comes the dull part," says whiny-tongued Damon.
"The scene with all the talking," adds smart-mouthed Daphne.
"Can you cut it a bit?" my son asks.
"Hush," I say, smoothing out Damon's coverlet. "No interruptions," I insist. I slip Daphne's papyrus doll under her arm. "When you have your own children, you can edit the tale however you wish. As for now, listen carefully. You might learn something."

By the burbling, tumbling waters of the River Simois, beneath the glowing orange avatar of the moon goddess Artemis, ten aristocrats are gathered around an oaken table in the purple tent of Ilium's high command, all of them bursting with opinions on how best to deal with this Helen situation, this peace problem, this Trojan hostage crisis. White as a crane, a truce banner flaps above the heads of the two kings, Priam from the high city, Agamemnon from the long ships. Each side has sent its best and/or brightest. For the Trojans: brainy Panthoos, mighty Paris, invincible Hector, and Hiketaon the scion of Ares. For the Achaean cause: Ajax the berserker, Nestor the mentor, Menelaus the cuckold, and wily, smiling Odysseus. Of all those invited, only quarrelsome Achilles, sulking in his tent, has declined to appear.

Panthoos rises, rubs his foam-white beard, and sets his scepter on the table. "Royal captains, gifted seers," the old Trojan begins, "I believe you will concur when I say that, since this siege was laid, we have not faced a challenge of such magnitude. Make no mistake: Helen means to take our war away from us, and she means to do so immediately."

Gusts of dismay waft through the tent like a wind from the underworld.

"We can't quit now," groans Hector, wincing fiercely.
"We're just getting up to speed," wails Hiketaon, grimacing greatly.
Agamemnon steps down from his throne, carrying his scepter like a spear. "I have a question for Prince Paris," he says. "What does your mistress's willingness to return to Argos say about the present state of your relationship?"

Paris strokes his jowls and replies, "As you might surmise, noble King, my feelings for Helen are predicated on requitement."

"So you won't keep her in Pergamos by force?"

"If she doesn't want me, then I don't want her."

At which point slug-witted Ajax raises his hand. "Er, excuse me. I'm a bit confused. If Helen is ours for the asking, then why must we continue the war?"

A sirocco of astonishment arises among the heroes.

"Why?" gasps Panthoos. *"Why?* Because this is *Troy*, that's why. Because we're kicking off Western Civilization here, that's why. The longer we can keep this affair going—the longer we can sustain such an ambiguous enterprise—the more valuable and significant it becomes."

Slow-synapsed Ajax says, "Huh?"

Nestor has but to clear his throat and every eye is upon him. "What our adversary is saying—may I interpret, wise Panthoos?" He turns to his Trojan counterpart, bows deferentially, and, receiving a nod of assent, speaks to Ajax. "Panthoos means that, if this particular pretext for war—restoring a woman to her rightful owner—can be made to seem reasonable, then *any* pretext for war can be made to seem reasonable." The mentor shifts his fevered stare from Ajax to the entire assembly. "By rising to this rare and precious occasion, we shall open the way for wars of religion, wars of manifest destiny—any equivocal cause you care to name." Once again his gaze alights on Ajax. "Understand, sir? This is the war to inaugurate war itself. This is the war to make the world safe for war!"

Ajax frowns so vigorously his visor falls down. "All I know is, we came for Helen, and we got her. Mission accomplished." Turning to Agamemnon, the berserker lifts the visor from his eyes. "So if it's all the same to you, Majesty, I'd like to go home before I get killed."

"O, Ajax, Ajax, Ajax," moans Hector, pulling an arrow from his quiver and using it to scratch his back. "Where is your aesthetic sense? Have you no appreciation of war for war's sake? The plains of Ilium are roiling with glory, sir. You could cut the arete with a knife. Never have there been such valiant eviscerations, such venerable dismemberments, such—"

"I don't get it," says the berserker. "I just don't get it."

Whereupon Menelaus slams his wine goblet on the table with a resounding thunk. "We are not gathered in Priam's tent so that Ajax might learn politics," he says impatiently. "We are gathered so that we might best dispose of my wife."

"True, true," says Hector.

"So what are we going to do, gentlemen?" asks Menelaus. "Lock her up?"

"Good idea," says Hiketaon.

"Well, yes," says Agamemnon, slumping back onto his throne. "Except that, when the war finally ends, my troops will demand to see her. Might they not wonder why so much suffering and sacrifice was spent on a goddess gone to seed?" He turns to Paris and says, "Prince, you should not have let this happen."

"Let *what* happen?" asks Paris.

"I heard she has wrinkles," says Agamemnon.

"I heard she got fat," says Nestor.

"What have you been feeding her?" asks Menelaus. "Bonbons?"

"She's a *person*," protests Paris. "She's not a marble statue. You can hardly blame *me* . . ."

At which juncture King Priam raises his scepter and, as if to wound Gaea herself, rams it into the dirt.

"Noble lords, I hate to say this, but the threat is more immediate than you might suppose. In the early years of the siege, the sight of fair Helen walking the ramparts did wonders for my army's morale. Now that she's no longer fit for public display, well . . ."

"Yes?" says Agamemnon, steeling himself for the worst.

"Well, I simply don't know how much longer Troy can hold up its end of the war. If things don't improve, we may have to capitulate by next winter."

Gasps of horror blow across the table, rattling the tent flaps and ruffling the aristocrats' capes.

But now, for the first time, clever, canny Odysseus addresses the council, and the winds of discontent grow still. "Our course is obvious," he says. "Our destiny is clear," he asserts. "We must put Helen—the old Helen, the pristine Helen—back on the walls."

"The pristine Helen?" says Hiketaon. "Are you not talking fantasy, resourceful Odysseus? Are you not singing a myth?"

The lord of all Ithaca strolls the length of Priam's tent, plucking at his beard. "It will require some wisdom from Pallas Athena, some technology from Hephaestus, but I believe the project is possible."

"Excuse me," says Paris. "*What* project is possible?"

"Refurbishing your little harlot," says Odysseus. "Making the dear, sweet strumpet shine like new."

Back and forth, to and fro, Helen moves through her boudoir, wearing a ragged path of angst into the carpet. An hour passes. Then two. Why are they taking so long?

What most gnaws at her, the thought that feasts on her entrails, is the possibility that, should the council not accept her surrender, she will have to raise the stakes. And how might she accomplish the deed? By what means might she book passage on Charon's one-way ferry? Something from her lover's arsenal, most likely—a sword, spear, dagger, or death-dripping arrow. O, please, my lord Apollo, she prays to the city's prime protector, don't let it come to that.

At sunset Paris enters the room, his pace leaden, his jowls dragging his mouth into a grimace. For the first time ever, Helen observes tears in her lover's eyes.

"It is finished," he moans, doffing his plumed helmet. "Peace has come. At dawn you must go to the long ships. Menelaus will bear you back to Sparta, where you will once again live as mother to his children, friend to his concubines, and emissary to his bed."

Relief pours out of Helen in a deep, orgasmic rush, but the pleasure is short-lived. She loves this man, flaws and all, flab and the rest. "I shall miss you, dearest Paris," she tells him. "Your bold abduction of me remains the peak experience of my life."

"I agreed to the treaty only because Menelaus believes you might otherwise kill yourself. You're a surprising woman, Helen. Sometimes I think I hardly know you."

"Hush, my darling," she says, gently placing her palm across his mouth. "No more words."

Slowly they unclothe each other, methodically unlocking the doors to bliss, the straps and sashes, the snaps and catches, and thus begins their final, epic night together.

"I'm sorry I've been so judgmental," says Paris.

"I accept your apology."

"You are so beautiful. So impossibly beautiful . . ."

As dawn's rosy fingers stretch across the Trojan sky, Hector's faithful driver, Eniopeus the son of horse-loving Thebaios, steers his sturdy war chariot along the banks of the Menderes, bearing Helen to the Achaean stronghold. They reach the *Arkadia* just as the sun is cresting, so their arrival in the harbor becomes a flaming parade, a show of sparks and gold, as if they ride upon the burning wheels of Hyperion himself.

Helen starts along the dock, moving past the platoons of squawking gulls adrift on the early morning breeze. Menelaus comes forward to greet her, accompanied by a man for whom Helen has always harbored a vague dislike—broad-chested, black-bearded Teukros, illegitimate son of Telemon.

"The tide is ripe," says her husband. "You and Teukros must board forthwith. You will find him a lively traveling companion. He knows a hundred fables and plays the harp."

"Can't *you* take me home?"

Menelaus squeezes his wife's hand and, raising it to his lips, plants a gentle kiss. "I must see to the loading of my ships," he explains, "the disposition of my battalions—a full week's job, I'd guess."

"Surely you can leave that to Agamemnon."

"Give me seven days, Helen. In seven days I'll be home, and we can begin picking up the pieces."

"We're losing the tide," says Teukros, anxiously intertwining his fingers.

Do I trust my husband? wonders Helen as she strides up the *Arkadia's* gangplank. Does he really mean to lift the siege?

All during their slow voyage out of the harbor, Helen is haunted. Nebulous fears, nagging doubts, and odd presentiments swarm through her brain like Harpies. She beseeches her beloved Apollo to speak with her, calm her, assure her all is well, but the only sounds reaching her ears are the creaking of the oars and the windy, watery voice of the Hellespont.

By the time the *Arkadia* finds the open sea, Helen has resolved to jump overboard and swim back to Troy.

"And then Teukros tried to kill you," says Daphne.

"He came at you with his sword," adds Damon.

This is the twins' favorite part, the moment of grue and gore. Eyes flashing, voice climbing to a melodramatic pitch, I tell them how, before I could put my escape plan into action, Teukros began chasing me around the *Arkadia,* slashing his two-faced blade. I tell them how

356

I got the upper hand, tripping the bastard as he was about to run me through.

"You stabbed him with his own sword, didn't you, Mommy?" asks Damon.

"I had no choice."

"And then his guts spilled, huh?" asks Daphne.

"Agamemnon had ordered Teukros to kill me," I explain. "I was ruining everything."

"They spilled out all over the deck, right?" asks Damon.

"Yes, dear, they certainly did. I'm quite convinced Paris wasn't part of the plot, or Menelaus either. Your mother falls for fools, not maniacs."

"What color were they?" asks Damon.

"Color?"

"His guts."

"Red, mostly, with daubs of purple and black."

"Neat."

I tell the twins of my long, arduous swim through the strait.

I tell them how I crossed Ilium's war-torn fields, dodging arrows and eluding patrols.

I tell how I waited by the Skaian Gate until a farmer arrived with a cartload of provender for the besieged city . . . how I sneaked inside the walls, secluded amid stalks of wheat . . . how I went to Pergamos, hid myself in the temple of Apollo, and breathlessly waited for dawn.

Dawn comes up, binding the eastern clouds in crimson girdles. Helen leaves the citadel, tiptoes to the wall, and mounts the hundred granite steps to the battlements. She is unsure of her next move. She has some vague hope of addressing the infantrymen as they assemble at the gate. Her arguments have failed to impress the generals, but perhaps she can touch the heart of the common foot soldier.

It is at this ambiguous point in her fortunes that Helen runs into herself.

She blinks—once, twice. She swallows a sphere of air. Yes, it is she, herself, marching along the parapets. Herself? No, not exactly: an idealized rendition, the Helen of ten years ago, svelte and smooth.

As the troops march through the portal and head toward the plain, the strange incarnation calls down to them.

"Onward, men!" it shouts, raising a creamy white arm. "Fight for me!" Its movements are deliberate and jerky, as if sunbaked Troy has been magically transplanted to some frigid clime. "I'm worth it!"

The soldiers turn, look up. "We'll fight for you, Helen!" a bowman calls toward the parapet.

"We love you!" a sword-wielder shouts.

Awkwardly, the incarnation waves. Creakily, it blows an arid kiss. "Onward, men! Fight for me! I'm worth it!"

"You're beautiful, Helen!" a spear-thrower cries.

Helen strides up to her doppelgänger and, seizing the left shoulder, pivots the creature toward her.

"Onward, men!" it tells Helen. "Fight for me! I'm worth it!"

"You're beautiful," the spear-thrower continues, "and so is your mother!"

The eyes, Helen is not surprised to discover, are glass. The limbs are fashioned from wood, the head from marble, the teeth from ivory, the lips from wax, the tresses from the fleece of a darkling ram. Helen does not know for certain what forces power this creature, what magic moves its tongue, but she surmises that the genius of Athena is at work here, the witchery of ox-orbed Hera. Chop the creature open, she senses, and out will pour a thousand cogs and pistons from Hephaestus's fiery workshop.

Helen wastes no time. She hugs the creature, lifts it off its feet. Heavy, but not so heavy as to dampen her resolve.

"Onward, men!" it screams as Helen throws it over her shoulder. "Fight for me! I'm worth it!"

And so it comes to pass that, on a hot, sweaty Asia Minor morning, fair Helen turns the tables on history, gleefully abducting herself from the lofty stone city of Troy.

Paris is pulling a poisoned arrow from his quiver, intent on shooting a dollop of hemlock into the breast of an Achaean captain, when his brother's chariot charges past.

Paris nocks the arrow. He glances at the chariot.

He aims.

Glances again.

Fires. Misses.

Helen.

Helen? *Helen*, by Apollo's lyre, his Helen—no, two Helens, the true and the false, side by side, the true guiding the horses into the thick of the fight, her wooden twin staring dreamily into space. Paris can't decide which woman he is more astonished to see.

"Soldiers of Troy!" cries the fleshly Helen. "Heroes of Argos! Behold how your leaders seek to dupe you! You are fighting for a fraud, a swindle, a thing of gears and glass!"

A stillness envelops the battlefield. The men are stunned, not so much by the ravings of the charioteer as by the face of her companion, so pure and perfect despite the leather thong sealing her jaw shut. It is a face to sheathe a thousand swords—lower a thousand spears—unnock a thousand arrows.

Which is exactly what now happens. A thousand swords: sheathed. A thousand spears: lowered. A thousand arrows: unnocked.

The soldiers crowd around the chariot, pawing at the ersatz Helen. They touch the wooden arms, caress the marble brow, stroke the ivory teeth, pat the waxen lips, squeeze the woolly hair, rub the glass eyes.

"See what I mean?" cries the true Helen. "Your kings are diddling you . . ."

Paris can't help it: he's proud of her, by Hermes's wings. He's puffing up with admiration. This woman has nerve—she has arete and chutzpah.

This woman, Paris realizes as a fat, warm tear of nostalgia rolls down his cheek, is going to the end the war.

"The end," I say.

"And then what happened?" Damon asks.

"Nothing. *Finis.* Go to sleep."

"You can't fool us," says Daphne. "All *sorts* of things happened after that. You went to live on the island of Lesbos."

"Not immediately," I note. "I wandered the world for seven years, having many fine and fabulous adventures. Good night."

"And then you went to Lesbos," Daphne insists.

"And then *we* came into the world," Damon asserts.

"True," I say. The twins are always interested in hearing how they came into the world. They never tire of the tale.

"The women of Lesbos import over a thousand liters of frozen semen annually," Damon explains to Daphne.

"From Thrace," Daphne explains to Damon. "In exchange for olives."

"A thriving trade."

"Right, honey," I say. "Bedtime."

"And so you got pregnant," says Daphne.

"And had us," says Damon.

"And brought us to Egypt." Daphne tugs at my sleeve as if operating a bell rope. "I came out first, didn't I?" she says. "I'm the *oldest*."

"Yes, dear."

"Is that why I'm smarter than Damon?"

"You're both equally smart. I'm going to blow out the candle now."

Daphne hugs her papyrus doll and says, "Did you really end the war?"

"The treaty was signed the day after I fled Troy. Of course, peace didn't restore the dead, but at least Troy was never sacked and burned. Now go to sleep—both of you."

Damon says, "Not before we've . . ."

"What?"

"You know."

"All right," I say. "One quick peek, and then you're off to the land of Morpheus."

I saunter over to the closet and, drawing back the linen curtain, reveal my stalwart twin standing upright amid the children's robes. She smiles through the gloom. She's a tireless smiler, this woman.

"Hi, Aunt Helen!" says Damon as I throw the bronze toggle protruding from the nape of my sister's neck.

She waves to my children and says, "Onward, men! Fight for me!"

"You bet, Aunt Helen!" says Daphne.

"I'm worth it!" says my sister.

"You sure are!" says Damon.

"Onward, men! Fight for me! I'm worth it!"

I switch her off and close the curtain. Tucking in the twins, I give each a big soupy kiss on the cheek. "Love you, Daphne. Love you, Damon."

I start to douse the candle—stop. As long as it's on my mind, I should get the chore done. Returning to the closet, I push the curtain aside, lift the penknife from my robe, and pry back the blade. And then, as the Egyptian night grows moist and thick, I carefully etch yet another wrinkle across my sister's brow, right beneath her salt-and-pepper bangs.

It's important, after all, to keep up appearances.

copyright acknowledgements

about the editor

Douglas Lain is a novelist, short story writer, and editor whose work has appeared in various magazines including *Strange Horizons*, *Interzone*, and *Lady Churchill's Rosebud Wristlet*. He is the author of two novels: *Billy Moon*, which was selected as the debut fantasy novel of the month by *Library Journal*, and *After the Saucers Landed*, which was nominated for the Philip K. Dick Award. He is also the editor of the speculative fiction anthology *In the Shadow of the Towers: Speculative Fiction in a Post-9/11 World*.

Lain is the publisher of Zero Books, which specializes in philosophy and political theory, and hosts the *Zero Squared* podcast, interviewing a wide range of fascinating, engaging people with insights for the new millenium: philosophers, artists, economists, and a diverse group of fiction writers. Lain lives in Portland, Oregon, with his wife and children.